*Daphne du Maurier*

DAPHNE DU MAURIER (1907–89) was born in London, the daughter of the famous actor-manager Sir Gerald du Maurier and granddaughter of George du Maurier, the author and artist. A voracious reader, she was from an early age fascinated by imaginary worlds and even created a male alter ego for herself. Educated at home with her sisters and later in Paris, she began writing short stories and articles in 1928, and in 1931 her first novel, *The Loving Spirit*, was published. A biography of her father and three other novels followed, but it was the novel *Rebecca* that launched her into the literary stratosphere and made her one of the most popular authors of her day. In 1932, du Maurier married Major Frederick Browning, with whom she had three children.

Besides novels, du Maurier published short stories, plays and biographies. Many of her bestselling novels became award-winning films, and in 1969 du Maurier was herself awarded a DBE. She lived most of her life in Cornwall, the setting for many of her books, and when she died in 1989, Margaret Forster wrote in tribute: 'No other popular writer has so triumphantly defied classification . . . She satisfied all the questionable criteria of popular fiction, and yet satisfied too the exacting requirements of "real literature", something very few novelists ever do'.

*By the same author*

*Fiction*

I'll Never Be Young Again
Julius
Jamaica Inn
Rebecca
Frenchman's Creek
Hungry Hill
The King's General
The Parasites
My Cousin Rachel
The Birds and other stories
Mary Anne
The Scapegoat
Castle Dor
The Glass-Blowers
The Flight of the Falcon
The House on the Strand
Rule Britannia
The Rendezvous and other stories
The Breaking Point: Short Stories
The Doll: Short Stories

*Non-fiction*

Gerald: A Portrait
The Du Mauriers
The Infernal World of Branwell Brontë
Golden Lads: A Study of Anthony Bacon,
Francis, and Their Friends
The Winding Stair: Francis Bacon, His Rise and Fall
Myself When Young
The Rebecca Notebook and Other Memories
Vanishing Cornwall

# The Loving Spirit

## *Daphne du Maurier*

with an Introduction
by Michèle Roberts

Alas – the countless links are strong
That bind us to our clay,
the loving spirit lingers long,
And would not pass away

E. BRONTË

virago

VIRAGO

Published by Virago Press in 2003
Reprinted 2004, 2005, 2006, 2007, 2008, 2009, 2010, 2011,
2012, 2013 (twice), 2014

First published in Great Britain in 1931
by William Heinemann

A CIP catalogue record for this book
is available from the British Library.

ISBN 978-1-84408-093-9

Typeset by Palimpsest Book Production Limited
Polmont, Stirlingshire
Printed and bound in Great Britain by
Clays Ltd, St Ives plc

Papers used by Virago are from well-managed forests
and other responsible sources.

MIX
Paper from
responsible sources
FSC
www.fsc.org    FSC® C104740

Virago Press
An imprint of
Little, Brown Book Group
100 Victoria Embankment
London EC4Y 0DY

An Hachette UK Company
www.hachette.co.uk

www.virago.co.uk

# Introduction

Daphne du Maurier takes her title from a poem by Emily
Brontë:

> Alas - the countless links are strong
> That bind us to our clay,
> The loving spirit lingers long,
> And would not pass away.

Emily Brontë seems to be talking about how hard it can
be to find the freedom of death if we are at all frightened of
dying, how the beauties of the world can exert their pull on
us right up to the end. Daphne du Maurier's lushly written
novel, on the other hand, salutes the necessity of death as a
conduit between the generations through which the loving
spirit can be poured. While it is a rapturous celebration of the
beauties of the Cornish landscape, in particular, it is also about
the drive towards abandoning the cares and duties of the daily,
material world in order to pin your faith on a transcendent
symbol and a love so intense it approaches the taboo, even
the perverse.

First published in 1931, *The Loving Spirit* is both a romance
and a family saga, a novel about thresholds and changes. It
begins with one marriage and ends, three generations later,
with another one. The heroines who brace the story, like book-
ends, are linked by their semi-mystical appreciation of the
power of love to inspire, save and heal. The presiding goddess
of this intense emotional landscape is Janet Coombe, whom
we meet, in the opening chapter, on her wedding morning.
She is about to marry her sober, God-fearing cousin Thomas,
a boat-builder, and has fled up to the cliffs above Plyn, her

village, and the harbour it shelters, to say goodbye to her old life and begin looking towards her new one.

Part of Janet fears her soul is 'sinful and wayward' for drifting off in daydreams: 'her heart would travel out across the sunbeams to the silent hills'. She is chided by all the village gossips for loving to play truant, for running and jumping, for answering back, for envying male freedoms. Her mother scolds her and beats her, but Janet insists on becoming a woman in her own way. Her beauty and strength attract all the local boys and from them she chooses Thomas.

She is doubtful about marriage, at first: 'No more could she lift her skirts and run about the rocks, nor wander among the sheep on the hills. It was a home now to be tended, and a man of her own, and later maybe, and God willing, the child that came with being wed.' So far, so mapped out. But then:

At this thought there was something that laid its finger on her soul, like the remembrance of a dream, or some dim forgotten thing: a ray of knowledge that is hidden from folk in their wakeful moments, and then comes to them queerly at strange times. This came to Janet now, fainter than a call; like a soft still whisper.

So Janet recognises her conflicted desires and destiny:

. . . and it seemed that there were two sides of her; one that wanted to be the wife of a man, and to care for him and love him tenderly, and one that asked only to be part of a ship, part of the seas and the skies above, with the glad free ways of a gull.

This opening chapter, having thus introduced the main themes and symbols of the entire novel, closes on an epiphanic note: 'she knew in her soul that there was something waiting for her greater than this love for Thomas. Something strong and primitive, lit with everlasting beauty. One day it would come, but not yet.' Of course I'm not going to spoil the story for the first-time reader by telling you what that is. Suffice it to say that it's the fuel for the entire book and drives it unflaggingly, through episodes of cruelty, treachery, war and loss, towards its peaceful and triumphant end.

How does du Maurier achieve her effects? To begin with, she's an accomplished storyteller, keeping the narrative racing along with plenty of colourful characters, dramatic incident, cliff-hanging chapter endings, mystery and suspense. More importantly, I think, she relies on the Gothic and Romantic elements of personage, narrative and landscape employed by Emily Brontë in *Wuthering Heights*. Her entire novel is a homage to that of her great precursor. Janet Coombe is a free spirit like Brontë's Cathy, and her wild, rebellious son Joseph has a lot in common with Brontë's anti-hero, Heathcliff. The great love between Janet and Joseph defies death, destitution, and wretchedness to the point of madness, just as Cathy's for Heathcliff does. *Wuthering Heights* could in no sense be described as a family saga, but it shares with *The Loving Spirit* the inbuilt necessity for the plot to be worked out over more than one generation. Du Maurier is conscious and proud of her debt to Brontë. At the beginning of Book One, her story of Janet, it's no accident that she quotes one of Emily Brontë's greatest poems:

No coward soul is mine,
No trembler in the world's storm-troubled sphere:
I see heaven's glories shine,
And faith shines equal, arming me from fear.

As in *Wuthering Heights*, the weather plays a crucial part. The Romantic Fallacy is in full swing. Storms at sea mirror storms in the human heart. Plants and creatures feel just as we do. Du Maurier invokes 'the glad tossing of the leaves in autumn, and the shy fluttering wings of a bird . . . a pale forgotten primrose that grew wistfully near the water's edge'. Imagining that flowers can share our wistfulness, or birds our shyness, is consoling, of course. This is what we might call the banal side of the Romantic Fallacy. But Brontë turned it around into a profound statement of mysticism, in which people dissolve into the universe to become one with it, and du Maurier follows her:

> . . . the spirit of Janet was free and unfettered, waiting to rise from its self-enforced seclusion to mix with intangible things, like the wind, the sea, and the skies hand in hand with the one for whom she waited. Then she, too, would become part of these things forever, abstract and immortal.

Only Brontë, I think, would not have said 'hand in hand': much too tame. Indeed, du Maurier is a much more sentimental writer.

Brontë's use of Gothic in *Wuthering Heights* allowed her savagely to satirise the genteel bourgeois world she despised, to dream of a hero brutal enough to overturn the established order, and to hint at some of the secrets festering underneath the placid surface of normal domestic life. Women writers have tended to take up the Gothic with enthusiasm, since it allows them to peer down the cellar stairs and up into the third-floor attic and reveal some of the bad things that go on in seemingly respectable houses. Du Maurier employs Gothic hyperbole and excess to permit her decent, hard-working, artisan characters to express their turbulent emotions in dramatic and even violent language, accuse each other of evil and madness, and knock each other down. No point fretting she's hamming it up; she's in a tradition as much theatrical as literary. To emphasise her novel's reach towards the timeless and the sublime she mixes in biblical phrases, cadences and rhythms, lots of archaisms, repetitions and inversions:

> And she strove to banish these thoughts . . . the cold rain shut outside and the damp misty hills, and the sound of the wild harbour water coming not to her mind . . . And Joseph looked down on Christopher, and stifled the nigh-overmastering impulse to kneel beside the boy and ask

him to place all faith and trust into his keeping, but it came to him that the boy might feel shy and embarrassed to see his father act in such a way.

Like other Gothic-influenced novelists, du Maurier uses the motifs of the form to conceal secrets as much as to expose them. Gothic circles around repression and may succumb to it. Du Maurier's rhapsodic descriptions of the love between Janet and her son Joseph hint at an incestuous element:

She longed for the other one to be with her tonight, he who was part of her, with his dark hair and his dark eyes so like her own. He who had not come yet, but who stared at her out of the future, and walked with her in her dreams.

On one level this son-lover is an animus-figure like those found in Jungian interpretations of fairytales, he who helps make a bridge for the woman into the wider world. On the level of modern psychobabble, poor Janet would be characterised as a dangerously possessive mother. Feminists might think the male principle is being over-valued and might want to deprecate a mother placing all her desires, potency and ardour in the lap of her son. But the Gothic romance can soar away from this sort of questioning, which is of course part of its charm. It is not necessarily a subversive form; it all depends on what you do with it. And to turn the question around: perhaps a forbidden love may be deftly imaged by separating the lovers into different generations and time-frames; or, perhaps, the enforced separation and ecstatic reunion of mother and son depicted here by du Maurier is simply a powerful image for the losses that afflict us all and for our longing to repair them.

*Michèle Roberts*
*2003*

# Contents

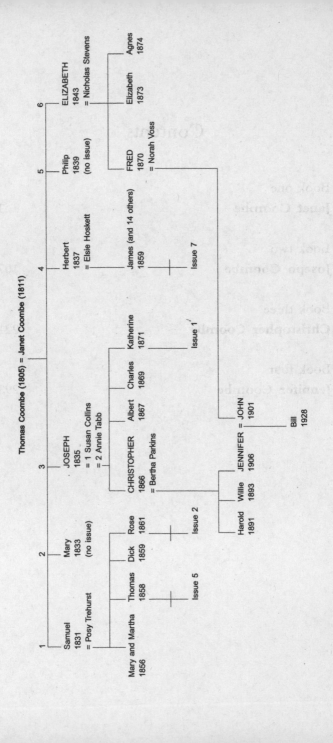

# Book One
## Janet Coombe (1830–1863)

No coward soul is mine,
   No trembler in the world's storm-troubled sphere:
   I see heaven's glories shine,
And faith shines equal, arming me from fear.

Vain are the thousand creeds
   That move men's hearts: unutterably vain;
   Worthless as withered weeds,
Or idlest froth amid the boundless main,

To waken doubt in one
   Holding so fast by thine infinity;
   So surely anchored on
The steadfast rock of immortality.

E. BRONTË

# 1

Janet Coombe stood on the hill above Plyn, looking down upon the harbour. Although the sun was already high in the heavens, the little town was still wrapped in an early morning mist. It clung to Plyn like a thin pale blanket, lending to the place a faint whisper of unreality as if the whole had been blessed by the touch of ghostly fingers. The tide was ebbing, the quiet waters escaped silently from the harbour and became one with the sea, unruffled and undisturbed. No straggling cloud, no hollow wind broke the calm beauty of the still white sky. For one instant a gull hovered in the air, stretching his wide wings to the sun, then cried suddenly and dived, losing itself in the mist below. It seemed to Janet that this hillside was her own world, a small planet of strange clarity and understanding; where all troublous thoughts and queer wonderings of the heart became soothed and at rest.

The white mist buried the cares and doubts of daily life, and with them all vexatious duties and the dull ways of natural folk. Here on the hilltop was no mist, no place of shadows, but the warm comfort of the noon-day sun.

There was a freedom here belonging not to Plyn, a freedom that was part of the air and the sea; like the glad tossing of the leaves in autumn, and the shy fluttering wings of a bird. In Plyn it was needful to run at another's bidding, and from morn till night there were the cares and necessities of household work – helping here, helping there, encouraging those around you with a kindly word, and sinful it was to expect one in return. And now she was to become a woman, and step on to the threshold of a new life, so the preacher had told her. Maybe it would change her, and sorrow would come her way and joy also for that matter, but if she held an everlasting faith in God who is the Father of us all, in the end she would know peace and the sight of Heaven itself. It was best to follow these righteous words though it seemed that the road to Heaven was a hard long road, and there were many who fell by the way and perished for their sins.

The preacher spoke truth indeed, but with never a word of the lovable things that clung about the heart. God alone is worthy of great love. Here on the hill the solemn sheep slept alongside of one another in the chill nights, the mother protected her young ones from the stealthy fox who steals in the shadow of the hedge – even the tall trees drew together in the evening for comfort's sake.

Yet none of these things know the love for God, said the preacher.

It might happen that he did not know the truth of every bird, beast, and flower, and that they too were immortal as well as human kind.

Janet knelt beside the stream, and touched a pale forgotten primrose that grew wistfully near the water's edge. A blackbird called from the branch above her head, and flew away, scattering the white blossom on her hair. The flaming gorse bushes breathed in the sun, filling the air with a rich sweet scent, a medley of honey and fresh dew.

It was Janet Coombe's wedding day. Even now her mother would be preparing the feast for the guests that were to come and her sisters laying her fine wedding gown upon the bed with longing awesome hands.

Soon the bells would peal over to Lanoc Church, and she and Cousin Thomas, her dear husband that was to be, would stand before the altar and be made one in the eyes of God.

Thomas's eyes would be lowered with beseeming reverence, and he would hearken to the good words of the preacher; but Janet knew her eyes would escape to the glint of pure light that shone through the church window, and her heart would travel out across the sunbeam to the silent hills.

The wedding service would seem dim and unreal, like the town of Plyn in the morning mist, and try as she could, she

4

would not be able to listen when she herself was elsewhere. It was the sinful soul in her that came not at the preacher's bidding; sinful and wayward as it had always been, since the days when she had been no more than a mite of a child, way back at her mother's knee.

For her sisters had attended school good and proper, and had learnt to sew and to read, but Janet was forever playing truant, away on the beach beyond the harbour. She would stand on the high crumbling cliffs, inside the ruin of the old Castle, and watch the brown sails of the Penlivy luggers that glittered on the far horizon.

'Please God, make me a lad afore I'm grown,' she would pray, and her no larger than a boot, with curls hanging round her neck. Her mother would scold her and beat her, and chide her for a great lump of a boy with heathenish ways, but it was all of no avail. Her mother might have spared the rod for the good it did her.

Like a lad she grew, tall and straight, with steady hands and fearless eyes, and a love of the sea in her blood. For all that she was a girl at heart, with her tenderness for animals and weak, helpless things, and it was this that made her have a care to her dress later, and pin a flower to her bodice, and comb her black curls off her forehead. The men would wait for her outside the gate of her father's house, and ask her to walk up the cliff path on Sundays; they'd stand with awkward hands and silly sheep's eyes, as if their tongues were too large for their mouths, but Janet gave them a laugh for an answer, and a toss of her head.

She would go with the lads if she could run with them, and climb the hedges, and have them admire her for her skill; but not to walk side by side with hands touching, for all the world like a pair of lovers. The time would come soon enough when she'd be wed, and have a husband and home to look after, and a bothering long skirt around her ankles, and a cap on her head, tidy and respectable.

It would be a man she'd want though, and not a great hulking boy with never a word to say for himself, and nothing

5

better to do than to hang around in hopes of a soft look or a gentle word. So reasoned Janet when she was eighteen past, and when her sisters were all for tying ribbons in their hair, and watching the men in church over their hymn books.

But Janet scorned their ways, though she was not better than them for listening to the preacher's words, for her thoughts travelled away across the sea, where the ships sailed into strange lands and distant countries.

Often she would wander down to the shipbuilding yard, at the bottom of Plyn hill by the harbour slip. The business was owned by her uncle, and though it was only small as yet, it was thriving steadily, and was growing larger every year. Besides, her uncle was helped by his hard-working nephew, young Thomas Coombe, Janet's second cousin.

Cousin Thomas was serious and steady, he had been to Plymouth to study, and he had a quiet way about him that impressed his uncle, and also the lazy good-for-nothing men who worked in the yard.

Soon, maybe, the firm would tackle heavier and harder work than the building of fishing luggers. Young Thomas would become a partner; on his uncle's death the business would be his.

He was a brave man, was Cousin Thomas, well-spoken and handsome enough, if you came to think of it. He had no time for love-making and walking up the cliff path on Sundays, but for all that he had his eye on Janet, and he thought to himself what a splendid wife she'd make, a worthy life partner for any man.

So it happened that young Thomas fell to calling at the house of an evening, and chatting to the father and mother, with his mind to Janet the while.

He pictured the house half-way up Plyn hill, ivy-covered and with a view of the harbour, and Janet waiting for him when the day's work was done, her children at her knee.

He waited a year before speaking his mind to Janet, he waited until she had come to know him as well as one of her own family, and trusted him and respected him the same.

Soon after her nineteenth birthday he told her father and mother that he wished to make Janet his wife. They were pleased, for Thomas was making his way in Plyn, and was as sober and honest as any parent could hope.

One evening he called at the house, and asked if he could see Janet alone.

She came running down the stairs, dressed neat and tidy, her locket pinned to her breast, and her dark hair parted smoothly in the middle.

'Why, Cousin Thomas,' she cried, 'it's early you've come to us this evenin', and supper not yet laid; and only findin' me for company.'

'Yes, Janet,' he answered quietly, 'an' I'm here special for a certain purpose, an' a question which I'm desirous to put to you.'

Janet flushed, and glanced to the window. Had not her sisters whispered something of this to her some evenings back, and she had laughed at them, heeding them not.

'Speak your mind, Cousin Thomas,' she said, 'maybe I shall not find it hard nor difficult to give an answer.'

Then he took her hand in his, and drew her to the chair beside the hearth.

'For twelve months, Janet, I've come here to your house regular, and watched your ways, and hearkened to your words. That which I'm preparin' to say to you now, is not the outcome of anythin' hasty, nor the result of wild thinkin'. It's twelve months I've seen you, and come to love you for your own true heart and simpleness, an' now the feelin' is strong upon me to speak my mind. It's that I'm wishful for you to be my wife, Janet, and to have you share my home and my heart; an' I'll work my life to bring you peace an' sweet content, Janet.'

She suffered her hand to rest in his, and thought awhile.

It seemed to her that she was scarce grown from a child to a girl, but that she must change into a woman – and forever. No more could she lift her skirts and run about the rocks, nor wander amongst the sheep on the hills. It was a home

7

now to be tended, and a man of her own, and later maybe, and God willing, the child that came with being wed.

At this thought there was something that laid its finger on her soul, like the remembrance of a dream, or some dim forgotten thing: a ray of knowledge that is hidden from folk in their wakeful moments, and then comes to them queerly at strange times. This came to Janet now, fainter than a call; like a soft still whisper.

She turned to Thomas with a smile on her lips.

'It's proud I am for the honour that you've done me, and me not worthy and wise enough, I reckon, for the like of you, Thomas. But all th' same it's terrible pleasant for a girl to hear with her own ears as there's someone who'll love and cherish her. An' if it's your wish to take me, Thomas, and bear with my ways – for I'm awful wild at times – then it's happy I'll be to share your home and to care for you.'

'Janet, my dear, there's not a prouder man than me in Plyn today, for sure, nor ever will be till the day I sit you for the first time by our own fireside.'

Then he stood up and held her to him. 'Since it's settled we'm to be wed, an' I've spoken to your parents t'other night, them being agreeable, I reckon it would be seemly enough and no harm done if I was to kiss you, Janet.'

She wondered a moment, for she had never kissed a man before, saving her own father.

She placed her two hands on his shoulders, and held her face beside him.

'No matter if 'tisn' proper, Thomas,' she told him afterwards, ''tis mighty good the feel of it.'

And that is how Janet promised herself to her Cousin Thomas Coombe, of Plyn in the County of Cornwall, in the year eighteen hundred and thirty, he being twenty-five years of age and she just turned nineteen.

Now the mist had lifted, and Plyn was no longer a place of shadows. Voices rose from the harbour, the gulls dived in the water, and folk stood at their cottage doors.

Janet still stood on the hilltop and watched the sea, and it seemed that there were two sides of her; one that wanted to be the wife of a man, and to care for him and love him tenderly, and one that asked only to be part of a ship, part of the seas and the sky above, with the glad free ways of a gull.

Then she turned and saw Thomas coming up the hill towards her. She smiled and ran to him.

'I fancy that it's sinful to greet your husband on the mornin' afore you'm wed,' she said. 'It's in the house I should be, preparin' for the church, and not here on the hill with my hand in your'n.'

He took her in his arms.

'Maybe there's folks aroun', but I can't help it,' he whispered. 'Janie, it's terrible strong the way I'm lovin' you.'

The sheep moved about the field, and the sweet scent of the gorse filled the air.

When would the bells start pealing over to Lanoc Church?

'It's queer to think as we shall never be parted agen, Thomas,' she said. 'Never at nights no more, an' in the daytime while you'm workin', and me fiddlin' with the house, our thoughts'll be with one another all the time.'

She rested her head upon his shoulder. 'Is bein' wed a mighty serious thing, Thomas?'

'Aye, sweetheart, but the holy state o' marriage has God's blessing, an' we needn't mind. Preacher has told me so. He was explainin' many things to me, 'cos there were some ways I was afeared to find uneasy an' hard. But I'll be good to you, Janie.'

'There'll be times when we'll chide each other, bad, and be short o' temper I'm thinkin', an' then it's regrettin' it you'll be, wishin' you was single once more.'

'No never, no never!'

'Funny to think as all our lives is to be here at Plyn, Thomas. No roaming for you an' me, same as some folks. Our children'll grow beside us, an' they'll be wed, and their children after them. We'll be old, and then the two of us at rest in Lanoc churchyard. 'Twill all happen, like flowers openin' their faces in summer, and birds flyin' south when the first leaf falls. An' here we be now Thomas, not knowin' no reckonin' of it.'

''Tis sinful to talk o' death, Janie, and life that is to be. Everything is in the hands o' God, we mus'n' question it. It's not our childrun's childrun I'm wantin' to be thinkin' of, but our own two selves an' us to be wed today. I love you sore, Janie.'

She clung fast to him, looking the while over his shoulder.

'In a hundred years there'll be two others standin' here, Thomas, same as us now – an' they'll be blood of our blood, an' flesh of our flesh.'

She trembled in his arms.

'You'm talkin' strange an' wild, Janie, keep your mind on us, and back from the days when we'll be dead an' gone.'

'It's not feared for meself I be,' she whispered, 'but feared for them as comes after us. Maybe there's many beings who'll depend on us – far, far ahead. Standin' on the top o' Plyn hill in the morning sun.'

'If you'm fearful, Janie, seek out the preacher and bid him soothe your mind. He knows best, and it comes from readin' the Bible o' nights.'

''Tisn' the Bible, nor the preacher's words, nor my everlastin' prayers to God that'll save us, Thomas; nor even watchin' the ways of birds an' beasts, nor standin' in the sun and listenin' to the quiet waves and the dear sight of Plyn with her misty face – though these be things of which I'm terrible fond.'

'What is it then, Janie?'

'There's words an' plenty for folks to talk, but I reckon in my heart there's but one thing that matters; an' that's for you an' I to love each other, and them as comes after us.'

They wandered down the hillside without a word.

At the house door stood Janet's mother, waiting for the pair of them.

'Where you'm been?' she called. ''Tis neither decent nor right, Thomas, to speak with her who's to be your bride, afore

10

you greet her in church. An' you, Janet, I'm ashamed of ye, runnin' up th' hill in your old gown on your weddin' mornin'. There's your sisters up in your room waitin' for to dress you; and folks'll be comin' in an' you not ready. Be off with you, Thomas, an' you too, Janet.'

Janet went upstairs to her little bedroom that she shared with her two sisters.

'Hasty, Janie,' they cried. 'Was there ever such a girl for losin' the time, an' on a day like this.'

They fingered the white gown on the bed with longing fingers.

'To think as in two hours you'll be wed, Janie, an' a woman. If 'twas me, I couldn' speak for the thought. You'll be aside Cousin Thomas tonight, an' not in here with us. Are you feared?'

Janet thought, and shook her head.

'If it's lovin' a person you are, there's nothin' to be scared of.'

They dressed her in her bridal gown, and placed the veil upon her head.

'Why, Janie – 'tis a queen you look.' They held up the tiny, cracked mirror for her to see her face.

How strange she looked to herself. Not the old wild Janet, who wandered on the seashore, but someone pale and quiet with grave dark eyes.

Her mother called from the stairs.

'You'll be faintin' unless you've some food inside o' ye. Come away down.'

'I'm not wishful to eat,' said Janet. 'But go down both of you, an' leave me a while. I'd best be alone at the last.'

She knelt by the window and looked across the harbour. In her heart were many strange unaccountable feelings, and she could name none of them. She loved Thomas dearly, but she knew in her soul there was something waiting for her greater than this love for Thomas. Something strong and primitive, lit with everlasting beauty.

One day it would come, but not yet.

Softly the bells pealed over the hill from Lanoc Church –
then louder; ringing through the air.

'Janie – where are you to?'

She rose from the window, and went away down where
the wedding guests were waiting.

12

# 2

It was as if a change came over Janet Coombe after she was wed. She was quieter, more thoughtful, and gave over running the hills in the old wild fashion. Her mother and the neighbours took note of this, and talked of the matter with many smiles and wise sayings.

''Tis having a man has changed her, and what more natural? She's a woman now, and wishful for nothing more than to do as her husband bids her. It's the only way with a girl like Janet, to rid her head of the sea an' the hills, and all such nonsense. It's young Thomas has found the way to quieten her mind, an' waken the rightful instincts in her.'

In a sense they spoke reasonably enough, for indeed with marriage and Thomas there had come to Janet a knowledge of peace and blissful content that she had never known, and could not explain to herself. It was as if he had the power to soothe with his love and care all troublous thoughts and restless feelings.

But this was only the result of the strange new intimacy between them, which would seem to change her for the while, but had done nothing to alter the wandering spirit in her.

For the moment it lay sleeping and at rest, while she gave herself up to her new-found pride and joy. She forsook the hills and the harbour, she ceased watching the ships on the far sea, but busied herself all day in her own house.

It was a pleasant spot that Thomas had chosen for their home, this ivy-clad house standing by itself away from the prying eyes of the neighbours. There was a garden too, where Thomas liked to amuse himself of an evening, with Janet beside him, her work in her hands. There was no more messing with rough boats for her now, but the mending and care of Thomas's clothes, and maybe curtains for the trim parlour.

She never ceased to wonder at herself, did Janet, for the pride and love she found in her heart for this home of theirs.

She remembered the many times she had mocked and laughed at her sisters, 'Why I'll never be a one for marryin' and wastin' my time with a house. 'Tis a lad I should ha' been, an' sailin' a ship.'

But now there was scarce a house in Plyn as spick and span as Janet's and for any wondering questions her sisters might put to her, they got a toss of her head for answer, and a swift reply from her sharp tongue, 'Aye, you may laugh as you will, but it's me that has the home of my own, and a husband workin' for me, while you have nothin' but soft-spoken lads who walk you along the cliff path o' Sundays.

'I can see you,' says she, 'yawnin' at their silly words, whilst I sit at my own fireside with Thomas beside me. And you can mind that.'

Indeed to hear her talk there had never been a house like 'Ivy House', with the tidy well-swept rooms, the big bedroom above the porch, the other rooms, 'for later on, maybe,' and her own smart kitchen. She was proud of her cooking, too, for she found once she gave a mind to it it, was nearly as fascinating as walking amongst the heather on the hills. Her saffron cake was as good as her mother's, declared Thomas, his heart swelling with pride for her.

'Now an' I come to think, Janie, 'tis better altogether. There's a lightness o' touch in your cakes like I've surely never tasted afore!'

Then she would hide her smile, and glance away from the look in his eyes.

'You'm forever flatterin' and makin' up to me,' she pretended. ''Tis my cakes you like, and not myself at all.'

Then he would rise from the table, and take her face in his hands, and kiss her till the breath nearly left her body. 'Stop it, stop it, Thomas, I tell you,' and he would sigh and put her away from him. 'It's terrible, Janie, the way I am.'

She would hold Thomas close to her in the darkness, while

14

he slept with his head against her cheek. She loved him for his strength and for his gentleness to her, for his special grave ways when he had the mood, and for the moments when like a clumsy child he'd cling to her, afraid of his own self.

'You'll stay mine, Janie, forever an' ever? Whisper it true, for the words are sweet to hear!' And she whispered them to him, knowing full well she'd be his loving, faithful wife till death came, but knowing also that there was a greater love than this awaiting her. From where it would come she did not know, but it was there, round the bend of the hills, biding until she was ready for it.

Meanwhile the first weeks passed and they became used to one another, and Janet grew accustomed to the presence of Thomas near her at all times, and his ever-ready wish to be close to her.

She busied herself with the house in the mornings, and if it happened that he was working hard she would take his dinner down to him herself in the yard, and sit beside him the while.

She loved the great trunks of trees, old and well seasoned, that lay waiting to be cut for planks, the sawdust on the ground, the smell of new rope and tar and the rough unformed shapes of boats. The thought would come into her mind that one day these planks would be living things, riding the sea with the wind for company; roaming the wide world over maybe; and she a woman in Plyn, with only a husband and a home. And she strove to banish these thoughts which belonged to the old wild Janet, and were not befitting to the wife of Thomas Coombe. She must remember that she wore a print gown now, and a smooth apron about her waist, and no longer a rough skirt for climbing the rocks beneath the Castle ruin. Sometimes of an afternoon she'd put on her bonnet, and walk up Plyn hill to her mother's house, where there'd be tea served in the front parlour, and neighbours coming in for cake and talk.

It was strange for all that to be treated by the women as one of themselves, when it was only a bit of a while since

15

she'd been scolded and chided for a mannerless girl. How many times had she put an eye to the keyhole of the parlour, holding her handkerchief to her mouth for fear of laughing, and listening to the chit-chat of the neighbours' voices? And now she was one of them, sitting as prim as you like with her cup and saucer in her hands, inquiring after old Mrs Collins' rheumatics, and shaking her head with the rest of them at the evil shocking ways of your Albie Trevase, who'd gotten the girl into trouble over at Polmear Farm.

'Seems as young folks have no respeck for themselves nor for others these days,' said Mrs Rogers. ''Tis runnin' and la'fin' an' go-as-you-please from mornin' till night. The lads won' wait till they're wed, good an' proper, nor the gals neither. You should pray God on your knees and thank Him you'm safe, Mrs Coombe,' turning to Janet, 'for your heathenish runnin' by yourself as a gal frightened your mother sore, it did.'

'All th' same, an' thankin' ye, Mrs Rogers,' said Janet's mother, 'my Janie was never one for havin' the lads take liberties with her.'

'No, I didn',' declared Janet, with all the indignation of a young bride.

'Mebbe not – mebbe not, I'm not sayin' as you did, my dear. You'm wedded now, an' can do as your husband bids you, without fearin' the wrath of God. It's treatin' him well that'll keep him, I tell you, an' if you forget it you'll find your Thomas slinkin' after the farm girls, same as young Albie Trevase. An' you can mind that, Mrs Coombe.'

Janet shook her head in scorn. They could say what they liked against her Thomas, there wasn't a quieter nor soberer man in all Cornwall for sure.

She kept her mouth shut too, and wouldn't answer the poking inquisitive questions they put to her. It was a common thing that all Plyn must know their neighbours' business, and they'd keep it up for hours, worrying the very life out of a poor body.

'If you feel sick-like in the mornin' an' queer, you'll tell your mother direckly, my dear,' said one of them, looking Janet up and down, for all the world like a sow on market day.

'Ef it's under your heart you feel it first, 'tes a lad for sartin',' said another.

'I can look after myself, thank you, without a word from here, an' a word from there,' retorted Janet, who hated their prying ways. Even Thomas himself seemed anxious over his wife's health.

'You're pale this mornin', Janie,' he would say, 'maybe you're feelin' tired and strange in yourself. You'd tell me, love, if there's somethin' – wud'n you?'

It was as if he were longing for her to admit it, yet afraid of her answer all the same.

'Why, yes lad, I'll not hide anythin' from you when the time comes,' said Janet, with some weariness.

True, she had felt tired and sick of late, but she thought it was nothing and would pass. Thomas knew better though. He held Janet close to him, and buried his face in her long dark hair.

'I thought I was proud an' content when I married you, Janie, but I had'n reckoned there'd be a moment as sweet as this. It's like if I were grander than any man on earth, Janie, because of lovin' you. Seems if I can see our lad on your knee, and us sittin' afore the fire.'

Janet smiled, and held his face with her hands.

'I'm glad to be pleasin' you, true,' said she.

Soon it was all over Plyn that Janet Coombe was 'in the family way'.

Her mother talked as if it were all her doing, and already the sisters chose little patterns of soft white wool to make the needful clothes.

Thomas sang at his work in the yard, with a smile on his lips, yet serious for all that, and looking ahead in his mind. Soon he would have a son, and in time the lad would work by his side and learn how to handle a saw, and to judge good timber. For of course the child would be a boy.

It seemed to Janet there was much fuss and ado for a small thing, and to hear the way Thomas and her mother talked anyone would imagine there had never been a baby born before.

As for herself she didn't know what to think, one way or the other. It was a natural thing to happen when folks got wed, and it would be pleasant and strange to have a child to dress and to care for. It made her happy too that Thomas should be content. She would sit in her rocking chair in the evenings before the fire, for it was getting on for winter now and chill at nights, while Thomas watched her with tender eyes.

It was peaceful there in her home, with the cold rain shut outside and the damp misty hills, and the sound of the wild harbour water coming not to her mind. The singing kettle, the supper laid ready on the table, the quiet flickering candles; and Thomas's hand in hers and the baby coming and all.

She felt soothed and restful, did Janet, and she wasn't afraid of the pain that would happen, in spite of the terrible tales the neighbours poured into her ears. There wasn't a happier home in Plyn than hers and Thomas's.

He read to her sometimes of an evening from the Bible, in his low grave voice, spelling out the difficult words carefully to himself beforehand.

'Fancy to think of all those folks begotin' each other, and them stretchin' in a long line through the ages,' she would say thoughtfully, rocking herself to and fro in the chair.

'If the first ones hadn' started nothin' would ha' come of it all. It's a great responsibility on two folks that has children. The Bible says, "Thy seed shall multiply for ever." Why, Thomas, folks'll come from us lovin' each other, on an' on, with no countin' them.'

'Give over worryin', sweetheart. You'm always thinkin' of a hundred years from now, and queer fanciful nonsense. Think of the lad that's coming to us. That's enough for your mind, I reckon.'

'I don't know, Thomas. It's mighty strange the ways of life an' love. People dyin' an' that.'

'But Janie, parson says all true believers, and them that has faith, goes straight to God in Heaven, amongst the angels.'

'An' s'posin' they leaves behind them someone they love, who's weak an' pitiful, an' has'n the heart to walk by hisself in the world?'

'God looks after 'un, Janie.'

'But no one could live in Heaven, Thomas, and be at peace, when sorryin' for the loved ones left behind. Think of them callin' out, askin' for help.'

'You mus'n talk so wild, sweetheart. The Bible speaks the truth. The happiness in Heaven is beyond our knowledge. Folks are so peaceful there, they don't give a thought to the sinful world.'

The wind blew around the house, sighing and tapping against the window pane, crying mournfully like a lost thing. The candles quivered and shuddered. Then the rain mingled with the wind, and the night air was filled with weeping and sorrow. Away below the cliff the sea thundered against the rocks. The trees were bent back with the force of the wind, and from the branches fell the last wet leaves.

Thomas drew the curtains close, and pulled the rocking chair nearer to the fire.

'Keep warm, love, and don't heed the wind an' the rain.'

Janet wrapped her shawl about her shoulders, and watched the firelight dance and flicker.

'I'll not bide in Heaven, nor rest here in my grave. My spirit will linger with the ones I love – an' when they're sorrowful and feared in themselves, I'll come to them; and God Himself won't keep me.'

Thomas closed the Bible with a sigh, and put it away on its shelf in the corner.

He must not chide Janet for her words, for women had queer notions at times like these.

He picked up the little sock that had fallen to the floor.

"'Tes terrible small, Janie,' he said anxiously. 'Will the lad's foot be no bigger than that?'

# 3

The long winter months passed slowly, Christmas came and went, and now the first breath of spring could be felt in the air. The sharp white frosts were no longer so hard in the mornings, and the very branches of the trees spread themselves into the sky, unfolding the tight round buds.

White lambs frisked in the fields above Plyn, and in the low sheltered places grew the pale primroses.

At Ivy House there was a bright atmosphere of mystery and expectation, for Janet Coombe was near her time.

Her mother was ever in and out of the place, with her fussy bustling air, lending a hand to the cooking and the cleaning to save her daughter work. Thomas's manner was sharp and impatient, giving hard words now and then to the men at the yard, and being short even to his good-natured, muddle-headed uncle.

They forgave him for it all the same, for these were anxious nervous moments for the young man.

Janet herself watched the fuss and commotion with a smile on her lips, and a laughing, wondering look in her eyes.

She didn't feel ill at all; it was only natural that the baby should come to her in the spring of the year.

Why, many was the time she'd helped carry the new-born lambs down from the fields, over to Polmear Farm; and seen the patient wounded eyes of the cows as they licked their sturdy little frightened calves, they shaking on their four legs.

It seemed to her that there was nothing more simple and homely than the birth of a young thing, whether it was a child in a cottage or a lamb on the hills. It was all the same in the end. The lambs cried for food and comfort, and nestled against the sheep who gave it them, while a woman clasped her baby to her breast. But she could not for the life of her see the reason for these nods and muttered whispers, and the tying of ribbons on the cradle in the bedroom, and her mother's meaning smile at inquisitive neighbours calling, and Thomas's agonized pleading that she should lie down and rest herself.

'I wish you'd away, all of you, and go about your business and let me be. I'm not feared o' pain nor trouble, and if I had my way I'd leave you to your ribbon-tyin', and soup-makin' and take myself to the quiet fields to have my baby, I would, 'midst the cattle and the sheep who'd understand.'

'Merciful Lord, if it's that you're thinkin' of, then bed's the place for you, and hasty too,' cried her mother, and she packed poor Janet upstairs without more ado.

Two days later, on 5 March, Janet's son Samuel was born.

''Twas a beautiful confinement,' declared old Mrs Coombe to the neighbours. 'Easier an' better than Doctor an' I'd ever thought. She bore it wonderful, the dear brave gal that she is, an' is goin' on splendid. As for the boy, 'tes a picture o' health, and the livin' image of his father.'

A string of flags was hoisted at the yard, and drinks given round to the men in honour of the event.

Janet lay back on her pillows, her dark hair pushed back from her pale face, her eyes fixed musingly on the baby in her arms.

What a queer mite of a thing it was, with its little bald head and watery blue eyes. She could not herself see any like-ness in it to Thomas, try as she did. She hoped she would remember to call it 'him', and not 'it'.

Still, it was pleasant and strange to feel a small warm body next to you, and to know it was yourself that had done it. And Thomas's face was a joy to see.

He tiptoed into the room with heavy creaky boots, his face very red, and his blue eyes nearly starting out of his head.

'Janie, are you'm feelin' terrible bad?' he asked her in a low hoarse whisper. She had to shake her head at him, and hide her smile, for fear he should be vexed. Then she drew back the coverlet, and showed him their bit of a lad, nestled in the crook of her arm. Thomas's mouth opened wide, his long legs nearly twisted themselves inside out, and he stood there gazing,

21

his smile stretching from one ear to the other. Janet could not help laughing at the sight of him, rocking there on his two feet with his red smiling face, and saying not a word.

'You've never seen a baby afore, I reckon,' she told him. 'Touch 'un, he's alive you know!'

Thomas stretched out a cautious finger – and laid it on his son's cheek.

The baby opened his eyes and blinked.

'Did you see him?' cried Thomas delightedly. 'Why, he knows me already.'

'Stuff an' nonsense,' said old Mrs Coombe. 'Why, the poor babe can't even see yet. Did you ever hear the like?' and she pushed him out of the room, for fear the man's silly ways should tire her daughter.

It was not long before Janet was herself again, and up and about the house.

Samuel was a good child, and gave very little trouble. He neither fretted nor wailed overmuch, but behaved himself as a healthy normal baby. Thomas could scarcely leave him alone for a minute, and begrudged the time spent down at the yard. To his immense pride and joy he was permitted to carry his son in his arms, on visits to the grandmother up the hill on Sunday afternoons.

Janet trudged beside him, thankful to be rid of her burden for a while. Thomas's step was firm and slow, he carried his head high, and every minute he'd be stopping to show the baby to a neighbour.

'Why, he favours you for sure, Mr Coombe,' they would say. ''Tes your very eyes in his little head, an' the same fair colourin'.'

'Now, do you mean it true?' smiled Thomas. 'Did you hear, Janie? Mrs Rogers here says she reckons the boy takes after me.'

'He surely do,' sighed Janet, for she had heard the same thing over and over again, and it had never surprised her that a baby should be like his father.

In her mother's house the child was handed round from neighbour to neighbour, and kissed by his aunts, and rocked on his grandmother's knee; while Thomas watched them with anxious, jealous eyes. 'Have a care now, you'll be droppin' him.'

Janet sat remote on the other side of the hearth, listening to the murmur of their voices as they spoke their baby language to the child.

She wondered at the amount of petting and smarming that went on, when she knew the lad was happiest alone in his cot, or when he lay naked after his bath kicking in her arms. It was queer that folks had not the sense to see it, and Thomas too, with the rest of them. But he was as weak as water, was Thomas, where young Samuel was concerned.

When Janet was undressing the baby in the evening, and he stretched out his small closed fists into the air, his proud father would take this as a sign of strength.

'Look, Janie, look at the muscle in his arms. That boy's goin' to handle a saw all right.'

And the first year passed, with the three of them together in the home, happy and content in one another.

In the autumn of 1831 old Uncle Coombe was laid low with rheumatics, and the whole care of the business at the yard fell upon Thomas. Now he took it upon himself to make changes and improvements where he would. The slip was enlarged, and the mud dredged away from the beach below, so that a larger type of boat altogether could be launched from the side in safety.

Orders came creeping in one by one for sturdy well-built fishing boats to withstand the winter gales, and Thomas had few moments to spare now for playing with his boy. The knowing ones in Plyn nodded their heads and pointed at him with pride, saying it was a fine thriving business young Coombe was building up for himself.

"Tes a good man, that Thomas o' yourn, young Janet,' they'd say to his wife. 'The lucky woman you are with sich a husband, an' a fine healthy boy i' the bargain.'

And it pleased Janet to hear them praise her husband, for the people of Plyn were ever ready to find fault with the smallest thing. Samuel crawled on the floor at her feet, and rolled on his back; he clutched at the sky with his hands and gazed at his mother solemnly, with his small, thoughtful face, so like his father's. Janet would wait to put him to bed until Thomas came home in the evening, and then he'd be laid in his cradle by the kitchen fire while the pair of them sat themselves down to supper, happy and content, to talk over the day's events.

'The big boat's gettin' along fine, Janie. We'll be puttin' the planks on her tomorrow forenoon. I'm mighty pleased with that timber we brought down ten months back from Truan woods. 'Tes the same that we'm usin' now. I reckon any boat I build won' go to pieces, unless they put her on the rocks, Janie.'

'They say, Thomas, you're buildin' faster an' better than ever did Uncle Coombe.'

'They say that, do they?'

'Aye, all Plyn is talkin' of it, 'cordin' to what I hear. I'm proud of you, Thomas.'

''Tes all for you an' the boy, Janie. Look at him, bless his heart an' his dear innocent face. Who knows, but he'll be workin' along o' his father afore many years, won't you, my son?'

Samuel kicked in his cradle, he would not go to sleep. He began to scream at the top of his voice.

Thomas rose to his feet, and knelt beside the cradle.

'There, Sammie, there; you mus'n' cry, my lovely boy.'

He took the clenched hand and kissed it. 'Hush, lad, hush. You'll be breakin' your father's heart if you take on so.'

Samuel screamed, scarlet in the face.

Janet smiled, and shook her head. She went to the cradle, and turned him over on his front, patting his little behind.

'What a fuss an' a pother,' she scoffed at her husband, 'just for a bit o' wind.'

Thomas sighed and hung his head. She knew more about babies than he did.

# 4

In the summer of the following year Uncle Coombe, who managed to hobble about on two sticks in spite of his rheumatism, was seized with a chill during a sudden spell of cold weather, and in less than twenty-four hours the old man was dead.

The business was now Thomas's, for better for worse, and it was for him to work hard and make it a real thriving concern. It was a great responsibility laid on the shoulders of a young man, and he but twenty-seven, but Thomas's nature was dogged and obstinate and he was not going to let himself be beaten.

It seemed that with the new cares upon him, Thomas's young lighthearted ways, that had indeed always been kept in control by his natural gravity, forsook him for good. He was a man with nothing of the boy left in him. He thought in terms of pounds, shillings, and pence, and though he professed to be working only for his wife and son, it must be admitted that they were not even in his mind when he glanced with pride at the sign above the yard entrance – 'Thomas Coombe, Boat Builder'. He had already made more of a name for himself in Plyn than ever his uncle had.

Janet had done well for herself when she married him, thought Thomas, and what more could any woman want than the home he had given her, and his care for her, and the boy in the bargain, with more to follow if it pleased God.

So much for Thomas, as he stood in his yard with his tall, upright figure, calling out sharp orders in a lofty tone to the men who worked for him.

Janet had seen the change in Thomas, but she did not blame him for it. To her the ways of a man were no mystery, she

25

accepted them as natural. That his work should now hold a prior claim was just; she would have despised him if he had been content to let the business care for itself in the old slipshod manner of Uncle Coombe's day, and he himself had mooned around the house because of her.

In the realities of life she saw straight before her, knowing truth from falsehood and that changes in people could be accounted for and observed, without bemoaning the fact and shutting her eyes to it. She knew that Thomas's love for her was solid and true, and that he would never look elsewhere than to her face for comfort; but she knew also that the strange exquisite worship – the sweet bewildered passion that sweeps a boy who possesses a woman for the first time had gone – never to return.

Samuel had strengthened the blood-tie between them, but no more than this. They would cherish each other in sickness and in health, walk through life sharing its pleasures and its sorrows, sleep side by side at night in the little room above the porch, grow old and frail, resting at last, not parted, in Lanoc Churchyard – but from the beginning to the end they would have no knowledge of one another.

Janet's feeling for Samuel ran parallel to her feeling for Thomas. The one was her husband, the other was her child. Samuel depended on her for care and for comfort until he should grow old enough to look after himself. She washed him and dressed him, seated him beside her in his high chair at table and fed him, helped him with his first steps and his first words, gave him all the tenderness and the affection he demanded from her. She gave to both Thomas and Samuel her natural spontaneity of feeling and a great simplicity of heart; but the spirit of Janet was free and unfettered, waiting to rise from its self-enforced seclusion to mingle with intangible things, like the wind, the sea, and the skies, hand in hand with the one for whom she waited. Then she, too, would become part of these things forever, abstract and immortal.

Because of her knowledge that this would come to pass,

26

Janet strove to banish despondency. She hid her loneliness, and always appeared willing and cheerful in the face of others.

It was as if she had two selves; the one of a contented wife and mother, who listened to her husband's plans and ceaseless talk of his great business, and laughed at her baby's prattle, and visited her own folk and the neighbours of Plyn, with a real pleasure and enjoyment of the happenings of her daily life; and another self, remote, untrammelled, triumphant, who stood tiptoe on the hills, mist-hidden from the world, and where the light of the sun shone upon her face, splendid and true.

These things were not conscious definitions in Janet's mind; introspection belonged not to the inhabitants of Plyn in the early days of the nineteenth century and to the twenty-one-year-old wife of a Cornish boat-builder. All she understood was that the peace of God was unknown to her, and that she came nearer to it amongst the wild things in the woods and fields, or on the rocks by the water's edge, than she did with her own folk in Plyn.

Only glimpses of peace came her way, streaks of clarity at unwakened moments that assured her of its existence and of the certainty that one day she would hold the secret for her own.

So Janet bided her time, and passed the days in the same way as all the wives in Plyn, with baking and cleaning, and mending her man's clothes and the boy's too. There was the walk to church of a Sunday and joining in the simple gossip of the neighbours afterwards, with a cup of strong brewed tea, and a slice of saffron or seedy cake and then home to supper, and the boy put in his cot and she and her husband to sleep sound beside one another till morning came.

In the spring of 1833, a fortnight after Samuel's second birthday, his sister was born.

She was fair and blue-eyed, very much like Samuel, and gave not more trouble than he had done at the same age.

The little girl was christened Mary, and Thomas was nearly as proud of his daughter as he had been of Samuel.

27

Though Thomas liked to think he had his own way over things, it was generally Janet who had the last say in the matter. She would fling a word at her husband and no more, and he would go off to his work with an uneasy feeling at the back of his mind that she had won. He called it 'giving in to Janie', but it was more than that, it was unconscious subservience to a quieter but stronger personality than his own.

He would never have admitted it, but he 'couldn't quite make Janet out', to use his own unspoken epithet. She was his wife and he loved and respected her, there was the home and the two children to bind them together, but her thoughts were a mystery to him. It was funny the way she would go off into silence sometimes, and gaze out of the window towards the sea, with a queer unbelonging look in her eyes.

He would notice this of an evening, when he had been sparing a moment to play with the children after the day's work, and there would be Janet, with her work on her knee, inside of herself as it were.

'What are you thinkin', Janie?' he would ask her, and she'd either shake her head smiling and make no reply, or come out with some nonsense or other such as – 'I'd been a man, Thomas, if I had my way.'

It was hardly encouraging to be told this. What could she want with being a man, when there wasn't a better home in Plyn, nor two sweeter children, nor indeed a more faithful, loving husband than himself?

'It's a puzzle you are to me sometimes, Janie, for sure,' he would say with a sigh, and then she would change her mood, like the sudden flash of lightning in summer, and come to where he'd be sitting with the children on the floor and maybe join in with them in their play or question him on real sensible matters that a man could answer, as to the work at the yard and so on. And then, perhaps, before he knew it, she'd be off again with some wild foolish saying, like expressing her pity for old Dan Crabb, who'd been caught at last in his smuggling tricks and sent off to Sudmin for trial.

'But, dear heart, the man is a villain, and an evil double-faced rogue i' the bargain; deceivin' His Majesty's officers, breakin' the law and raisin' his hand against honest, peaceable folk.'

'Aye, Thomas, but it's a man's game, for all that.'

'You call it a man's game, do ye, a sneakin' rotten thing like smugglin'. Why, I would'n shake the hand of one o' them, for fear of contamination.'

'I reckon I would then, an' follow him too. It's often I've pictured the life to myself. A pitch-dark night in Lannywhet Cove, an' no sound but the waves breakin' on the shore. Then a faint light glimmerin' through the blackness, and oars creakin' stealthy-like. There'd come a whistle, faint an' low, an' your boots would crunch on the shingle as you crept to meet the boat. There'd be voices murmurin', while the stuff was unloaded, and then a shout and a cry from the top o' the hill, and wild confusion on the beach; an' you'd be runnin' for your dear life, your hair in the wind, with nigh six revenue officers pantin' at your heels. That's livin', Thomas, and dyin' all in one – no reckonin' o' time.'

She laughed at his shocked, pained face.

'Will ye chide me for a shameless, brazen woman?'

And he would answer her, solemn as a judge: 'Why, Janie, how you do run on.'

The two children gazed at their mother; Samuel holding on to his father's hand, and the baby Mary safe in his arm, the pair were the picture of each other and Thomas all over again. Janet smiled to see them so, the three of them belonging to her, and part of her too, maybe; but the rest of her stole from the warm, cheerful room, and the dear kindly faces, and fled away, away, she knew not whither, beyond the quiet hills and the happy harbour of Plyn, through the seas and the sky – away to the untrodden air, and the nameless stars.

# 5

Next Christmas snow fell on Plyn. It lay light upon the hills and the fields, like the touch of a white hand protecting the earth. Even in Polmear Valley the stream was frozen, and the dark trees looked scarred and bleak against the sky. Then the sun shone from the blue heaven where there was never a cloud, and the hard frosts went with the melting snow, leaving but a thin pale covering in their place.

Thomas went up to Truan woods and brought down with him great bunches of holly with flaming berries. With them he mingled pieces of ivy that could be spared from the house, and together he and Janet placed bits here and there about the rooms, and Thomas cleverly fashioned a bent branch of holly into a rough cross, and hung it above the porch.

Janet busied herself in the kitchen, baking in preparation for the day of general rejoicing; there was to be company in the afternoon for tea, and she knew they would make short shrift of her cakes and puddings and pasties, and maybe expect a cup of hot broth too before they took their leave and went into the chill night.

Thomas sat by the fire with his Bible on his knee, and the two children clung to Janet's skirts the while, pleading for a taste of that which smelt so good in the pan on the hob.

'Now leave your mother alone, there's good children, do, or it's never a taste of the puddin' you'll get till Christmas Day is come an' gone,' she scolded, and their father couldn't but help to show his powers of authority, and called sharply to Samuel, 'Now, let your mother be, Sammie, and you and your sister give over plaguin'. Come here to your father, and listen while I reads the good book to ye.'

They obeyed silently, the boy dragging his little sister along the floor, she scarce able to walk. Thomas read aloud in his careful voice the first chapters of St Matthew, but it was not likely that two babies of their age could know what he was about, and they sat at his feet quietly enough playing with a rag doll that was shared by the pair of them.

Janet straightened her back and rested awhile, her hand on her hip. After she had tidied up and laid the supper, and the children put to bed, it would soon be time for finding her bonnet and shawl, and while a kindly neighbour sat in the house to mind things, she and Thomas would set out side by side across the frosty hill to Lanoc Church for the midnight service.

Somehow she had no wish to go tonight. She did not care to listen to the parson's words, nor to join in singing the hymns with the others, nor even kneel by the altar rail to receive the Blessed Sacrament. She had a mind to slip away in the darkness, and run for the cliff path that overlooked the sea. There'd be a moon over the water, like a path of silver leading away from the black sea to the sky, and she'd be nearer to peace there than on her knees in Lanoc Church. Nearer to something for which there was no name, escaping from the world and losing herself, mingling with things that have no reckoning of time, where there is no today and no tomorrow.

She was thinking, "Tesn't a churchy worshipful feeling in me tonight, 'tes a wish to be alone with the moonlight on my face.'

Then she took herself away and began to lay supper on the table, thinking the while of an excuse for staying from the service. It was Thomas himself who gave it to her.

'There's shadows 'neath your eyes tonight, Janie, and your face has a pale wearisome look. Are you feelin' poorly?'

'I reckon it's the cookin' and all that bendin' over the stove; it's put a pain across my head an' my back. Maybe it's better if I bide in the house, Thomas, and let you go to Lanoc without me.'

'I hate to be leavin' you, dear, the first Christmas Eve I've done so since we was wed.'

''Twill be better so, all the same. I can't be sick tomorrow, with the folk comin' an' all.'

So it was arranged, and when the bells called softly through the air from Lanoc beyond the fields, Thomas went alone, his lantern in his hand, while Janet watched him climb the hill from the shelter of the porch, the holly cross creaking and sighing above her head. The neighbour, whose presence was no longer needed, bade her good night and a happy Christmas, and went her way. Janet was now alone in the house with the two children, who were sleeping soundly in the room above. She prepared some hot broth for her husband when he should return from the church, cold and hungry from his prayers and his walk.

She wrapped her shawl about her shoulders and leant from the window. A faint film of snow still lay upon the ground.

The moon was high in the sky, and there was no sound but the moan of the still water lapping the rocks beyond the harbour. Suddenly she knew that she must go to the cliffs, and follow the call of her heart.

She hid the key of the door in her bodice and left the house. It seemed to her that there were wings to her body that bore her swiftly away from home and the sleeping children, away up the steep, narrow street of Plyn, to the white-frosted hills and the silent sky.

She leant against the Castle ruins with the sea at her feet, and the light of the moon on her face. Then she closed her eyes, and the jumbled thoughts fled from her mind, her tired body seemed to slip away from her, and she was possessed with the strange power and clarity of the moon itself. When she opened her eyes for a moment there was a mist about her, and when it dissolved she saw kneeling beside the cliff with his head bowed in his hands, the figure of a man. She knew that he was filled with wild despair and bitterness, and that his poor lost soul was calling to her for comfort.

She went and knelt beside him, and held his head to her breast, while she stroked his grey hair with her hand.

Then he looked up at her, his wild brown eyes crazy with fear at himself.

And she knew him to belong to the future, when she was dead and in her grave, but she recognized him as her own.

'Hush, my sweet love, hush, and cast away your fear. I'm beside you always, always, an' there's none who'll harm you.'

'Why didn't you come before?' he whispered, holding her close. 'They've been trying to take me away from you, and the whole world is black and filled with devils. There's no truth, dearest, no path for me to take. You'll help me, won't you?'

'We'll suffer and love together,' she told him. 'Every joy, and sorrow in your mind an' body is mine too. A path will show itself soon, then the shadows clear away from your spirit.'

'I've heard your whispers often, and hearkened to your blessed words of comfort. We've talked with one another too, alone in the silence of the sea, on the decks of the ship that is part of you. Why have you never come before, to hold me like this, and to feel my head beside your heart?'

'I don't understand,' she said. 'I don't know where we come from, nor how the mist was broken for me to get to you; I heard you callin', and there's nothing kept me back.'

'They've been long weary days since you went from me, an' I've not heeded your counsel, nor deserved your trust in me,' he told her. 'See how I'm old now, with the grey hairs in my head and beard, and you younger than I ever knew you, with your pale girl's face and your tender unworn hands.'

'I have no reckoning in my mind of what is past, nor that which is to be,' said she, 'but all I know is there's no space of time here, nor in our world, nor any world hereafter. There be no separation for us, no beginnin' and no end – we'm cleft together you an' I, like the stars to the sky.' Then he said: 'They whisper amongst themselves I'm mad, my love, my reason's gone and there's danger in my eyes. I can feel the blackness creepin' on me, and when it comes for good, I'll neither see you nor feel you – and there'll be nothin' left here but desolation and despair.'

He shuddered and trembled as a cloud passed over the face of the moon, and it seemed to her he was a child in her arms crying for comfort.

'Never fear, when the black fit seizes you, I'll hold you as I hold you now,' she soothed him. 'When you can neither see nor hear, and you're fightin' with yourself, I'll be at your side and strivin' for you.'

He threw back his head and watched her as she stood, white against the sky with a smile on her lips.

'You're an angel tonight,' he said, 'standing at the gates of Heaven before the birth of Christ. It's Christmas, and they're singing the hymn in Lanoc Church.'

'Fifty years or a thousand years, it's all the same,' said Janet. 'Our comin' here together is the proof of it.'

'You'll never leave me again, then?' he asked.

'Never no more.'

He knelt and kissed her foot-prints in the snow.

'Tell me, is there a God?'

He looked into her eyes and read the truth.

They stood for a minute and gazed at each other, seeing themselves as they never would on earth. She saw a man, bent and worn, with wild unkempt hair and weary eyes; he saw a girl, young and fearless, with the moonlight on her face.

'Good night, my mother, my beauty, my sweet.'

'Good night, my love, my baby, my son.'

Then the mist came between them, and hid them from one another.

Janet stood by the Castle ruin, the sea lapped the rocks beneath her, and across the water stretched a path of silver. Nothing had stirred nor moved, nothing had changed. A second maybe had passed since she had stood there, but no more.

Yet she had travelled half a century, out of the world into space, into another time. She neither wondered nor feared, she was only filled with a great love and thankfulness.

Then she turned away from the sea, and made her way

from the cliffs down the steep hillside to Plyn. It was past midnight, and Christmas day had come. She paused to listen for a moment and across the air came the faint sound of voices, as they sang the last hymn in Lanoc Church. The song came sweet and low, the voices of simple people who brought glad tidings to the world.

The church tower was lighted with a streak of gold.

> Hark! the Herald Angels sing
> Glory to the new-born King,
> Peace on earth and mercy mild,
> God and sinners reconciled.
> Joyful all ye nations rise,
> Join the triumph of the skies,
> With the Angelic Host proclaim
> Christ is born in Bethlehem.
> Hark! the Herald Angels sing
> Glory to the new-born King.

And Janet smiled, and looked to the east, where high in the sky shone a star like the star of Bethlehem.

# 6

E arly in the new year Thomas Coombe took Janet for a visit to Plymouth. He had been well paid for the turning out of a smart cutter in November, and pleased with his work and the money in his pocket, he considered there would be no harm in spending part of it on a holiday for himself and his wife. In those days it was quite a journey, especially in winter, and they were obliged to make their way by carrier's cart to Carne, and put up there for the night, going on to Plymouth next morning by coach – arriving there in the afternoon.

The two children were left in the care of Janet's mother.

Janet had never in her life been away from Plyn before, and she was nearly dumbfounded at the big town. Thomas was delighted at her astonishment, and took much pleasure in showing her all there was to be seen, and professing himself the best guide in the world. He liked to show his familiarity with the names of the streets and the shops, though it was a good few years since he himself had been there.

'Why, mercy, Thomas,' she would say, 'how ever is it that you can recollect so many names, when all the streets look so alike, an' us never losin' ourselves at all.'

''Tes quite simple, Janie,' he boasted. 'It don't take a man like me long to get the hang of a place. I dare say it seems difficult for you, comin' from Plyn with no knowledge of anythin' bigger.'

'Well, I don't know about that,' says Janet, her chin in the air, 'an' it's terrible high an' mighty you'm considerin' yourself, all said an' done. Anyway, I knows the cliffs an' the woods round Plyn better'n you ever will, I reckon. If there's ever a

36

bit of a mist, you'll be goin' round an' round in a circle, an' me home hours ago, layin' the supper.'

Thomas remained silent, for by now he had learnt Janet would ever have the last say in a matter. Nevertheless she was awed by the shops, and approved of Thomas's choice of a warm grey cape for her, and the pretty trim bonnet to match.

'Fancy the price,' she whispered in his ear, 'why 'tis no less than highway robbery.'

'I like you to have the best, my dear,' he said, as proud and lofty as Squire Trelawny himself. Many a man turned to look at her in the streets, as she walked with her arm in his.

She was a good-looker, was Janet, with her thick dark hair, her wide far-seeing eyes, and the determined mouth and chin. She carried herself like a queen. Thomas was aware of the glances cast at her by the many sailors about Plymouth, and he looked to see how she would take it. Generally she would walk beside him unaware, but once some fellow, probably the worse for drink, lurched purposely against her, and brushed her new cape with his dirty fingers.

Thomas wanted to interfere, but Janet took the matter into her own hands, and the sailor, expecting her to shrink back with a cry of fear, had a taste of her temper instead.

'You've forgotten your manners, my man,' she said swiftly. 'In Cornwall 'tes polite to take off your hat when you walk into a lady,' and before the man had time to reply she had seized his cap from his head, and flung it into the dirty water of the harbour. 'That'll clean the cobwebs for you,' she told him, and gathering her skirts in her hand, she made her way along the street, with Thomas behind her blushing and a little ill at ease.

''Twas my place to have done that, Janie,' he reproved her. 'I admire you for your pluck, but 'twas scarcely a womanly action.'

'Would you have me leavin' his dirty paw on my new cape?' said she, in a proper fury, yet smiling in spite of herself at his red face. 'If you don't keep quiet I'll be sendin' your hat over to join his!' And Thomas knew that she'd keep her word, and care not a jot for his discomfort.

Nearly five days they were in Plymouth, and then time was up for them to be back.

Thomas placed their two bundles ready for leaving, when Janet, who had been looking out of the window in silence, suddenly spoke.

"Tes really fine an' glorious weather for the time of the year,' she said in a careless tone.

Thomas agreed, little realizing that he was falling into a trap.

'It's as calm on the water as if it were summer, I'm sure,' she went on. 'With a fine breeze we'd be in Plyn before night-fall, where as it is we'm obliged to delay in Carne for the evenin', till the cart comes for us tomorrow forenoon.'

'Aye, the waste of it. In summer there's boats go to and fro this part o' the coast, but o' course there's none this time of the year,' he told her.

'Ah! that's where you're wrong,' said Janet. 'There's a boat goes today. While you were fiddlin' in here, I went outside and spoke to the captain. The boat sails at noon, an' we'd be in Plyn by this evenin' for certain.'

Thomas rubbed his chin doubtfully. Janet had her chin in the air, and a glint in her eye he knew well.

'Supposin' it came on to blow hard?' he said weakly.

'Well, what if it did. I'm not afeard, are you?'

He made a last effort to withstand her.

'There'd be no room for us, Janie, we'd be i' the way.'

'Oh! no, there's no use in sayin' that, Thomas; it happens I've arranged it all with the captain, he'll take us willing.' And with that she seized the two bundles in her hands, bade a smiling good-bye to the lodging-keeper, and stepped from the house across the road, calling to him over her shoulder.

They made their way towards that part of the harbour where their boat was moored alongside the quay. Thomas had expected that Janet would have pleaded for one more glance at the shops before they turned their steps in this direction, but he was mistaken. His wife was not going to waste her

38

time over ribbons and stuffs when there were ships to be seen.

She lingered about the quays, admiring the forest of tall spars stretching to the sky, and surprised him with her knowledge of the names of the spars, and various parts of the rigging.

'You thought I spent my time learnin' to sew an' to cook, did you,' she said scornfully, 'an' me playin' truant all the while, an' running to the beach, with nothin' in my mind but to learn all I could about a ship.'

'It's a queer thing how you ever came to be the woman you are, Janie,' marvelled her husband.

She laughed and slipped her hand in his.

'I'm not so much changed, for all that,' she said softly.

At length they came to the ship *Watersprite*, and climbed aboard.

The captain made as if to help Janet, but she shook her head indignantly, and seizing her skirts in one hand and the rope in the other, she mounted the rough ladder that was hanging over the side. Once on deck she looked about her in interest, instead of descending at once to the cabin, which, as Thomas whispered to her, was the proper place for a woman. He himself fell to criticizing the lines and the build of the little ship, though he was careful to say nothing aloud.

In spite of what the captain had assured them, it was well two hours before they were under way, and nearly five in the afternoon.

'We shan't be home before midnight if we're home at all,' said Thomas, and he glanced uneasily at the sky where the clouds were gathering fast from the south-west.

'Looks like a change in the weather,' he said to the captain.

Janet was enchanted at the idea of a rough voyage, but Thomas was thinking of the children at home, and cursed himself for his weakness in giving way to her.

It was too late now to turn back, they were out of the Sound and heading for the open sea, with Rame Head away on their quarter.

'If it comes on thicker we shall have a job beatin' against it, eh, captain?' said Thomas.

'Oh! no, there may be a squall or two,' laughed the sailor, 'nothin' to hurt. There's no anger in it, as far as I can see. Should it come on bad we'll try for St Brides instead.'

But Thomas had no desire to spend the night at St Brides, and he scarcely trusted the captain's ability to find the entrance to the little harbour after dark, with the great projecting island outside it, barely a quarter of a mile to the westward.

It was dark soon and raining. Janet had been persuaded to go below, and to keep herself warm by the side of the small stove.

Thomas stayed with her, every now and then going on deck to find out what progress had been made.

The boat was rolling badly but neither of them was ill. They sat in silence, listening to the creaking and straining of the mast, and the sound of the wind and the rain.

Janet saw by Thomas's face that he was uneasy in his mind, and she blamed herself, but all the same there was a wild feeling in her heart to think she was on a ship in the middle of the sea, and that the wind held danger.

She would have liked to be on deck with the men, hauling at ropes and blistering her hands, or clinging with all her strength to the straining wheel.

'Why wasn't I born a man?' she thought. 'To be up there now i' the midst of it,' and she felt the fact of her sex to be like a chain to her feet, as bad as the hampering petticoats around her ankles.

She longed for the other one to be with her tonight, he who was part of her, with his dark hair and his dark eyes so like her own. He who had not come yet, but who stared at her out of the future, and walked with her in her dreams. They would not be sitting like two prisoners in the cabin, they would be standing together on the deck, with their hair wild and soaked by the wind and the sea, and laughter on their lips. She could picture him with his hand on the wheel, and his eyes every now and again cast aloft to watch the trim of his sails, and then descending upon her with one warm swift glance.

Long legs and square shoulders like Thomas's, but heavier

built and stronger. Then a beckon of his free hand to her, and his arm about her waist, and throwing back his head and laughing the way he did.

She knew the sound of his voice, low and careless-like, and the very smell and feel of his flesh.

Janet closed her eyes and prayed.

'Oh! my love, come soon – for it's weary and sore I am of waitin',' and when she opened her eyes she saw Thomas her husband standing before her, like the shadow and the reflection of the one she loved.

He came and knelt beside her.

'There's more beauty in your face tonight, Janie, than I've ever seen,' he whispered. 'Do you love the sea and a ship so well?'

She placed her hands on his shoulders, and drew him to her.

'It's something that's stronger than myself at times,' she said to him. 'Like in olden days when a woman felt the call upon her from God, to forsake all, her home, her life, an' maybe her lover too, for the sake o' givin' herself into His keeping, secure from the world within a convent's walls; the like of it comes to me, to wander forth from Plyn an' you an' our children, an' to sail away in the heart of a ship, with only the wind an' the sea and my dreams for company.'

He held her close, caressing her timidly with shy, nervous hands.

'You'm not unhappy, Janie, you'm not regrettin' we're wed, an' these few blessed years we've had together.'

'No, dear lad, nor never will.'

'Maybe I haven' been by your side as often as I should, these last times, since the business has been all my care. It's been over-much in my thoughts, I reckon. But Janie, my own dear wife, you're the light o' my eyes an' the sweet of my heart – I love you for your dear strange thoughts an' ways though I can't understand them; you wouldn' leave me altogether for your dreams, promise me you wouldn', and take yourself where I'd not be touching you no more.'

41

'Would you be lonely for me, lad?'

'Why, Janie, don't you reckon how I'd hunger for the feel o' you at nights, your blessed tender body which belongs to me, an' the touch of your hand on my heart, you in the house, your care for me an' the childrun – you, the livin' breathin' thing which means home to me.'

'No – I'll never roam from you i' the flesh, Thomas – I know as Janet Coombe belongs to her man, an' her childrun, an' Plyn itself. I'm rooted there like the trees in the shelter of Truan woods, an' nothin' can tear me from you.'

He leant his head against her, content with her answer, and Janet saw him resting against her in death as he did now, like a child asleep, while her restless spirit haunted the deep, flying with the gulls, and the song of the sea on her lips.

The captain appeared down the companion-way, and glanced into the cabin.

'You're welcome to turn in here an' make yourselves at home, you know. We shan't be in Plyn afore one or two i' the mornin', with this wind, but there's no danger an' you can sleep in peace till I calls you.'

Janet rose to her feet.

'Let's take one look at the sea, Thomas; I'm hungry for the feel of the air on my face.'

Together they climbed on deck and watched the scene around them. The wind had shifted more to the west, and the rain had ceased. The night was black save for the light of the stars. The ship plunged her way through the seas, happy and alive. No sign of land – nothing but the sea and the sky, and the sound of the wind in the sails. Janet stood in the bows of the ship, her cap streaming out behind her, her dark hair wild and tossed.

She looked like the figurehead of a ship.

Thomas caught his breath as he looked at her. She moved with the sway of the vessel, as though she were part of it. Thomas stood by her, and was aware of himself, troubled by her beauty. 'Janie,' he whispered, 'Janie.'

Beyond him, beyond the ship, beyond the sea she heard

someone call, loud and triumphant, out of the darkness – like the voice of the wind.

'It's now that I'll come to you, NOW – NOW.'

She held out her hand, and felt Thomas beside her.

'Janie,' he was saying, 'Janie.'

She turned away from the sea, and drew his hand to her lips.

'Love me tonight.'

They went from the deck, and the ship plunged on through the darkness, one with the wind and the sea.

I n the latter part of the spring there were several bad gales off the Cornish coast, and many fine vessels foundered. Thomas Coombe, being shipwright as well as boat-builder, was busier than he had ever been in his life. He engaged more men to work under him, and there was never a moment when some vessel was not lying on the beach beside the yard slip.

Little Samuel, who was now five, spent most of his time watching his father and the men at their work. He was given an old blunt tool to play with, and was nimble enough with his fingers, for all his lack of years.

Sister Mary had already passed her second birthday, and toddled about after her mother, with fat unsteady legs.

Janet blessed them for the lack of trouble they gave her, she feeling giddy and ill at times now, with another baby on the way. Both her sisters had married that year, and three weeks after the wedding of the youngest, old Mrs Coombe had died.

Janet said little to Thomas about her health. He was proud at the thought of another addition to his family, but his work at the yard prevented him from looking after his wife, and he was never in the house, except for his evening meal, and then straight to bed to sleep like a log.

Never before, either with Samuel or with Mary, had Janet felt so weak and tired in the early months. She was more concerned for the child than herself, and was afraid it would be born prematurely and die. The feeling of peace and security she had known before the birth of the two other children was not with her this time.

Her old wild, restless longings rose within her, and she

wanted only to leave the house and her family, and take herself away into some silent far-distant place.

She no longer sat in the rocking chair, her work in her hands, content with the peace and warmth of her home, she would wander restlessly about the house, miserable at her weak state.

When the summer came, and the days were warm and long, Janet would leave the house and taking the children with her, climb laboriously to the top of the high cliffs above Plyn, and sit there for hours, watching the sea.

She longed for freedom as she had never longed for it; a throb of intense pain shook her being when she saw a ship leave the harbour of Plyn, her sails spread to the wind, and move away like a silent phantom across the face of the sea. Something tore at her heart to be gone too.

As the months slowly passed this feeling became stronger and more vital, not a day passed when Janet did not find some moment or other for making her way to the cliffs, and turning her head to the wind and listening to the sound of the sea. More than ever in her life she felt the urge and the desire to use her strength and to move swiftly, then she looked at her ugly misshapen body and bowed her head in her hands for shame that she had been born a woman.

Her nerves, usually calm and unruffled, were jagged and on edge.

The house seemed empty to her, she found no peace within its walls – it gave her nothing. She was short with Thomas and hasty with the children, they were all part of the chain that bound her to Plyn. Back to the cliffs she would roam, restless and miserable, searching for what was not; frightened at solitude yet craving it withal – her soul as sick as her body, and alone.

So the summer months drew into autumn, the early mornings were chill and drowned in a white mist, while at nights came the sharp frosts, heralding the approach of winter. Truan woods and the trees round Plyn were a riot of colour, and then the first leaves fell, shivering, rustling, a pale covering for

45

the earth. The seaweed broke away from the rocks, and floated dull and heavy on the surface of the water. The rich brown and yellow autumn flowers became sodden with the soft autumn rain, and drooped their heads upon lean stalks.

Harvest was gathered in, the apples stripped from the orchards and stored in the dark lofts.

The birds seemed to have vanished with the summer sun, only the everlasting gulls remained, wheeling and diving for fish in the harbour, the long-necked solitary shag, and the stout busy little puffins. The river was silent, save for the whisper of the trees when the leaves dropped to the ground, and the weird mournful cry of the curlew as he stood at low tide on the mud banks, searching for food.

Dusk came early, soon after six o'clock, and the people of Plyn closed their doors and their windows against the cold damp mist, leaving the night to wrap its shrouded blanket about their sheltered homes, heedless of the weeping sky and the lonely baleful owls.

So the last week of October drew to a close.

The damp still weather changed of a sudden one afternoon, great purple clouds gathered from the south-west, and a low ugly line ran along the sea's horizon. With the turn of the tide the strong wind changed to a gale, and descended with all its force upon Plyn.

High mountainous seas broke against the rocks at the harbour mouth, and swept their way inside the entrance. The spray came up over the Castle ruins, and the water rose above the level of the town quay, flooding the ground floor of the cottages grouped there on the cobbled square.

The men shut their women folk inside their houses, and made their way to the harbour slip, to see to the safety of their boats. It was the last day of October, 'All Hallowe'en', and usually a beacon was lit on this night, and the custom followed of feeding it at midnight with driftwood, and then proceeding through the town, but tonight this was abandoned – for no one would venture forth into such a gale unless on duty bound.

Thomas Coombe was down at the yard, watching the rising tide with apprehension and longing for the turn, when no more damage could be done. At Ivy House the children were put to bed and already asleep in spite of the howling wind. Janet had laid the supper and was awaiting Thomas's return.

The rain had now ceased, only the wind and the sea shouted in unison. Every leaf was scattered, and the broken branches swung in the trees, creaking and shaking like the rattle of a ship's shroud. Something was dashed against the window and fell, sending Janet's hand to her side with the shock of the sound. She opened the window to see, and saw the dead body of a gull with its two wings broken.

The wild air tore at her curtains and blew to darkness the flickering candles. The fire hissed and shrank in the grate. Then Janet felt the movement of the live thing stir within her, she felt the striving of one who would break his bonds and be free.

And to her, too, came the call for liberty, the last desperate longing of a soul to seek its freedom, and the anguish of a body cast from its restraint.

She threw up her hands and cried aloud, and the wild mocking wind echoed her cry – 'Come with me,' called the voice out of the darkness, 'come and seek your destiny on the everlasting hills.'

So Janet wrapped her shawl about her head, and conscious only of the pain that gripped her and the struggle of spirit and body, she stumbled away into the wild wet wind, with the call of the thundering sea in her ears.

Down in the yard Thomas and his men watched the slackening of the tide, and when they saw it retreat slowly inch by inch, angry at the forces which compelled it, they knew that the premises were safe for the night until the following morning.

'Well, lads, it's been a hard forbiddin' watch for us. What do ye say to a cup o' somethin' hot up to the house? The wife will have it ready and waitin'.'

The men thanked him gratefully, and marched by his side

47

up the hill to Ivy House, half bent with the weight of the wind at their backs.

'Hullo, no lights,' said Thomas. 'She's surely never gone to bed.'

He made his way into the house, the men at his heels.

The room was just as Janet had left it, with supper on the table, but the fire was low in the grate, and the candles blown out.

'That's queer,' muttered Thomas, ''tesn't like Janie to leave a room in such a state.'

One of the men looked over his shoulders.

'Seems as if Mrs Coombe left everythin' hasty-like,' he said. 'Suppose she's been took bad, she's very near her time, isn't she, Mr Thomas, beggin' your pardon?'

Fear clutched at the heart of Thomas.

'Wait,' he said, 'I'll see what she's about.'

He went to the bedroom over the porch and opened the door.

'Janie,' he called, 'Janie, where are you to?'

Samuel and his sister were sleeping sound, there was no movement in the house. Thomas ran downstairs, breathing hard.

'She's not there,' he stammered, 'she's not anywhere; she's not in the house.'

The men looked grave, they read the fear in his eyes. Suddenly he clutched at the table for support, his legs weakening. 'She's gone to the cliffs,' he cried, 'she's gone out into the gale, crazy with the pain.'

He seized the lantern in his hands and ran from the house, shouting and calling to the men to follow him.

Folk came to their doors. 'What's all the pother an' noise?'

'Janet Coombe's trouble is upon her, an' she's gone to the cliffs to lose herself,' came the cry.

Men donned their coats and found lanterns to join in the search, and one or two women besides, sorrowful and anxious at the thought that one of their kind should suffer. The group staggered up the hill after Thomas, already a long way ahead.

48

Borne through the air came the chime of midnight from Lanoc Church, the final notes loud and triumphant with a gust of wind.

'All Hallowe'en,' whispered the folk amongst themselves, 'and the dead risin' from their graves to walk the earth, an' the evil spirits of all time fillin' the air.'

And they huddled close together and called for God's mercy and protection, with horror in their hearts for the plight of Janet.

They gathered beside Thomas at the summit of the cliff, where the gale nigh shook them from their feet, and the black sea crashed against the rocks.

Hither and thither tossed the pale lanterns, searching the ground. 'Janie,' cried Thomas, 'Janie – Janie, answer me.'

No sign of her on the bare grass, no sign of her in the tangled ferns.

Now the rain came once again, blinding the eyes of the searchers, the boiling waves dashed themselves to pieces, sending cloud after cloud of stinging spray on to the cliffs above.

The wind tore at the ground and the trees, wailing and sobbing, and cried like a thousand wild devils let loose in the air.

Then a faint shout came from Thomas, who held his lantern high above his head, and the light fell slantways upon the figure of Janet beside the Castle ruin.

She was crouched half kneeling in the grass, her hands flung out and clenched, her head thrown back. Her clothes were drenched with the spray and the rain, and her long dark hair fell wild about her face.

On her cheeks were the marks of her own tears, and those of the rain from Heaven.

Her teeth were biting into her torn lips, and blood ran at the corner of her mouth. The light in her eyes was savage, primitive, the light of the first animal who walked the earth, and the first woman who knew pain.

Thomas knelt by the side of Janet, and took her in his arms, and carried her away down the bleak hillside into the

49

town of Plyn, and so to her home and laid her on the bed.

All the night the storm raged, but when at length the wind ceased, and the sea quietened its mournful clamour, peace came to her.

And when Janet held her wailing baby to her breast, with his wild dark eyes and his black hair, she knew that nothing in the whole world mattered but this, that he for whom she had been waiting had come at last.

# 8

'Joseph, leave your brother alone, will 'ee, tormentin' him like the little devil you are.'

'No, I won't. He's got my boat, an' he's goin' to give it back to me,' said the boy firmly.

'I only wanted to see it for the shape,' cried Samuel, wiping the tears from his face. 'I haven't done 'un no harm. Get away, Joe, you're hurting.'

The two boys were struggling on the floor, Samuel, the eldest, held down by his younger brother. Joe's black hair fell over his face, he threw back his head and smiled, a dangerous gleam in his brown eyes.

'Give it me, or I'll smash your face in,' he said softly.

'No, you don't, my lad,' shouted his father, and Thomas sprang to his feet from his armchair by the fire, and pulled the two boys apart; Samuel pale and shaken, Joseph reckless and laughing.

'Is this the way you behave on the Sabbath? Has'n' church taught you no better'n that? For shame on ye. Samuel, you go to your room an' to bed without your supper, but you, Joseph, you'll take a beatin'.'

Samuel went quietly up to bed, crying to himself, ashamed of his bad behaviour; and Thomas was left alone with his second son.

Although he was only seven, Joe was tall and big for his age, nearly as tall as Samuel who was eleven. As he stood there, with his dark eyes fixed on his father's, his head thrown back and his chin in the air, he looked so much like his mother that Thomas turned away for a moment, then he hardened himself.

'Do you know you're a bad evil boy?'

51

The child made no answer.

'Baint you goin' to reply to your father when he asks you a question? Say you'm sorry at once, will ye?'

'I'll say I'm sorry when you gives me my boat, an' not afore,' said the boy coolly, and he stuck his small hands in his breeches and tried to whistle.

His defiance staggered Thomas. Never had Samuel behaved like this, or either little Herbert or Philip, the two youngest boys. Only Joseph persisted in getting his own way above them all, as if there was something in him that made him different to the others. He looked different too, with his dark wild appearance; his clothes were always in holes and his boots through at the toe.

Two or three times a week he played truant from school, or was complained of in some way or other, generally for fighting. It seemed as if Thomas had no authority over him at all. Only Janet knew how to handle him. Since his birth seven years ago on that dark October night, this small bit of a lad had dominated the household. He had needed more careful rearing than either Samuel or Mary, and during the first few months of his existence the house had rung with his screams and his yells. There had never been such a baby for making a noise. Only when his mother held him close to her and whispered to him, was he quietened. Once he grew out of his babyhood he threw off his first temporary frailty, and developed into a strong sturdy boy. Ivy House was seldom still or peaceful now, it resounded with either his laughter or his rages. He was not spoilt, there was no attempt made to pamper or give in to him in any way, it was just the boy's personality that threw a sort of glamour about him, and there was no gainsaying him.

With the development of his character he seemed to open also that of his mother's. From the moment of his birth Janet had altered. The soft pliability of temperament that had obeyed Thomas's wishes during the first years of marriage had flown to the winds, and with it the solitary melancholy part of her that had seized her later. She had emerged stronger, braver, utterly fearless in mind, soul, and body, with no humble wishes to please her husband only and to care for his home, and no half-conscious longing and vague desires in her mind. Now she was no more a girl half sure of herself, puzzled at the world; she was a woman of past thirty who had already brought five children into the world.

Thomas, who had hitherto ruled home and business with no doubt about it, found himself placed gently but firmly in the background. It was Janet who had the first say and the last say at Ivy House, and now it had come to be the same down at the yard. It was Janet who suggested a change here, or an improvement there, it was Janet who ordered this and refused that. Of course, Thomas was the head of his own firm, and he gave the orders, but all the men under him and the folk of Plyn knew that his wife was behind him. Any man who had been slacking at his work invariably straightened his back and clutched his tool with an uncomfortable fear in his heart when Janet came down to the yard, with young Joseph following close behind her.

'Well, Silas Tippet,' she would say, 'you've been an uncommon length o' time over that piece o' plankin'. What's the reason for it?'

'Well, I can't say, Mrs Coombe,' mumbled the man, red as fire, 'we'm tremendous busy down here, if you ask Mr Coombe he'll tell 'ee . . .'

'Stuff an' nonsense, man,' said Janet sharply, 'that boat's promised by June the first, an' on that date 'twill be ready. It's nails that is wanted in that plank, an' not the drops of beer from your pocket, so see.' – And she swept away like a regular queen, with young Joseph's hand in hers.

And by June the first the boat would be ready for sure.

At Ivy House and in the yard there were only two people that mattered – Janet and Joseph. Always the same couple running the house and running the business – Janet and Joseph.

But in the year 1842 Joseph was still but a lad of seven, and known then to be 'terrible wild', while Janet was famous for two things in Plyn, her beauty and her temper.

Back in Ivy House Thomas stood in the parlour, his stick in his hand, and Joseph before him. 'Come here an' take a beatin',' he said gravely.

'I won't,' said the boy, and folded his arms.

Thomas took a step towards him and seized his collar in his hand, then he bent the child over and gave him three hard cuts with the cane.

Joseph fought like a little devil, and catching hold of his father's wrist he bit it, breaking the skin and bringing blood.

Thomas dropped his stick with a cry, not of pain but of horror, at the action of his son.

He was white with the shock, none of his children had ever done such a thing. 'God will punish you in His own way,' he said quietly.

Joseph seized his coveted boat from the table, and with a shout of triumph he climbed out of the window, preferring it to the door, and was gone.

Upstairs poor Samuel knelt by his bed, his face in his hands – 'Please God, make me a better boy,' then he undressed, folded his clothes, and climbed into bed, the sheet over his head.

Thomas sat uneasily by the fire. When would Janet be back and what would she say?

She had gone to tea with Sarah Collins, taking with her Mary and Herbert, and little Philip.

Thomas reached for the Bible on the shelf, always his consolation, and unfortunately the book opened at the Commandments, and his eyes fell on the line – '. . . for the sins of the fathers shall be visited on the children, even unto the third and fourth generation of them that hate me . . .'

He sighed and shook his head. He had always loved and trusted God, he could think of no action in his life that could deserve the pain that Joseph had brought upon him. He had always been so proud of his family, too. Good, hard-working Samuel, gentle patient Mary, kind stolid Herbert – even quiet baby Philip with his small refined features; none of them had ever gone against his word, except Joseph.

Janet and Joseph – Joseph and Janet – the pair of them together controlled everything.

Thomas listened, he heard footsteps and voices in the garden.

It was the family returning. Janet swept into the room, the children following. They were chatting and laughing, pleased with their afternoon.

Janet was smiling, her eyes were bright and there was colour in her face.

'Were you thinkin' us was never comin'?' she asked gaily. 'The children enjoyed themselves that much I had'n the heart to bring them away.' Then she noticed the disorder of the room, the cane flung in the corner – Thomas's grave face with his wrist bandaged. She took it all in at a glance.

She bit her lips, her eyes hardened, her chin stuck in the air like her son's when he was angry.

'Where's Joseph?' she said at once.

Thomas rose to his feet and pulled himself together.

'We've had a very unhappy afternoon here,' he said slowly. 'Samuel and Joseph started fightin' over Joseph's boat, and I was obliged to separate them. I was sorely angry, on the Sabbath an' all, that they should behave so bad. I sent Samuel to bed sayin' he was to have no supper, an' as Joseph wouldn' say he was sorry I gave him a beatin'. Look what he's done to my wrist – bit it.'

He uncovered the wrist, and showed it to his wife, as if it were her fault. Mary slipped away and ran upstairs to Samuel, Herbert's lower lip drooped and tears came into his eyes, while little Philip alone seemed unperturbed. He crossed the room to a cupboard where he kept his toys, and played quietly in a corner.

'Where's Joseph now?' inquired Janet.

'I don't know,' replied Thomas sullenly. He was hurt that no notice should have been taken of his wrist. 'He jumped out o' the window, an' made for the beach, I reckon.'

Janet left the room and went upstairs to the room the three boys shared together.

Samuel was sitting on the bed, with Mary at his side.

'He's terrible sorry, mother, to have behaved so bad,' said his sister swiftly.

Samuel and Mary were devoted to one another.

'Tell me what happened, Samuel,' said Janet quietly. She knew he would speak the truth.

'I got hold o' Joe's boat, to see how 'twas finished off,' sniffed poor Samuel. 'I'm tryin' to make a model meself, an' I was'n' doin' it no harm. Then up came Joe and gives me a bang on the head. "Leave 'un alone," he says shoutin' at me, and before there was time, though I wanted him to ask for it proper, he'd knocked me over. 'Course we started fightin', an' then Father pulled us apart.'

'Did Joseph hurt you?' asked Janet, feeling him.

'No, I don't think so.'

'Yes, he did – the naughty boy,' cried Mary. 'Sammie has a bump on the back o' his head, feel it, mother.' In truth there was a small swelling, but nothing much.

'You can get up, Samuel, and come downstairs. There's no need for you to go to bed hungry, when you're a growin' boy. I see it wasn't your fault about the fightin'. Now Mary, 'tend to the supper if you can, there's a good girl, an' I'll go see where Joseph's to.' And with these words she left the room and went from the house. She knew where Joseph would be. Down on the rocks below the Castle ruins, with the boat she had given him, sailing it in the wide pool. It was low tide, and she made her way to the pool over the rocks, without climbing the steep cliff path and down again.

Sure enough, there was Joseph, up to his waist in water, poking at the boat with a long piece of stick.

He shouted with joy when he saw her, and waved his hand. 'Come an' see,' he cried, 'she's sailin' beautiful.'

Janet's lips twitched as she looked at him, and she smiled.

All his clothes would have to be dried and mended again, and his boots patched. She knew the feel and the touch of them so well. He ran to her, his face flushed and eager, clutching hold of her with his wet sandy hand. A lock of dark hair fell over

56

his face. He jumped up and down beside her in impatience.

'She's called "Janie" after you,' he laughed. 'I scratched it on the stern of her with Mary's pen. Won't she be cross? Look – there's never been such a boat, now has there?'

He pulled her towards the water, splashing her with his muddy feet.

But at that moment a gust of wind caught the superb 'Janie', and tossed her out of his reach into the deeper water.

'Hi – come back,' shouted Joe at the pitch of his lungs, 'come back, will 'ee.' He splashed after the boat, always just out of his reach.

'Joseph – come here at once,' said Janet. She knew there was deeper water ahead, and Joseph could not yet swim.

The boy ran back to her as soon as he heard her voice.

'Mother – I'll be losin' the boat,' he whispered.

She seized the stick he had thrown aside, and lifting her skirts she climbed on to a ledge of rock. 'Here, Joe, you stand in the shallow part, an' I'll push her towards you.'

The boy obeyed.

'Plunge the stick in deeper,' he shouted, wriggling with impatience. 'Look, there's a ripple formin'. We'll get her yet.'

Janet clung to the ledge with one hand, and poked at the boat with the stick.

'Wait a minute,' she cried excitedly, 'my hair's fallin' down.'

The boy giggled. 'Never mind, love, 'tend to it after. Sail in "Janie", my beautiful boat. We'll rescue you, never fear.'

'Don't make so much noise,' said Janet, shaking with laughter, 'you'll bring the coastguards on us. Come on, "Janie", what a time you be.' She gave a last lunge at the boat with her stick. 'There – clutch her, Joe, she's comin'.'

The boat sidled along into Joseph's waiting hands.

'Hurrah—' he shouted – 'I knewed your namesake 'ed save ye.'

Janet sat down on the rocks, and began to arrange her hair.

As soon as she screwed it up, Joe pulled it down.

'Gee-up – will 'ee – you're a horse with a mane,' he said, pulling at the loose strands. 'Come up – 'tes market day.'

Janet tried to pinch his legs with her hands, but he danced round her, avoiding them.

'Look out, there's coastguard' – he warned her.

'Mercy on us – where?' said Janet, glancing up at the cliff. There was nobody there. Joseph rolled on the ground, sick with laughter, and she darted at him, slapping him and tickling his ribs, until he begged for mercy. Then he flung his arms round her, biting her neck softly.

'I'm goin' to be a wild horse tearin' you to pieces,' he told her.

'You'll do nothin' of the sort, my son,' said Janet, setting him on his feet. 'Help your mother to put herself in order.'

He stood by her side and watched her as she smoothed her hair and dress. Suddenly she remembered why she had come to fetch him. She took hold of his hands and drew him before her.

'You've been fightin' your brother Samuel, an' you bit your father,' she said gravely, watching his eyes.

He nodded, and swallowed hard.

'You've made them both unhappy an' sore with your cruelty. Samuel meant no harm, an' your father acted justly. I'm goin' to punish you, Joe.'

He said not a word, but began to breathe rather heavily.

'I'm goin' to take your boat away from you. You see that high ledge up there? That's where your boat is to be put, out of your reach. When not a scar remains on father's wrist you shall have it back. I'm bein' fair, Joseph, aren't I?'

Joseph blinked. He was very red in the face and his lip was shaking.

'Yes,' he said.

'You'll ask father's forgiveness and you'll shake hands with Samuel. Promise me?'

'Yes.'

She placed the boat safely on the ledge, where the rain could not harm it. When Joe could no longer see it, he looked at his mother with swimming eyes, and pushed his head into her shoulder, feeling for her hand.

58

She gave him her handkerchief and he blew his nose loudly and rather slowly. Janet looked away, pretending not to see the tears.

'Shall we be goin'?' she said.

'I've muddied your dress,' he told her, and tried to scrape it away with the handkerchief.

There was a dirty tear-mark on his cheek, and his nose was running.

She caught him to her suddenly and held him close.

# 9

The children were playing down in the yard. Samuel had been given a broken saw and a couple of old planks. He laid the planks against the side of the slip, and grasped his saw firmly in his right hand.

'Now jest watch me,' he said gravely. Mary knelt by his side, her doll in her arms, her eyes fixed proudly on her brother. Herbert had half a dozen rusty nails in his hand which he held open for Samuel.

'Tell me when you want 'em, an' I'll hold 'em steady for ye,' he said, pleased to be able to help. Up and down went the saw, and the planks fell neatly in two.

'See where I marked the board with white chalk,' cried Samuel, proud of his steady wrist. 'I didn't move not quarter'n inch one way or t'other. Give us the nails, Herbie, there's a good lad.'

The three fair heads bent together over the planks. Then there was a shout and a yell, and Joseph leapt from behind the shed in the midst of them.

The children cried in dismay.

'Take care. Joe, you'm spoilin' our game.'

The boy kicked the planks carelessly with his toe.

'Don't mind 'bout your silly stuff. Listen to me. You know old Tim West's boat?'

The children nodded.

'I've cut her moorin's, an' brought her round to the ladder. Don't say a word, no one's noticed. Come on.'

'I don't think we ought to . . .' began Mary. 'What d'you say Sammie?'

Samuel looked doubtful. He was the eldest, and had a stern conscience.

'You'm afeared,' laughed Joe scornfully.

That settled the matter.

'All right – we'm comin',' said Samuel hastily, flushing all over his face.

They crept down the ladder at the back of the yard, and landed with a splash into the bottom of the leaky boat.

Joe seized the paddles before Samuel could get at them, and though they were far too long and heavy for him, he pulled the boat awkwardly from the slip, and out towards the harbour entrance. No one at the yard noticed their departure. Yes – one. A small figure wormed its way out from behind an empty tub, and watched the boat disappear behind the cliff.

It was Philip, the youngest boy. He was much smaller than Herbert, although only two years his junior, and his features were small too, and clear-cut. His hair was sandy-coloured, and he was the only one of the Coombe children who had narrow small eyes, deepset, and close together.

He ran swiftly out of the yard, and made his way up the hill to Ivy House. Half-way he stopped, a sudden thought had come to him. Playing in the gutter was a boy of his own age.

''Member what I see you doin' in Church las' Sunday,' he said, whispering in the boy's ear. The other one flushed and wriggled.

'Yes,' he whimpered.

'Well, you'm to go up to Ivy House and say as you'm seen my brothers an' sister pull away in Tom West's boat from the yard; an' if you don't I'll tell on 'ee.'

'I'll go,' said the frightened boy, scrambling to his feet.

'Mind, you'm to say you've seen it yourself. Don't say as I said so.'

The boy ran away up the hill, and Philip disappeared in the other direction.

Meanwhile Joe and the others were well to the entrance of the harbour. The water was grey and choppy, and the wind blowing straight in from the south.

Mary was frightened and began to cry. Herbert was white

61

in the face, he felt seasick; while Samuel glanced uneasily about him.

Only Joseph was perfectly happy. He caught a crab with his oar, and the water splashed over his face. He threw back his head and laughed. 'Wish there was an' old mast an' some canvas to her,' he said. 'We'd sail her to France.'

'I reckon we'd better be turnin', Joe,' said Samuel, who had noticed the larger seas ahead and guessed something of the unseaworthiness of their craft.

'Hoo!' scoffed Joe, 'there's nothin' to hurt,' and he attempted to pull a wider stroke, with the result that the rotten oar snapped in two, knocked him off his seat, and escaping from its thole-pin it floated away on the water.

'Now you've done it,' shouted Samuel. Mary screamed and clung to him. Poor Herbert, who had struggled manfully with his stomach, gave way with the increased rocking of the boat, now that there was no pulling to steady her, and he leant over the side and was sick. Joe glanced about him, and remembered the force of the flood-tide would wash them steadily towards the rocks, where the white waves were breaking.

'Here,' he said calmly, 'move yourselves to the centre thwart. I'll try an' scull her in.'

He shifted the remaining oar to the cleft mark on the transom. But the big heavy oar was too much for him to handle, and he could not keep it in its place. Samuel came to his aid, but made a worse mess of things and before many moments had passed the remaining oar had smashed and gone out of his reach.

Mary was now crying bitterly, and Herbert too, between his bouts of seasickness.

Samuel turned pale, and held his sister's hand fast. Joe whistled and stuck out his chin. ''Tes me as has done it. Must get 'em out of it,' he was thinking.

The tide was bearing them steadily towards the rocks.

He saw clearly that there was no way out. The idea came to him that if he tied the boat's painter round his waist and tried to swim to the cove inside the entrance, he might be able to guide the boat to safety. A forlorn hopeless thought, but the one remaining chance. He was not afraid of the water; he had learnt to swim last summer. He threw off his clothes and hitched the rope round his middle.

'Don't do it, Joe,' said Samuel, who grasped what he was about, 'you'll be sucked under for sure.'

Joe winked, and was about to plunge in, when something made him raise his head.

He glanced towards the cliff and saw his mother climbing down the rough loose crumbling stones and earth. She must have been sitting on the top of the hill with the baby Lizzie, and had seen their plight.

Joe never turned his eyes away from the small black figure. Supposing she slipped . . .

He waited, ready to throw himself in the sea. He cast away the painter from his waist. What did the boat's safety matter now? Samuel, Mary, and Herbert could be drowned for all he cared, and dashed against the rocks.

The only thing that mattered was for his mother to reach the ground in safety.

He made no attempt to call to her, he knew that she was making for the narrow cove on the harbour side of the cliff, where a boat belonging to one of the crabbers was moored about twenty yards from the shore in deep water. She would swim to it, cast away the buoy, and come to their rescue.

He knew all this instinctively. From the cliff's side Janet raised her eyes and saw him looking at her as he stood in the bows of the rough unsteady boat. She smiled.

She was not afraid of falling, she had climbed every part of this cliff as a girl. The only thing that hampered her were her long skirts and petticoats.

'I'm coming, Joseph' – she said and she knew he was waiting for her. The sea sounded loud and cruel beneath her, the wind blew at her hair – the stones and the earth crumbled beneath her feet and hands. A gull screamed nearby, rousing his fellows, and they flew about her head – crying and beating their wings.

She cursed them aloud, caring not at all. Her heart sang. This was danger. She loved it. Janet was happy.

She had complete faith in herself and she knew she would reach Joseph in time.

At last her feet touched the sand in the cove, and she cast aside her dress and tore away her shoes. Still Joseph stood motionless in the bows of the boat.

Janet waded out into the water, and waved her hand.

'There's nothing to fear, childrun – I'm comin' to you.'

She swam steadily towards the crabber's boat, and with some difficulty hoisted herself aboard, her wet garments clinging to her, her hair streaming down her back.

She unclasped the mooring hook from the boat, and cast the rope and cork buoy into the water. Then she seized the paddles, and pulled towards the helpless drifting boat, now barely thirty yards from the sea-swept rocks.

'Have the painter ready,' she called to Joseph, and he waited, the rope in his hands – the other children cowering and trembling in the stern of the boat.

Then as she drew near enough, he flung it to her, calling 'Catch, 'un' – in a high unsteady voice. She caught it, and quickly made it fast to her own boat. Then she seized hold of the paddles once more, and towing the children's boat astern of her, Janet pulled away from the waiting rocks to the sheltered calm waters of the harbour. It was then that Joseph Coombe fainted for the first and the last time in his life.

As they rounded the bend, she saw Thomas in the yard boat with nigh half a dozen men coming to meet them. Her husband was white to the lips.

'What ever come over ye?' – he called to her, trembling with fear that she or one of the children might be hurt.

'All's well,' said Janet quietly – 'there's no harm done.'

'I was comin' down from the house,' cried Thomas, 'an' Harry Tabbs' little boy came runnin' to say Joseph had cut the painter o' Tim West's boat, and was pullin' out o' the harbour with the others. I rushed down as fast as ever I could an' launched this boat. Just as we was climbin' in, along comes

Mrs Collins with Lizzie in her arms. "I found the mite cryin' on top by Castle ruins," says she, "I'm fearin' some harm's come to her mother," but I had no time to wait.'

Soon they were back by the yard slip and all was explained. 'Bain't you ashamed, Joseph?' said his father harshly, 'and you other wicked childrun for followin' his advice?'

'Leave them alone,' said Janet swiftly, 'they've had punishment enough, I reckon.'

The little party toiled up the hill towards the house.

Philip was waiting in the parlour, his book *Tales of Jesus* on his knee. Kind Sarah Collins stood by, with Lizzie in her arms. 'My poor Janet,' she exclaimed, 'come at once and dry yourself, my dear.'

'Where was you, Philip?' asked Thomas wearily.

His children were too much for him.

'I's been readin' here quiet, father dear,' said little Philip meekly.

'You'm the only good one o' the bunch,' sighed Thomas, and he took Philip on his knee and gave him a piece of cake.

The other children huddled by the fire, profoundly wretched and miserable, wondering how Mr Tabbs' boy had been able to see them escape. Father would never have known, and now he would be displeased with them for over a week.

They wouldn't have been drowned, anyway, with mother coming to their rescue.

Mother always came in time.

And little Philip watched them calmly from his father's knee, wiping the crumbs from his mouth. 'Can I have 'nother bit o' cake, father dear?' he asked.

Upstairs kind Sarah Collins was putting the baby to bed. In the boys' room Janet knelt by her son's bed, with Joseph crying in her arms, sobbing with grief.

'I was fearin' you'd fall,' he choked, burying his face in her neck. 'There's never been nothin' that hurt my heart afore, till I seen you climbin' down that cliff. I shan't never forget it — never — never — till I die, you comin' down the bare side o' it — with the gulls beatin' and cryin' in your face.'

65

She kissed his wet eyes, and smoothed back the hair from his face.

'Hush, my love – no harm will ever come to mother. Remember that – I'm here to take care o' you. You know 'twas wrong to take out the old boat, an' your sufferin' from watchin' me down the cliff will learn you not to be so wild an' reckless in your ways.'

'I'll never be bad again – mother. But 'tis a fever that comes on me at times, to get out in a boat an' away – not carin' where – just away on the sea with the wind in my face.'

He put his arms about her neck.

'You understand. I know there's only you can understand – the wicked roamin' spirit of me.'

They clung to each other in the dark room.

'When I'm grown you'll come away, won't you?' he whispered. 'We'll have a boat of our own, and we'll sail where the wind takes us. You know there's nothin' in my mind but the want o' that, don't you?'

'Yes – Joseph,' she whispered back.

'I'm not goin' to stay i' the yard 'longside o' father, with Sammie an' Herbie,' he said. 'I'm goin' to be a sailor like I've told you many a time. And when I'm Master o' my ship – *Janet Coombe*'s her name – you'll be with me – at my side facin' the danger an' the wonder of it. Promise you'll come – promise?'

He took her chin in his hands.

She closed her eyes.

'I promise.'

'Do you know my ship will be the fleetest ship in Plyn – an' in the bows of her, flauntin' the world with her eyes an' her mouth, there'll be your figurehead.'

Janet knelt with him pressed close against her.

Into both their minds came the vision of a ship with her white sails spread. Joseph laughing with the wind in his face, and in the bows of the vessel, her hands clasped to her breast and her head thrown back – the figurehead of Janet.

'Will you be proud?' whispered the boy.

She raised her head and looked into his eyes.

# 10

If it were possible it seemed that the incident of the help-less boat and the last-minute rescue bound Janet and Joseph even more closely together. It was not only the tie of flesh and blood that made them part of one another, nor even the knowledge that their minds and their bodies were cast in the same mould; it was like a union of spirit defying time and eternity – something that had existed between them before birth, before their physical conception of each other. Janet continued to be a devoted faithful wife to Thomas, and a kind and careful mother to her other children, but with Joseph there was an understanding and a love that held the rare strange quality of immortality. Frequently she read his thoughts and his wishes before he had expressed them; a shadow scarce passed before his face but that she knew the reason. His joys were her joys, and she shared with him his childish sorrows. He was her second self, he was to do all the things which had been denied her because of her sex. He loved the sea and the ships with the same passion that she did, and because he would be a man he would become a sailor, and she would see through his eyes all those dreams she had imagined when she was alone.

Now she knew she would never be alone again; separation from Joseph would not take him from her. He knew this too; no words passed between them to speak of these things; a smile in passing, a touch of her hand, a glance at him across the table and he was aware of the flood of warmth that came to him from her and he rejoiced in his soul, accepting her gift to him.

When his father and his brothers and sisters were in the room, when they were sitting at their meals around the table, Joseph was disturbed and thrilled by his feeling of a conspirator. His mother sat with the teacups in front of her, her hand raised, her elbow crooked so that the stuff of the dress she wore folded in a thousand pleats, her fingers clasped round the handle of the teapot. Lizzie, the youngest child, sat by her side, a pale delicate little girl with something of Janet in her face, and Samuel the eldest boy on her right. Joseph would place himself where he could see the light of the lamp swing upon Janet's head, like a halo of gold above her dark hair.

He looked around him, his father talking, biting his food slowly and thoughtfully, Samuel and Mary discussing some question the teacher had brought up in school, Philip sneaking something from Herbert's plate while Herbert listened to Samuel with an open mouth.

Joseph smiled to himself. 'They none of 'em know, they don't understand,' and then he would watch Janet's head as she lowered it for an instant to attend to Lizzie. He willed her instinctively to look up, and in a second she would raise her eyes and glance across at him, meeting his eyes, sending a light through him that gripped him in its power, soft, compelling, stronger than life.

'Are you wantin' more tea, Joseph?' – and he would hold out his cup, trying to touch her hands with his fingers – 'Please, mother.'

Then they smiled at each other, over the top of the teacup, recklessly, blindly, as if they held a secret and defied humanity. He noted with a sting of pride the change of her voice when she spoke his name.

To his father the tone of it was kind and tender, to his brothers and Mary warm and cheerful, with something gentler in it, perhaps, for little Lizzie, but for himself there was a note that was his alone by right, something between a whisper and a caress, as though she was kneeling in the dark beside him, holding him to her. 'Joseph' – she would say – 'Joseph.'

Often in the daytime when the household work was finished and done, and Thomas was still down at his business in the yard, Janet would allow Mary and Sam to go out in charge of the younger children, bidding them take special care of Lizzie who must not tire herself; and then when the house was silent and still she would straighten her hair before the little mirror in her bedroom, and search for her shawl and bonnet. She would hear someone tiptoe to the door, and knowing who it was a warmth would come to her heart, but she would hum some line of a song and fiddle with her things, pretending she had not heard.

Suddenly she would feel her elbows gripped behind her, and a head laid against her back – and then her elbows released, and two arms would creep under hers and feel their way upwards. She would laugh and free herself, then feel his hair with her hands and lay her face against his cheek.

'Why baint you gone with the others?' she whispered.

'Why be you puttin' on your out-door clothes?' he whispered back.

'You don't know anythin',' she would say. 'As it happens I'm goin' to pay a visit to Mrs Hocken, who is poorly they tell me, an' she's expectin' me to cheer her, poor soul.'

'I'm terrible sorry Mrs Hocken'll be disappointed,' said Joseph carelessly, ''cos it happens you're not goin'.'

'No? – an' why not, son?'

'You know without tellin' you'm comin' out with me,' he answered.

'No – I'm not,' she pretended.

'Yes – you be,' said Joseph.

And they would steal quietly from the house for fear the others had not gone, and then avoiding the main street of Plyn, they would climb a narrow path that ran behind the houses, to the cliffs and the Castle ruins. They would sit there watching the sea, she with her back against the wall, her legs tucked under her, and he lying full length upon the grass, his chin in his hands, chewing a piece of straw the while, and ever and anon turning his eyes from the horizon to look at her face.

She told him of her childhood, and her longing to be a man, and the wild desires that used to come over her, like the cattle and the sheep in the hills at odd seasons, to break pasture and leave the quiet peaceful life for adventure and unknown things. He held her hand and understood, for these desires

69

were his also, and one day he was certain that they would realize them together.

'Go on speakin'; he would implore her. 'Never stop tellin' me your wishes an' your thoughts – and the stories of your feelin's as a girl. It's as if I'd always known about 'em, and was rememberin'.'

He asked her to describe her figure and her face.

'Are you changed much since then, was you thin an' wispy, like little Liz will be?'

'Yes – something like Liz maybe, but never weak in health. More like you, Joseph.'

He bit hard on his straw, kicking his heels with pride.

'I reckon there's more beauty to you than anyone in Plyn, now at this minute, but all the same, I'd dearly loved to have seen you then, slight an' frail, not much bigger'n Mary.'

She looked down at his head and tried to remember the vision of him on the hill – tired, middle-aged, with his weary, haggard eyes; and there now at her feet was this boy, with his dark hair and his wild care-free spirit.

His path was mapped out ahead of him, hard maybe – narrow and tortuous in places, but she would be beside him.

They sat together, silent and thoughtful. He untied the strings of her bonnet, and taking it off, he laid it on her lap.

'I want to watch the wind playin' with your hair,' he said slyly; but she knew what he was about, and drew away from him, for in two seconds he would have drawn away the pins as well, and brought her hair tumbling about her shoulders.

'Why do you act so?' she sighed happily, not angry, but content with his ways.

'I don't know.' He lay on his side and ran his finger along her arm. 'When I go to sea, I'll buy you jewels an' clothin' from foreign parts, lace too, and scent. I'll conceal 'em from the Customs, act as a smuggler, an' bring 'em to your room i' the dark o' the night. We'll wrap the garments about you, an' I'll clasp the jewels round your throat an' wrist. The scent shall go beside your eyebrows an' your ears, and maybe, a tiny drop i' the hollow of your hand.'

'What more will ye bring, Joseph?'

'Baint ye content with that, you graspin' angel? We'll not be tellin' anyone o' course. 'Twill be a close secret for you an' me, when the rest of folk's in bed an' asleep.'

'Where will ye sail to, son?'

'I reckon as I'll be crossin' the world, from "China to Peru" like they say in the poetry book at school. I'll see great cities, thronged with folk dressed rich an' grand, with dark queer-coloured skins. There'll be palaces and kings, there'll be mountains reachin' to the sky, an' forests that stretch from country to country, silent save for the song o' birds an' the grave rustlin' leaves. But best of all is the sea itself, with never a sight o' land for days, an' the big waves breakin' astern of you. Wind like a slap on your cheek, an' a sting from the rain.'

'Will you love this most?'

'More than anythin', exceptin' you waitin' for me on the top o' Plyn hill. Even afore we left the Lizard, I'd know you would be there. No cities, no oceans, there'd be nothin' like the sight of you, here, by the Castle ruins. You'd come alone, without father, without Sam or the others – you alone, for me.'

'You wouldn't be sorry to be back?' she asked, knowing his answer.

'What d'you think?'

He was silent a while, then spoke again, chewing his straw.

'I've in my mind's eye the model of my ship. I can picture the shear of her, an' the long graceful lines. Her sails spread to the wind. She'd run like a devil if I let her, laughin' with the joy of escape, but a touch of my hand an' she'd under-stand, obeyin' my will, recognizin' I was her master an' lovin' me for it.'

He leant over and watched Janet with narrow eyes, sweeping the whole of her.

'What is it, Joseph?' she asked, conscious of his gaze.

He laughed, and spitting out his straw upon the ground, he reached for her hand.

'Women are like ships,' he said.

71

# 11

As the children grew older, so did the little town of
Plyn thrive and flourish.
Already it was changed from the Plyn that Janet
had known as a girl, and as she had seen it as a whole from
the top of the hill on her wedding morning. The old quiet
air of peace and calm seemed to have departed, it was no
longer a small village nestling at the foot of the hill, with the
water from the harbour coming nearly as far as the cottage
doors at high tide. In the old days the harbour had often been
empty save for the old fishing luggers belonging to the folk
of Plyn, and when the men came back from their fishing or
down from their work in the fields, they would lean over the
wall by the slip of Coombe's yard, and gossip over their pipes,
the nets spread out to dry on the cobbled stones, and naught
to watch save the gulls diving for fish in the water, and the
smoke curling from their cottage chimneys, with the women-
folk at their doors.

Then the rooks would rise like a cloud from the trees above
Squire Trelawney's house, and circle in the air, calling to one
another.

When Janet was first wed she and Thomas would stroll in
the fields above Plyn on summer evenings, and watch the
orange patterns that the sun made in the water. No sound
came from the harbour then; maybe from time to time the
soft splash of an oar, as someone pulled his boat away from
the seaweed, and made his way along the narrow pill that led
to Polmear.

They would watch the dark form of his boat slowly dissolve
into the shadows and the gathering twilight. The sun would
lighten the farthest hill with a touch of flame for one instant,

leaving a glow upon Plyn that caught the glass of the cottage windows, and shone bravely upon the slate roofs – then the sun would sink beyond the tall beacon, that stood on the high sheer cliffs above Pennybinny Sands. The colour lingered yet on the water, and beside them in the fields the last rays touched with gold the sheaves of riotous corn. Silence fell upon Plyn, with now out of the dusk a voice from the cobbled square calling a name, or the bark of a dog from the farm in Polmear Valley. If it was Sunday the bells from Lanoc Church called the folk of Plyn to evensong, and the people would walk along the footpath that led over the fields to the Church above Polmear. Before supper the younger ones, lovers, or newly wed like Janet and Thomas, would climb the steep hill to the Castle ruins, and wait for the moon to rise, white and ghostly, making a magic channel of the water, that crept away to the horizon like a narrow pointing finger.

Such was the peace and the silence of Plyn, lost by itself, far from the clamour and cries of a city. Then little by little the changes came. The importance of the china clay was discovered and the mines were started. Rough jetties were built where the river and harbour meet, and the clay was brought there.

Ships came to Plyn in numbers to load with the clay, and often now the harbour was a forest of masts, awaiting their turn at the jetty.

The people of Plyn were delighted with the growth of the town – trade would make them prosperous and rich. Only the old folk grumbled, disliking the change.

'What be us wantin' with ships an' clay?' they muttered

'There's nothin' now but hammer and crash i' the harbour, from mornin' till night. Why can't they leave Plyn alone?'

New houses were built up the hill, straighter and more severe than the old cottages at the water's edge, and they had plain gaunt windows hung with lace curtains. The quaint latticed windows of the cottages were considered old-fashioned and rough, and instead of the roofs being tiled with the soft grey slate, they were black and shiny. Queen Victoria was now on the throne, and in the parlours of the Plyn houses her likeness would hang, with that of the Prince Consort at her side.

Plyn was no longer a lazy, sleepy harbour, but a busy port, with the noise of ships and the loading of clay. The ship-building yard of Thomas Coombe was important in Plyn. Large vessels were launched from the slip now, ships of over a hundred tons, schooners, barquentines, and the like.

Thomas was now forty-eight, little changed in character, but his work had told on him; his shoulders were bent, and there were tired lines beneath his eyes. He thought only of the business, and the name he had made for himself in Plyn. He was devoted to his wife and his family, but the business came first. They still lived in Ivy House. Nothing had been altered here, the large warm kitchen was the same, where they all sat around the table and had their meals.

Mary had helped her mother make new curtains for the parlour, and in the corner of the room was a harmonium which she had learnt to play.

Samuel had joined his father down at the yard, and proved as honest and clever a workman as Thomas had been at his age. He was indeed his father's right-hand man, and Herbert too, ever eager to copy his brother, was learning the trade beside him. Soon perhaps the board above the yard would bear their names as well – 'Thomas Coombe and Sons'. That was the dream always present in the minds of Samuel and Herbert.

Mary remained at home in Ivy House, cheerful and willing, desiring nothing better than to remain there all her life and look after the needs of her father and brothers.

Philip seemed to have no wish to join his brothers later at the yard; he was a queer secretive boy with his own friends and his own ideas, and he spoke little, spending most of his time reading in a corner.

Lizzie was now a dear unselfish little girl of ten, who seemed fond of everybody, and was made a general pet by the household.

What of Joseph? At eighteen he was taller than his father and his brothers, with square powerful shoulders and a massive chest. Except for Lizzie, he was the only dark one of the Coombe family. His hair was thick and curly, already whiskers were growing on his cheeks, and he looked older than his brother Samuel, who was twenty-two. He had not yet learnt caution. There was not a man in Plyn he would not have fought for the pleasure of it, nor any wild escapade of which he did not make himself the leader. Old people shook their heads when Joe Coombe's name was mentioned.

The girls of Plyn blushed when he looked at them in church, which he had made a point of doing, and they would gather in groups, giggling, and whispering excitedly when he passed them in the street. 'He's treated Emmie Tippit shameful,' whispered one. 'Aye, an' now they say he's turned down Polly Rogers,' whispered another. Who would be the next victim, they wondered. One of them, perhaps. The secret longing rose in their hearts and would not be stilled.

It was high time Joseph went to sea. He was going, too; very shortly now he was to join the *Francis Hope* as apprentice under Captain Collins, Sarah Collins's husband.

Joseph felt that the first ambition of his life was to be realized. To go to sea, to leave Plyn behind him, and all the stuffy ill-natured folk who would not let him do as he wished. He was not afraid of roughing it in a cramped barquentine, of being treated possibly worse than a dog, of being soaked to the skin for hours on end, little enough to eat and a few wretched hours of sleep; this was a man's life, and in spite of having to obey orders from morning till night, it was a free life. He laughed at Herbert and Samuel, who seemed content and proud of themselves after a day's work down at the yard. What did they know of real work? Icy gales and shaking sea-drenched canvas, slippery decks in the darkness, hard ropes that tore your fingers, the waves and the wind fighting in unison against your life, the cries and oaths of roughmen. None of his family envied him, save one, Janet, his mother. At forty-two she was unchanged; the years had not left their mark upon her. There were no lines beneath Janet's eyes, no grey threads in her hair.

Her figure was still that of a young woman, for all the six

75

children she had borne. Her eyes were bold and fearless like her son's, and her chin was perhaps more determined than ever. She alone envied Joseph. There was nothing she desired more than to be at his side on his first ship, and to share his discomforts and his dangers.

Before he came to her, before he was born, she had always known that the sea would claim him, as it would have claimed her had she been a man.

She was proud that Joseph was to be a sailor, but her heart was sick and cold at the anguish of parting. She despised herself for her weakness, she who had no fears of death nor danger. Her reason told her to be still and unmoved, she would follow Joseph in the spirit; but her body claimed his body, she could not bear that his eyes would no longer light upon hers, nor his voice whisper in her ear, nor his arms hold her close. She must fight against this weakness, fight with all the strength that was in her, and conquer herself.

She made no attempt to hide her pain from Joseph; they had never hidden anything from each other.

They said little during these last days. They pretended to busy themselves with Joseph's new clothes. Joseph was never still for a moment. He ran wild about the countryside to prevent himself from thinking, he fought the farmer's son over to Polmear Farm, and was chased by the labourers, he made love to three girls in Plyn on the same day and forgot them a moment afterwards. He disturbed his brother and his father who were working on a new boat down at the yard. He spoilt Mary's cakes that she had baked so carefully for supper, he hid Lizzie's doll behind the harmonium where she could not reach it, he took Philip's books and chucked them down the dried-up disused well at the bottom of the garden.

His spirits were wilder and higher than they had ever been in his life, he sang and shouted at the top of his voice, he broke a chair in the parlour, the house shook with his noise and his clatter.

'There won't be no peace till you'm gone,' cried Mary indignantly.

76

'Hurrah – hurrah – only one more day now,' shouted Joe, his eyes shining, his hair falling over his face.

Only Janet understood that this was a blind, a last defiance, a pretence of strength, and every now and then his eyes would meet hers across the room, savage, miserable – 'I love you – love you – love you.'

He saw her lower her head, and the colour drain from her face, leaving it white and pitiful. She clenched her hands, and turned away, looking into the fire. 'Careful – now, Mary, with the hot plates,' she said in a steady voice.

He could bear it no longer. He ran from the room and left the house, climbing the steep hill to the cliff like a madman, the angry futile tears brushing his cheek, blaspheming God aloud. The trees tossed in the wind, the hedges moved, the sheep cried sorrowfully from beyond the fields. He saw none of them, he saw only Janet's face and her dark eyes looking up into his. He felt her cool hands on his forehead, her low voice speaking his name. He knew the sound of her footsteps, the rustle of her skirt.

He remembered the strength of her arms when she carried him as a little boy, and the sweet clean smell of her as he pushed his head against her bodice. He remembered looking up at her, holding her hand; running madly to her to climb in her lap and to mutter some nonsense in her ear. She kneeling beside his bed at nights and tucking him safely, while Samuel and Herbert slept like logs in the corner.

How they laughed and whispered like conspirators in the darkness and he would watch her steal from the room like a pale ghost shielding the light with her hand, her eyes shining, her finger on her lips.

Joseph reached the top of the cliffs, and he flung himself on the ground, tearing at the earth with his hands, groaning and kicking like one in a physical pain. 'Hell and Damnation – Hell and Damnation—'

Back at Ivy House Janet sat at the head of the table, while the family gathered round for supper.

Thomas looked about him frowning.

'Wherever's Joseph to? The lad is that wild with his goin' away tomorrow, there's nothin' to be done to him.'

'Leave him alone,' said Janet, softly. 'I reckon he's finishin' his packin' in his room.'

She knew well he had run from the house and was now cursing and blaspheming by the Castle ruins.

'Oh, no, he's not,' put in Philip, sneering. 'He went up the hill as fast as he could go. He'll be meetin' some of his girls to kiss 'em for the last time.'

'High time he went to sea,' murmured Thomas thoughtfully.

Janet looked across at her youngest son. What was this queer strain of his nature that made him mean and sly at times? He was the only one of her children she did not trust. He had more intelligence than the others, but there was something indefinable in his character that made her shudder. He was harmless at present, but when he grew to be a man, what then?

She wondered if the difference in him was owing to her weakness after he had been born. She had not been able to nurse him.

Thus she had never felt that he belonged to her.

She turned her eyes away from Philip, and glanced at the clock on the wall. Joseph would be hungry. She knew that sitting with his family would be irksome to him this last evening, and he would want only to be left alone with her. At that moment Joseph came into the room. His clothes were bespattered with mud, and there was an ugly red mark on his cheek.

Janet knew this meant he had been weeping.

The family glanced at him. They thought he had probably cut himself, falling by the stile.

Only Philip laughed quietly to himself. 'Did she scratch you so hard, Joe?' he asked.

'Be silent, Philip,' said his mother sharply, and she handed Joseph his plate.

He sat down without a word, and never spoke throughout

78

the meal. The others took no notice of him, they were used to Joe's queer changes of mood.

When supper was cleared, they all sat round the fire as they did every night. Janet and Mary took their sewing on their laps, while Lizzie learnt a new stitch from her sister. She alone seemed to sense something of the agony in her mother's eyes and Joseph's, and once she went across to her brother and squeezed his hand. He looked up at her in surprise, and noticed for the first time that her expression was like to Janet's. He pulled her curls softly and smiled. 'I'll be bringin' ye back a new dolly for sure,' he told her. Thomas sat in his armchair opposite his wife, with a book in his hands. He narrowed his eyes at the small print, and fumbled for his glasses. How old he was compared to the Thomas who had kissed Janet on the top of the Plyn hill, over twenty years ago. Yet he saw no difference in himself.

Herbert and Samuel were cleaning Samuel's gun in a corner of the room, Philip was counting the money in his money-box. He always had more silver than any of the others. Joseph was standing at the window, his hands in his pockets, only his back view visible.

The old clock ticked and coughed on the wall, the fire settled sluggishly in the grate.

Thomas turned a corner of his book, and then laid his head against the back of the chair, and took off his spectacles. His eyes fluttered, he sighed, he opened his mouth wide and yawned horribly.

'Think I'll be goin' up, dear,' he said to Janet.

'Yes, Thomas,' she answered. 'It's your bedtime, too, Lizzie.'

There was the sound of Lizzie's light patter in the girls' room, and the heavy sober tread of Thomas in the room over the porch.

A board creaked loudly now and then. One by one the others moved off to bed, and soon Janet and Joseph were left alone.

She laid aside her work, and poked at the dying fire. The room felt chilly, drear. Joseph put out the lamp, and snuffed the candles. He drew aside the curtains, and the light of the moon made a white pattern on the carpet. Then he came across the room, and knelt beside Janet in the darkness.

'Do you know how much I love you?' he whispered.

'Yes, Joseph.'

He held her fingers and kissed the hollows of her hands.

'I reckon I've never realized before what the losin' o' you meant.'

She rested her head on his shoulder when he said this.

'You won't be losin' me, Joseph. This baint a real partin', 'tes a reason for you to find yourself, an' lead the life that's suited to you.'

"Twon't be a life away from you. 'Twill be a misery an' an anguish, turnin' me to stone till I'm by your side again.'

'Hush, Joseph, I won't let you say these things. Cowardice is no man's business, 'tisn't for the likes o' you an' me.'

He dug his nails into her hand.

'Call me a coward, do you?'

'Yes — we'm both cowards, an' I'm filled with shame at myself.'

He put out his hand and felt her chin.

'I knew it would be stickin' i' the air,' he smiled. "Tisn't no good, don't let's be brave for our last few hours together. Bravery's no mortal use to me now. I want to lay here all night, and cry at your feet, and worship you in a still an' silent way.'

He bent his head, and she laughed in the darkness, and kissed the back of his neck.

'How long are you goin' on bein' a child like this?'

'Always — never. I don't know.'

'Why baint I a man to come along wi' you?' she sighed. 'I'd be at your side i' the daytime an' learn a sailor's life. I can picture the sway o' the vessel as she leans to the wind, an' in rough weather the grey seas sweepin' the deck. Bare feet, bare head, an' the taste of salt on your cracked lips. At night the kiss of wind an' rain, the shouts of men through the darkness, and then sudden, when a great cloud broke away loose from the sky, there'd be one wild white star.'

'Come with me,' he said. 'I'll find you clothes – pretend you're Sam; come along to keep me company.'

'You'll never be lonely, Joseph. Promise you'll never be lonely?'

'Aye, I promise.'

'What's to be done about darnin' your socks an' the like? An' you won't be fed proper. Oh! sudden, the fear an' dread of it all comes upon me – you goin' away without me like this.'

'Mother, dearest love – there'll be nothin' to hurt. Look, it's me the brave one now, an' you all pale an' tremblin' like a lamb i' the fields.' He took her in his arms and rocked to and fro.

'Where's your proud chin now?'

''Tes all a sham, an' always has been through my life,' she whispered. 'You know that, don't you?'

She laughed through her tears.

'Stop it, will you?' he said. 'Here's fine talk about bravery. Listen, every night at this hour, whatever I'm doin' and wherever I be, I'll look for a star in the sky; an' when I judge as there's a star pointin' his finger over Plyn I'll close my eyes and say good night to you.'

'Joseph, what made you think o' that?'

'It came to me by the Castle ruin tonight, and gave me comfort; and at this same time when I'm away on the sea, you'll lean out o' your room over the porch; an' the star that's direct above you will be the star I'm lookin' at.'

'I'll remember, Joseph. Every night. Will you never be forgettin'?'

'Never – never.'

She took his face in her hands and smiled, while the moonlight cast a shadow in his eyes.

'My baby – my sweet.'

The ashes fell in the grate, and the clock ticked slow and solemn on the wall.

★   ★   ★

81

Although the next day was Sunday the wind held true from the north, and Captain Collins determined to sail with the evening tide. Joseph's things were got on board and stowed away by his hammock in the fo'c'sle. All the family came down to the slip to see him off, and bid him farewell. Thomas shook him warmly by the hand and blew his nose rather too heartily, when he saw him climb into the boat with his companions, and pull for the ship.

He was fond and proud of his handsome son for all his wild ways. The boys clapped their brother on the shoulder and chaffed him for a sailor, while Joseph kept up his jokes and his laughter until the end. Mary slipped a couple of hot saffron buns into his pocket, and Lizzie gave him a spray of white heather she had discovered on the hills. Janet stood a little apart from the others, chatting quietly to one of the men whom she knew. Joseph hung back too, and made some cheerful remark to his father about the weather.

The last minutes were passing, flying now – faster – faster; they fled away in a hopeless tangle of time. Joseph took a step towards Janet. The men were waiting in the boat below, ready to push off for the ship.

He grasped her hands and kissed her hurriedly, roughly on her neck behind her ear. 'I can't find my speech somehow,' he muttered, 'there was somethin' – many things – I was goin' to have told you. All gone now – I've no thoughts in my head.' He swallowed hard. Janet looked over his head. There seemed to be no feeling in her heart. Her limbs were turned to stone, her tongue refused to move. She noticed that Mary's bonnet was hanging a little crooked. It gave her a drunken, foolish appearance. She must remember to tell her.

'Yes,' she said, and that was all.

'Don't – don't get catchin' cold or anythin', remember the evenin's are chillsome now,' he told her desperately.

'No – oh! no!' Janet listened with surprise to her own voice, dull and cold.

'Good-bye.' She looked at him in horror, her eyes sweeping

his face, her hands clutching foolishly at her shawl. 'Are you goin'?'

He turned from her and jumped with a shout into the boat.

'Give us an oar, an' let's pull like the devil.'

The boat swung away across the harbour, and he was gone. Suddenly the bells began to peal for evensong from Lanoc Church.

Usually they were soft and mellow, breathing a whisper of peace and content, but now they clanged loudly, furiously. They ran in Janet's ears, hideous, monotonous, never changing their ceaseless clamour, falling over each other in a wild confusion of sound.

Thomas came beside her and held her arm.

'Feelin' faint, love?' he asked kindly. 'Don't 'ee start worryin' over the lad, he'll soon find his feet, I reckon.'

She shook her head silently, unable to speak, she put her hands over her ears.

'It's them bells,' she cried suddenly. 'Won't they never cease, never?'

The children were looking at her curiously.

'Come to church, mother dear,' said Mary, 'and we'll all pray that Joe is returned safe and sound to us.'

Thomas pulled out his watch.

'We ought to be startin',' he began awkwardly. 'Us has never been late in our lives as far as I can remember.'

They waited on the slip, a kind, hesitating little group, unequal to the occasion.

Janet drew her cloak about her, and fastened it at the neck.

'No – we mustn't be late.'

They walked back along the slip, and turned up the hill. The bells were hushed for a moment, and now another sound rose from the harbour; the hauling and rattling of chains. It was the *Francis Hope* weighing anchor.

The Coombes walked hurriedly to the stile that led across the fields. They tried to speak easily and naturally, but all were aware of their mother's silent grief. Poor Thomas blundered tactlessly, meaning to cheer and to comfort.

'Ah! well, we'll miss the lad's voice about the house for sure. 'Twill seem a different place without him.'

The bells started once more, screaming and insistent.

Janet tried to shut her mind to the sound, to put away every thought from her. It was autumn, the time of the year that she and Joseph loved the best. The ripe corn was cut, and the rough edges that were left were short and prickly stubble to the feet. The hedges were bright with hips and haws, and in the gardens in Plyn drooped the scarlet fuchsias. Down in Polmear Valley below Lanoc Church the golden bracken was waist-high and soft lichen clung to the branches of the trees. The farms smelt of manure, and of the bitter wood smoke that rose from the bonfires of the fallen leaves. The swollen brook murmured loudly over the flat grey stones. The evening was grey and cold, the air hinting of mists arising from the river banks. In the elm tree by the church a thrush sang of the autumn, his note sweeter and more plaintive than in spring.

By the gate the family turned, and looked towards the harbour. Already the ship was clear of the land, and every sail set. Her bows were turned to the horizon, and Plyn lay behind her. Soon the land would be astern like a dark smudge in the coming dusk, and the lights would be swallowed up in the darkness.

'Well, there goes the last of Joseph,' sighed Thomas.

The ship slipped away like a bird upon the surface of the still water. The bells ceased ringing. Janet Coombe led the way into the church, followed by her husband and her children. She sat through the service dumb and unresponsive.

The setting sun caught the western windows in a beam of light. She knew this same beam would cross the path of the ship that sailed away. The little church was hushed and peaceful. Centuries old, it still held the presence of those folk who had knelt there in years gone by. The stones were worn with the knees of humble people, now in their graves, their names long buried and forgotten. Those who worshipped there beside Janet would one day in their turn come to the same unbroken silence and rest.

Their voices murmured in prayer now, as they responded to the preacher. Joseph in his ship thought of them kneeling there in Lanoc Church, and of his mother's pale face turned to the lattice windows.

The *Francis Hope* plunged on, with her stern lifting to the sea, and the fresh wind hissing in the flattened sails.

In Lanoc Church the voices sang loud and true, resounding in the old rafters, and with them the plaintive organ rose and fell.

> Jesu – lover of my soul
> Let me to Thy bosom fly,
> While the nearer waters roll,
> While the tempest still is high.
>
> Hide me, O! my Saviour, hide,
> Till the storm of life be past,
> Safe into the haven guide
> O! receive my soul at last.

Janet sang with the rest, but her heart stole away from the sound of the hymn and from the voices of the people, beyond the bowed heads and the quivering candles; all she saw were the stars of heaven, and the lights of a ship upon a lonely sea.

# 12

During the months that followed, Janet tried to accustom herself to Joseph's absence. At first it was as though all mortal feeling had left her. She felt as if she herself were dead, and that some mechanical being had taken hold of her limbs and her mind, to continue her life in the same narrow channels as before. Her body was like an empty husk, the nerves and the senses were departed. Outwardly there was no perceptible change, save that her head was carried somewhat higher; she wrapped herself in a cloak of pride to mask her grief.

For all her declaration and her certitude that a physical separation could mean nothing to her and Joseph, she was torn and shattered by the very longing for his presence. Wherever she walked in Plyn it seemed to her that she was treading in his footprints.

The hills and the cliffs resounded with his clamour, the marks of him were in the wet sand beneath the rocks, and in the breaking of the waves upon the shore. Wherever she turned she found herself searching for some sign of him, as though there was some double torture for her in the places where he had been that gave to her a bitter comfort.

The nights were long and tedious. Janet would be awake hour after hour, with Thomas slumbering heavily at her side, and she would turn her head to the chink of air that came through the curtained latticed window, and watch for the white star in the dark blanket of the heavy sky. She tried to send herself through space to the ship upon distant waters, and to stand beside her beloved as he watched through the night on the silent deck. She knew that his thoughts and his soul were with her, but these were not enough for her pitiful human wants. She cursed the weakness of her flesh that hungered for his nearness and his touch, she fought against the demand of her eyes to dwell upon him. To touch his hands and his body that was part of herself, to smell the familiar scent of sea and earth and sun that clung to his clothes, to taste the salt spray that washed from his skin, all these she claimed; but they were taken from her, leaving her half-asleep and a shadow of a woman.

The home she had made for him was hollow and denuded of warmth, it lacked the one reason for its existence.

At times the want of him gripped her like the pain she had suffered in the bearing of him, and she would leave the house and her children and climb once more the hill to the Castle ruins. No sound came from her, she made no gesture of despair. Her cheeks were free from the queer comfort of tears. All that she did was to stand with her back against the wall, her head uplifted, her eyes fixed on the hard grey line where sea and sky meet.

At home in Ivy House new events took place, were recognized and passed into the natural scheme of daily life.

Samuel began to wait at the garden gate of Silas Trehurst the coastguard on Sunday afternoons, and at half past three the coastguard's daughter Posy came down the path, and after chatting awkwardly for a while, the gate would click and slam, and Miss Posy would be walking up the hill on Samuel's arm.

The faithful Herbert aided his brother in the very difficult composition of love notes, and often in the evening the pair of them would sit in the corner of the parlour, with pens, paper, and ink, and Samuel would frown heavily and struggle with his writing, while Herbert encouraged him and searched for words in the dictionary.

Mary did not bother herself about the young men of Plyn, she preferred to busy herself in Ivy House, and to attend to the wishes of her father and mother.

One day Philip arrived for dinner and announced his intention of becoming an office boy in the shipbroking firm of 'Hogg and Williams' in Plyn.

His father stared at him in amazement.

'Don't ye want to be joinin' your brothers down to the yard?' he asked, bewildered at his son's decision.

'No, thank you,' said Philip quietly. 'I've been an' seen Mr Hogg myself, an' he's quite willin' to take me. The pay is not much to begin with, but I'll be gettin' a rise later on if I suit him.'

'Well, I'm blessed!' said his father, leaning back in his chair. 'Goin' off by yourself an' arrangin' things.' He was secretly proud of his son's independence.

'What d'you say, Janet?' He turned to his wife.

'I think Philip knows what he's about right enough,' answered Janet. 'I reckon as he'll always go his own way through life, and get what he wants. Whether 'twill make him happy or not is another matter.'

She glanced curiously at her youngest son, with his sandy hair and his narrow deep-set eyes. Philip looked up at her and down at his plate again. Janet was aware of a strange mute antagonism to herself and all she loved. Doubt and a little seed of fear were planted in her heart by her own child. She looked, with uncertainty and a grain of horror, into the very distant future. Then she turned her mind back into the present, and gave her thoughts to Joseph, far away upon the sea. She wondered whether he would be back in time for her birthday in April. Always it had been his delight to spend this day alone with her. They made it the excuse for the first picnic of the year.

Surely Joseph would return to Plyn in the spring? From time to time she had news from him, from the great scattered ports in America, and she would walk with his letters held close to her, because they were something of himself. They were strange passionate letters, breathing a love of the sea and an enthusiasm for the life he was leading; telling of his hardships, of the harsh weather, of the ceaseless toil from morning till night which scarce left him time for reflection; the fight they had with a storm in mid-Atlantic when his companions feared that the end had come, and he himself, though wet, exhausted, dog-weary, and aching in every limb, was filled with a zest and worship that would not be denied, for the rough and dangerous calling he had chosen. In spite of it all, he felt the lack of her by his side every minute of the day and night. He worked hard, he said, throwing himself with ardour into every branch of knowledge, so that he should become a skilled seaman. Captain Collins was teaching him something of navigation, he was sure it would not take him long to acquire a second mate's ticket, but that he must serve four years as apprentice first apparently, according to the rules of the Board of Trade. He must try not to become restless and impatient waiting for it. No new scene passed before his eyes but he thought of her, and he was filled with a longing that she should be with him to share these things. He looked for the star at night which he judged to be above her head in Plyn, and he bade this star keep watch over her, and save her well and unchanged for when he should return.

So Janet waited during the first months of the year in hope and expectation for a letter to say he would be home by April. At last one came, uncertain of the date of return, but he added in post-scriptum: 'There is a calendar in the fo'c'sle, and I have marked with a red cross the 10th of April. The men here inquired of me the reason for doing this, and I told them that on that day I must be back in Plyn, for I had a tryst with the woman of my heart, and that the gales of the Atlantic could not gainsay me in the keeping of it.'

This was the last letter that Janet received, and then the month of March drew to a close. At any day now the *Francis Hope* was expected in Plyn, and every evening Janet climbed to the Castle ruin, and shading her eyes with her hand she waited for the first sight of a white sail emerging on the rim of the horizon.

Sometimes Lizzie came with her, or one of the boys when they could spare time from the work in the yard, and once Thomas stood by the side of his wife, a proud important figure with a new telescope under his arm, which he had bought specially for the occasion. And still no sail appeared.

On 9 April Janet climbed with a sick and weary heart to

the top of the hill, and for two hours she waited there against the walls of the ruin, with the east wind blowing her hair and her skirts and a green white-edged sea thundering and breaking on the rocks below.

These would mean head winds for a ship coming up-Channel, and a hard beat against it to make Plyn. She waited there until the sun set like a wind-swept ball of fire behind the short flaked clouds, and the smoke rose from the chimneys and the lamps were lit, and dusk crept upon Plyn, blotting out the sea.

And the *Francis Hope* came not. So Janet turned away, and walked down the steep hill where the dogs ran about the gutters sniffing for food, and children played and screamed, and peaceable comfortable folk stood at their doors with no care upon their shoulders, and no wrinkles beneath their eyes.

The lights showed through the curtains of Ivy House, and the cheerful smoke curled from the chimney. Her husband and her children were waiting for her, the supper laid upon the table.

The clock ticked on the wall, and all was as it had been. She watched their kindly happy faces gathered round the fire, chatting with unconcern, content and unaware.

'They are of me,' she thought, 'and I belong to them. But my heart lies in the bows of a swaying plunging ship, and my thoughts are in the keeping of my beloved.'

The evening wore away, the firelight dimmed, and the candles shrunk into themselves. The children went to their rooms, and Janet lay once more beside Thomas in the bed they had shared for nearly twenty-five years. She saw herself once more a bride, held close to his heart and her arms about his neck, and now he was nearly fifty and his face looked lined and worn on the pillow beside her.

Perhaps there was no end to a living moment, and even now her young self slept secure in the arms of Thomas, on some other plane of time, like the undying ripple on the surface of still water.

A soft wave of tenderness for him swept her, and she took hold of his hand and held it to her heart.

But he grunted and moved uneasily, turning his back to her and breathing heavily in his sleep. Then Janet laid aside his hand gently, and watching for the chink of light through the curtain she saw the star, and it seemed to lighten her heart; thus she was comforted and so fell asleep.

Just before daybreak she awoke, startled by the sound of something striking against the window pane. She sat up in bed and saw the grey dawn steal into the room, and a flat round pebble lying at her feet.

In a moment she was leaning from the window, heedless of the cold still air, her two dark plaits hanging about her like a young girl.

He stood there in the shadow of the house, his hand upon the thick strong ivy, his face upturned.

'Joseph,' she whispered. 'Joseph.' For a moment he gazed at her, saying nothing, watching the light that was aflame in her eyes.

'Thought I'd be forgettin' your birthday?' he called softly. 'Didn't I vow we'd drop anchor in Plyn harbour before the sun rose over Polmear Hill, before the gold rays lit the tower of Lanoc Church? The *Francis Hope* 'as been safe an' snug an hour since; we creepin' in with the break o' dawn to the sleepin' harbour, an' you forgetful in your bed.'

He mocked at her, laughing, and then when she shook her head and a tear rose in the corner of her eye, he seized hold of the thick ivy branches that clung to the face of the house, and swung himself up, hand over hand, to the ledge of the window where she waited motionless.

And that was how Joseph returned to Janet in the spring of the year, as he had promised her.

91

# 13

There were many partings after that first one, and many returnings.

Joseph's boyhood lay behind him, and it was too late now for him to go back on the calling which he had chosen. Not that the wish ever came across him, for it seemed to him that he was predestined for the sea and he knew that there was no other life which would suit him so well; but he could see the suffering that lay behind Janet's eyes every time he went from her, and on his return the hollow marks in her cheek and the shadows told their own tale.

If only it were possible to take her away with him. If he learnt his trade with all the energy and the force in his brain, he would rise steadily to the highest position, and there would be nothing to prevent him from laying his Master's certificate in Janet's hands, and welcoming her aboard their own vessel.

He whispered these ambitions to her when on his brief holidays at Plyn, and she watched his eyes and trusted him, knowing no power could gainsay his dream.

They spoke together of the ship that should be built for her, of the strength of her timbers, made from the very trees in Truan woods. The family ship, that would carry the Coombe fortunes. The time had not yet come, perhaps in six, ten years she would be built by his father and his brothers, and then Janet would be the soul of her and Joseph her master. Meanwhile they visioned her in their minds, they drew pictures of her with the stub of an old pencil, they calculated her size, her cargo capacity, her rig, the cut of her sails. Thomas and the sons were told of the scheme and they were filled with delight at the thought of a Coombe ship, commanded by a Coombe, to bring them wealth and glory from foreign parts.

Thomas made a model in his workshop, and exhibited it with pride to the fond gaze of his family. Part of the wealth that Thomas had saved and was to be distributed among his sons at his death, was to be used for the building of the ship. This was solemnly agreed to one Sunday at Ivy House, when Janet and all her children were present, and Thomas concluded with a moving prayer to God that at some future date, when work was not pressing on their hands, he and his sons should build the ship, and that she should be named after their dear mother and his beloved wife.

And as he spoke he placed before them the model, and taking a knife in his hand he scratched upon her stern the words: '*Janet Coombe* – Plyn'.

Then he blew his nose heartily and kissed his wife and his two daughters on both cheeks, and shook hands affectionately with his sons.

'We'll put our best work into her,' he said, his voice strong with emotion. 'Samuel, Herbert, and I. Let us hope that she shall be Joseph's first command, and may he always bring her safe and sound to port. While Philip perhaps will see to our interests in the firm of Hogg and Williams.' So all were to have a share in the vessel, and they lived now for the day when their ship would be launched in Plyn Harbour, no vague dream but a living reality.

Happy and content they gathered round the harmonium in the parlour to uplift their voices and give thanks to God.

Mary seated herself at the instrument, her gaze fixed solemnly on the hymn book in front of her, while behind her stood Thomas, his honest face uplifted with his hands on his youngest daughter's shoulders. His tall sons stood by his side, and Joseph, over-topping the lot, smiled above their heads to Janet, the ship's namesake, and she answered him with her eyes. So the existence of the *Janet Coombe* was launched into being, though as yet the trees were unfelled in Truan woods, and there was nothing to show of her but the model on the parlour table.

Thus the years passed by in Plyn, with little events and

little changes to break the monotony of the days. Samuel was wedded to pretty Posy Trehurst, and they moved into a little cottage only five doors from Ivy House, so that Samuel could still be near his family and close to the yard for his work. They were married in Lanoc Church, where Thomas and Janet were wed before them, and as Janet watched her fair solemn son standing at the altar-rail beside his bride, a tremor and a sigh came over her for the days that were no more.

It might have been Thomas himself, twenty-five years back, with his long twisting legs that never knew where to place themselves, and his serious round blue eyes.

'Janie,' he had called her, 'Janie,' trembling at himself and now he was this bent, frail, middle-aged man kneeling in the pew, peering at his prayer book over his spectacles; and standing in the place where he had stood was their grown-up son, whom she had cradled in her arms.

And as she watched Samuel through a mist of foolish tears she saw, not the strong proud bridegroom, but a high gateway beyond the fields of Plyn, and running to her arms in a torn jersey a little weeping lad.

Why had Posy chosen this hymn for the wedding day? As Janet sang she saw through the window the uncared-for stones, and the tangled grass in the churchyard.

> Time like an ever-rolling stream,
> Bears all its sons away;
> They fly forgotten as a dream—
> Dies at the opening day.

Unconscious of the irony of their words Samuel and Posy sang before the altar, their hands clasped, their thoughts filled with hope and expectation of the life before them. They were a quiet, loving couple, never to know the sublime path of passion nor the depths of great sorrow, and Janet blessed them in her heart.

Meanwhile her other children had grown up, or were growing up, besides Samuel.

94

Mary was still at home with no thoughts of marriage, while Herbert, fired by Samuel's example, was keeping company with Posy's cousin, Elsie Hoskett. They were not married, however, until 1858, when Herbert was twenty-one.

Philip had already risen from his position of office-boy, and was now a clerk to the firm of Hogg and Williams. He was still quiet and undemonstrative, was a hard worker and respected if not particularly liked by his brother clerks.

Now Joseph was so much away Janet was glad to have a companion who resembled him a little in thought, and Lizzie was a happy, high-spirited girl, by no means slow-witted, but she was young for her age.

In time twin daughters were born to Samuel and Posy, greatly to their parents' pride, and were named Mary and Martha. It was strange to Janet to hold her first grandchildren in her arms, and to wonder what their lives would be. Would Plyn be very changed when these two babies were old women? Would they love much and suffer much? Somehow she felt their lives would be serene and untroubled, and all would be well for them.

There were still no grey hairs in Janet's dark head, and no wrinkles to her face, but the repeated absence of Joseph made its mark upon her, and though she was not yet fifty there was a strain upon her heart, weakening it, gleaning little by little the strength from her pulse, so that this vital part of her became weary and tired without her knowledge. Often now a dizziness came upon her when she climbed the hill to the cliffs, and she would stop half-way, wondering the reason for her pounding temples and her quick breathing. A doctor would have sounded her heart anxiously, and shaken his head with a grave face when he had done so, prescribing some medicine to calm though it could not cure; but Janet Coombe had no faith and no love for doctors, so she had little idea that month by month she was growing steadily weaker and her heart more life-weary, so that any great shock of joy or sorrow would be the end.

The one moment for which she lived was the launching

of the unbuilt ship, named after her and for the day when
Joseph should attain his Master's certificate. The days that he
spent in Plyn were passed at her side, every minute and every
hour he could spare, but the time was all too short. He had
served as second mate aboard the *Francis Hope* and then, to
his great joy, after passing the necessary examination, he was
recommended by Captain Collins, and became first mate of
her sister ship, the *Emily Stevens*. The promised day loomed
on the horizon, he wrote letters of love and enthusiasm to
Janet, begging her to tell his father and his brothers that it
was time that the ship was started. But Thomas and his sons
were still too occupied with the list of orders on their hands,
for when the moment came they wished to give their full
time to the promised ship, and to put into her their best work
and the best material.

Herbert was the next to marry, solid, painstaking Herbert,
and though he did not copy his brother to the extent of giving
twins to his wife, he certainly never lost heart in the hopes
of doing so, for when he died at the age of eighty-three, he
was the father of fifteen children. If Janet had been alive she
would have remembered her words to Thomas on her wedding
morning: 'There's many as will depend on us, in the years to
come.' But all this was to happen many years after, and now
Herbert was a fine upstanding young fellow of twenty-one,
and his wife the same age as himself.

Now that her children led their own lives, and could fend
for themselves, the time began to hang heavy on Janet's hands.
Mary was only too pleased to take on the responsibility of
keeping the house, and seeing to her father's wants, and slowly
Janet gave up the task to her capable daughter.

She longed for Joseph more than ever now, to be with him
continually, to forsake him never. She was nearly fifty and she
had seen nothing of the world. Her old wild spirit, undaunted
and fearless, claimed its rightful place beside Joseph. They were
born to share danger and joy together, the sea that held so
strong a hold on him, had woven its spell about her too, and
though she was a woman and middle-aged she dreamt not of

a warm fireside and an easy chair, but of a lifting deck and a straining mast, grey seas beneath a wind-swept sky. There, where sky and sea mingle, and where no land beckons, she felt her youth and her strength would return to her, but to live without Joseph in Plyn meant a desolation of soul and body, and at times when her weak heart betrayed her failing strength, she felt the supreme courage ebbing from her.

Every time he left her he took something of her life's blood away with him. Joseph had no other wish in his mind but to gain his Master's certificate, and then all the regulations in the world would not stay him from bearing her away.

'You believe in me, don't you?' he said to her. 'You know that I'll reach the top soon, and that nothing can stay my course? I reckon I can figure out what my father felt in his heart when he led you to the house he'd made for you, but even that pride of his will be as dust compared to what I'll feel and tell you, when you step aboard my ship and call it home.'

'Joseph, my love,' said she, 'when that moment comes it'll be a gull as flies with you, an' no human.'

'The ship will be your ship, and her ways your ways,' he told her. 'You'll be in command an' I'll obey your wishes. There'll be no star for me to bid good night to then, no lonely watches with the moon for company. The winds'll blow because of you an' the seas laugh for joy, I guess, when they see your figure at my side upon the deck, an' your hair a' tossin' out behind you like a veil, an' the stars in heaven shamed by the light o' your eyes.'

'But Joseph, I'm old, I'm nearly fifty, why do you say these things to me?'

'You old?' He laughed and held her close. 'It's not now that I'm goin' to start tellin' you the pictures in my mind, but later – when we'm on the ship and Plyn lies far back like a forgotten dream, then I'll hae you remember the words about bein' old, so see.'

Why were they so bound together, she and this son of hers? Would she ever know, would she ever come to a full understanding of the reason for things? Life was strange, mixing folk wrong and leaving them to shift for themselves as best they may. Joseph was twenty-five now. There was scarcely a girl in Plyn who was not in love with him by now, and told him of it too, to his very face. He laughed and loved them, and left them, in an incredibly short space of time, and his affairs were as many as his escapades as a boy. Janet made no attempt to stop him, she knew that such things were as necessary to him as the food he ate and the air he breathed. He told her of his adventures in foreign ports, and all she did was to laugh and bid him teach the girls of Plyn what he had learnt. His brothers were sober married men, who heard with shocked astonishment of Joseph's evil ways, but it was little he cared for their opinion. As for the good folk of Plyn they pursed up their lips when sailor Joe was mentioned, and locked their daughters in their bedrooms after nine o'clock. Such precautions were no hindrance to Janet's son though, and if he saw a pretty face that stirred him, he'd find a way to it, for all the locked doors in the world. Parents would heave a sigh of relief when he had sailed away again, and their worry at an end. It was no use to attack his mother on the subject. She stood up for him, the shameless woman, and saw no harm in what he did. Once Mrs Salt had stopped her in the street, but it never happened again.

'Now listen here, Mrs Coombe,' said the angry woman, 'I'm not goin' to have your Joe get my Lilly into trouble, d'ye hear?'

'Ah – I hears you, Mrs Salt,' replied Janet, her chin in the air, and her hands on her hips.

'Well, then, Mrs Coombe, if your boy goes gallivantin' with my gal after dark, and doesn' bring her back till past eleven, it's not at the moon they've been lookin'.'

'I hope you'm right, Mrs Salt. If your gal goes out with my Joe and only looks at the moon, well, that girl's a fool in my opinion, an' aint worth her Salt – beggin' your pardon for the play o' the words.'

'Well, I never did,' said the furious mother. 'Ye bad shameless woman. To urge your boy to seduct my innocent gal.'

'If seducin' is the word you mean, Mrs Salt, you can save your breath,' laughed Janet. 'If your Lilly goes up to woods with my Joe, 'tisn't for the first time, I reckon. Your little pitcher has been to the well before, an' you can mind that, my dear. Good-day to ye, Mrs Salt.'

And away walked Janet with her head in the air, for all the world like her son himself.

Nobody ever got the better of her when she had made up her mind to outface them. Besides she knew that there was not a girl in Plyn who did not wait her opportunity to throw herself at Joseph's head. 'Seducin' indeed,' she thought. 'It takes two to play at that game, an' there's not a girl yet been brought to trouble which didn't know full well what she was about. There's no more preventin' young folks hungerin' after one another when they're left to themselves on a dark hillside, than ye can stop the gulls from matin' down to Lannywhet Cove i' the spring o' the year.' So reasoned Janet Coombe of Plyn in Cornwall in the year 1860. She knew that human nature was stronger than convention, and that no tight lips and sermons in the world could gainsay a man when he went with a girl. These things were as simple and as natural to her as they were to the sheep and the cattle in the fields. It was a tide of something that swept all before it, a power from which there was no escaping.

When Janet looked upon Joseph her son, and saw his flushed cheek, the damp curl on his brow, and a restless gleam in his eye, she took herself back to an evening on a Plymouth boat, when the land lay dim on the quarter and the sea and the sky were wild, and she stood in the bows of the vessel with Thomas her husband who murmured her name 'Janie', low and hushed. She remembered the touch of Thomas's hand, and how she had turned to him on the swaying deck, with the song of the wind and the water in her ears, and bade him love her.

Joseph stood at her side because of this, and the same blood that ran in her veins that night belonged to him now, and would pass to his children, and his children's children.

'I will die,' thought Janet, 'and Joseph too. But because o' the beauty of a night at sea our flesh an' blood will not pass away — but part of us will breathe this same air that we have breathed, and walk where we have trodden.'

## 14

The ship was to be built at last. The dream was to be realized. The little model placed so proudly on the mantelshelf of the parlour at Ivy House was to find a magnification of itself, take shape and form down at the yard, and instead of a toy would be a living vessel made for the rough seas and the forbidding gales, a thing to carry cargo and human lives in her keeping. Joseph was home, and Janet beside him, when the first timber was brought down the river from Truan woods. Great giant trees they were, whose trunks had withstood the storms of centuries, and whose branches had swayed in the wind before Janet's father opened his eyes upon the world.

The Coombe brothers took the great boat belonging to the yard and chose their well-seasoned timber, and then back again down the river to the harbour with the trees in tow.

Two years the ship took in the building, and into her was put the best work of Thomas and his two sons, Samuel and Herbert. Every day the sound of their hammers rose to the ears of Janet, sitting above at Ivy House.

Her children were grown up and married; Lizzie the youngest girl was twenty now and would soon be thinking of a wedding day.

Both Samuel and Herbert had families of their own. Philip, though barely twenty-three, was raised to the position of second clerk in his shipbroking firm, and he was still unmarried. Mary, too, remained at home. But they were all grown up, with their own interests, and Janet realized that she was past fifty.

All she lived for now was to see her ship launched and Joseph as its master. The years would roll away from her as if they had never been, and she would stand at the deck with Joseph at her side.

Scarce a day passed during these two years but that she visited the yard, and watched the progress of the vessel. Slowly the ship took form, first a mere gaunt skeleton which was fashioned bit by bit from the bare framework.

She was to be carvel-built with a square stern, and the length of her was ninety-seven feet. Her main breadth was twenty-two feet, and her depth, a little over twelve feet. Thomas and his sons reckoned that when she was finished she would be about a hundred and sixty tons gross. She was to be rigged as a two-masted top-sail schooner. A great moment it was when the framework of her was finished, and she stood with her mighty ribs waiting to be planked. Then every man in the yard was summoned to the work, and Plyn resounded with the ceaseless hammer and crash as the nails were driven into the sturdy planks.

Janet stood over them, a smile on her lips, a hand on her hips, a tall, lithe figure for all her fifty years. Should any man down his tools, it was: 'Were ye weak when your mother cradled ye, my lad, to give way so soon?' and the fellow would glance up ashamed and meet her keen unwavering eye. There was no standing against her, and no one cared to, for that matter, for she had a way with her that it was impossible to resist.

Unknown to Plyn and herself, however, the strength of her heart declined day by day. As the ship, her namesake, took shape and became a thing of strength, so did Janet's body weaken and her pulse slacken.

She could scarce drag herself to the top of the hill now without a faintness coming upon her, without strange black shadows dancing before her eyes. She took no notice of this; she imagined it just the natural change in her life because she was past fifty.

It would not be long now before the ship was launched from the slip, and Joseph was her master.

When he returned in the late spring of 1863 he was startled

at the change in her that none but himself could perceive. There were no silvered hairs, no lines, but a general appearance of frailty as though the strength in her had departed; her skin was stretched white over her cheek bones, and the blue veins showed clearly on her temples. He was frightened and uncertain what to do with her. The thought of possibly losing her he banished from his mind like an evil nightmare, and to make up for it he unwittingly tired her with his love, never leaving her a moment, and thus so much happiness was exhausting to her, pulling her down still further. Instead of calming her and soothing her, his presence acted like a drug that fortifies for the instant, creating an impression of renewed vigour and strength, but leaves its patient weaker than before.

She gave herself up to the enjoyment of Joseph with every ounce of power left to her. He enveloped her with his love and devotion until she became dazed and overwrought: it was too strong for her, but she had arrived at the state when she could no longer exist without it. He was at Plyn for some time now, until he had passed his examination at Plymouth, after which he hoped to take command of the new ship to be launched in the summer. The strain of these weeks was almost more than Janet could bear, and when he set off for Plymouth to sit for his examination she waited in a fever for his return. They passed the days in silent agony until the result should be known to them.

At last one morning there arrived an important-looking document, and Joseph made straight to Janet's side so that they should see it together. They unfolded the stiff parchment, stamped with the red seal of the Board of Trade.

'WHEREAS it has been reported to us that you have been found duly qualified to fulfil the duties of Master in the Merchant Service, we do hereby in pursuance of the Merchant Shipping Act 1854 grant you this Certificate of Competency. Given under the Seal of the Board of Trade this ninth day of August, 1863.'

Janet held out her arms to him with a cry – he had passed. Joseph, her son, not yet twenty-nine, was a Master in the

103

Merchant Service, the equal of middle-aged men like Captain Collins. There were great rejoicings that day at Ivy House. Janet seated at the head of the table with Joseph on her right hand, and gathered about her the grown-up sons and daughters, and her grandchildren, Samuel's two daughters and his young son, and Herbert's little boy. The next event would be the launching of the ship. Thomas and his sons, including Joseph, held a private consultation when Janet was not present, to decide the all-important matter of the ship's figurehead.

They agreed that it must be taken after Janet herself, but it seemed there was no one in Plyn who was skilled enough to undertake such a task. So a well-known carver in Bristol was commissioned to build the figurehead, and a likeness of Janet as a young woman was sent to him.

The father and his sons rejoiced in their secret, for Janet would know nothing of it until the day of the launching, as the figurehead would be bolted on to the ship's head the evening before.

The last weeks in August had come, the last nails were driven into the planks. The decks were laid and the hull painted. Her masts would be stepped when she was in the water, and there she would be rigged and fitted out for sea.

The *Janet Coombe* was ready to be launched. Her two years of waiting were over, and as the great black ship lay on the slip biding for the high spring tides, it seemed as if her very timbers called for the first embrace of the sea which she would never leave again.

The evening of 1 September was arranged for the launching, just before sunset, when the tide was at its highest. All Plyn was in a fever of excitement, because with the launching of a new ship everybody automatically took a half-holiday, and this ship was to bear the name of Coombe itself.

The evening before, a Sunday, all the family were assembled in the parlour. The weather was warm, and Janet, who was overtired with the preparations, and scarce able to realize that the great day would dawn tomorrow, sat in her chair before the open window, while the cool air played on her face. She would have climbed the hill to the Castle ruins if she had had the strength, but she was too weary. She lay back in her chair, looking down upon the harbour, and let her thoughts wander as they willed.

It seemed to her that in all her life this was the moment for which she had waited. Two other moments only would perhaps equal it. The night on the boat from Plymouth, and the morning she first held Joseph in her arms. But tomorrow her ship, built because of her, would be claimed by the sea, and she would step upon its decks and give her blessing. Life would hold no more for her than the beauty of that moment. Dusk was creeping over Plyn, over the quiet town and the sleeping harbour. Behind, cloaked in shadows, were the hills and the valleys that she loved so well. A supreme feeling of peace and contentment came upon her, she was filled with a love of all things, of people and of places, of Thomas her husband, of her children, and Joseph beyond them all.

From the parlour came the strains of the harmonium. The family were grouped round Mary as they had done for so many years, to sing the Sunday hymn. As the night descended and the stars shone upon Janet's uplifted face, her children opened their voices to their God. 'Abide with me! fast falls the eventide; the darkness deepens; Lord with me abide! When other helpers fail, and comforts flee, Help of the helpless, O abide with me. Swift to its close ebbs out life's little day; Earth's joys grow dim, its glories pass away; change and decay in all around I see; O Thou who changest not, abide with me!'

As Janet listened, sweet and clear above the voices of the others was that of Joseph – 'Abide with me.'


It was close to sunset, and the tide had made its highest mark. The red light of the sky glittered upon the houses, and the parting smile of the sun lingered upon the water. All Plyn was gathered about the slip to watch the ship plunge into the sea. The yard was decorated with flags, and thronged with folk.

A chair had been brought for Janet, and she was seated upon it, her hand on Joseph's arm. Her eyes were upon the figure-head of the ship. It was Janet herself, Janet with her dark hair and eyes and her firm chin; dressed in white with her hand at her breast.

As she looked on it for the first time her heart throbbed in her bosom and her limbs trembled. This was herself, this was she fulfilling her dream, placed there in the bows of the vessel which bore her name. She forgot everything but that her moment had come, the moment when she would become part of a ship – part of the sea for ever. Mist came into her eyes. She saw nothing of Plyn, nothing of the people about her – only the ship hovering on the brink of the slip wait-ing for the plunge.

She heard none of the cheers; in her ears were the call of the wind and the cry of the waves. Beyond the hill the sun glimmered for an instant – a ball of fire. A great shout arose from the people: 'There she goes!' The harbour rang with their cries and the mighty crash as the vessel struck the water. At the sound a shudder passed through Janet's body and she opened her arms. Her eyes were filled with a great beauty, like the light of a star, and her soul passed away into the breathing, living ship. Janet Coombe was dead.

# Book Two
## Joseph Coombe (1863–1900)

No later light has lighted up my heaven,
　No second morn has ever shone for me;
All my life's bliss from thy dear life was given,
　All my life's bliss is in the grave with thee.
E. BRONTË

# 1

When Janet Coombe died Thomas turned to his eldest daughter Mary for comfort and care. She helped him as best she could with gentle looks and tender words, and little by little his faith was restored to him and his affection for his daughter increased; Samuel and Herbert reigned supreme down at the yard, and with their own growing families and separate homes, there was no time for them to give way beneath the strain of losing a devoted parent.

Philip left home and moved to rooms in the middle of the town, near to his firm of Hogg and Williams. Here he could have absolute independence, unbothered by his many relatives. Lizzie felt keenly the blow of parting with her mother, and for a time she weakened considerably in health, but with her coming to convalescence came the presence of one Nicholas Stevens upon her little sphere, and this good man, some fifteen years older than herself and a farmer from up Truan way, was to aid her to recovery; and though she had lost her mother she was to find a devoted and faithful husband.

Joseph was different. His brothers and sisters had to live motherless, his father without a wife; but with the passing of Janet something of Joseph's immortality had perished. He must walk through life henceforward with the certain knowledge that there was no reason for his existence, and that wheresoever he trod and in what dubious company, he would inevitably march alone. The blessed love, his one and only salvation, was extinguished.

During those first weeks Joseph worked hard, never allowing himself a moment in which to relax.

There was much to be done. The ship had just been launched, and there were many necessary formalities to be gone through which Joseph, as her future master, took upon himself to arrange. Nor was she yet ready for sea, and it was some four months before she would be finished and fitted out. This was the business of Samuel and Herbert, Thomas Coombe being too dumbfounded with grief to help, and Joseph lent them a willing hand, suggesting improvements here and there, which his years of sea experience qualified him to give.

When Janet was buried that soft September afternoon, the sun shone upon the windows of the church, and the tall grass blew gently in the west wind. There was no sadness in the air. A blackbird sang joyfully on the topmost bough of the elm tree and from two fields away came the glad shouts of schoolboys as they played. The men were working as usual on the jetties; a ship passed out of the harbour laden with clay, bound for a distant land. People moved to and fro like little dots on the Town Quay; the smoke rose from the chimneys; and beyond the harbour entrance were scattered a few fishermen in their small open boats, spinning for mackerel.

Henceforward Janet Coombe would be a little name carved on a still grey tombstone, until the winds and rain of many years should bring it to obscurity, and then covered with moss and the tangled roots of ivy the letters would fade away, and she would be as unremembered as the fallen trodden leaves of past summer and the melted snow of a vanished winter.

The family stood by the open grave, Thomas supported by Samuel and Mary, with the others weeping at his side.

Joseph watched them, dry-eyed and still; he saw the white surplice of the parson blowing in the wind; he looked into the heavens where the loose clouds fled across the sky, he heard the eager voices of the boys as they played in the field near by.

Dust unto dust. There was no reason then for life – it was only a fraction of a moment between birth and death, a movement upon the surface of water, and then it was still. Janet had loved and suffered, she had known beauty and pain, and now she was finished – blotted by the heedless earth, to be no more than a few dull letters on a stone.

Joseph watched the gravel fall in upon her coffin, stones and earth together hiding it from his view, then the whole was strewn with wreaths of brilliant autumn flowers.

As the little crowd dispersed from the side of the grave, Joseph threw back his head and laughed aloud. A few turned back to gaze on his solitary figure, torn with mirth over his mother's corpse.

It was not until the *Janet Coombe* started on her maiden voyage that a measure of consolation came to him.

The desolation of Plyn where Janet was no more lay behind him like a cast-off dream, and here stretched the calm and solitary sea, the love of which had run in his blood even before birth. The sea held danger, much beauty, and the elusive quality of unknown things in its keeping; here perhaps, when the winds shouted and the high sea swept him forward, there would come to him for one moment forgetfulness, and with it the zest of living once again. This ship was her namesake and her life's dream; they had planned it together as their means of escape to perpetual freedom – and now Janet was dead. This ship was alive, sweeping her way over the surface of the water like a carefree gull, with Plyn a dark line far astern on the horizon; but Janet was dead. She would have been beside him now, treading the sloping deck, turning her head aloft to watch the mighty spread of canvas, listening to the kiss of spray as the vessel tossed the sea from her bows.

And Janet lay in Lanoc churchyard. She could not see, she could not touch, she could not feel; all her promises had vanished in the air.

'I will never forsake you.' Had she said those words? If there was any truth in beauty, any power in love, should she not be there at his side, whispering in his ear, holding his hands with ghostly fingers? He was alone, save for the watch, and the man at the helm.

So Janet had been wrong; there was no force stronger than death; and survival was but another falsity in the general scheme of things, a fairy tale for frightened children who had never learnt to walk in the dark. He was alone then, but for his ship which had come to him like a legacy from her. For the sake of her blessed memory the ship should not be unworthy of her.

Joseph glanced around him, up at the wide sky with the grave placid stars; beside him at the dark swift water; and then with a word to the helmsman he went below to the cabin, where his supper was spread on the narrow table, and the lamp swung in its gimbals above his head. He was joined by the first mate, and after a little while, when they had eaten and drunk, Joseph turned in. All was silent. The watch on deck, busy with their own thoughts, spoke not to one another. The helmsman watched his compass, while the mate paced up and down beside him, the sparks from his pipe brushing away into the air.

And unknown to all save the wind and the sea, with the spray leaping to kiss her eyes and the breeze alighting on her hair, the figurehead of Janet Coombe smiled to herself in the darkness.

# 2

The maiden voyage of the *Janet Coombe* lasted some months. She sailed first to St John's, Newfoundland, laden with china clay from Plyn, and from thence she proceeded with fish down to the Mediterranean, a very important freight at that time of the year, when the Catholic inhabitants of these southern ports were fasting for Lent. Then she filled with fruit, and there was a gallant race to London of schooners, barquentines, and brigantines, all eager to be the first to deliver their perishable cargo. The first home was *Janet Coombe*, who signalled for a pilot two miles before Gravesend, with her rivals still half a day astern of her down Channel.

From London she ran up to Newcastle in ballast, and there loaded with coals for Madeira; from thence to St Michaels for fruit and back to London, from whence she crossed the North Sea to Hamburg. Nearly a year had passed since she sailed from Plyn harbour, but time meant little to Joseph now.

There was no peace to him save on the decks of his own ship, of whose capabilities and speed he was justly proud, and he journeyed from one port to another with but one desire in his mind, to escape somehow from the spectre of loneliness that haunted his still moments.

While he was at Hull he received the following letter from Samuel:

Plyn. 13 November 1864

My dear Brother—
As requested I have much pleasure in dropping you a few lines to say that we settled yesterday and that we had a goodly number present, all of whom, both ladies and gentlemen, were highly pleased at the success of

113

yourself and the vessel, and your first year's work; and I believe it was the heartfelt wish of all that the same good fortune would smile upon you in the future. I need only add that yourself and vessel are now spoken very favourably of and I trust, and know, that you will do your best it may continue so. The *Francis Hope* is waiting at Falmouth for orders, and as it is probable she will be sent to Hamburg, all being well, you will be there together.

We are all in good health and hoping to get your sailing letter soon. Wishing you a prosperous and quick passage with our best love, believe me,
Your affectionate brother,
Samuel

Joseph smiled as he folded the letter, and put it away. He pictured them all at Plyn, solemn and unchanged, going about their work from day to day with few cares and worries, knowing nothing of the misery that gripped him always, nor of the dogged wish which swept upon him at times, to lose himself in adventure.

They would all forgather at Ivy House on Sunday evenings, with Mary seated at the harmonium, and offer up their voices to a God that did not exist. He did not know in his mind whether he pitied them or envied them.

There was a security in their life, a steadfastness of purpose which he would never know. But they knew nothing of the lifting power of a ship, of the scream of a gale in torn rigging, of the force of a tempest-swept sea which could fling humanity to destruction.

So Joseph pocketed his letter, and made sail for Hamburg, to whose port come men from every corner of the globe, where the richest merchants rub shoulders with the poorest sewer rat, where adventure beckons over the tall masts of crowded ships and loses itself in the sinister dock-side houses.

He knew no thrill like the entering of a strange harbour. First the dawning of an unfamiliar coast-line, then the hail of the pilot who came to take charge, the entering of a wide river which led to the port beyond.

If it was dark there would be the dim outlines of other ships at anchor, the rough voices of men, calling one another in a foreign tongue; and then suddenly the glare of lights, the throb of humanity, the shape of tall buildings outlined against the sky. There would be a scurry of feet in the darkness, a sharp cry from the pilot and the rattle of the heavy clanking chain. *Janet Coombe* was anchored in unknown waters.

Then, when all was safe and snug, Joseph would look about him, and let his eyes travel towards those challenging lights, which called to him to forsake the deck of his ship. Amidst those lights moved danger and romance, beneath those dark buildings dwelt poverty and suffering, love and death.

Joseph threw back his head and breathed the air which was a mixture of ships and tar and water, together with the smell of food and drink and tobacco, of people touching one another, and the disturbing scent of women. So Joseph looked upon Hamburg for the first time, and the figurehead of the *Janet Coombe* gazed proudly across the still waters to the city beyond.

Joseph was a month in Hamburg. He explored what he could of it, between visits to his broker and seeing to the general business of arranging a freight, and it was always the docks that interested him most. Joseph liked to lose himself amongst this crowd, pick up a few scattered words of their language, and drink with them in the thick atmosphere of the overheated cafés.

There was no need to speak sentences and search for phrases; a common understanding united every man there, for there was but one topic of conversation, one search which brought them here together. Women, always women.

A smile, a nod, a gesture, the chinking of money, this was the bond between them, while their restless eyes searched through the crowded room, and their restless feet beat time to the tune played by the scraping fiddler. On his last night in Hamburg, for they were to sail next morning for Dublin, Joseph left the broker's office and made his way down to that

115

part of the docks where lay the *Janet Coombe*. The pilot was coming aboard at six o'clock, and long hours at sea stretched once more before him. The reasonable thing to do would be to go to the ship right away, and turn in, snatching a few last precious moments of sleep.

But Joseph found little rest in sleep, and small comfort in reason. Here in Hamburg the lights glittered through the open doors of the cafés, the dark figures of men lurked in the corners of the street, and next to him on the pavement a woman murmured something, brushing against him with her skirt. Below him lay the docks, and the silent ships at their moorings. Tonight perhaps there would be something in the air, and an answer to a closed secret. So Joseph smiled, and bade reason fly to the winds, and he disappeared along the lighted streets in search of adventure, the inevitable adventure which means one breathless, intoxicating moment of intolerable pleasure — but so unchanging — so always the same.

Joseph stood by the crowd at the door of a café watching the people inside. There was a little stage at the corner of the room, where a Negro girl was dancing, and heaped against the walls were tables where the men were seated. The floor space in the middle was intended for dancing, but at the moment it was filled with women, parading up and down, like animals at a show. Joseph pushed his way round the room and sat at a table, while a hustled waiter stood at his elbow for orders. Joseph drank his beer thoughtfully, his eyes searching the crowd of women on the middle of the floor. Two Portuguese were settled at the next table. One had a white, pasty face, with protruding eyes and a dirty tuft of beard. He muttered excitedly to his companion, and clutched his glass with puffy, trembling hands. Joseph watched him as he drank his beer, and disliked him.

The Negro girl had finished her performance. There were a few shouts and some half-hearted clapping, then the men rose from their tables and fought to get to the women in the centre of the room. Music struck up from the band in the corner, and dancing began. Couples pressed against each other, unaware of their ugliness, their greasy faces, their fixed, meaningless smiles. The men knew only that beneath the tangled petticoats and the trailing skirts was a woman. Nothing mattered but that.

Joseph pushed his glass away. The face of a girl stared up at him over the shoulder of a man. A girl with dark hair and eyes, and a provocative tilted nose. She moved well, and Joseph could picture the lines of her body. Suddenly she shook her shoulders and laughed, calling out something in German to a woman who passed. Just for a fraction of a second she reminded him of someone – of something; she was like a clue to an invisible secret, and then it was gone again. He noticed the tight bodice drawn across her full breasts.

Then Joseph knew that he wanted this girl. She moved with her companion to the table by his side, and he saw that the man was the Portuguese.

Joseph rose, and laid his hand upon the girl. No matter if the lights rocked a little above him, or the floor sloped like a deck beneath his feet. The Portuguese shouted an oath and seized a knife. Joseph swung his fist into the man's face, laughing as he did so. The Portuguese crumpled at his feet, his face smeared with blood. 'Come on,' roared Joseph, 'have ye had enough?' He wanted to fight, to seize the tables and chairs and swing them across the room, to break the limbs of other men and trample their skulls beneath his feet. Then the girl laid a hand on his arm, she laughed up at him. People crowded round him threateningly. Joseph shook himself free, and pushed his way out into the street with the girl hanging at his heels like a dog. He stood unsteadily on the pavement and looked into the girl's face.

Five o'clock in the morning. The girl lit a gas jet, which spluttered feebly and cast a sickly yellow glow about the dark room. This was reflected on the carpet, on the smeared window pane, on the face of the girl, as she moved about the floor treading heavily. She poured some water into a basin. Joseph sat on the edge of a chair, his head in his hands. He reached

117

for his coat and fumbled in the pocket, from whence he took his pipe and pouch of tobacco, and a handful of change. He laid the money in a heap beside a photograph of a child on the mantelpiece. The girl's back was turned to him, he saw nothing but a bent figure encased in ugly stiff corsets, drawing on a pair of long black stockings. Joseph lit his pipe and moved towards the door.

Groping his way down a dingy staircase he opened the outer door, and let himself into the street.

Joseph felt the longing rise in his heart for Plyn. He wanted to look upon the quiet waters of the harbour, and the little cottages clustered about the hill, with the blue smoke curling from their crooked chimneys. He wanted to feel the cobbled stones of the old slip beneath his feet, where the nets were spread to dry in the sun, and where the blue-jerseyed fishermen leaned against the harbour wall. He wanted to hear the sound of the waves, splashing against the rocks below the Castle ruins, and the rustle of the trees in Truan woods, the movement of sheep and cattle in the hushed fields, the stirring of a rabbit in the high hedges that bordered the twisting lanes. He longed once more for the faces of simple folk, for the white wings of the crying gulls, and the call of the bells from Lanoc Church. Joseph stood on the side of the dock and saw the sharp outline of his ship, her two masts pointing to the sky. He raised his lantern and flashed it on the figurehead in the bows. The light fell upon her face. Her white dress was in shadow, and her two small hands folded upon her breast.

And as he watched, it seemed to Joseph that she smiled upon him and whispered in the air, 'Did you think that I'd forsaken you. Did you think I was crumblin' to dust in the churchyard? My son, my beloved, I've been at your side always, always – here, part of the ship, part of yourself, and you didn't understand. Open your heart, Joseph, an' come to me. There is no fear, no ugliness, no death – only the white light of courage and beauty and truth. I'm alive an' free, an' lovin' you as of old – Joseph – Joseph.'

He felt warmth steal into his cold heart and strength return to his spirit. The grim spectre of loneliness faded away.

For a moment Joseph was drawn into the light, beyond good and evil, beyond the flesh to the high places – and he opened his blinded eyes and looked upon the living Janet.

A passing sailor saw a man, with a lantern raised, scanning the empty face of a weather-beaten figurehead.

3

'Well, Joe, you're not greatly changed for all your travels, an' we're right pleased to see you back amongst us again.' Samuel smiled at his brother, while Mary poked the parlour fire into a warm blaze. Thomas Coombe sat in his usual place in the armchair, with the inevitable Bible on his knee. The other brothers and their wives had joined the circle, and were looking proudly at their sailor relative.

The curtains were drawn, the supper was cleared away, the hymns had been sung, and the clock ticked as slowly as ever on the wall.

Joseph stretched out his legs and sighed. It was good to be back. He gazed at the dear, familiar faces, and asked for all the Plyn gossip.

'Sammie's twin girls are a picture o' health,' said Mary, loyal as ever though secretly a little jealous of Posy. 'The'm raisin' ten now, you know, an' doin' splendid at school. Take after their father somethin' extraordinary.'

Samuel blushed proudly.

'Then little Tom is more delicate, but a dear boy for all that, an' his brother Dick is taller than him already.'

Funny to think that dear, sober Samuel was the father of four children, while quiet, painstaking Herbert, seated with his wife near the harmonium and beaming at Joseph, had been married scarce seven years and had already three boys and two girls, and it seemed that dark-haired Elsie, his wife, was expecting again.

Philip had dropped in at Ivy House to take a look at Joseph and to discuss the bills for the *Janet Coombe*. He was now second clerk at Hogg and Williams, and was inclined to take the business side of the family ship into his own hands. The brothers and sisters were a little afraid of him, he was so superior, 'quite the gentleman' they said amongst themselves.

Lizzie was courting Nicholas Stevens, and Joseph at once took a liking to this bluff genial farmer, with his blue eyes and his hearty handshake.

Why had he sometimes despised this little crowd, thinking them narrow and foolish? After all, they were part of Janet as he was himself. She had been the mother of them all. They none of them resembled her, though, unless it was Lizzie with her black hair like his own, and her large eyes. He was fond of Lizzie, and glad that she would make a home with her handsome farmer, for all the difference in age between them.

'The girls o' Plyn are in a ferment that you're back again,' laughed Mary. 'You'll have them chasin' you about the place lest you take care.'

'I should think Joe wants a rest from women when he comes home,' remarked Philip dryly. 'Besides, they must seem poor enough compared to the ladies of the Continent.'

Joseph glanced at his sandy-haired, narrow-eyed brother. Queer chap he was, with that strain of bitterness. Nothing of Janet in him.

'Why don't ye give the wild ways a miss, Joe,' suggested Samuel. 'You're old enough now to have had a good time, and seen all ye want. If I was you I'd find some nice girl in Plyn an' settle down, same as me an' Herbie has done. It 'ud do you all the good i' the world to have a wife, an' childrun of your own.'

Thomas looked up from his Bible and peered at Joseph over his spectacles.

'As ye sow, so shall ye reap,' he said firmly. Nobody quite knew what he meant, but they were used to their father's ways by now.

'There's no need for you to leave the sea, Joe,' put in Mary, who was an ardent matchmaker. 'You can remain Master of the *Janet Coombe*, but Samuel's right about you marryin'. It's a wife you need to steady you, an' a neat tidy home o' your own.'

Joseph smiled and shook his head. 'I reckon I'm not the marryin' sort,' he said. The idea clung to his mind, however, and though he professed to laugh at the suggestion, he thought it over when he was alone. What was against it anyway? He knew that he would never be able to love a woman. His heart and his soul were given to Janet – Janet and the ship. But he could feel affection and tenderness, he could experience that warm, contented sensation that someone was waiting for him in a lighted cottage, that he was not entirely unwanted, that someone perhaps might give him comfort and a home, and a kindly devoted nature. It would be grand, too, to see boys growing up around him, his own boys. Janet's boys. Funny – queer. Yes, he must think about it.

Joseph spent these first days quietly enough at Plyn. He went for long walks about the country, looking up the old haunts where he had rambled as a boy, when Janet had been by his side. It was still winter, and there was no sign of spring in the air as yet. He liked to trudge over the wet fields and the desolate hills, with the soft rain blowing about his face, and the squelching mud soaking his boots. Often he stood in the corner of Lanoc Churchyard, where Janet's grave lay sheltered in the long grass, beside the thorn hedge and the elm tree. Could it be true that she lay beneath the soaking earth, heedless of him and of his need for her, or was his vision of beauty the real truth, when he stood on the dock-side at Hamburg and looked into her face? He clung to the stupendous grandeur of this thought. Meanwhile his own personal life stretched out before him, days and nights that must be faced with courage, and he knew too well how often he would fail. So Joseph turned away from the silent grave, and made his way down to the busy world of Plyn, with the noise of the jetties and the ships, and the voices of folk who called from their cottage doors. Mary would welcome him with a kind smile, and push him a chair next his father's on the hearth; but more than ever Joseph began to think of the idea of a wife and home of his own, where he could feel himself at perfect liberty on his return from the sea.

Ivy House was still too full of memories. He could not look up to the ivy above the porch, because it was *her* room. Her voice echoed on the landing, and in the kitchen. He could not sleep in his bed without turning his head towards the door where she should come, softly on tiptoe, a candle in her hand. Memories that tugged at his heart, and weakened his strength. Unconsciously he missed, too, all the little attentions which she had made so dear to him. She had cared for his clothes and his food, giving him always the best of everything, and making him aware of love.

Mary was a loyal affectionate sister, but she gave him none of these things. To her he was just one of the family, and must shift for himself.

Joseph was lonely in a hundred ways. Parts of him that had never grown up called out for sympathy, understanding, and care.

Perhaps he would find this in marriage. He would not take any of these laughing pretty girls, who watched him walk up Plyn hill with a blush on their cheeks and a glance from their lowered eyes; but a woman with a brave and loving heart, who would know how to calm his restlessness, who would give him a home, and not a haunted dwelling. He would be good to her and respect her, she would be the mother of his sons. So Joseph reasoned as he gazed upon the harbour from the garden at Ivy House, and as he watched the movement on the water he saw that the *Francis Hope* was anchored off the Town Quay. He had missed Captain Collins at Hamburg, and now he would be able to make up for it, and they would have a chat on old times.

Joseph seized his hat, and made his way along the street to the house where the Collinses lived. Sarah, the captain's wife and Janet's former friend, was ill, it appeared, and in bed. This was told him by the boy who opened the door.

'Grandfather's upstairs with my Grannie, Captain Joe,' said the boy, 'but Auntie Susan is in the parlour and will give you a cup of tea. Grandfather'll be down directly, and glad to see you for certain.'

Joseph entered the house and wiped his feet on the mat. He remembered being brought to tea here as a lad, and playing with the young Collinses. The boys were all grown up now, sailors like himself, and the child who had let him in must be a son of one of them. Susan he could recollect but vaguely. She was the eldest daughter, three years older than his own brother Samuel, and had not entered much into their games in the former days. She must be thirty-five now. Strange how the years fled without your reckoning them.

'Come on, do, Captain Joe,' called a voice from the parlour, 'the kettle's on the boil and I dare say you'd like warmin' up after this dirty weather. Terrible it's been now all the month, an' father arrived home to find our poor invalid upstairs. Sit right down, and put yourself at ease.' So this was Susan. A kind, motherly woman with patient hazel eyes, and quick capable hands that moved swiftly about the tea table, laying the cups and saucers.

'Why, you'm wet, I declare,' she said, pointing to his streaming boots. 'Let's have 'em off right away, and put to dry in the kitchen. Give me your coat as well. That's better, isn't it? Was there ever such foolish, careless creatures as men?'

He laughed up at her, and his eyes followed her as she moved about the room, her trim, rather plump figure, the twist of her humorous mouth, and the brown hair that curled beneath her white cap. He stretched his feet to the fire, and drank his tea. He felt well, comfortable, and he liked this woman who showed no sign of embarrassment at the rough sailor in his shirt-sleeves, with his stockinged feet stuck in the fender.

She was no beauty, neither was she young, but there was something appealing about her for all that, and her voice was soft and low. He was content to be there in this house, and see her bend over the fire, and laugh at some remark of his, and then brush her hair away from her brow with an impatient gesture.

It reminded him of someone – something – No, he didn't remember. Must have been an idle fancy.

After a while Captain Collins came down, and two of the sons came back from their work in Plyn, so the parlour was filled. When at length Joseph rose to go Susan Collins went with him to the door, and helped him on with his dried coat. 'Now keep out o' mischief, an' don't go catchin' any chills,' she warned him laughingly.

'I'll know where to come if I do,' he told her, and he was pleased to see the colour come into her cheeks, and a dimple show at the corner of her mouth. 'Good evenin',' she said, shy for the first time.

Joseph returned to Ivy House and found the fire out in both the rooms, his father and sisters having gone to Samuel's for the evening. His supper was waiting for him in the kitchen, cold and unappetizing. He wished himself back in the cosy parlour at the Collinses' house; and hastily swallowing his supper he climbed to his cheerless bedroom, and after reading for a while, he dropped off early to sleep.

After that day Joseph found himself often calling in to have a chat with Captain Collins. This was the excuse he made for going there, but more often than not the old man would be above in his wife's bedroom, and Joseph would find nobody about but Susan.

Thus it happened that many times now Joseph would sit by the fire in the kitchen, while Susan baked her cakes and her bread, and saw to the needs of her household.

In a month's time Joseph would be sailing again, so he made the most of his days while he could.

One afternoon he arrived and went round to the back door as usual. He tapped softly on the window, 'Where are you to, Susan?'

'You must let yourself in, Joe,' she called, 'for it's bakin' day an' I've my hands all messed with the flour, an' the yeast.' He went into the kitchen, and she raised her face from the stove, rather hot and red, while her hair fell in curling untidy wisps about her forehead. Her sleeves were rolled up, and he noticed the full white arms with a dimple in the elbow.

'O' course you would choose now the moment to come in,' she reproached him, 'wi' me in such a state. Why don't you take yourself off with one o' the gay girls up the hill, instead o' laughin' at me and idlin' by the fire, takin' me mind off the work.'

She pommelled at her bread, kneading it and punching it with her capable fists.

'Mother'll be up agen in a day or two,' she told him, 'an' I'll have finished wi' all this, unless she feels the need o' me.'

'Well, if she does, I reckon Cathie can help her,' said Joseph, watching her closely.

'But I like it,' exclaimed Susan, wiping a spot of flour from her chin. 'I'm not young enough to care for gallivantin' about Plyn, this is when I feel happy an' at ease.'

'You can continue till the end o' your days,' said Joseph, gazing at her arms, 'but you won't be doin' it here.'

'Why ever not, pray?' scoffed Susan, wringing the dough from her fingers.

'Because you're goin' to marry me an' do it in your own kitchen,' said Joseph, and he rose to his feet and put his arms round her, and kissed the white flour marks away from her mouth.

'Why, bless me,' began Susan weakly, and struggled to get free. 'What's marryin' got to do wi' the likes o' me, you wild ridiculous lad.'

'Everything in the world, my dear,' laughed Joseph, 'and I will not let you go until you promise to be my wife, and quickly too, because I want a week of married life before I sail.' And that was how Joseph Coombe proposed to Susan Collins in the year 1865.

So it was arranged, and before the night was passed the news was all over Plyn that Joe Coombe was going to marry Susan Collins, whom nobody ever thought would find a lover, with her homely face, and she past thirty-five.

126

''Twill never last,' declared the pretty girls of Plyn. 'To think o' Joe bein' tied to a dull quiet body like Susan Collins. Why, she's five years older'n him, an' maybe more.'

Nevertheless, Susan, flustered and overwhelmed by her impatient lover, made haste to see to her clothes and be ready in time. Joseph found a house close to the Methodist Chapel. He too was busy with his ship *Janet Coombe*, for she was to sail to St Michaels a week after his wedding day.

Thus the days passed like a flash of lightning, and on the 17th day of March, Joseph and Susan were married in the little grey Methodist Chapel, for old Captain Collins was a staunch Wesleyan and would not have his daughter wed in church.

For a week Joseph devoted himself to the task of making his wife happy and content, which was easy and pleasant enough; and he felt proud of her and his home as he thought things over on his last night in Plyn. Queer to think he must consider himself as 'settled down' now, and a married man with responsibilities. He bent over her as she lay asleep in the crook of his arm. They were to look after one another through life, she was to share his luck and his misfortunes. Did she care for him greatly, he wondered? Would she understand his moments of wretchedness and desolation? He longed so much for her to wake and to drag his head down upon her breast, and to run her fingers through his hair, and whisper to him that he would be safe with her. Tomorrow he was starting off once more on his lonely path, on his own ship that understood his ways, and where he could give himself up entirely to that strange mixture of dreams and reality that was the essence of his inward life.

But it would be good to know that here in Plyn a woman waited for him, to whom he longed, in some helpless way, to be a child as well as a lover.

'Susan,' he said softly, 'Susan.'

She stirred in his arms and opened her eyes. 'Still awake, Joe?' she murmured sleepily. 'Try an' sleep, my dear, for you've a long journey afore you i' the mornin'.' She stretched and settled herself once more in his arms. 'An' here's me dreamin' I'd burnt the Sunday cake to ashes, an' parson comin' to tea . . .'

Joseph lay awake until the morning. Below in the harbour the figurehead of Janet waited, her eyes turned to the horizon, and the ship strained at the moorings which kept her from the sea.

# 4

Once more on the decks of his ship, the interests of his little world were cast aside from Joseph's mind, as dim and as unreal as the smudge of Plyn astern of him. His wife and his home were nothing but make-believe, the fancies of one who was not sure of himself, and who created these things to serve as a protection and a means of escape from himself. They could be loved and cherished for a while, but the real life was here, far from the cries and worries of humankind. Here Joseph lived with a strange indefinable sense of freedom, beside the rough simple men who obeyed his will and shared his dangers.

The routine life in the *Janet Coombe* was much the same as the first year. She made a quick passage to St Michaels, and from thence back to London with fruit, the race again being won by Joseph's ship, having met with favourable winds the whole passage, and also by a stroke of luck securing an early freight. In London she loaded with coals to Madeira, proceeding in ballast to St Michaels again, from where she returned with a cargo to Dublin. Freights were firm for St Michaels at this time, and the ship returned to Plyn for a few days only, filling up almost at once with clay and taking her departure once more.

Thus Joseph, who had only spent a week of married life, was obliged to sail again with scarce three days added to the original week, and those few hours mainly filled with settlement of the new cargo, and paying off the ship's accounts. The business was always transacted with Philip at Hogg and Williams, and Philip, though not yet thirty, was hinting at his rise to the position of head clerk in the near future. Mr Hogg was an elderly man, with no sons to follow him, and he trusted

129

most of his affairs in the hands of the head clerk, who was about to retire for reasons of ill-health. It was into this man's shoes that Philip was to step. Williams, the other partner in the firm, was a pleasant easy-going sort of man, and the young clerk expected to have little or no trouble in dealing with him. Philip was clever and far-seeing; he already looked ahead to the days when old Hogg should succumb to his age, and by judicious foresight and careful investment the young man intended to save enough money to buy the partnership, when it became vacant. None of his family knew of this intention. He kept his concerns private, and no one knew of the little store of wealth that was accumulating year by year. He lived extremely quietly, almost meanly, and his expenses were practically nothing. The only clue to his as yet modest fortune was that he possessed most of the shares of the *Janet Coombe*. He and Joseph between them held four-fifths of the shares, while the remaining fifth was owned by Samuel and Herbert, whose stock of money naturally was in the business in the yard. Mary and Lizzie also held a small interest.

Philip looked forward to the time when he might control much of the shipping in Plyn, and when he would command respect from his brother Joseph himself.

Joseph was unaware of the secret animosity of his youngest brother. He had never had any particular liking for him, but had not given the matter much consideration. Philip led his own life; they were not likely to come into opposition against each other.

Only Janet had foreseen trouble. She had read it often in Philip's eyes.

Meanwhile the *Janet Coombe* had sailed again, and did not drop anchor in Plyn until the first week of October.

Joseph was in a fever of impatience to be back, for Susan was already seven months gone, and he knew she was anxious for him to be with her when her time came. Joseph was strangely excited at the thought of being a father. He had not thought it possible that such a thing could stir him. He had never taken much notice of Herbert's and Samuel's children, and had laughed when one of his brothers went about Plyn with an important face, half pride and half concern, that meant his wife was expecting an addition to the family. He had joked with them on the 'trials of marriage', and asked them if they did not envy a free sailor like himself, with no cares and responsibilities.

Now he was surprised at his own tenderness towards Susan, and caught himself watching her with anxious worried eyes as she moved slowly about the house, fearful lest she should do herself some damage and harm the child that was within her. This child would carry Janet's blood in his veins, and his own too. There would be something indefinably precious about him that Joseph could not explain. It was as if Janet herself had been present at his creation, and was sending him as a messenger of consolation, as another tie to bind them more strongly together.

The weeks dragged slowly for Joseph. He could scarcely conceal his impatience, and fretted at what he considered to be an unnecessary waste of time.

Susan smiled at him and said little. She was facing her ordeal with courage, for to a woman of past thirty-five it was no small matter to bring a child into the world. But she was too happy to be overcome by vague fears. She had longed all her life to be a wife and mother, and that Joseph Coombe, the most splendid man in Plyn, should have chosen her for his own, never ceased to be a cause for wonder and glory. She would suffer ten times over if it should bring him any pleasure.

The baby was due in Christmas week, and the *Janet Coombe* would be sailing for St John's, Newfoundland, in the very first days of January.

The Christmas festivities came and went, and on New Year's Day Joseph was standing in the little garden at the back of the house in a half-hearted attempt to do some digging, his spade in his hand. It was in the early part of the afternoon, and he was thinking of laying aside his tools and going into the kitchen to ask Susan to make him a cup of tea, when he

131

heard a murmur come from her bedroom window. She was leaning out, and waving her hand to him.

He threw away his spade and ran to her.

'What is it, are you taken bad?' Her face was pitiful, and contracted with pain, but she managed to summon a smile for him.

In a moment he was gone from her and running up the hill. Soon he returned with the doctor.

Why was the man so slow, when perhaps the child's life was in danger? To his fury, he was shut away from the sick-room, and told to take himself off.

Helpless and raging Joseph made his way to the *Janet Coombe*, and as he looked upon the figurehead of his ship it seemed to him that calm came to him. The eyes of Janet smiled into his, and bade him to lay aside care and distress. She understood what this thing meant in his life, she knew the great value he placed upon the birth of this child, bringing them both, as he would, nearer together. The evening came and still Joseph stayed by his ship, wrapping himself in the atmosphere of Janet, and then refreshed and steadied he turned his back on the harbour, and walked along the quay to his house. The doctor was standing on the doorstep.

'You've got a splendid little boy,' he said, 'and your wife is rallying wonderfully. You can step upstairs an' see 'em both, but only stay a minute, mind.' Joseph burst into the bedroom, with a smile on his lips. He had felt like this before, when he had returned to Janet after a voyage, and she waited for him with open arms. He had known the same sensation on a wild night at sea, when for hours he had battled with wind and sea, and by his own skill had brought his ship to safety. This was the thrill that came to him when he anchored in strange waters, and looked for the first time on a new land where the city lights rose and beckoned with mysterious fingers.

Another adventure . . .

He crossed the room and leant over the bed where Susan lay, pale and weak, upon her pillows. Then he turned without a word and gazed down upon the cot, where the baby was sleeping.

'We'll call him Christopher, won't we, Joe, since he's come to us at this holy time,' murmured his wife.

'Yes,' said Joseph slowly. He was looking on his son for the first time. He had a tiny red face and his head was covered with soft fair hair.

'Takes after his mother, I should say, eh?' cried Mrs Joliff.

Joseph waited and then the child's eyelids fluttered, and for a moment opened wide.

The colouring and indefinite features were Susan's right enough, but the eyes were the eyes of Janet.

# 5

When Joseph returned from his voyages, it was not with a light in his eye and a boyish step that he flung himself ashore, as in the old days with no desire in his mind but to reach Janet's side as soon as he may; this new Joseph was a man of past thirty, Master of his own vessel, who sat in the stern sheets of a gig while the boat was pulled to the quay by his seamen; and who was greeted with respect by the shopkeepers, before he made his way to the house hard by the Methodist Chapel. Here he was just as much master as on his own ship, and every word was accepted as law and the truth from Susan.

Now all was changed. Joseph would come into his house, and Susan would be standing there in the hall, anxious to relieve him of his raincoat, and fearing the splashes of dirt on the spotless floor. Then she would fling open the door for him, and wait for him to pass into the stiffly furnished parlour, with the hard upright chairs of plush, the white antimacassars on the back, and the pot of 'everlasting' fern on the bamboo table by the window.

Joseph was proud of his parlour; it was furnished in the latest style and much admired by the people of Plyn, but for all that he wondered sometimes why the old kitchen at Ivy House had been so homely, with the soft candlelight instead of the gas lights; and the rug for him to lie by the fire had been more soothing than his armchair here. He would sit with his feet on a footstool, while Susan placed a little table at his elbow for his tea, and she herself took up her work on the opposite stiff, hard chair, and prattled on about the local gossip of Plyn, while Christopher, a somewhat fretful baby, moved restlessly in his cot.

With the first excitement of the baby over, he was aware of a certain amount of flatness and staleness about this married life. Nothing unexpected ever happened. The meals were orderly and punctual, his clothes were mended and brushed, and then the days spread themselves emptily before him with little to fill them. Joseph had imagined that once married the hours in Plyn would fly like the wind, and with difficulty he would leave his home for the discomforts and danger of the sea. On the contrary, he found the time heavy on his hands, with Susan busy about the house, and now he was used to her there was no excitement in watching her bake, and cook his dinner.

Then he was shocked to discover that Christopher's crying got on his nerves. He reproached himself greatly for this, for like Janet he disliked irritation in any form, but sometimes when he sat in the parlour with a book in his hand, in a hopeless attempt to read, the boy started his fits of crying in the kitchen next door, and as the child droned on like a mewling cat, Joseph would fling his book to the floor with a muttered oath, and leave the house to get away from the sound.

Lizzie was the only one of his family who made a companion, and he wistfully asked her to come for a stroll or a row in the harbour, and sometimes she went with him, but not often, for she was very much wrapped up in her farmer, and they were to be married quite shortly. Then Joseph rambled about by himself, and finally returned to his home where his wife was waiting, with his restlessness unappeased.

It was with a feeling of great relief, though cursing himself for his own inability to enjoy his home, that he stood again on the deck of the *Janet Coombe*, and sailed away from Plyn harbour, alone with his sea and his dreams once more.

In 1867 another boy was born, Albert, and two years later a third, christened Charles.

Joseph's desire for sons was thus being fulfilled, although to his disappointment he found he was unable to take a

135

great deal of interest in them during these early stages. He was at home in Plyn for barely four scattered months in the year, and these three boys, who followed so closely upon one another, were scarcely more than babies, and clung to their mother, intimidated and nervous of this big strong man with his rough hair and beard, who pinched their ears and tickled their chins, and spoke to them in a deep voice which they were too scared to answer. Joseph realized that, being away at sea as often as he was, it was difficult to appear little more than a stranger to his children. He would have liked to drop down on his hands and play with them, rolling them over like puppies; be, in fact, entirely free from self-consciousness towards them. Something kept him back though, shyness perhaps, and a fear that they would not understand his ways. Susan was no help in this matter either. She was for ever cautioning the children not to make a noise before their father, telling them how hard he worked on that cruel rough sea, so that they should have this lovely home to live. When father returned from his travels he liked to sit quietly and rest, said Susan, and he would be angry if they disturbed him with their silly games and chatter. Everything that father did was right, and if they were quiet, good little children in his presence, then he would be pleased and proud of them.

So, coupled with Joseph's natural shyness and Susan's unintelligent but well-meaning training, the children grew up in fear of their father, and spoke to him timidly always, waiting for a chance to escape and play by themselves, or run to their mother to whom they were devoted.

Often Joseph would sit in the parlour after tea, and hear their voices in the next room, and a longing came over him to have them next him, and hold them on his knee, his own boys, Janet's boys. When he first thought of marriage and children of his own, it was with the idea of their companionship.

He wanted to carry the lads on his back, and chase them about the hills and beaches of Plyn, show them how to sail their toy boats, and watch their faces lighten at his approach. Of course, they were very young, as yet, too young to want anyone but their mother, he supposed, yet it hurt him that they never came to him of their own free will.

'Where are the children, my dear?' he would say carelessly to Susan of an afternoon, 'I don't seem to have seen anythin' of them the livelong day.'

'I reckon they'd be worryin' you, Joe, with their noise an' their clatter,' replied Susan, laying aside her work. 'You know what children are when they get playin', there's no holdin' them. I sent them in the garden to be out o'your way, but I'll fetch 'em in.'

'No need to worry, Susan,' mumbled Joseph, picking up his paper, 'they'll be happy out there by themselves.'

'Nonsense, dear, if you want to see the children they shall come in at once. They must learn to obey their father's wishes, that's the first thing I tell 'em always.' So saying she would bustle out of the room, and Joseph would hear her marshalling the little boys up to their bedroom to be washed and brushed, whispering to them that 'Father wants to see you in the parlour.'

So Joseph, who would have enjoyed to see them muddy and dirty, and running in to him with cries and laughter, their tongues not moving quickly enough to explain to him all they had seen and done, would stand with his back to the fire, his pipe in his mouth, while Susan ushered in two tiny round-eyed boys.

Then his wife perhaps would run upstairs to give an eye to the baby, and he would be left alone with these two, wondering what to say.

His heart went out to Christopher the eldest, with his slim well-built little body, his fair hair, and his brown eyes – Janet's eyes.

Janet would have known how to deal with these babies; she would have taken the pair of them under her arm and made for the fields, setting them to run bare-headed and bare-footed in the long grass, while she knelt beside them her dress

137

and her hair blown by the wind, inventing some wild and very wonderful game.

His mind instantly flashed to his own boyhood, when even as a little lad no bigger than Christopher now, he had plunged into water up to his waist, his hair falling over his face, tugging at Janet's hand while they both shouted with laughter at her trailing petticoat, and the pickle they were in. Christopher would have blushed scarlet with shame if he had seen his mother's hair come down. Something had happened to the world since he had been a boy. It was for the best, he supposed with a sigh, but it turned him bitter and sore at times. And now he stood in his own parlour with these two round-eyed little lads before him.

'Been playin' nicely together, Chris an' Albie,' he said, making his voice as gentle as possible.

'Yes, thank you, father,' they replied seriously.

'There's good youngsters.' He scratched his head wondering what to say next.

'Well,' he said after a while, 'you can play in here if you like, an' make as much noise as you want.' He smiled and sat down. Would they perhaps come to his knee?

The children said nothing, they stood silently by the door, uncertain whether he meant them to stay or to go away. Then Susan came down and they ran to her at once.

'Well, now,' she said, 'have you answered your father nicely when he spoke?'

They clung to her hand, while Joseph sat alone by the fire, wretched and uncomfortable.

'Show me your play,' he suggested, flushing a little, watching Susan's eye and wanting to hold Christopher next to him. Immediately the boys disappeared and returned in a minute with a toy horse. Joseph thought of his old moth-eaten rag monkey, and how he had slept with it until he was twelve years old.

'Ah!' he said cheerfully, 'that's a very fine animal, I'm sure. I reckon he can gallop to Plymouth an' back in no time.'

Christopher stared up at his father in wonder, and squeezed Albie's hand. 'S'only a toy,' he said politely.

138

'Oh! I see.' Joseph roared with laughter, and then pulled himself together, afraid of appearing a fool before his boys.

'There now,' declared Susan, clapping her hands, 'isn't father funny, joking with you.'

The children summoned up a laugh at once.

'This is terrible,' thought Joseph. 'I don't seem to know how to treat 'em at all.' He began to feel in his pockets.

'Here's a nice bright penny for you both,' he said, bending down and twisting a curl in Christopher's hair.

'Thank your kind father, dears, immediately,' cried Susan. 'Was there ever such spoilt childrun, I wonder?'

'Thank you, father,' said the pair together. What queer little mortals they were, impossible to get a word from them separately. He wondered what Chris thought about, whether he knew he was going to be a sailor. Oh! well, they were only babies after all. He yawned, and took up his paper which he had already read from corner to corner. 'Run back an' play i' the kitchen, or you'll fuss your father,' said Susan.

Joseph made no attempt to keep them back, he saw how eager they were to get away. He drummed his boots in the fender moodily, wondering whether to go out or not.

What was the use, though? There was nowhere to go.

Lizzie was married now, and the mother of a baby boy. Joseph liked the old rough farmhouse where they lived, two miles from Plyn, on the road to St Brides. Lizzie was always ready to welcome him, but he had been there only two days ago, and it looked odd to be always going there, as if he was not made comfortable at home. He watched Susan as she drew the curtains and trimmed the lamp. Her three children had aged her considerably, she was forty now, and looked more. There were many grey streaks in her hair. She looked more worn than Janet had done at fifty, with six children. Not that he minded this. He had chosen her for the qualities of wife and mother, and not for youth and beauty. Joseph yawned again and stretched himself.

'Sleepy, dear?' asked his wife, ready to turn down the bed upstairs if he wanted a nap.

'Think I'll go along an' take a look at the ship,' said Joseph, and he went from the room.

It was better outside in the fresh air, with the wind on his face. It had been stuffy in the parlour, and difficult to breathe, and his legs were cramped from sitting still. Not quite dusk yet, but the men were coming back from their work at the jetties, and the lights were beginning to shine in the windows. He glanced at the yard, and saw that his brothers had closed down for the night. They would be up in their homes now having a late tea. He went down the slip, and cast the painter of a small pram. He jumped into this, and seizing the paddles pulled swiftly against the tide up harbour towards the buoy where the schooner was moored. This was better than being inside the house with those queer little brats and Susan. The tides were springing, and he had to work his boat carefully along the edge of the harbour, out of the run of the channel. From the entrance to Polmear creek the tide was ebbing swiftly, and there was a hint of an easterly wind. This meant a strain on Joseph's muscles, and he enjoyed it. He was bare-headed and the wind blew his hair over his eyes. He had to keep shaking his head to push it back. He chewed a quid of tobacco, and every now and then he spat into the water. The pram shot ahead in spite of the tide, and before long he reached the buoy, and lay on his oars, glancing up at the figurehead. A gull was perched on the foremast, facing the wind, and uttering a weird triumphant cry. The ship had just had her bottom scrubbed, and a coat of paint all over. She was ready to move up to the jetties for her load of clay and then away to sea again. She looked smart and trim, and worthy of her name as the fastest schooner in Plyn. Only the figurehead of Janet had been left untouched. The colour was a little faded now from the friction of the sea, but the features were unchipped and unspoilt as on the day she was launched.

Joseph stood up in his boat, holding the water with one paddle. 'Hullo, my beauty,' he called softly.

Dusk sank upon Plyn. The gull lifted his wings and flew

away. The harbour was deserted. The hour chimed out from Lanoc Church, borne on the easterly wind. Only Joseph remained, a still figure in his boat, watching the shadows creep along the figure-head above him.

## 6

A daughter was born to Joseph and Susan in 1871, and this completed their family.

Susan was seriously ill at the birth of Katherine, and the old doctor warned her that she must be very careful in the future if she wanted to be sure of her life. Suspecting that she would say nothing to her husband, and would in all probability keep the matter to herself, making light of his words, the doctor determined to tackle Joseph himself.

Joseph returned to Plyn three weeks after his daughter had been born, and was amazed to see the man's long face, and that he still visited Susan and the baby every day.

'Why, she'll be up and about soon, surely,' he said. 'The house is very uncomfortable with a woman hired in to do the work, and to only give an eye to the children now and again. My wife is strong and healthy, isn't she?'

'Your wife is past forty, Joe,' said the doctor seriously. 'She's borne four children now, and this one has all but killed her. Unless she takes very great care of herself from now on, I won't answer for the consequences.'

'Thank you, doctor,' said Joseph slowly, and turned into the house. He supposed he had been selfish and inconsiderate, but all said and done he did not consider he had been entirely to blame. After all, Susan had never complained, she had never said a word to him about weakness in health. He could not be expected to guess this sort of thing, when he was away at sea for nearly eight months in the year. Supposing something happened to Susan and he was left with this young family on his hands. What in the world would he do with them? And Lizzie was married, no possible hope in the thought that she would come and live in the house.

Susan would always be something of an invalid in the future. What a hopeless outlook it was going to be. She would just act as his housekeeper and bring up the children. No more than this.

'Doctor says you've been worse than poorly this time, my dear,' he began awkwardly. 'Somehow I didn't come to realize things, bein' away so much, and then just at home for short whiles now an' agen. I ought to have known that . . .' He broke off in confusion, afraid to hurt her by alluding to her age. He had always made a point of ignoring it. 'I reckon that men don't figure matters out the same as women do,' he went on, trying to be as gentle in his words as possible. 'Sailors, too, are a selfish, careless crowd, seldom givin' a thought to others. I've been as bad as any o' them. We'll start things different in future, an' you must get well quick an' get out in the air, 'twill pull you together in no time.'

'That's what's been the worryin' of me up here,' cried Susan fretfully, 'to know as you're back an' I can't look after you. I know the house'll be all upside down, an' nothin' like comfortable for you. The place not clean nor tidy, in all likelihood, and the boys runnin' wild. You'll be that irritated you'll be wantin' to go off to your ship again. Oh! dear – oh! dear.'

'There, there, dear,' said Joseph, taking his wife's hand. 'Everythin' is in perfect order, all shipshape an' Bristol fashion. I'm perfectly happy an' content, an' the boys no worry. Susan, my love—' He was stumbling to tell her how sorry he was for bringing her to this state, how he cursed himself for a selfish blind ruffian, and that in the years to come, from now onward, he would love her devotedly and selflessly, protecting her and caring for her. Perhaps it was not too late to start some sort of companionship, nothing physical nor passionate, but a deep understanding born of mutual trust and affection. This poor tired-eyed woman was his wife, Christopher's mother; who had slaved and worked for him while he had grumbled and groaned that she could not share his dreams.

143

'There now,' she choked, blowing her nose, 'now you're vexed with me for givin' way, and quite right an' proper too, for you to feel like that. I'm a stupid selfish woman, who gets silly little fads into her head, an' you're too good to say you mind the house upside down, though I know well you hate it. Never mind, dear, I'll be up soon, and all will go on as before.'

Joseph rose and stood above her helplessly. She had misunderstood him again, and another fresh ideal had flown to the winds. He realized that there could never be anything permanent or truthful about their relationship. Husband and wife. Queer. Had Janet lived thus with his father? No, he believed there had been moments of beauty between them.

He looked at the baby girl whom his wife was trying to soothe. Poor little thing, with her blue eyes like a kitten. Why could he feel no sort of emotion towards his children, except – Christopher. And Chris was a shy sensitive boy, who didn't seem to understand.

'I've made a mess o' things, somehow,' he thought, but aloud he said to his wife, 'Don't take on, dear, you'll soon be better now, an' the little girl is a dear, I can see.'

Then he went downstairs and sat alone in the stiff parlour.

Joseph was nearly a month in Plyn before sailing again, and he enjoyed this holiday ashore more than he had ever done since Janet had died. As Susan had feared, the house got upside down, and this was what appealed to her husband, though she never had any idea of it. It amused him to take off his boots in the fender and put his feet on the mantelshelf. He left the parlour, and spent his time in the kitchen when he was not out-of-doors. The meals were late and badly cooked by the woman who came in daily. Time did not matter, and he could wander in to one of these scrappy suppers and smoke all the time, with an old wet jacket on his back, and a newspaper in his hand.

He started to make a great pet of Christopher, and would take him off for walks alone, leaving Albert and little Charles to play together in the garden. He crammed the lad's pockets

144

with fruit and pennies, he went to the shops and bought him buns and sweets. The boy was quick to see the favour shown to him, and soon lost his early fear of his father. He saw that he had only to express a wish for something, and he was immediately given it.

Joseph imagined that by giving in to him like this and winning his affection, he was paving the way to the wonderful companionship of the future, the dream of which clung to his mind. Christopher would understand him as Janet had done.

Already the boy ran to him with a smile on his face, and told him his troubles and his wishes.

Once a dog barked loudly in the street, and the little fellow flung himself against his father with a cry of fear, clutching at his knee, burying his head against his trousers.

'There, there, Chris sonny, father has you. He won't let the brute harm you,' said Joseph, running his hand through the child's curls, lifting him up and kissing his cheek. 'My boy mustn't be afraid of animals. Stop cryin', sweetheart, an' we'll go and buy you some sweets.'

The crying stopped instantly.

'Can't ye keep the dog under control?' shouted Joseph angrily to the owner. 'My son is a nervy little chap, an' this sort o' thing is enough to make him ill.'

The boy snuggled his head in his father's shoulder.

'Can I 'ave pepp'ment?' he whispered.

'Bless you, you can have the whole shop,' said Joseph.

He had never imagined he could feel like this, just because the boy was next to him, and asked him for something.

Joseph sailed next time happier than he had been for years, feeling that now at last there was somebody who mattered to him, somebody who would welcome him on his return with a solid depth of love in his heart, and who as he grew older would become his one reason for living, apart from the ship and the sea.

It was during these years that the fruit trade was at its height, and the *Janet Coombe* was one of the many schooners

145

who raced from St Michaels or the Mediterranean back to
the Thames or the Mersey with this perishable cargo.
Sometimes freights ran as high as £7 a ton, and there would
be numbers of schooners alongside Joseph's ship near London
Bridge, waiting to discharge. Passages were made as far as
Smyrna and other eastern ports, where the cargo would be
currants.

Sometimes the *Janet Coombe* would be out to St Michaels
and back in seventeen days, for Joseph was a desperate carrier
of sail, pressing his little vessel under every rag he could set;
and when other ships would be held up by a westerly gale
he would thrash his way down Channel, hanging on to his
canvas until the last possible moment.

It was a hard life and a rough life, and through his men
sometimes cursed him for a driver, they were proud of him
right enough; and when they arrived at St Michaels and found
the stores full of fruit and scarce another vessel in port, they
could afford to laugh at the caution of the other skippers,
hove to or brought up somewhere till the gale moderated,
while the slippery-heeled *Janet Coombe* had nipped in and got
the best of the market.

When the steamers began to capture the fruit trade and
freights became scarce for a sailing ship in the western isles,
the *Janet Coombe* loaded with salt or clay for St John's,
Newfoundland, and after fighting her way across the Atlantic
she would fill with salt fish and travel down to the
Mediterranean ports with her cargo, sometimes taking only
sixteen days for her passage back.

During these races, and the battles against wind and sea,
Joseph forgot Plyn, and Christopher, and lived only for the
zest of this life, which needed all his strength and endurance,
and a keen mind alert to danger and unforeseen disaster. The
old quiet days at Plyn were nothing but a dim memory, this
was the life for which he had been born, he, and this ship
that was part of him.

These were the days when Joseph was conscious of really
living, and not merely eking out a solitary existence as he did

on shore, try though he might to forsake loneliness and cleave to his family. Here on the ship Janet was with him, but at Plyn he found her not. Christopher was only a boy, and though in the years to come he would be an ever-present joy and consolation, yet at the moment it was impossible to make him understand everything, for all his affectionate ways.

When Christopher was twelve, there came an incident that was like a sharp blow to his father, and though Joseph reasoned with himself and pretended it was just childish nonsense, he was aware after this of a queer bitterness that clung to him, and a disappointment in his heart half sorrowful, half afraid. It happened that in the spring of that year the *Janet Coombe* made the record for the fastest passage from St Michaels to Bristol, and the ship remained there for the space of a few days to unload, after which she was to return to Plyn in ballast.

Susan's sister Cathie had married a shopkeeper in Bristol town, and there Joseph lodged for his visit. Cathie had been spending a little while with her sister in Plyn, and was returning in time to look after her brother-in-law. It was then that Joseph suggested that Cathie should bring back Christopher with her to Bristol, so that he should be able to sail with him on the *Janet Coombe* to Plyn.

During the few days at Bristol Joseph wondered rather that Christopher did not show more interest in the unloading and the life of the quayside. If he himself as a boy had been given the chance of a visit to Bristol, he knew it would have been impossible to drag him away from the shipping and the wharves, and that he would have gone hungry rather than miss the sight of a barque leaving the port, or the entrance of a full-rigged ship.

Christopher, though exceedingly affectionate and pleased to see his father at meal-times, seemed perfectly content to be taken by his aunt to look in the shop windows of the town, and to carry her basket for her, never once suggesting that he should change his walk in the direction of the harbour.

Again, nothing seemed to please him better than to be allowed to stand behind the counter in his uncle's own shop, and be permitted to help serve the customers.

At last the boy bade farewell to his uncle and aunt, and stepped aboard the *Janet Coombe* with his father. It was fun running about the deck and talking to the men, also it was a fine morning. After a day, though, the ship seemed a trifle cramped. It started raining, and Christopher, who hated getting wet, went below to the cabin. It was so small and stuffy, and such a squeeze too at night, sleeping in the poky bunk alongside of father.

He didn't fancy the food much, though he was too polite to say so. Joseph appearing for a moment down the companionway roared with laughter at his small pinched face.

'Feelin' her roll?' he said, bringing an atmosphere of wet oilskin into the close cabin. 'We're in for a dirty night, so I reckon you'll be a bit squeamish-like. Never mind, 'twon't take long afore you have your sea-legs. Lie down in my bunk an' take it easy, though speakin' for myself, I got over it as a boy by climbin' on deck an' layin' my hand to some work. You'll find me on deck should you want a breath o' air.'

Christopher had no intention of going on deck. He lay on the bunk groaning and sniffing; every lurch of the little vessel was agony to him. Being in ballast of course the *Janet Coombe* pitched much worse than if she had been carrying a cargo, and they were reaching that part of the ocean where the Atlantic meets the Channel, and there was a heavy cross sea. All night it continued thus, with poor Christopher below. It wasn't fair, he ought to have been told sailing was like this. Father was mean and unkind to bring him.

Early next morning, when still dark, the ship had cleared the rough and tumble of Land's End, and was now well advanced in the Channel with the Lizard lights ahead, and a stiff sou'westerly breeze and a big following sea.

The movement of the ship was changed, and she frisked along now like a mad spirit, kicking her heels at the weather astern. Joseph wanted to see his boy beside him and hear his

148

glad shout of delight. He went to the head of the companionway and yelled to his son.

'Come up, Chris, and watch the night. Now the motion's easy you won't feel ill no more. Come up, lad, when I tell ye.'

The boy was shivering in his bunk. He had got over his sickness for the moment, but he did not want to leave the warm cabin for the cold cheerless weather on deck. He wanted to be home in bed or in the shop at Bristol.

However, the habit of obedience was too strong for him, and he climbed out of the berth and struggled up the companionway. The night was pitch dark. The gale was howling in the rigging, it tore at his legs and thrashed him in the face with a stinging blow, and the bitter rain blinded his eyes.

'Father – father,' he screamed in terror. Joseph made a dive for him and held him tight by the arm. He was smiling, and shook the spray from his streaming oilskin. His beard was wild and tangled, his face rough and hard with the clinging salt. To the boy he seemed mad and reckless, bringing them to a frightful death.

'Look,' shouted Joseph pointing astern, 'baint that the grandest and most wonderful sight my Chris has ever seen? Tell me you'm happy, son, tell me you're a real proper sailor an' proud of the ship that belongs to us both?'

The lad peered over his father's arm, and to his horror he saw a terrible black sea like a dark falling cliff rising in the air, and making towards them.

They were going to be drowned – they were going to be drowned.

'Take it away,' he screamed, 'take it away – I hate it, I hate the sea. I always have. I'm afraid – I'm afraid.'

'Christopher!' cried Joseph, 'what are you sayin', son – what d'ye mean?'

'I don't want to be a sailor,' sobbed Christopher. 'I hate the sea and I hate the ship. I'll never go again. Oh! Father – I'm afraid – I'm afraid.' The boy tore himself from his father's grasp, and scrambled once more down the companionway, screaming at the top of his voice in rage and fear.

Joseph watched him stupidly, and held out a trembling hand to the rail. He was stunned, unable to think.

And the *Janet Coombe* sped on, one with the wind and the sea.

# 7

For the first time, in the forty-three years of his life, Joseph knew shame and humiliation.

Better to land the boy in Plyn and send him up to his mother without another word, and he himself to shake clear of the lot of them for ever, and sail away, out of the sound and hearing of them, alone with his ship and the spirit of Janet.

These were the first bitter thoughts of Joseph. Later he stole softly down to the cabin where the boy was sleeping, and he watched the tear-stains on the pale handsome little face with mingled sorrow and compassion, swearing by the love he bore for his ship to forget his son's words and to love him as before. Then suddenly the lad opened his eyes, and a flush of shame came over young Christopher for the look he noticed on his father's face, which meant he was sorrowful and distressed. For a moment he longed to jump from the berth, and fling his arms around his father's neck and ask him to help him to conquer his distrust of the sea, but he thought his father would push him away with a frown, and bid him not be a child.

And Joseph looked down on Christopher, and stifled the nigh overmastering impulse to kneel beside the boy and ask him to place all faith and trust into his keeping, but it came to him that the boy might feel shy and embarrassed to see his father act in such a way.

Thus a minute passed, waiting for the chance to unite father and son in a bond which would be close and unbreakable, but the minute passed in vain, never to return, and from henceforward Joseph and Christopher Coombe walked apart with a wall between them, a wall which could not be surmounted

151

because of the pride of Joseph and the weakness of his son.

So the ship anchored in Plyn with the words of union unspoken.

Four years passed, with Joseph Coombe passing a few months here and there on shore, before he set sail again.

The harbour resounded with the hammers of shipwright and builder, and the noise of the clay-loading at the jetties. Samuel and Herbert Coombe were never still down at the yard, and they were joined now by their own grown-up sons: Thomas, Samuel's eldest boy, and James, the first of Herbert's youngsters to grow up, in a family of twelve, with five more yet to come.

Samuel's second son, Dick, a strong hefty young man, was now second mate under his uncle Joseph, and proving himself a fine sailor. Joseph was fond of his nephew, but he longed for his own boy Christopher to be in his place.

In September of 1882 Joseph Coombe dropped anchor in Plyn harbour, after discharging his cargo at London. He was content with the thought of a few weeks at home before going away again. As he watched his men making all snug, below and aloft, he glanced over the bulwark and saw Christopher and brother Herbert Coombe pulling out towards him in a boat. This had never happened before, and he knew at once that something was amiss. Thank God, Christopher was safe, that was his first thought. He remarked the boy's pale, unhappy face, and Herbert's grave expression.

In a few moments they were both on the deck beside him.

'Prepare yourself, dear Joe, for bitter and melancholy news,' said Herbert, his eyes filling with tears. 'And grieved indeed am I that it has fallen on me to break it to you.'

'Out with it quick!' said Joseph gruffly.

'Your dear wife, Susan, has left us yesterday,' said Herbert gently. Christopher at once burst into tears, and walked away. 'She was took bad just after tea, and though the boys ran at once for the doctor, and came to me and Samuel, she passed away by six o'clock. Oh! brother, this is a wretched home-coming for you.'

Joseph wrung his hand without a word, and going over to

Christopher, he kissed the boy's head. Then he climbed into the boat, and the others followed him.

As he gazed down upon his wife's face, now white and silent for evermore, Joseph was possessed with a great pity that she should be gone from her children, but for himself he felt no emotion.

He had never really loved her; he had used her as a way of escape from his own loneliness. And now she had fled beyond him, seeking her own salvation, and not at his side. Poor Susan, she had given him seventeen years of affection and care, and now it was over. She had given him Christopher. . . . He turned away, and as he went down the stairs he wondered what would come to the home and the children without her. The boys would soon be able to fend for themselves, but Kate was merely a child.

The problem was happily solved by his two nieces, Mary and Martha, now tall and strapping young women of twenty-six, suggesting that they should come and keep house for him. Thus, the matter was lifted from his mind.

Another surprise was in store for Joseph on his return, besides the sad hearing of his wife's death. He went down to the broker's firm on the afternoon of his arrival home, and found brother Philip seated at the desk in the office which had always belonged to the senior partner.

'Why, Philip,' exclaimed Joseph, 'what in the name of thunder are you doing here?'

'Merely sitting at my own desk in my own room,' replied Philip. 'I'm sorry to hear of your wife's death; I'm sure she will be a very great loss to you. However, Time the great healer will perhaps – hum . . .' he pretended to sort his papers.

'Listen, Philip, I don't seem somehow to get the hang o' this,' said Joseph frowning, 'what's come to Mr Hogg?'

'The old man died a month ago, and I have bought up the partnership.' Philip leant back in his chair and watched his brother's astonished expression with cool enjoyment. 'You see, Joe, while you and my brothers have spent your time marrying and raisin' large families, I have quietly put by with no one but myself to keep, and here I am, aged forty-two, a partner

153

in this business and a moderately rich man, and my own master in the bargain. Samuel and Herbert are already middle-aged men, and you, I suppose, make some sort of existence on the family vessel?'

'No need to sneer, Philip,' said Joseph quietly. 'I've no reason to be ashamed of my calling, which is the finest in the world, and a man's job, what's more. You can be the gentleman of the family for all I care, and welcome to it if it brings you any satisfaction.'

'Thank you,' said Philip, with a superior smile. 'Incidentally, I suppose you are aware that the remainder of the family have sold their shares of the ship? You and I are joint holders now.'

'But that's goin' agen the original agreement,' cried Joseph, smashing his fist on the desk. 'We was all to share equal, an' everyone to have a benefit.'

'Perhaps so, but the others being, I imagine, in the need of ready money, competition is fierce, you know, in Plyn, were only too willing to hand over their rights to me. Any objection?'

Joseph had no reply to this. The procedure was entirely legal, but he mistrusted Philip.

'No,' he said, shortly.

'By the way, how's that eldest son of yours shaping?' inquired Philip carelessly. 'He's old enough to go to sea, I suppose?'

Joseph rose from his chair and seized his hat. He longed to hit his brother in the face, with his sneering attitude, and his hints against Christopher. 'My boy will be ready when I want him an' not afore,' he said and made for the door.

'Well, Joe,' called Philip as a parting shot, 'I gather you are a happy man with this big growing family of yours. However, I'm glad I've been single and free during the best years of my life. No ties or anything. Now I have an established position though, I may look around me and choose some beautiful young thing to share my home. I'm still a comparatively young man, you see. Good day to you.'

Joseph laughed as he left the building. So that was why Philip had lived so much in retirement all these years. He would control much of the shipping in future, he supposed, if he was buying up shares in this manner. Well, he could hang himself for all Joseph cared.

The next few weeks in Plyn Joseph spent much of his time up at Nicholas Stevens' farm, where his sister Lizzie was always pleased to welcome him and give him a meal. He liked the happy, friendly atmosphere of this place, and the obvious mutual devotion of Lizzie and her kind husband. They were three in the family, two girls and a boy. Joseph found himself much attracted to this lad, Fred, who though only twelve or so was a keen, intelligent youngster, with ready answers and a lift to his chin which reminded him of Janet.

Thomas Coombe was now seventy-seven, a frail tremulous old man, who could just manage to creep down the road to the yard now and again, to see how things were going.

He would sit on a bench and puff at his pipe, making some remark from time to time which nobody would notice, and follow with his eyes his namesake and grandson, Thomas, Samuel's eldest son, in whom he liked to see himself all over again. And then Mary would appear to fetch him home, a stout middle-aged woman whose expression and character had changed very little in all these years; she had still the same affectionate self-effacing character. Joseph's heart always beat faster when he approached the path to Ivy House. At times he was a boy again, playing in the front garden with his eye on the kitchen window, from which Janet would peep, waving to him, taking her mind off her work; and at other moments he was a young man, returning from the sea, knowing that she was there waiting for him. He could never look at the room above the porch without remembering his first home-coming from the *Francis Hope*, when she appeared with her girl's plaits at the window, and he had climbed up to her, hand over hand, by the thick-branched ivy. Nearly thirty years ago.

One afternoon Mary met him at the door with a worried expression on her face.

'Father's poorly,' she told him. 'He's up in bed and seems so weak. I don't know whether 'tis tiredness only or if I should call the doctor. Come up and see what you think.'

155

He found his father propped up by pillows, his face white and sunken, his eyes gazing vacantly to the open window, and his thin hands plucking nervously at the sheet. The veins stood out on his temples, and his lips were blue. 'Is that you, Sammie?' he murmured.

Joseph knew at once that his father was dying.

'Fetch the doctor,' he said in a low tone to Mary, and she went at once, frightened and distressed.

'It's Joe, father,' he said gently, and going towards the bed he took his father's hand. 'Be there anythin' I can do for ye?'

'Back from the sea, boy, eh?' Thomas Coombe peered up at his son. 'I can't see ye without my spectacles, but I'm sure you'm well and hearty, an' glad to be home. Give my compliments to Captain Collins, that worthy man.'

'That's right, father. Why not try an' get a little sleep, dear?'

Thomas moved his head fretfully about the pillow. 'I ought to be down at the yard,' he said. 'They'll be launchin' that new boat tomorrow forenoon, and I'm blessed if those boys will do it proper. The Squire will be vexed if anythin' goes wrong, an' your brothers haven't the experience that's mine.'

Squire Trelawney had been dead twenty years, and his nephew lived up at the House now.

Joseph felt the tears coming into his eyes. They rolled down his cheek and into his beard.

The afternoon quietly faded, and the sky was streaked with crimson and golden patterns. They shone upon the surface of the harbour water. From the yard came the steady clanging of hammers, as planks were nailed into the ribs of some new ship. Presently Mary returned. The old doctor was dead, and this new one was a younger man, and a stranger to Plyn. He held Thomas's wrist and felt his pulse.

'I can't do anything for him,' he said gently. 'I'm afraid his time has come. There's very little life left, you see, and I think he will be gone in a few hours. There will be no pain. Would he care to see the parson?'

Mary threw her apron over her head and began to cry

156

softly to herself. Joseph saw she would be the better for something to do.

'Go down to the yard and tell Sam and Herbie to come at once, and Philip too if you can find him at the office.'

Then when she was gone he took his place once more at Thomas's bedside. The old man muttered sentences from time to time, but it was impossible to catch what he said. The orange light dwindled in the sky. Long shadows crept across the floor. Suddenly the sound of hammers ceased down at the yard. Joseph knew that his brothers had been told.

With the silence Thomas spoke in a clear, firm voice.

'They've stopped work for the night,' he said, 'the boys will be comin' home to supper.'

'Yes, father.'

'I reckon as all will be quiet now, till mornin' agen, won't it Joe?'

'Aye, that's so, dear.'

For a few minutes there was silence, and then Thomas spoke again.

'I don't fancy as I'll read the Bible, not just at present. Seems as though my eyes is come over terrible dim, and I'll fancy restin' awhile. Maybe Mary'll read it later on, when I feels refreshed.'

'Just as you like, father.'

The house was very still. Down in the parlour below the old clock was ticking on the wall. Joseph could hear the sound through the thin boards of the floor.

Quietly the other brothers made their way into the room, followed by Mary. Philip had been impossible to find, and it was too far to run and fetch Lizzie. The tears were flowing fast down Herbert's cheeks, but Samuel knelt beside the bed and whispered in a low tone: 'Be there somethin' you require, father?'

Thomas felt for his head in the gathering dusk.

'That you, Sammie? I'm glad you'm come. You'll have a tidy wrist for the saw if you practise hard, sonnie, but you must always heed my advice in all things, so see.'

His voice wavered uncertainly, he tried to raise himself on the pillow. 'How the evenin's do draw in for sartin, we'll be havin' the light for supper now regular. I can mind the time when 'twas sweet to feel the fall o' dusk on Plyn, and me, as a young chap in a tidy way, callin' your mother up to Castle ruin . . .'

He leaned back exhausted, and closed his eyes. The breathing came slow and harsh now, difficult to control. The three men waited beside their father, with Mary at the window. For a long time he did not speak, and the room was quite dark. No one thought of lighting a candle.

Then he spoke once more, his voice sounding immeasurably tired, and coming from far away.

'Janie,' he said, 'Janie, where are you to?'

Joseph bent low over the bed and watched his father's eyes. They opened wide and looked into his.

'You'll not be forsakin' me, lass, I'm thinkin'. We'll bide a tidy while together, you an' I. D'you know that it's terrible strong the love I have for you, Janie, leavin' me all of a tremble at times like a flummoxed lad.' He held out his two hands and covered Joseph's eyes, and then sighed gently and so fell asleep.

Thomas Coombe was buried beside his wife Janet in Lanoc Churchyard, next to the thorn hedge and the old elm tree. Their tombstone stands today, high above the waving grass, with long stems of ivy clustered about their names. Beneath the inscription are these words in faded lettering:

'Sweet Rest at Last.'

In early spring the first primroses nestle here, and the scattered blossom falls from a forsaken orchard beside the lane.

## 8

Albert Coombe had gone to sea beside his father the Skipper, and his cousin Dick. Charles was at a training camp for soldiers away in the Midlands somewhere. Only Christopher remained at home, pleading his health as an excuse for not going to sea. He was working down at the yard with his uncles and his three cousins, and imagined that he was wasting his time. Christopher could not banish the demon of restlessness that was ever at large within him. He loathed and detested the thought of being a sailor, his only experience these eight years ago had never been forgotten. He read the disappointment in his father's eyes. Every time Joseph returned the son was aware of the unspoken question that never passed his lips. 'Will you come with me this time?' Then ashamed, miserable, half-rebellious at heart, Christopher would show his father that even if he was a poor sailor, he would make a splendid workman. Secretly he disliked the business, he dreamt of leaving Plyn and seeking his fortune farther afield, but had no idea how this could come about.

Meanwhile, the father must have patience. Joseph was now fifty, and had not yet wearied of the sea or of his ship. He was as strong and as powerful as he had ever been, with little trace of grey in his dark hair and beard. He had never known a day's illness. The only thing that troubled him occasionally was his eyesight. At times his right eye became sore and bloodshot, and the pupil greatly distended in size. He had no idea of the cause of this. Every now and again this eye would fail to register, as though there was a film partially obscuring the sight, and then all would be clear again, and the shooting pain that was part of the trouble would also pass away. Joseph said nothing of this to anyone; he refused to admit to himself that there might be anything serious connected with it, as obstinate as Janet herself had been with her faltering heart. Nothing mattered but that the *Janet Coombe* still held her high reputation as the fleetest schooner of Plyn, and that son Christopher would soon become a man.

Just before Whitsun of 1885, Joseph returned to Plyn after an exceptionally long voyage. He had been twice to St John's, Newfoundland, for fish, which had to be taken down to the Mediterranean, and then had secured good freights from St Michaels to the Mersey, making three runs. It was now the latter part of June, and he looked forward to a peaceful, happy time while at home before setting forth again. Christopher pulled out to the *Janet Coombe* as soon as the ship dropped anchor. Joseph looked about him with pleasure. There were several boats rowing up and down the harbour, and some children were bathing in the Cove beneath the Castle. Real glorious summer weather. He promised himself some days' fishing round the bay, with Christopher perhaps at his side.

'Well, Chris, son,' he said, 'it's good to be back again for a spell, eh Albie? You shore folk don't appreciate home like we poor sailors.'

Christopher flushed, and bit his lip. Joseph noticed this at once, and cursed his tact. Poor dear lad, after all it was only his health that kept him from the sea.

'What's the news, son?'

'Sister's well, and brother Charlie writes pleased enough from barracks. Both aunties are in good health an' lookin' forward to seein' you up home. We've a lot of work on at the yard, and cousin Tom and James and I are working on a boat from morning till night, so I'm fearin' I shan't be able to be with you as much as I'd hoped, father.'

'Never mind, Chris, I like to know as you'm busy, an' your uncles are pleased with you.'

'They say that Uncle Philip is courting at last, but who the party is I cannot say.'

'Philip courtin'?' Joseph threw back his head and roared

160

with laughter. 'The man is crazy. Why, I reckon he doesn't even know how to handle a woman. If he gets one it'll be for sake of his riches, and not for his lovely person.'

The boys laughed, and Joseph went off to the office highly amused at the thought of his youngest brother in love.

Philip received him with his usual superior smile, and waved him to a chair. Joseph made no bones about the matter, and tackled him at once. 'So you'm goin' to bow to petticoat rule at last, be you, Philip?' he said, winking, and holding out his hand.

Philip went a dark crimson.

'I have no idea what you mean,' he said slowly.

'Oh! come, my dear fellow, none of your airs an' graces with me. Let's have a look at the lady, I'll soon tell you if she's bed-worthy or not.' Joseph nearly choked with delight to see his brother wince at his expression. It reminded him of the old days when he had hurt his feelings over some book.

'There old chap, I didn't mean to be aggravatin'. I'm sure I'll be highly pleased to see you settle down and be human, an' your wife'll be a lucky woman. Now to business.'

Joseph would have thought no more of the matter, and, indeed, at once dismissed it from his mind. But Philip had taken his jest in the wrong way. He was filled with loathing for this conceited, cocksure elder brother, who had always had any woman he had fancied.

He resented his height and his still obvious powers of attraction, he would have lost half his fortune to see Joseph show some signs of middle age. When the accounts of the ship were settled, and Joseph was preparing to depart, Philip, like a narrow-minded, spiteful woman, could not resist flinging a venomous dart.

'It's true I may be settling down shortly, Joe,' he said, 'and I look forward to many happy years beside a young wife. I'm in the lucky position to be able to give a woman anything she may take a fancy for, a large house and servants. I wonder you don't marry again, some good hard-working soul of your own age. You're fifty, aren't you, brother? You'll have to think of retiring soon and letting a younger man take your place. Good afternoon. My respects to your family.'

'Dirty little worm,' thought Joseph to himself. 'By Jesus, I'd like him to see who's the younger man when it comes to a fight, him or me. He's not quarter of a man, an' can only fall back on words to keep his countenance.'

Nevertheless Joseph could not forget his brother's closing sentence. He climbed up to the Castle ruins and thought it out. Yes, heavens above, it was true in a way. He was fifty, a middle-aged man, and he had never realized it.

His boys were grown up or nearly, and yet he still felt as young as they did. Philip was a fool. A man is as old as he feels, and Joseph felt thirty, at times younger. He leaned back on the grass, and lit his pipe. Pity Katherine the child was not yet at a more companionable age, but she was still at school. Anyway, she was a queer little thing. The two nieces were well-meaning, but a trifle heavy on the hand. He must look up Lizzie tomorrow, and see how that attractive boy was shaping.

From where he lay he could see *Janet Coombe* riding to her buoy. What a beauty she was, with her sheer, and her long lines. Janet's ship . . . He sighed and closed his eyes, longing for her at his side.

The bell chimed out the hour from Lanoc Church; he supposed he must make an appearance at his home, and also call on the brothers at the yard. He emptied his pipe, stretched himself, and rose to his feet, wondering idly where Christopher had vanished to.

Suddenly a faint cry caught his attention.

He looked towards the direction from where the sound had come, and saw someone huddled in a little heap by the stile to the cliff walk. He at once walked to the spot, and saw that the person was a girl, with a basket on her arm filled with primroses, and she was weeping, clutching at her foot.

'What's come over you, my dear?' he inquired, and knelt beside her, feeling her ankle.

The girl ceased sobbing, and looked up at him from under

her hat. He saw a pair of large troubled hazel eyes, and coils of red golden hair twisted about her ears.

'I hurt my leg jumping the stile,' she said shyly, 'an' when I tried to walk it pained me something terrible.'

'Ah!' said Joseph, not taking his eyes off the golden curl that crept about her cheek.

'That's a bad business. Let me touch it an' see if 'tes strained.'

He moved his hand about the foot and ankle, and the girl seemed to show no sign of pain.

'I reckon it's not strained, merely a twist,' he said, wishing she would look up at him again.

'I'm glad of that,' she smiled. 'Maybe if I bide here awhile I'll be able to walk home.'

'Not on your life,' said Joseph coolly, and he picked her up in his arms as if she were no more than a child. The girl blushed, and Joseph noticed this. He also noticed the long golden lashes that swept her cheeks when her eyes were lowered. He tightened his hold, and her head rested on his shoulder.

'Tell me your name if I may be so abrupt,' he asked her.

'Annie Tabb, Captain Coombe.'

'How d'you know who I am?' he said curiously.

'Why, mercy, everyone knows you in Plyn,' she smiled.

'Are you Reuben Tabb's daughter?'

'Yes, for sure, the second girl. There's eight in family.'

Joseph had been at school with Reuben Tabb, and this was his child. That took him back a bit, a good many years. Oh, hell, he was middle-aged, Philip was right. As old as this girl's father—

'And what's your age, Miss Annie, makin' so bold as to inquire?'

'Just turned nineteen, Captain Coombe, but folks say I look younger, which is most vexing.'

Joseph glanced at her pouting mouth and laughed.

'D'you like to be old?' he said, teasing her, 'and crawl about the town with a shawl on your shoulders and a lace cap on your head?'

'You're playing with me, Captain Coombe,' the girl turned away her head and frowned. 'I mean I likes to be taken for a young woman and not a silly child.'

'That's easy enough,' whispered Joseph slyly, watching her face. She was blushing again, and biting her lip.

'Where d'you live?'

'Just round the corner, the third house over there with the cream curtains. Oh! please let me go, I shouldn't care for folks to see us, and I'm sure I can walk – now.'

'Why not let me take you a little farther – as far as the gate?'

'No. Oh! no.'

Joseph put her down.

'Are you feelin' strong?' he asked her.

'Yes, honest, Captain Coombe. 'Tis nothing at all, for the fuss I made up the field.'

She held out her hand to him.

'You've got a nice load of primroses here, I see,' said Joseph, searching about for some reason to detain her.

'Yes, they're my favourite flowers.'

'Will you be wantin' any more, I wonder?'

'Oh! certain. I expect I'll be goin' up tomorrow to the hedges to get another basketful.'

Joseph took a handful and examined them carefully. 'Why, these baint nearly fresh enough. You don't find the best 'uns in the cliff hedges. Now down by Polmear Valley there's some beauties, only you'd never get there by yourself, with all those prickly brambles and one thing an' another.'

'There now, what a pity!' she sighed. The golden curl slipped a little down her cheek.

'Listen here,' he said carelessly, 'you mustn't go ruinin' your clothes down i' the Valley, all by your lonesome. And it's wicked to waste such primroses. I'll walk that way with pleasure, if you've a mind for the stroll, an' see you don't scratch those pretty hands of yours.'

'Oh! Captain Coombe, I wouldn't think . . .' began the girl, casting down her eyes demurely, and hanging her head. 'Did

you ever?' she thought to herself, and her heart beat excitedly because of this tall handsome sailor, with his warm eyes
that made her heart feel daft like a bleating sheep.

Joseph made great pretence of sighing, watching her out
of the tail of one eye.

'Ah! well, it can't be helped. The flowers must fade for want
o' pickin'. Good evenin', Miss Annie.'

He was turning away when she called him back.

'Wait – wait a minute, Captain Coombe. P'raps if 'tes fine
tomorrow evenin', I'll be walkin' that way with a basket.'

She spoke a little breathlessly, the colour flaming into her
cheeks. Joseph looked at her feet, and allowed his gaze to
travel up the whole of her until he reached her eyes.

'There's somethin' tells me there won't be no rain tomorrow, an' it's terrible pleasant to rest in the shade of the Valley,'
he called softly. Then he went away, and strode down the road,
while she watched him out of sight.

Joseph rolled a quid of tobacco and stuffed it in his cheek.
And Philip had said he was fifty . . . What a cursed fool the
man was; why, he felt twenty-five, younger than he had ever
felt in his life. He threw back his head and laughed. It was
good to be back in Plyn.

> O! where are ye goin' to, my pretty maid—
> O! where are you goin', my honey

he whistled, and waved his hand to an old man leaning over
a garden gate. He was young, young . . .

Joseph woke the next morning with a strange feeling in
his heart. He sprang out of bed and wondered why it was he
pulled aside the blind with such an eager hand to glance at
the blue sky overhead, and note the direction of the wind.
Then he remembered Annie Tabb, and cursed himself for a
fool, though pleased enough for all that.

Joseph sang as he dressed before the open window. He was
overcome suddenly with a love for Plyn and a joy of living.
Long days stretched out before him, with Christopher perhaps

busy, but somehow he felt that his hours would not be lonely or empty. He went down to breakfast in a very cheerful frame of mind, chatted gaily with his two nieces, who were so alike he could scarce tell them apart, walked with his daughter Katherine up to school and bid her be a good girl and learn her lessons well, then strolled round to the yard for a chat with his brothers Samuel and Herbert.

At four o'clock Joseph turned his back on Plyn, and strode away over the fields as though his legs would not carry him quickly enough, although he knew he was an hour before his time.

As he heard five strike from Lanoc Church above him, he emptied his pipe and straightened his collar, and looked towards the path that led to the stile on which he leaned. His hands were hot and his feet were cold. Damn her, she wasn't coming, the little flirt. At twenty past five he saw a figure with a basket on her arm making her way through the fields. He took a newspaper from his pocket and pretended to read.

When Annie reached him he pretended not to see her. The girl put out her hand timidly and touched his arm.

'Captain Coombe,' she said shyly.

Joseph made play of starting, and lowered his paper. 'Bless my soul,' he said, 'so you've turned up after all. Well, I must say I never expected you.'

Annie pouted and withdrew her hand. 'If you don't care for my company I won't worry you,' she answered, deeply hurt, and was for drawing off by herself. But Joseph calmly took her basket from her, and without a word lifted her over the stile, putting her down the other side, flushed and indignant.

'You've rough manners, Captain Coombe, with never as much as by your leave,' she began.

'It's a way we sailors have,' he told her, hiding his laughter, and set off along the Valley with her beside him.

The world could go hang now for all he cared.

It was a funny thing that with two of them at the work they should take so long to fill one basket, and also rest as

166

often as they did. Then Annie saw some tall wild iris growing the other side of the stream, and cried out that she wanted
them and must have them. So Joseph strode through the water,
soaking his boots, and began to pluck them for her, and then
came over very foolish and said she must come there with
him, for he was no hand at distinguishing the ones she liked.

'No, I can't, for 'tes dirty, an' I've no mind to be bedrag-
gled in my best gown.'

'Oh! 'tes your best, is it?' said he. 'Well, I'm mighty pleased
at the compliment, for there's few women who'd risk their
skirts down in the Valley, because a sailor asked for her
company.'

Then Annie protested she had not put it on for him, but
Joseph, conceited fellow that he was, cared not a jot for her
denial, and asked whether she'd join him over the stream.

'No, I'll not be wettin' my feet;' she shook her head, and
with two splashes he was at her side again, picking her up in
his arms and bearing her across. 'Least said, soonest mended,'
he whispered in her ear, and proceeded to stagger under her
weight and breathe loudly, and protest she was too much for
him.

Then Annie said no one had ever called her heavy before,
and he vowed if any other man had as much as touched her
he'd knock his face in for him. So they both laughed, and
then came to rest on a bank where the iris grew next the
stream, and Joseph spread his coat for her to sit on, while he
squatted on the edge and took hold of her hand, saying she
had wounded it on a thorn.

"Tisn't true, Captain Coombe,' said Annie, ''tes a middlin'
sort o' scratch that I did hasty-like last night with my brooch.'

'Well, I must see the brooch,' said Joseph. 'Is this it?' and
he bent towards the fancy piece of jewellery that was pinned
at the lace collar round her neck.

'Yes,' she murmured; 'no, you can't touch it,' for he was
about to unclasp it, and that would mean him leaning very
close indeed, which would make her come over awkward,
though she hoped for it all the same.

167

He sat back on his heels, and watched her, while she rested, a little disappointed that he had made no attempt to kiss her, which was just as Joseph intended her to feel; and when he glanced at her for an instant, and saw the look in her eye, he smiled to himself and knew he would have her.

And the evening passed very pleasantly, with no love-making in words, and in a flash it seemed they were walking home across the fields, both remembering the four stiles that had to be crossed, and glad that there was no other way back to Plyn.

Joseph went with her to her garden gate, very correct and as he should be, and said they must go walking again some time when it suited her, and then, as there was no reason for him to linger, he made his way down the hill, sending Annie to her room in a flutter of excitement to peep at herself in the glass and watch him from her window; while he saw nothing of the houses he passed, nor the neighbours, nor the ships at anchor in the harbour, nor even heard the voice of Christopher calling him from the yard, but only a girl that had never been kissed yet by any man.

# 9

Joseph was in love. He was more blindly and passionately in love than he had ever been in his life. He could not remember having wanted anyone as he now wanted Annie Tabb of Plyn, just nineteen, and only five years older than his own young daughter. His age made little difference to him.

His marriage with Susan had been the result of a longing to be understood, an unconscious craving to rest his head in her lap and forget his loneliness. In this she had failed him, and perceiving his tenderness unwanted he had loved her casually, carelessly, without feeling, and the last eleven years of their married life he had been no more to her than the bread-winner, and she his housekeeper. Now, all the natural instincts, repressed for so long, were awake once more, and Joseph could neither sleep nor eat for the one thought that tormented him night and day – that he must have Annie, and that nothing in the whole world mattered but this. He worshipped her youth and her beauty, he longed to be able to share this and become part of it. In the old days women and girls had been the same to him, he had thought nothing of their years but only of a certain look in their eye which meant they understood what he was after. Now, all was changed.

The thought of Annie's innocence and inexperience tormented him. Why had he never understood this before? Joseph did not realize that his fifty years made these qualities so precious, and that twenty years back he would have scorned them as worthless and uninteresting. At thirty he desired Susan, older than himself, to care for his wants. Now at fifty he desired Annie, like a symbol of spent youth in which to recover himself, to turn his back on the spectre of age which lay ahead, and to linger in this fair land of promise by his side.

169

So while son Christopher toiled in the yard, restless and discontented, aching for some sort of freedom, Joseph the father hung about by a certain garden gate, one moment believing himself in heaven, and the next unwittingly plunged in the depths of despair. There seemed to him no possible reason why a beautiful young thing like Annie Tabb should return his passion, unless it was from sheer concentration and will-power on the part of himself, thought Joseph, as he paced to and fro at the top of the hill – after the child had kept him waiting for nearly three-quarters of an hour, and then when she did appear with a heightened colour and shining eyes, excusing herself, his dark mood instantly vanished and he was certain that it would only be a matter of days before she gave way to him. Often in the evenings now they would stroll across the fields to Polmear Valley, Annie making the excuse at home that she was walking with a girl acquaintance, for she doubted her parents' approval of this bewildering friendship with Captain Joe, who, for all their difference in age, would scarcely be accepted as a suitable companion by those who remembered his early escapades. She herself had often listened to the shocking tales her aunts told one another, middle-aged married women now, of twenty and thirty years back when Joseph Coombe had run wild in Plyn, and though this bearded widower was respected enough now, she could not help feeling secretly that he was little changed, especially when he looked in her eyes and held up his arms to lift her over a stile. The thought that she was playing with fire, of whose power she was uncertain, thrilled young Miss Annie, and turned her head. What did it matter after all? Folks hadn't noticed them walking of an evening, and she didn't care about anything as long as she knew her handsome skipper was waiting for her at the top of the cliff path. All his family had noticed Joseph's high spirits, but they none of them guessed the reason. Christopher was greatly relieved to see his father made no attempt to question him on when he would go to sea, and Albert, surmising that the *Janet Coombe* would not be sailing again for some weeks, took the opportunity of slipping away and visiting his brother Charles in camp.

Mary and Martha found their uncle excessively pleasant and agreeable this time, and not nearly as frightening and overbearing as he was generally. Even Katherine forgot her natural awe, and looked upon her father as someone human after all, instead of a tall gruff stranger, who hardly recognized her when he passed her on her way from school.

Joseph scarcely knew himself. He began to dress with greater care, and to take some sort of a pride in his appearance. He noticed with satisfaction that his dark hair was free from grey.

There was a glorious spell of weather at the moment, and he would wake up in the mornings and hear the gulls shouting 'Annie,' and the waves calling 'Annie' as they broke against the rocks; even the soft summer breezes whispered her name, and the air was full of her.

In a week it would be Whitsun and holiday, and this was the limit of time he had imposed upon himself. On the Saturday before the holiday Joseph had occasion to step into the office of Hogg and Williams (the name had not been changed) to see his brother Philip over some matter of insurance which was due. To his surprise Annie Tabb came out of the door as he was about to walk in. She flushed when she saw him, and would have made her escape, but he barred her way and would not let her pass.

'Why, whatever are you doin' in the office?' he asked jokingly. 'Thinkin' of becomin' a shipowner?'

'No, Captain Joe,' she said. 'And there never was such a man as you for askin' questions, one way an' another. I had to go in with a message to Mr Coombe from my mother.'

'Sakes alive!' said Joe. 'So you know brother Philip, do you? And what do you think of him?'

Annie twisted her handkerchief. 'I consider him a real gentleman, and very agreeable. He's always polite and attentive, and knows just the sort of things a girl requires. Look, he gave me this bracelet for my birthday.'

171

Joseph frowned, very much taken aback. 'How long have you known him?' he asked, somewhat roughly.

'Why, deary me, I really forget,' laughed Annie affectedly. 'He often comes of a Sunday up to our place and drinks a dish of tea with mother and me. I must have told you that before now, Captain Joe.'

'That you never have, Miss Annie, I'll lay my oath on it.'

'Well, it ain't such a grand matter for all I can see, Plyn bein' a smallish place an' neighbourly. An' now I must be steppin' along back.'

'Don't you forget you'm comin' to the fair with me Monday night?'

'No – there, I never promised.'

'I reckon you did, you little flirt.'

'An' don't call me names, or I shan't speak to you. We'll see about Monday – I'll think it over.'

He would have none of this play though, and held out his arm to prevent her.

'You've got to say "Yes" about the fair Monday afore you leave this buildin'.'

'Oh! Captain Joe, you're impossible.'

'Say "Yes" – Annie.'

'Well, I never did – it's Christian names now, is it?'

'Say "Yes" an' quick about it, or you'll be late home, I reckon.'

There was a silence for a moment while they both pretended to be angry.

'Oh! bother you. I'll come,' said the girl at length, never having had any intention of refusing, of which Joseph was well aware. So he stepped aside and allowed her to pass, and then walked into his brother's office, smiling foolishly like a drunkard. Philip was seated at his desk, idle for once, with his hands clasped behind his head, and gazing apparently into space. He too was smiling, but neither brother was aware of the other's appearance.

'How do, Joe?' said one.

'Well enough, thank ye, Philip,' replied the other.

172

'Weather's very seasonable. I hope it holds over the holiday.'

'Aye, 'twill be a sore pity if it should come to rain, spoilin' folks' enjoyment an' all.'

Both brothers hoped to end the interview as soon as possible, for they were neither of them at ease in one another's company.

'Well, that's that,' said Joseph, as he blotted some document, and wiped his inky fingers on his handkerchief. Writing and signing anything was a labour he detested.

Philip scanned it carefully, and placed it away in a drawer. He glanced at his brother, and grudgingly admitted to himself he had never seen him in better health.

'What do you find to do with yourself in your spare time, Joe?' he inquired with some curiosity. 'Plyn must seem a dull little hole compared to places abroad.'

'It baint so bad for all that,' smiled Joseph, 'an' I find my hours filled pleasantly enough. You're the queer one, Philip, a regular dark horse in my opinion. Nobody ever sees you when you've shut up the office. D'you still read as much as you did in the old days?'

'Yes – a pretty fair amount, but I've been thinking of other things lately. I'm not so old that I make myself into a hermit, you know. I'm still a comparatively young man.'

Joseph was tickled at this. He remembered the story of Philip's courting, which he had put out of his mind.

'I s'pose you'll be springin' a marriage on us all, sudden like, one of these days, Philip?' he laughed.

The brother made no attempt to conceal a smile of satisfaction.

'Perhaps, Joe – perhaps. In fact I may say it is extremely likely that I shall take the plunge in the near future.'

'Providin' the lady is willin' of course,' teased Joseph.

'Providing she is willing, naturally. But I think I can safely say I have no fears on that score.'

'Well, it's a wonderful consolation when you're in love to know that the sentiment is returned,' pondered Joseph.

173

'Though I often consider uncertainty is part of the excitement myself.'

'What a statement coming from a man of fifty,' said Philip cuttingly. 'Haven't you put all these ideas out of your head yet?'

Joseph laughed.

'Never make certain of a woman until you've got her, Philip,' he said. 'There's all my years' experience for you, an' wishin' you luck.'

'Oh! nonsense, Joe, things are changed nowadays. It's position that a woman seeks, and a house and servants; if a man can offer his future wife these things, there's no need to bother about anything else, she'll come to him willingly enough.'

'Think so? I rather doubt it, Philip. There's mighty little consolation in fine furniture if you've a cold bed-companion. Let's hope you'll make a good job of it, though I reckon a few lessons from an expert would do you no harm.'

'It's evidently impossible for you to rise above coarseness, Joe,' said Philip. 'I admit her youth is a very great attraction to me, and her physical appearance is – blinding, to say the least of it. I'm convinced I have only to say the word and she will accept. Besides, I have a certain amount of influence with her family.'

'When are ye thinkin' of gettin' yourself spliced, then?' asked Joseph.

'Well, I haven't actually decided,' replied Philip coolly. 'I had thought of speaking my mind after the holiday.'

Joseph visualized the conventional scene. Philip standing in the parlour, very stiff and formal, with the young lady seated in a chair, as prim as butter. A fine Whitsun triumph. While he, Joseph, would be riding a whirlie horse with his girl before him, then carrying her away to the silent cliffs. What was Philip saying?

'. . . so I am quite certain she will not refuse me. Every girl wishes to better herself, and she'd be a little fool if she turned me down. Here, Joe, I've got her likeness here in my desk. Stole if off her mother. I suppose she's young enough to be your daughter . . .'

Joseph looked over his brother's shoulder straight into the face of Annie Tabb.

'Christ Jesus—'

'Yes – she's a little beauty, isn't she? It doesn't do her justice though. Now if—Why, where on earth . . .' Philip rose to his feet in astonishment and ran to the door. But Joseph was gone. He was half-way along the street, and already turning the corner and up the hill. He reached the summit just as a girl was about to turn in at her garden gate.

'Hullo! You again, Captain Joe?'

'Come here,' he said unsteadily. 'You'll have to be late for your dinner, because I want to talk to you. Come away to the cliff for a minute, I won't keep you long.'

He was dragging her by the hand. 'What in the world has come over you?'

He made no answer, but waited until they came to a seat, some distance from the Castle, where he sat her down beside him.

'My brother Philip has been making love to you,' he began at once.

Annie started, and shook her head. 'No, he never did. He gives me things now an' again, an' visits us too, but he's never did nothing that wasn't proper.'

'I'm not talking of anything proper or improper,' said Joseph impatiently. 'All that matters is that he fancies himself in love with you. Did you know of this?'

'No – I don't think – I can't say. He's always very attentive.'

'Listen, child; did you know he was going to ask you for yourself?'

'Oh! Captain Joe – really . . .'

'In marriage, Annie, in marriage. He wants to make you his wife.'

The girl's eyes opened wide in astonishment. 'Mr Coombe wants to marry me?' she exclaimed. 'I can't believe it. Why, he's quite the gentleman.'

'You like that, do you, eh? You like him for it, you're pleased,

175

I can see. You fancy yourself in a lace dress and a flunkey to wait on you. That's it, is it?'

'No, Captain Joe, don't flummox me so – I can't think at all, I can't. I've never given a thought to Mr Coombe.'

'Ha! you say that, do you? Well, you must have been pretty fresh and easy with him to make him talk as he has done. So you're goin' to marry him, then, an' become a fine lady, with a carriage of your own?'

'I never said so.' The girl was nearly in tears. 'Mr Coombe is polite an' kind, but I've never fancied him for a husband. Besides, I don't want to wed yet awhile.'

'Ah! you'll keep him danglin', will 'ee, like a poor fish on the end of a line, until you've made up your mind what material you'll have for a weddin' dress. Then when he hires enough servants to kneel at your feet, you'll give in, eh, and make a present o' yourself to him for all he's done for you?'

'Oh! stop it, Captain Joe, I'll lose my wits in a minute, with you going on at me so.' The tears began to roll down her face. 'Oh! dear – oh! dear, what a fuss an' a pother, I scarce know where I am.'

Seeing her tears, Joseph lost control of himself, and seizing her in his arms he laid her across his knee, and kissed her hungrily and angrily, until her hair broke from its band, and fell about her shoulders, and she lay still, with her face pressed in his shoulder weak and helpless.

'You'd go to him, would you,' whispered Joseph, 'him with his parson's face an' his parson's ways, just for the sake of a pretty dress an' a fine house. You'd go to him without knowin' anythin' of the meaning of love, an' never learnin', an' never carin'. You'd go, where I couldn't hold you like this – and this – and this . . .'

'No – no—' cried Annie. 'You mustn't, oh! Joseph, what's come to me – I love you – yes I do – indeed I do.'

He kissed her again and again, exhausting her, stirring in her a flood of misery and pleasure and emotion that she did not understand. Then he pushed her away from him, and she found she could scarcely stand, and her legs were trembling beneath her, while her heart was throbbing in her breast. Her hands shook as she arranged her dress and her hair, and there was a queer, gnawing pain inside her.

He watched her, his eyes narrowing.

'Well, are ye goin' to tell him you'll be his wife? Run then, don't lose him, he'll be gone unless you'm quick.'

'I don't want to marry him, you know I don't. Why are you trying to make me so miserable?'

'He'll make you a fine husband an' give you a tidy home, with everythin' in the world you need. You'll be a fool to refuse him.'

Poor Annie was ready to burst into tears again.

He kissed her once more, and she leaned against him, unable to walk, unable to do anything but what he asked her. She had no will, no strength left in her, only a wish to be held next him and loved.

'Philip must have his chance fairly,' said Joseph. 'I'm not goin' to sneak in behind his back. This afternoon you'll have to come down with me to the office, and choose between us. You'll have to speak the truth to his face. Do you promise, Annie?'

'Oh! I promise – I promise.'

'Well then, now go along to your dinner, an' don't worry your little head about things. We'll fix it between us.'

So poor Annie stumbled away to her home, filled with emotion and swaying like a sleepwalker after this first experience of physical love, while Joseph tramped across the cliffs with no thought of food or repose, trying to quieten the restless longing that had got the better of him, and which would not rest for all his bidding.

That afternoon the pair of them went down to the gloomy building next door to the Post Office, where Philip lodged.

Annie was left in the hall, while Joseph knocked on the parlour door.

Philip was lying on a hard-backed sofa, with a handkerchief over his face. Joseph smiled. His brother evidently believed in taking care of himself.

177

Philip flung away his handkerchief and rose to a sitting position, his smooth, sandy hair rumpled for once, his mouth open in surprise.

'Where have you sprung from, Joe, and what did you mean by running away like that this morning? Is anything wrong?'

'I should certainly say there is,' replied Joseph, pulling forward a chair for his own use.

'Look ye, Philip, I'm not agoin' to mince matters, I believed in plain speakin' an' plain dealin'. You can't marry Annie Tabb, the girl belongs to me.'

The brother stared incredulously; then hardly aware what he was doing he drew his handkerchief from his pocket, and wiped his hands slowly. 'If this is your idea of a joke, Joe, it's in exceedingly poor taste, I'd have you know.'

'Cut out this gentleman stuff, Philip, I've got no time for it. It's not my way to joke about something of such deadly importance, you fool. I tell you I've been courtin' that girl this last fortnight or so, an' I mean to have her, whether you like it or not.'

Every vestige of colour drained from Philip's face. He looked shrunken and wizened, like a fair rat. He clutched at the arm of the sofa, never taking his eyes off his brother's.

'Say that again.'

'I say I'm goin' to have that girl, an' she's promised herself to me. I'm very sorry to break up your happy schemes, old fellow, but I'd no idea that my Annie was your intended. If you'd only be a little more open, an' not so mighty secretive about your affairs, there'd be none of this springin' things on you now. I reckon there's nothin' more that I can say, except the position is an embarrassin' one for both of us, an' the sooner we put an end to it the better.'

Philip sat motionless on the sofa, then he began to speak slowly and softly.

'You damned swine,' he said. 'So that was your idea, was it? To slink behind my back and make love to the woman I wanted for my wife; to deliberately steal her from me . . .'

'Hold fast, brother,' shouted Joseph. 'I never knew until this

178

mornin' when you showed me her likeness that Annie was the girl you had a fancy for. Do I look like a thief?'

'What difference does that make? All I know is that you've chosen to step between me and Annie Tabb, you, a middle-aged sailor with a grown-up family.'

'Curse your insultin' tongue. Bain't ye only four years younger'n me, Philip? Where's the difference, eh – show me the difference? You'll not get Annie for all your flimsy fortune an' your boastful talk. She'll have none of you. Annie,' he called, 'Annie, come here an' tell him so.'

'Good God, you've had the impudence to bring her to this house?'

'I have that.'

Annie appeared in the doorway, very flushed and confused.

'Now, Annie,' said Joseph, 'I can't get my brother to understand you refuse to marry him. Do you mind tellin' him so yourself?'

'Oh! dear – I don't know – what can I say? – I never . . .'

Philip rose from his sofa and went towards her.

'Miss Annie,' he said, 'this is perhaps the most important moment of your life, and you must think carefully. You have known me for some months, a great deal longer than you have known my brother Joseph. I have made no attempt to frighten you or to rush you into an engagement. I had decided to speak to you early next week, and ask you to be my wife. You would, by accepting me, hold a high position in Plyn, and I should be able to offer you anything you wanted. You would never regret taking such a step. And now you intend to throw this aside, with not so much as a thought, because my brother, a rough sailor, has chanced to throw his eye over you, and has amused himself by telling you things he will forget in a few weeks' time.'

'Pay no heed to his smooth words, Annie,' said Joseph, seizing her hand. 'You're too beautiful an' too young to be content with the things he promises. I tell you they're empty an' cold, the gifts he'd fling on you, makin' you a pretty stuffed doll for his own pleasure with no care for your natural feelin's.

You'm born for love, Annie, an' beauty, an' the blessed things of this earth. He'd sit you in a high chair with a jewel at your throat, and your body starvin' the while; while I'll give you no fancy trinkets but hold you in my arms next my heart. Come to me.'

'Oh! deary, Oh! deary,' cried Annie, 'what can I say, when there's none to counsel. It's terrible hard for a girl, who'd no wish to be wed yet a while, to be plunged like this i' the midst of trouble, till she's nigh borne off her feet with the flurry o' words.'

'Think, child, think,' said Philip. 'I'll not hasten you, nor worry you. I'll make you one of the richest ladies in Plyn, which Joseph can never do, remember that.'

'Don't you want to be loved, Annie, don't you, eh – don't you?' whispered Joseph.

'Oh! please, please, let me think by myself,' said the girl, with tears in her eyes. 'I'm certain I do love you, Captain Joe, but I must think it out alone as Mr Philip says. Let me go now, an' after the holiday I'll give you my answer, I promise.'

'Come, that's fair enough, I reckon,' laughed Joseph. He had no doubt that he could win her. 'What do ye say, brother?'

Philip walked to the window, his hands behind his back.

'I'll break even with you, one day. This is something I won't forget. Now go out of this house, and take her with you. I want to be alone.'

'Good day, Philip,' said Joseph, and he strode from the building with Annie following close behind him. 'So you needs must think by yourself, my girl?' he asked, frowning down on her. 'Well, don't you take too long over it, that's all I plead. An' one thing more. There's no slippin' away from me Monday night at the fair, eh? No more harsh words then, but a quick forgettin' of all this business.'

So he turned on his heel and left her.

# 10

All day long the sun had shone on the merrymakers of Plyn, for it was Whit Monday, and a great holiday. The harbour had been alive with pleasure boats to watch the racing up the river and back.

At last evening was come, and many of the people pulled for home, but the younger and more restless ones made for the excitement and the crowds of the town quay, before the old 'King William Inn'.

The fair had come to Plyn.

There were booths huddled close together on the cobbled square, there were coconut shies, and Aunt Sallies, and dart-throwing, and 'Try your weight', and numberless little stalls for sweets and refreshment.

The centre of the attraction was the merry-go-round. Here gathered the thickest of the crowd, sailors from off their ships, foreigners some of them, and boys and girls escaped from home, lovers making the most of their time. And the barrel organ squeaked out the rollicking popular tune, 'Champagne Charlie is my Name'.

The night was dark and windy, loose clouds blew across the sky, hiding the stars. The lanterns flickered, and folk lost one another now and again amongst the throng. 'Where are you, Nancy Penrose?' 'Has anyone seen my Jan?'

The air was filled with excitement and adventure, whispers in the dark, and the touch of hands.

Round and round staggered the painted horses, the wretched fellow sweating as he turned the handle.

> Oh! you girls, you naughty young girls,
> Why don't you try to be good, be good?

181

> Why will you flirt with so many young swells,
> And not with the men you should, you should?

The barrel organ thumped and trilled, while folk rode the horses, swaying in time to the music.

Joseph sat astride his horse, with Annie propped up before him. Christopher was away the other side of the quay, flinging darts with a young Danish sailor.

So Joseph swayed to the lively tune with Annie's hair blowing about his face, and his mouth nearly touching her mouth, and she half drunk with the night and the flaring lights, caring not at all what should become of her.

Round and round they went, laughing, singing, joining in the riotous clamour of sound.

> Oh! you girls, you naughty young girls,
> Why don't you try to be good, be good?
> Why do you flirt with so many young swells,
> And not with the men you should, you should?

Joseph drew Annie closer to him, burying his face in her hair. 'Sweetheart, I love you – I love you, come away now, now at once. I can't wait for you no longer.'

'No – Joe, I mustn't. Oh! I can't.'

'Yes.'

'No – don't ask me.'

'Yes – I say.'

'Oh! Joe, how can we? Where would we go? We mustn't.'

'Yes – come away, now, over the water, to my ship. Darling, I can't go on without you – come.'

'Joe, please . . .'

'Annie, my beautiful Annie, I love you, quick, down into the boat waitin' at the steps, and over to the ship.'

Protesting, half afraid, half excited, Annie allowed herself to be pulled away by Joseph from the thick pressing crowd, and handed into the little boat. The water was dark and rough, and the careless wind tossed at her hair and her skirts.

'Joe, let's go back.'

'No, I say. Annie, it's so wonderful, so wonderful.'

The boat shot away into the darkness, over the tumbled harbour water, towards the black ship anchored at the far buoy. Joseph pulled like a madman, his face wet with the spray, his heart thumping, his eyes shining.

The loose clouds blew away from the sky, showing a misty star. In the middle of the harbour the wind and the tide caught them, carrying them towards the ship as powerfully as a mill stream leads to a waiting weir.

Annie crouched in the stern, her hands and her eyes burning, her knees trembling. What was going to happen, why did she feel so weak and helpless, and yet seized with a queer excitement? Joseph did not care.

The lights of the quay faded away, the music sounded but faintly in the distance.

> Oh! you girls, you naughty young girls,
> Why don't you try to be good, be good?

From his window Philip Coombe watched the crowd contemptuously. Once he had seen Joseph and Annie hand in hand, and then they had disappeared in the direction of the fair. He drew the curtains close and then went and sat alone by the empty fireplace, with only his thoughts for company.

The little boat in the harbour swung against the side of the ship, and two figures crept up the ladder that was hanging over the side.

'Joe, what have I done – what have I done?' whispered Annie.

Joseph took her face in his hands. The *Janet Coombe* was deserted save for them. High above his head swayed the riding light. Plyn lay away across the harbour. This was one of Joseph's moments, splendid, triumphant.

He carried her away below to the silent cabin.

★  ★  ★

183

Some five days later they were married by licence at Sudmin.

The sudden marriage caused a great upheaval in the Captain's home circle. Joseph moved into his old home, Ivy House, which had stood empty since Thomas's death, for Mary had not wished to remain there alone, and she was now living with Samuel and his family. The services of his twin nieces were of course no longer required.

Christopher was deeply shocked at his father's marriage.

He took an instant dislike to Annie, he suspected that she was shallow and foolish for all her prettiness, and was convinced that she would never bring any permanent happiness to his father.

These ridiculous lovers at Ivy House made him feel hot and embarrassed. He spent all the time he could down at the yard pretending he liked his work, and privately determining that sooner or later he would leave Plyn, and seek his fortune elsewhere.

Albert, sick of waiting for the *Janet Coombe* to sail, shipped in another vessel, and left his father to his fate.

Charles wrote from Africa sending his respects to his stepmother – and Katherine was delighted to have a companion who was something nearer her own age.

Joseph was like one who walks with his head in the sun above the clouds; and his feet on the edge of a precipice.

For six weeks he lived, careless of time and money and everybody but himself and Annie. Ships left harbour and returned again, the full bloom of summer was upon Plyn, but still the *Janet Coombe* remained at her buoy, forlorn and deserted.

One day towards the beginning of July, Dick Coombe, now first mate of the family vessel, went up to supper at Ivy House, determined to speak tactfully to his uncle the skipper. He was unmarried himself, and slightly contemptuous of the way his uncle had fallen a victim, allowing himself to be ruled by a petticoat instead of acting Master of his ship.

It was a warm lovely evening, and he found Joseph and Annie seated in their garden.

'Well, nephew, glad to see you,' said Joseph, without looking up. 'Nice sort o' weather, isn't it? Annie an' I have been sittin' here all day, that idle we're almost ashamed of ourselves, ain't we lovie?'

'Oh! Joe, it's been delicious, I'm sure I couldn't have moved a step if I tried,' said Annie, gazing at her husband with swollen eyes of devotion.

Joseph yawned and stretched himself. 'Well, I've got indigestion, I know that. It's a good twenty-mile walk I need, only I can't make the effort. Sit down, Dick lad, an' smoke, Annie doesn't mind tobacco.'

His nephew obeyed, watching his uncle as he lit his pipe.

He decided at once that Joseph had put on weight; there was a certain loose flabbiness round his neck that had never been there before, and there were pouches under his eyes. His right eye, that Dick had sometimes suspected worried him on board ship, was bloodshot, and the pupil dilated.

'The *Mary Hawkins* left this morning at 9 o'clock,' he said quietly, 'bound for the Mediterranean. Freights are firm at the moment, and the stuff's waitin' down there, rotting, for ships to take it away. Did you see her go? There was a fine breeze, I reckon she'll make a quick passage.'

Joseph moved a little uneasily in his chair. 'No,' he said carelessly, 'no, I wasn't up. Matter of fact, I haven't been down the harbour lately. Are the jetties filled?'

'Aye, packed, every one. There's vessels moored down opposite the town, waitin' their turn. I saw Captain Salt s'mornin'. The *Hannah Lee* all but beat your record passage to Bristol, just over a week ago. They're all talkin' of it down in Plyn.'

He was a clever fellow, was Dick. Joseph roused himself at this bit of news, and looked at his nephew with interest.

'The *Hannah Lee*?' he said. 'Well, I reckon she must have smartened up a deal since last we raced in company. D'you mind that time we left Plyn together? Why, we beat them five miles from the Deadman to the Lizard. Only a few weeks back, too.'

'Gettin' on for three months, sir,' said Dick, calmly puffing at his pipe.

'Three months,' exclaimed Joseph, something bewildered. 'Have I been married then over nine weeks? The devil indeed! How the time does fly. Why it seems only yesterday, Annie heart, don't it?' He reached out his hand to take hers.

'Yes, my love,' she replied.

'Captain Salt sails again early i' the week,' went on Dick unperturbed. 'His schooner is up at No. 2 now, taking in ball clay. She's goin' to Newcastle, an' then out to St Michaels in ballast, to catch the trade. They all say she'll be first home again.'

'Ha!' laughed Joseph scornfully. 'She wouldn't stand a chance 'longside o' my *Janet Coombe*. I s'pose Jimmie Salt knows that.'

'Aye, I told him so. But he said he'd beat her fair an' square, now *Janet Coombe* has nigh twelve weeks' weed on her bottom. Offensive old fellow, is Cap'ain Salt. He said the *Janet Coombe* was gettin' quite a landmark where she lay, an' some stranger t'other day inquired if she were a relic o' the French wars.'

'Blarst his impudence,' roared Joseph. 'I'll teach Jimmie Salt better manners, by thunder. Annie, treasure, did ye hear that?'

'How shocking, deary me,' said Annie, who hadn't been listening, but was wondering if she ought to go in and see to the supper. She rose now and left them, while Joseph stamped up and down the garden path, calling Jimmie Salt every name under the sun.

During the days that followed Joseph's manner changed. Worry had crept into his mind. He found himself wandering about Plyn and the harbour, catching snatches of conversation here and there, and fancying he heard insults directed at himself and his ship.

He would speak in the inn to skippers returned from St Michaels, boasting of their quick passages and favourable winds.

Then the weather changed, and there was a fortnight of fierce sou'westerly gales. The rain streamed in the little garden, and Joseph prowled about the kitchen and parlour.

The *Julia Moss* was lost off the Lizard, with all hands, and another brigantine put into Plyn with her bulwarks stove in, and under jury rig. Joseph thought of the battles in mid-ocean on the deck of his *Janet Coombe*, and how she had fought and withstood every gale, never drowning a man yet, bringing them all to safety.

And the old restless longing rose in Joseph, to depart once more with the wind and the sea, to the life he loved, and to which he belonged. Once more he must stand on the deck of his ship with Janet for company, and danger lurking near, with the water surging beneath him, a shout in his ears, and above his head a wild wet star.

Not even the clinging arms of Annie could keep him back.

So he put his wife from him with scarce a sigh, and with a light in his eyes Joseph weighed anchor once more on board the *Janet Coombe*, and on a summer's evening, Master and ship went away down harbour, borne by the wind and the tide – outward bound.

# 11

Gradually Joseph slipped back into his old routine on board ship. Hours of energy and hours of peace. The companionship of men, the life they shared together, the sharp struggle against a sudden tearing gale ending in victory, the safe anchorage within a strange harbour, where the lights beckoned, and away again once more, to the infinite horizon.

The months sped on as they had always done, with never a regret for the vanished honeymoon, save a queer sensation that the tide of passion had run its course, and was now spent, inevitably. Thus reasoned Joseph in the back of his mind, and put his bride away from his thoughts, knowing she was possessed, certain of her.

When he returned, bronzed and weatherbeaten, he was a husband who claimed his wife, but no more than this.

In 1886 Annie's baby was born, and died a few hours later.

Joseph himself was touched by his wife's grief, but the loss meant little to him. He had already brought up one family, and the thought of a possible second brood was not to his fancy.

And now another trouble was creeping into his life. Joseph's eyesight was failing him.

Sometimes he could scarcely stand for the ache in his head, and the shooting pains in his right eye. This eye was always red and bloodshot now, the lid swollen and the pupil magnified. A mist came over it at times, and now started on his left eye, though the pain in this was less severe.

He began to find it impossible to focus objects, a dark patch leapt and danced before him, obstructing his view. Sometimes the sight was clear, and then the shooting pains would come again and the dark patches, and he would be unable to read the compass under the light of the binnacle.

When this happened for the first time, he went below to the cabin, and sat awhile in silence, helpless, like a lost child, then he summoned his nephew Dick and told him of his fears.

'Come, sir, it can't be much; perhaps you've strained your sight somehow, and it will come all right by degrees.'

The man did his best to hearten the skipper, but he was afraid there must be something seriously wrong for all that.

'I don't know, Dick,' said Joseph, his head in his hands, 'this ain't anythin' sudden like, it's been creepin' on me gradual an' slow. I've felt it for months back, an' arrant coward I've never said a word to no one. Then my marriage − well, I reckon that put the whole matter out o' my mind. An' now it's come upon me in full force, worse than ever before. What am I goin' to do, Dick, tell me, what am I goin' to do?'

'Have a heart, Uncle Joe,' said Dick. 'Maybe 'tisn't as bad as you think. As soon as we gets back to Plyn you take train to Plymouth an' see a doctor. It's wonderful what medicine can do nowadays.'

And so he went on deck, leaving Joseph alone.

The *Janet Coombe* anchored in Plyn harbour on the first day of February 1888. How word had spread among the crew of the skipper's trouble was a mystery, for Dick had mentioned nothing of it, but nevertheless by the next morning it was all over the town.

Joseph sent Dick to the office to settle accounts with Philip, for ever since his marriage to Annie, he had never spoken to his brother.

Philip Coombe at once questioned the mate about the skipper's eye trouble. 'What's this story of my brother's blindness, eh?' he asked. 'He'll have to see a doctor, you know.'

'Oh! there's no cause for alarm,' replied Dick coldly. 'You know how things get round in Plyn, whether they're true or not. Uncle Joe's had headaches, that's all, he's goin' over to Plymouth, I believe, to buy some stuff to cure 'em.'

'Hum,' said Philip. 'It's all very well for you to keep calm,

189

young fellow, and pretend to send me about my business. It happens this *is* my business. I've got equal shares in the ship with my brother, and I'm not going to risk my money in a vessel that's skippered by a crock. Joe will have to retire.'

'No one can make the skipper retire unless there's a doctor's certificate provin' he's unfit for work,' said Dick swiftly.

Philip laughed and rose from his seat.

'This will break him up,' muttered Dick, half to himself.

'Better that, than break up the ship,' was the cruel retort.

Dick made no attempt to relate this conversation to Joseph, but later in the day he met his cousin Christopher, and taking him aside, he explained the gravity of the situation.

Christopher was shocked beyond measure. 'This will be a terrible blow to my father,' he said slowly. 'God knows what will become of him, Dick. You know what a restless fellow he is. Life ashore will be hell for him. Even my stepmother will find herself unequal to the task of keeping him content. Do you really and truly believe this eye of his will be blinded?'

'I don't know, Chris. It looks bad from outward appearance, but one can't depend solely on that. The only thing to do is to get him to Plymouth and have him properly examined. I reckon we all three had better go together, you're the only one of the family he'll listen to. I have to come up before the Board of Trade as you know, to try and secure my Master's ticket. If the skipper gets notice to quit I'll do my level best to take on his job, and prove a credit to him if I can. It's a rotten sad business though.'

'You're a good chap, Dick,' sighed Christopher. 'I wish to God I was more like you. It's me that ought to be doin' this. What a rotter I am.'

'Nonsense, lad, I'm nearly eight years older than you, that's all. You'll find your feet soon, and your father will be no end proud of you. Dad says you work steady at the yard, and so do Tom an' the others.'

'Maybe, Dick, but I hate the work, an' there's the truth.'

'Come to sea, Chris, it's the only life for a man, and you'd please the poor skipper then.'

190

'What's the use? I'm just an out-an'-out waster, I know. Oh! hell, cousin, I swear I'll make good in time, and my father won't have cause for shame.'

A week later, Joseph, accompanied by his eldest son and his nephew, took train to Plymouth, where Dick went straight to sit for his Board of Trade examination. Joseph watched him go, remembering his own feelings twenty-five years back, filled with hope and strength, and the knowledge of Janet waiting for him in Plyn. And now he was fifty-three, with his youth behind him.

Joseph stayed alone in the doctor's room leaving Christopher in the hall. He was there exactly half an hour. Christopher heard his step coming slowly down the stairs, and raising his head saw somebody bent and frail, who stared before him as one lost in a desolate place.

Without a word they left the house together and walked away, anywhere, it did not matter, wherever their feet should lead them. They went to a hotel, for they had eaten nothing since breakfast early that morning. It was now half past three in the afternoon. Christopher heaped the food on to his father's plate, as though he were a child. Joseph tried to smile, but the muscles of his face seemed stiff and frozen. An atmosphere of shadows clung about him. Christopher turned away, and struggled with his own meat, forcing the food down his throat, thinking helplessly of the life that awaited Joseph at Plyn.

When they had finished Christopher paid the bill, and they made their way outside again into the false sunshine. Dick was waiting to see them off at the station. He was staying five days in Plymouth. Then Joseph spoke for the first time.

'How did 'ee manage at the exam, Dick?' he said.

'Middlin' well, thank you, Uncle. I trust that I'll satisfy them all right.'

'That's good.' Joseph looked out of the carriage window beyond him. 'You see, I want you to be the new skipper of the *Janet Coombe*,' he said.

The two men knew then that the end was come. The sea and the ship would know Joseph no more.

'I'll do my level best, Uncle Joe.'

The train sped away, carrying father and son.

Christopher took his father's arm.

'Can't they save your eyes at all, father?' he whispered.

'I don't know,' said Joseph. 'Don't worry, boy.'

The tears were slowly trickling down Christopher's face.

'Father, can't I do anything?'

'All right, Chris, dear lad. It's like comin' to the end of a dream, that's all. It's only the ship I mind.'

Grey clouds gathered, and rain pattered against the carriage window.

# 12

The first weeks after the *Janet Coombe* had sailed without him, Joseph seemed to sink into a coma of depression from which it was impossible to rouse him.

Annie was no help to him. She was frightened at his change of mood, and did not understand. Age, which Joseph had always despised and thrust from his mind, was now coming upon him.

Ivy House remained to him and the quiet strolling along the cliffs above the harbour. Joseph found some measure of content up at the rambling farm, with his sister who understood him better than his own family, and her boy Fred who possessed the strength that had been Janet's.

Queer, unaccountable thing this business of heredity.

Meanwhile, unknown to his father, Christopher was planning to go to sea.

He saw himself standing in his father's place, admired, respected, a little feared, carrying on the tradition of Coombe strength and gallantry.

Christopher had studied his father during the last months, he had learnt something of the love that had existed between Joseph and Janet, and he began to understand why this father of his had expected so much from the son.

Christopher told Joseph one evening when they sat together by the Castle ruins.

'Father, the *Janet Coombe* will be home in less than five weeks time, and I want to ship in her when she sails again.'

Joseph stretched out his hand to Christopher as though he were a little lad again.

'I knew you would go,' he said. 'It's stronger than you, Chris, it's somethin' in your blood there's no strugglin' agenst.

I've waited so long for you to tell me this.'

'I'll do anything to make you proud of me, father, and I swear you will be before long.'

'I know. Oh! Chris boy, you've done a lot for me today, I'll never forget.'

'Thank you, father. I'm glad – I'm glad.'

The pair went down the hill together, the father with his arm round the son's shoulder.

Once more Joseph took heart, and the next weeks fled rapidly until the *Janet Coombe* was anchored again in Plyn harbour.

Christopher himself could scarcely wait for the time to pass. He was getting away from Plyn at last, and entering upon a strange unknown life. Never mind the risks, never mind the discomforts, this was freedom of a sort, and better than the drudgery at the yard.

The day before he sailed, the young man had occasion to go into the shipping office, and there he met his Uncle Philip, who showed himself surprisingly good-tempered.

'Going to sea, Christopher?' asked Philip. 'I can't somehow see a smart chap like you settling down to life on a rough schooner.'

The young man flushed awkwardly. 'I trust I shall make a success of it,' he said.

Philip Coombe looked him up and down, and leaning back in his chair, he picked his teeth with his penholder. An idea had come into his head.

'Your father is glad about this, I suppose?'

'Yes, Uncle; well, I admit it was to console him somewhat that I came to the decision.'

'I imagined that. I suppose you know where you are bound?'

'St John's, I hear, and then the Mediterranean. I've always had a wish to see some of these places, and it's queer to think I shall soon be there.'

'Hum! no doubt the shore will seem a splendid thing after the Atlantic. You'll discharge your Mediterranean freight at London. Ever been to London?'

'I've only been as far as Bristol,' replied Christopher, some-what ashamed.

'Ah! London's the spot for a young man like you. You'd fall on your feet there right enough. Something of a dreamer, aren't you? London is the stepping-stone for the ambitious. Many a penniless boy has won fame and fortune in the capital, boys who, but for seizing their opportunities, would have spent their lives before the mast in some old vessel, such as you intend to do.'

A shadow seemed to lay itself across Christopher's heart.

'I hope to work my way to the top of my trade, Uncle,' he said in defiance. Philip Coombe whistled and shook his head.

'Don't you want to strike out on a line for yourself, be somebody? Is your ambition to be eventually the Master of a little schooner? She will be out of date when you get your ticket, some time in the nineteen hundreds. You're not as bright as I thought. Go off on your sailing ship and stay there as long as you like, but don't forget that London is waiting round the corner.'

Christopher left the office, his mind perplexed with a hundred new doubts and fears, as his uncle had intended it should be.

The next three months Joseph passed peaceably and contentedly; it seemed to him that perhaps the future could be made splendid and worth while, and he looked forward to his son's return.

It was quite possible the *Janet Coombe* would anchor in Plyn harbour early in the new year. His father would prepare a great welcome for him, especially as it would, in all probability, fit in with the boy's twenty-third birthday.

As the time drew near Joseph trembled with impatience to see his son again, and to hear from him a detailed account of the voyage and the behaviour of the ship.

He thought of little but this now, and when the brothers and Annie complained that the 'sailor-boy' seldom wrote beyond a line now and again to say he was well in health, he defended him stoutly, saying that Christopher had better things to do than spend his watch below in scribbling to his family. He was training to be a man, and learning a man's job. Let him be. Time enough to hear his news when he returned.

So Christmas came and went, and still no sign of the *Janet Coombe*. The weather had been severe, with several gales in the Channel, and there were some uneasy nights in Ivy House. Then the ship was reported safe in London, and Joseph breathed again. It would not be long now. The ship had only to discharge her fruit cargo, when she would return in ballast to Plyn. The boy would be late for his birthday, but never mind that, he would receive a warm welcome from all his family, as both the brothers were at home.

On the morning of the third of January, Joseph was standing in the garden inspecting the weather some half hour before the midday dinner, when a boy entered the gate with a note in his hand.

'A message for you, Captain Coombe, from the office,' he said. Joseph tore open the letter with a frown.

Could you please come down and see me at once? I have something of importance to tell you. – Philip Coombe.

What on earth did the fellow want? He had not spoken to him for over three years, not since his marriage in fact. He made a point of cutting him deliberately in the street. Well, it must be urgent he supposed, it was not like Philip to be the first to break the silence. He seized his cap, and made his way down the hill to the office, calling to his wife not to wait dinner, as he might be late.

He had not been inside the office since that day when he had looked over his brother's shoulder and seen the photograph of Annie. He chuckled to himself at the remembrance. He, Joseph, had won her, and Philip had lost. It had been easy enough. Well, he wasn't going to have his brother notice his decline in strength, so he straightened his shoulders and entered

196

the once familiar room with something of his old swagger.

'Well,' he said, 'I must say I did not expect to hear from you. However, here I am, an' out with your news, because it's cold weather, an' I'm anxious to get back to my dinner.'

Philip watched him, and rubbed his hands softly.

'Still the same attitude of defiance I see, for all your changed appearance,' he said smoothly. 'Well, I'm very sorry, Joe, but there's a bad knock in store for you. This wire has just come through to the office. I felt it my duty to entrust it to you personally. Read it, brother, by the light, for I know you see with difficulty.'

Joseph took the wire and read the following message:

Handed in at London. Friday evening. Christopher Coombe deserted ship this evening. Obliged sail without him, one hand short. Due Plyn probably early in week. – Richard Coombe, Master.

'Wherever's Joe?' worried Annie. 'Nearly three o'clock an' not back yet. I've a mind to clear away. Seen your father, boys?'

Charles and Albert shook their heads. 'Can't fathom out where he's gone,' said Albert, 'lest he's up on the cliffs, but then it ain't like him to be late for his meals.'

'He told me not to wait, but never said how long he'd be;' Annie went to the window. 'S'comin' over misty, too, I'm in a way about him.'

Katherine looked up from her sewing.

'P'r'aps he's gone up to Aunt Lizzie at the farm,' she suggested.

'Scarcely likely.'

Five minutes later they heard a slow dragging footstep coming up the garden path.

'Is that him now?' asked Charlie.

''Tisn't Joe's step. He treads firmer than that, for all his poor sight,' said Annie.

But the door opened and Joseph stood before them. Not the Joseph that any of them knew, but a man with tortured

197

eyes. His hands were shaking. He leaned against the door, his hand to his side.

'Joe,' whispered Annie, 'what's come over you?'

The boys leapt to their feet.

'Father, good God! . . . What's happened?'

He waved them away with his hand.

Then he spoke slowly, weighing up his words with care.

'I forbid you to ever breathe the name of Christopher again, here in this house or in Plyn, or amongst yourselves. He may die in the greatest poverty and distress before I ever lay a finger to help him. I swear before you all I will never look upon his face again. And if you wish to know the reason – look there – that's why.'

He threw them the crumpled telegram, and without another word he went to his room above the porch, and locked the door.

# 13

U p and down his room paced Joseph, with his mind wrecked and his soul wounded, and below, his family sat trembling for him, but unable to help, unable to heal.

So the day passed, with the endless footsteps overhead, and the night, too, which Annie spent with Katherine in her room, and only at daybreak did the sound cease, and Joseph give way to bodily fatigue.

When he arose the next day his face was set in harsh lines, and his eyes were cold and empty.

The name of Christopher was never mentioned, whatever the son's reasons were for leaving the ship, the father never knew. Letters arrived, but were put away by him, the seal unbroken.

The atmosphere of Ivy House changed, it became heavy and unbearable. Joseph was the stern master whose word was law. There was no laughter, no gaiety.

Albert and Charles were only too glad to escape, Albert to his ship, Charles to his regiment. Annie and her stepdaughter were left to care for this dragon of horror that had once been Joseph. If their natures had been stronger, if they had been possessed with some grain of courage and light, they might have succeeded in bringing him back to himself. But they were timid, cowed; they ran hither at his bidding, and bowed their trembling heads before him. He forbade them to wander from the house unless it was to shop, and then they must be back at a certain fixed hour. If they were a minute late he would wait for them on the doorstep, his watch in his hand, his mouth ready to open and curse them.

They were permitted to visit relatives once a week, but no

one was invited to the house, no neighbours could have the pleasure of their company. Katherine was forbidden to speak to young men; she saw that her chances to marry were remote and nigh hopeless. No one had the courage to seek her out for fear of Joseph. She saw herself doomed to a lonely, bitter spinsterhood, beside this terrible father.

Annie he treated as a slave, as a wretched servant; slowly her health and youthful spirits dwindled, her eyes became wan and lustreless, her cheeks pale and thin.

They had no boy now at Ivy House for the rough work, they were obliged to do it all themselves.

Too frightened to complain or to withstand his tyranny, they scrubbed the stone floors and carried the coals from the cellar, while he stood over them, watching, laughing at their feeble efforts. He would drag Annie to the looking-glass, and show her the thin, tired reflection of herself.

'Twenty-three? You look forty. No man would sigh for you now, I reckon.'

He never touched them or beat them, his cruelty was more refined than this, more subtle. They dreaded the meals alone with him, when they were obliged to hearken to his words, and listen to the tales of horror he told them.

And all the while he gazed before him with his cold, blank eyes that seemed to hold no knowledge of their presence, eyes that looked into what unknown depths of desolation, they dared not know.

Most of all Annie feared the nights by his side, when sometimes he would walk up and down till dawn talking aloud to her, preventing her from sleep, and at other times he would torture her with his questions as to her doings and thoughts on the previous day, leaving her no privacy.

The two girls clung together in the daytime, and asked in despair what possible consolation he received from his way of living and his utter negation of life. There was no answer to this. The flickering spark of sanity that lingered yet in Joseph asked himself this question, in self-loathing and utmost horror, and then backed away from itself, leaving him a prey to the waiting demons who dragged him apart. He could not stop himself now, he must go on inevitably to whatever end fate held in store for him. There was no backward path, nor returning.

A year passed thus, and then began the start of another.

He had no knowledge how long this existence of his would last, he only knew that he must wait until the end should come.

In the spring of 1890, Annie knew that she was to have another child, and she summoned up what little courage she had to tell her husband.

As he listened to her he watched her with his cold, heavy eyes, and then when she had finished, and murmured some pitiful appeal that he would show a sign he was not angered, he turned his back on her and shrugged his shoulders.

'Why should I be angry? Go away, Annie, an' let me be. I'll not say anythin' to the child I reckon, when it comes. I care for none of these things.'

Nevertheless when she had crept from the room his eyes followed her, and he had half a mind to call her back and give her a tender word. But she had gone upstairs, and he would not have her return, and think she had won him by her news. Yet something had stirred within him at the thought, something of the old blind idealism that lay crushed beneath his dead heart. Another son to replace the lost son. Something of himself that had not gone astray, but remained as a light of hope and as a promise of past beauty.

He said little to his wife, but he was less harsh now as the months drew on.

It was about this time that Annie became friendly with Philip Coombe once more. She was passing his office one afternoon on her way to the shops, and he came out of the door and stood before her. He had avoided her since her marriage, and this was perhaps the first time he had come against her, face to face. Annie lowered her eyes and would have walked on, but he spoke to her and she had not the heart.

'Annie,' he said, 'let me speak to you.' He held out his hand which she took nervously, glancing over her shoulder as she did so, murmuring something about her husband.

'Don't be afraid. Come inside.' He led her inside the office and shut the door.

Annie burst into tears, and covered her face with her hands.

'Don't give way,' said Philip, 'that won't help you now. Besides, I am not going to blame you for your wretched marriage. I warned you at the time, but you were too young and too ignorant to understand.'

Annie rocked backwards and forwards in her chair, the tears flowing fast.

'There's none save my stepdaughter Kate as known what we've been through,' she choked. 'How we've survived it I can't tell. These last two years – Mr Philip, what have I ever done that I should be so punished? Maybe it's the wrath of God on my head from havin' acted so wanton with Joe before we was wed. Oh! dear, I was a bad girl, now I thinks it over cool. I was swept off my feet, I never thought . . .'

'Of course you were not to blame. It was that damned brother of mine, who deserved every ounce of misery that has come his way.'

'Well, Mr Philip, I would feel wrong to blame him entirely. Poor Joe was greatly lowered in spirits when his eyes failed, an' then the trouble over Chris comin' on top o' that. He's never recovered from the blow of it.'

'I suspected as much, Annie. The ship returns regularly, but he does not as much as pull up the harbour to look at her.'

'That's so, Mr Philip. And at one time he thought of little else but his precious old schooner, neglectin' me for it even; I used to feel hurt an' sorry, but I've learnt my lesson now.'

'Does Christopher Coombe ever write?'

'Ah! he writes to his brothers, an' he's written to his father many a time, but Joe leaves the letters unread. He's cruel an' hard-natured is Joe, Mr Philip.'

'I had rather see you dead, Annie, than unhappy with him. Why don't you leave him?'

'Where would I go, Mr Philip? A woman can't leave the

man she's wed, and I couldn't somehow, for all the misery he's caused. He's helpless with his eyes, too.'

'Sentimentality, ridiculous sentimentality. Why, you're but five-and-twenty, you must not waste your life. There is no need to leave Joe helpless, the proper place for him in Sudmin, and you know it.'

'Oh! Mr Philip – not the asylum? Oh! how terrible. You surely don't mean the asylum?'

'I'm afraid I do, Annie. My brother is not responsible for his actions, and I'm in favour of having him placed in the care of authorities, where he can do no damage.'

'No, Mr Philip. We must not think of it. Joe is strange and cruel in mind, but he has done me no bodily harm. There would be no just reason to shut him up.'

'He will become worse.'

'I think not.'

'What makes you say that?'

'He is better already, Mr Philip, there's somethin' of his old self returning since I told him my news.'

'What news?'

'There's to be another child at Christmas.'

Philip rose from his chair beside her and went towards the window, turning his back. He stood in silence.

'I want you to look upon me as your friend, Annie, always; and to come here whenever you wish. The next months will not be easy ones for you; please have no hesitation in coming to me if you are unhappy. Will you promise?'

'Yes, Mr Philip.'

'And call me Philip – we are friends, are we not?'

'Thank you – Philip. And now I must go.'

'Good afternoon, Annie.'

So the summer passed, and autumn fell once more, the days shortening and the weather becoming cold and wild. Joseph spent most of his time in front of the little kitchen fire at Ivy House. He clutched feebly to the hope that the arrival of this child would prove his salvation. He found his mind wandering at times, losing the thread of his thoughts, and then the blackness would threaten to engulf him. He would bury his head in his hands, and press his fingers into his temples.

He had no idea of his wife's visits to his brother's office. She went there now regularly, sometimes twice a week, and had come to look forward to these hours as the only bright moments of her life. Slowly and subtly Philip planted in her the longing to be free once more, the longing to leave Ivy House and her husband.

All through those long months of cruelty and hardship, the thought of deserting him had never come to her mind, and now that he was showing himself more gentle towards her, the wish took birth, whispered by Philip. Joe would never recover, the presence of a baby could not fail to irritate him; things might even become worse than they had ever been, and Joe savage. No, Philip perhaps was right, although it seemed hard. Joe would be better in Sudmin Asylum. Better for himself, and better for his family. She had promised to trust in Philip, and she would. He was her dear friend, her true friend. He was always so noble, so unselfish. When Joe was put away in Sudmin, properly attended to by nurses and doctors, far happier and more comfortable than at Ivy House, so Philip had said, then this dear friend would do everything in his power to make her happy.

October drew into November, and November to December. The child was expected during Christmas week.

Annie was very weak these last weeks, no doubt the result of the wretched preceding years. Katherine was anxious, and the doctor looked grave.

'She must be kept very quiet, and free from any irritation or worry,' he told the stepdaughter. 'I don't like the way things are turning out. Should she experience any shock at this critical time, the result will be disastrous. Yes, she may get up, and walk a little. That will do her no harm, rather the reverse. But see that she is not worried in any way.'

On Christmas Eve Annie felt strong enough to walk down to Plyn to see Philip, leaving Katherine at home, and her husband off visiting his sister Lizzie. She made her way slowly down the hill, through the town, to the large house on Marine Terrace where Philip Coombe lived, entirely alone save for his housekeeper and a manservant, husband to the woman.

This day Annie lay on the sofa while Philip poured out the tea, and she stayed until after six o'clock, when she feared Joseph might be starting back from the farm; so she went, Philip kissing her hands gently and bidding her be of good cheer.

Neither of them noticed that she had left her handkerchief in the corner of the sofa, a gift to her from her husband on the first anniversary of their marriage.

Joseph did not leave the farm until half past ten. It was a fine clear night, with a full moon shining over the water, and frost in the air. There were groups of people about the street, excited at the thought of the next day's festivities, and most of them preparing for the midnight service at Lanoc Church across the fields. Later the bells would start to peal, and they would trudge away up the hill and along the path, swinging their lanterns in their hands.

As Joseph passed down the road below Marine Terrace he saw a light in the end house, and the figure of his brother pacing up and down before the window. And as he watched the pacing figure it came to Joseph that the night was Christmas Eve and in a few days his son would be born. His life would be changed from thenceforward, he would put aside from him rancour and hatred.

Joseph stood for a moment uncertain and then climbed the steps of the house and rang the bell.

A sleepy manservant answered. 'I'm Mr Coombe's brother; I've come to bid him a Happy Christmas,' said Joseph softly, and he pushed the man aside and opened the door of the room where he had seen the figure. Philip started with a cry of surprise at the sight of his brother. His thoughts at once leapt to Annie.

'What in God's name brings you here, brother, at this hour? Something has happened at your home? Your wife?

Joseph smiled and shook his head. He sat down on the sofa.

'I've come o' my own accord, Phil. I've come to say I . . .' then his eyes fell on the handkerchief in the corner at his side. The words fled from his mind, and he sat there, staring stupidly, pointing.

'What's Annie left her handkerchief there for?' he began in a dull voice, and then his brain reeled, and he began to tremble. 'Annie's been here, Annie's been in this room. Tell me the truth – speak, or by Jesus I'll wring it from you.' Philip paled, as his brother stumbled from the sofa, and made towards him.

'Have a care, Joe, or you'll be sorry.'

Joseph paid no attention, he leaned over Philip, his eyes blinking.

'How long has Annie been i' the habit o' visitin' you?' he shouted.

Philip shrugged his shoulders and smiled scornfully.

'Oh! so you've come for a scene, have you? Well, you won't have it. Clear out of my house.'

'How long has Annie been friendly with you?' repeated Joseph, his fists ready to swing, the longing rising in him to smash this man's face, smash it to a pounding, pulping jelly. Then tread on it, crush it, see the blood run swiftly . . .

Philip moved to the other side of the room.

'Annie has been my dear friend for some months,' he said softly, 'since you took to treating her like an animal I have been doing my best to make up to her for it.'

'Annie's come here for months, you say – Annie has dared to deceive me? . . .'

'Of course she has deceived you, you dirty brute, with your swine's ways. Annie has never loved you.'

'You damned liar – you.' The ideas fled hopelessly through Joseph's mind, jumbled, huddled, tearing at his brain, leaving no clearing, no space for him to think.

'Don't you know Annie's with child?' he said.

Then Philip laughed; Joseph watched the grin spread over his face, watched the teeth spread in a lifeless mask.

'You ask me that? You have the courage to ask me that? You're mad – you're insane – you're only fit for the asylum.

206

Joe, deceived all these months, Joe the wronged husband. You're mad, I tell you – mad.'

Something crashed in Joseph's brain at the words, he swung his fists and smote his brother in the eyes. Philip fell to the ground and lay still, like a dead thing.

Then Joseph stumbled from the building, he ran up the hill towards Ivy House, seeing nothing, the black specks dancing before his eyes.

The bells were pealing for the midnight service at Lanoc Church, he heard them not, the folk were making their way towards the fields, he saw them not.

He flung open the door of his house, and climbed the stairs to the bedroom over the porch.

'I'll get you now,' he called. He lit a candle and bent over his cowering wife.

'Kate,' she screamed. 'Kate, run for help – quick – quick.'

The girl rushed into the room in her nightgown. 'Father,' she called, 'Father, what are you doing—? Remember the doctor – oh! Father have a care.'

Joseph held the light above his head. 'So you've deceived me have you? You've been to Philip, you've gone with Philip.'

'Oh! Joe, dear, I meant no harm, I swear to you. He's been so kind I . . .'

'You've deceived me, eh? Bain't that enough?'

'Forgive me, Joe, forgive me. Yes, I have deceived you, but let us talk of this another time. Oh! Kate, dear, I feel so ill – so ill – run for the doctor.'

'So you don't love me, eh – Annie? You've never loved me – that's what he said – well, is it true?'

'Oh! Joe, let me be – let me be. I can't tell you all now, forgive me – I did wrong but I was weak – please Joe.'

'Deceived me, did ye – deceived me – by God I'll make you suffer for it.'

Annie stumbled from the bed and crouched against the wall, covering herself with her hands.

'Go on then – go on then,' she cried, 'murder me an' your own innocent child. I'll not stop you. But before I die I'll tell

207

you this, I hate you – yes, I hate you, an' I'll curse you for what you're doin' to me now. You'll know no rest nor peace after this – you'll come to a greater loneliness than ever before. Folks'll shun you worse than now. You're hated and feared in Plyn, an' always have bin. There's once I lived for the glamour of your eyes, but I've never loved the cold proud heart of you—'

Joseph swayed on his feet, and dropped the candle to the floor.

'Janet,' he cried – 'Janet' – 'Janet'. The house rang with his cries. 'Janet,' he called, 'Janet, come to me.'

Then he ran from the house and climbed to the Castle ruin on the cliffs.


He knelt on the hard, frosted ground, bowed in grief. And suddenly there came to him the touch of a hand upon his head, and the living presence of one beside him. He raised his troubled eyes, and saw his beloved beside him, not as he had known her, but young and slim, no more than a girl. She held him to her and murmured words of love. Then he knew that she belonged to the past, when he was unborn, but he recognized her as his own.

'Hush, my dear love, hush, and cast away your fear. I'm beside you, always, always an' there's none who'll harm you.'

'Why didn't you come before?' he whispered holding her close. 'They've been tryin' to take me away from you, an' the whole world is black an' filled with devils. There's no truth, dearest, no path for me to take. You'll help me, won't you?'

'We'll suffer an' love together,' she told him. 'Every joy and sorrow in your mind an' body is mine too. A path will show itself soon, when the shadows clear away from your spirit.'

'I've heard your whispers often, and hearkened to your blessed words of comfort. We've talked with one another, too, alone in the silence of the sea, on the decks of the ship that is part of you. Why have you never come before to hold me like this, and to feel my head beside your heart?'

'I don't understand,' she said. 'I don't know where we come from, nor how the mist was broken for me to get to you. I heard you callin', and there's nothin' kept me back.'

'They've been long weary days since you went from me, an' I've not heeded your counsel, nor deserved your trust in me,' he told her. 'See how I'm old now, with the grey hairs in my head and beard, and you younger than I ever knew you, with your girl's face and your tender unworn hands.'

'I have no reckoning in my mind of what is past, nor that which is to be,' said she, 'but all I know is there's no space of time here, nor in our world, nor any world hereafter. There be no separation for us, no beginnin' and no end – we'm cleft together you an' I, like the stars to the sky.'

Then he said – 'They whisper amongst themselves I'm mad, my love, my reason's gone and there's danger in my eyes. I can feel the blackness creepin' on me, and when it comes for good I'll neither see nor feel you – and there'll be nothin' left but desolation and despair.'

He shuddered as a cloud passed over the face of the moon, and it seemed to him he was a child in her arms, crying for comfort.

'Never fear, when the black fit seizes you I'll hold you as I hold you now,' she soothed him. 'When you can neither see nor hear, an' you're fightin' with yourself, I'll be at your side, strivin' for you.'

He threw back his head and watched her as she stood, white against the sky with a smile on her lips.

'You're like an angel,' he said, 'standing at the gates of Heaven before the birth of Christ. It's Christmas, and they're singin' the hymn in Lanoc Church.'

'Fifty years or a thousand years it's all the same,' said Janet, 'our comin' here together is the proof of it.'

'You'll never leave me again, then?' he asked.

'Never no more.'

He knelt and kissed her footprint in the frost.

'Tell me, is there a God?'

He looked into her eyes and read the truth.

They stood for a minute and gazed at each other, seeing themselves as they never would on earth. She saw a man, bent and worn, with wild unkempt hair and weary eyes; he saw a girl, young and fearless, with the moonlight on her face.

'Good night, my mother, my beauty, my sweet.'

'Good night, my love, my baby, my son.'

Then the mist came between them, and hid them from one another.

There were no thoughts now in Joseph's mind, no knowledge of what had happened before. He went quietly down the hill, his memory and his reason gone, and let himself in to Ivy House without a sound, creeping silently to the old room he had lived in as a boy, which had remained empty since Christopher had departed. Then he undressed, and lying down on the bed, he fell asleep. He heard nothing of Annie's low moaning, nor the soft weeping of Katherine, he was not even disturbed by the arrival of the doctor, and the general movement about the house.

He slept until late the following morning, Christmas Day. When he awoke he rose and dressed himself, and descended to the kitchen. He found something to eat, and sat himself down by the empty grate. People came in and bothered his quiet reflection, he bade them leave him alone, and let him sit there in peace. No, he would not move, he would not go out. Would they please let him rest there in peace? He would do no harm.

There was a girl weeping by the doorway, her apron to her eyes. He offered her some of his bread, for he was sorry to see these tears. Then her face crumpled up, and she moved away. He wondered who she was, and why there were so many folk coming and going about the house.

A man came to him, saying he was a doctor. Well, he wanted no doctor. There was nobody ill. Someone took hold of his arm, and told him that his wife and new born child were dead.

He shook his head and smiled.

210

'I am not married, I have no child – you have made a mistake.'

Then he turned his back on them, and spread his hands to the empty fireplace. 'Would someone light a fire, perhaps?' he suggested. 'The mornin's are cold this time of the year.' But they went away and left him. They must have forgotten. It may be he had been dreaming all the while. Never mind though, he would lay the fire himself. This he did, and when the cheerful blaze crackled and burnt he rubbed his hands, and laughed. He hummed to himself, remembering snatches of old tunes.

He found the rocking chair from the parlour, and brought it into the kitchen. Now he could rock backwards, forwards – backwards, forwards. He could watch the bright fire, listen to the clock, listen to his own voice singing. That was very nice, that was very pleasant. Did somebody say it was Christmas? Well, fancy that, who would have known?

Backwards, forwards – backwards, forwards. Someone looked in at the door.

Joseph waved his hand. 'Merry Christmas – Merry Christmas,' he called.

There were no days, no nights. . . .

Philip Coombe was seated at his desk, his head bandaged, and his wrist bound. He was reading aloud a postcard.

Dear Mr Coombe,

I see I cannot get to Plyn before 11 o'clock in the morning.

You had better have someone ready with a trap at noon, so that we can start right away, to get to Sudmin as soon as possible.

Yours in haste,

R. Tamlin

PS – Have you found out if there is room in the asylum, if not, you had better wire immediately.

211

'This Tamlin is a male nurse, who will act as an escort,' said Philip, laying the card on the desk.

Samuel and Herbert Coombe nodded, their expressions grave, their eyes sad.

'Is it really necessary to remove Joseph?' began Herbert.

'Can't you see for yourself?' exclaimed Philip impatiently. 'Hasn't he killed his wife, his poor child, not to mention his deliberate and vicious assault on myself? The man is dangerous – a raving madman, I tell you. Let there be no mulish sentimentality among you, brothers. Joe is to go to Sudmin this morning. I have wired to the asylum, and they are expecting him. My word is final.'

They groped for their hats and took their leave.

At noon a trap was waiting outside the door of Ivy House. There were little knots of people clustered in the roadway. At the sight of Philip Coombe they moved away, alarmed at his stern face and authoritative manner. With him was a big burly man, a stranger to Plyn. They went into the house together. The sun was shining in a cloudless sky, the blue harbour water flickered, and on the branch of a tree a robin sang. Children's voices sounded on the beach below the quay.

A tug-boat was steaming slowly in past the entrance, with a schooner in tow. The sun caught the topsails in a patch of colour, before they were furled on the yard. There were shouts from the deck, and the rattle of halyards as the mainsail was lowered. Then the clanking of the anchor chain. The figurehead stood out white and distinct on the bows of the ship. The *Janet Coombe* had returned to Plyn.

Ten minutes later Philip Coombe and the male nurse came out from Ivy House, holding Joseph between them. He made no attempt to struggle or break away, he allowed himself to be placed in the trap, and his coat buttoned up to his chin. He blew on his hands to warm them, he smiled with pleasure at the restive horse. Then he sat still, a big hunched figure, dumb and unresponsive, heedless of those around him. Philip and the keeper were talking in low tones; Katherine was weeping in the doorway.

212

Joseph looked over his shoulder to the harbour below him. The keeper climbed into the trap with Philip, and the driver took his place. The little party moved away down the hill, and through the street of the town.

As they passed the quay Joseph saw the schooner in mid-harbour, anchored safely and her stern to the buoy. She was standing in a patch of sun. For a moment the light flickered in his eyes, shone strong and true, a recognition of love and beauty; then he shivered and the light was gone, leaving a heavy, cold haze instead. The houses shut the harbour from sight, and the trap sped away along the road to Sudmin.

# 14

For five years Joseph Coombe was an inmate of Sudmin Asylum. He would probably have remained there for the remainder of his life had it not been for the efforts of his sister, Elizabeth Stevens, and her son Fred to have him released.

In October 1895, Fred Stevens, passing through Bodmin, suddenly decided to call at the asylum and demand to see his uncle, on chance. To his surprise he was admitted, and on inquiring after Joseph's health, he was informed that the patient was doing very well, that in fact he could have been released three years ago, but that his family preferred to keep him in the care of proper authorities, and paid handsomely for doing so.

Fred knew at once that the 'family' was Philip. He was taken upstairs to the ward where Joseph was seated before the open window.

The nephew was greatly shocked at the devastating change in his uncle's appearance. His hair and beard were white, although he was but sixty years of age, and the whole contour of his face had altered. The cheeks were sunken and the brown eyes dimmed.

Fred went over to where he was sitting and took his hand.

'Uncle Joseph,' he said gently, 'have you forgotten your nephew Fred?'

Joseph moved in his chair and blinked his eyes, peering up at the young man.

'Why, Fred,' he said in his old strong voice, 'this is pleasant indeed. I'm delighted to see you. Why have you never been before? I've been staying here some time, you know. Everybody is very kind, I'm sure, but I wish I could go home. Will you ask them if I may go home?' He smiled timidly like a lost child.

'There now, Uncle. Don't you fret. I'll see what can be done about having you home. D'you want to return to Plyn?'

'Yes, please, nephew. They're all kind here, but home is best. Yes, home is best.'

Fred left him soon after this, and demanded to see the Governor of the asylum. There were many matters to be gone through before his uncle could be released, but he was determined to overcome all difficulties. In spite of Philip's objection, there was no possible reason for confining Joseph any longer.

The family were told of the approaching release, and Ivy House was opened once again. Katherine had no objection to return and look after her father, now that it was proved he was harmless, and as gentle as a child.

So Joseph was fetched away from Sudmin Asylum one fine morning in November, and brought home to Ivy House where Katherine waited anxiously on the doorstep.

He was happy and contented to be back. He could remember nothing of his life, nothing of the first terrible years at the asylum, all he knew was that this was his home, and here he had come to rest.

He didn't want to move anywhere, he was content to stay where he was. Sometimes he could climb his way slowly to the top of the cliffs by the Castle ruin, leaning on his daughter's arm, and when he reached the summit he sighed, then stood with his cap in his hand, letting the soft breeze play with his white hair and beard.

He liked it on summer evenings best, just as the sun was sinking in the west, behind the beacon landmark; when the crimson patches were reflected on the water. There would be a still hush, and now and again the sound of sheep calling one another in the distant fields, or the lowing of cattle. The smoke rose from the chimneys of the grey houses, and with it an evening mist, like a gentle shroud. Children played on the quayside. Then a boat would draw into the harbour, returned

215

from the fishing grounds, with a cloud of gulls in the wake that stretched behind like an orange ribbon.

The peace and calm of Plyn. Joseph would sigh, and hold his daughter's arm. 'You know, Kate girl, I've travelled far, an' I've travelled wide, I've seen the riotous coast of Africa with her glittering surf an' her tossin' palm trees; I've lain becalmed in the lazy waters o' the tropics; I've known the cold of Arctic nights an' the rare white light that leaves a man dumb with wonder; I've gazed at the snow-capped mountains of the north; vast, Kate, lonely an' mysterious. But 'tis a queer thing, an' a true thing, that wherever I've been, an' whatever I've seen, there's nothin' like the sweet beauty o' Plyn harbour when the sun be setting, and the shadows fall, an' the white gulls fill the air with their joyous clamour. It's home, Kate, that's all I reckon.'

In the May of 1900 Joseph became very feeble, and Katherine saw that he had not long to live. His mind wandered, and he scarcely knew what he was about. She had to dress him, and attend to his wants as though he were a child. Both Albert and Charles were away, and Fred was shortly to be married.

There was no one to whom Katherine felt she could turn, for she never spoke to Philip Coombe.

Then one day a letter arrived with the London postmark. She tore it open with eager hands, for she had recognized her brother Christopher's writing. He wrote apparently overcome with a wave of homesickness, longing to see all their dear faces again, and especially his father's. He asked if his father would ever forgive him? He had written so many times to them and had never received an answer, he had but poor hopes that this letter would ever reach its true destination.

Poor Christopher. Then he had heard nothing of the trouble there had been, nothing of those years at the asylum. Katherine read over the letter carefully, then after turning the matter over in her head she resolved to write to her brother without saying a word to anyone. She would write to him imploring him to come home at once, as his father was in weak health, and she feared the worst. So Katherine shut herself up in her room and composed a long letter to Christopher, giving a full account of the years since he had been gone, and then she put on her hat, and slipped to the post with it herself.

Two days later a wire came for Katherine. Luckily Joseph was in the parlour and did not see the boy coming up the garden path, and the wire was from Christopher saying he would take the train on the Saturday and be with them.

On Friday evening, 28 May, Katherine left her father safely seated in the garden of Ivy House, and made her way down into the town to tell her Aunts Mary and Martha that Christopher would arrive the following day.

It was drawing on for evening, and the sun was setting, lighting the roofs of the houses of Plyn and the hills above, and smoothing a wide orange path over the sea that lost itself on the horizon. Joseph moved restlessly in his chair, and pushed aside his rug. He did not wish to sit there any more, he was cramped and stiff.

He turned his face towards the setting sun, and felt the gentle warmth of it strike his dim eyes, while his hair was blown by the west wind. He could hear the cries of the gulls and the dull lapping of the harbour water. Beyond this was the sea, grey, silent, colourless save for that orange band, like a last trailing whisper of the setting sun.

And the longing rose in Joseph to look upon the sea once more, to touch the water with his hands, to be borne by the waves to some far-distant resting place where the wind blew everlastingly, and the white surf thundered. He yearned to taste the salt upon his lips, to hear the sighing murmur in his ears, and following the sun track, he would come upon the ship that waited for him. Somewhere, beyond the land, beyond that line where sea and sky mingled, the *Janet Coombe* lifted her face to the heavens; alone amidst the silence of the ocean she tossed and plunged, glorious and free, her two masts pointing to the stars.

Joseph rose from his chair, casting it away. He went from

217

the garden; he left the house standing empty and forlorn, with the golden light on the windows.

His eyes could tell him nothing, but his senses led him to the shipbuilding yard, quiet and deserted till morning. A boat was moored to the ladder at the bottom of the slip. For thirty, forty, fifty years a boat had been fastened there from custom, night after night. Joseph remembered this; like a ray of light at the back of his mind, the memory had opened itself to him. He lowered himself slowly, heavily, into the boat, and untied the painter with stiff, fumbling hands. Then he grasped the paddles in his hands and pulled away to the harbour mouth. The tip of the sun hovered above the rim of the distant hill for a moment – flickered, whispered, and was gone. The pathway shivered in the lost light, and the red glittering patches faded into mist, and were sunk, swallowed in the hands of the gathering dusk.

Joseph was a little lad again, a child in a boat for the first time, grasping the heavy oar while his mother guided his straining wrists.

Joseph was a boy, a laughing, reckless boy, who pulled a quick, impatient stroke, and smiled into the eyes of Janet, seated in the stern.

Joseph was a young man, filled with the zest and wonder of life, craving adventure, scorning danger, drunk with the glory of wind and sea.

Joseph was the master of his ship, eager to reach her decks again and forget the empty days on shore, wanting no more but the rattle of shrouds and the hiss of a gale in close-reefed sails.

Joseph was a husband, showing off his skill to Susan, marvelling with open mouth, her baby in her arms.

Joseph was a father, and Christopher tugging at his knee with scared brown eyes and sun-kissed hair, pointing at the angry waves that loomed ahead.

Joseph was a lover, watching the loveliness of Annie, who, ashamed of the light, hid her eyes with her hands to make herself more secret.

Joseph was an old man, weary of living, calling for release, seeking salvation on the lonely waters where his beloved waited.

Joseph was none of these things, he was a spirit who had cast aside his chains and triumphed over matter, he was a soul who had climbed from the depths of darkness and despair to the high and splendid hills.


Night fell upon the ocean, and the winds and the sea rose in unison. The storm clouds gathered and battled in the darkness. The lightning flashed in the rain-streaked heavens, and the waves shouted.

And a sea, larger than his fellows, rose above the surface and flung itself upon the boat.

Joseph threw back his head and laughed, as the planks were torn and tossed into the sky.

Then he spread out his hands, and the waters covered him.

# Book Three
## Christopher Coombe (1888–1912)

Often rebuked, yet always back returning
    To those first feelings that were born with me,
And leaving busy chase of wealth and learning
    For idle dreams of things which cannot be;
I'll walk, but not in old heroic traces,
    And not in paths of high morality,
And not among the half-distinguished faces,
    The clouded forms of long-past history.
I'll walk where my own nature would be leading;
    It vexes me to choose another guide:
Where the grey flocks in ferny glens are feeding;
    Where the wild wind blows on the mountain side.

E. BRONTË

# 1

When Christopher Coombe left Plyn on his first voyage, that August day in the year 1888, it was with a dogged determination to succeed. He would skipper the *Janet Coombe* as his father had done before him, and as his cousin was doing now, and if a young man had courage, coupled with brains and skill, it would not take so very many years either.

So decided Christopher, Joseph's son, at the age of twenty-two, as the ship was towed from Plyn harbour by the puffing tug-boat, and then when well clear of the land she made sail for St John's, Newfoundland, far away across the grim Atlantic.

It was in strange company that Christopher now found himself. There were four other seamen besides himself and the cook in the fo'c'sle, while the skipper and the mate of course berthed aft.

The crew of a small schooner were something different to the crowd on board a big clipper ship, where a man could remain unmolested if he wished, as long as he was smart enough to his work, but in the cramped quarters of a vessel in the fish or fruit trade there was no getting away from your companions, and precious little time for repose, with the constant cry of 'All hands!' when up it was on deck to struggle with the bellying canvas, your nails torn and your eyes blinded by rain, and a kick in the pants for your pains if you bungled the job. Soaked to the skin, with an empty stomach and aching limbs, dizzy with seasickness, poor Christopher would stumble up from the fo'c'sle with the others, to find a pitch-black night and a screaming wind, the topsail carried away, and a new one to be bent. It seemed to him that they were battling with half a gale, as the ship

223

plunged heavily into the trough of the sea, as he lost his way in the confusion on deck, and his feet as well, rolling into the lee-scuppers with a thud that nearly cracked his head in two. But no, this was apparently no more than a rattling fine wind, and hopes were expressed that it would continue thus across the Atlantic.

Sick, giddy, the young man clung to the nearest shroud, until someone yelled in his ear to climb aloft and make shift about it.

What was he expected to do when every rope felt alike, hard, damp, and swinging? How could he fight at these tight sodden knots with his fingers numb and his nails torn? Somehow he scrambled up the narrow slippery ratlines, knowing that the faintest slip would send him into that black churning sea, and then fought his way along the yard, with some wretched idea of helping the two hands who had arrived there before him, and who shouted incomprehensible directions that failed to register in his dazed mind. If this was a fair wind, what in heaven's name was a gale?

Poor Christopher, he was soon to know, for they were scarcely five days from the Lizard when the weather changed, and it was over twenty-five days before the ship made the port of St John's, having beat against head winds most of the way, and been obliged to steer a more northerly course to avoid the full force of these. One of the crew told the new hand that this was a poor passage, but at least the masts and rigging were free from ice, which was a constant occurrence during the winter months. And this was only September. These wretched thirty days had done nothing to help Joseph's son in his love for the sea. He was noticeably thinner from the poor food and the lack of regular sleep, while his skin was an agony to him from the unaccustomed exposure.

Too proud to admit his sufferings, the young man wrote a scrappy sort of letter home, giving a bare account of the voyage, and mentioning little of his reactions to it, beyond saying he was as well as could be expected, after such a gruelling passage.

The *Janet Coombe* did not remain long in St John's before she was away again, with her cargo of fish, bound for the Mediterranean. The next two months were hard and bitter ones for the young seaman. After unloading at Oporto they proceeded once more across the Atlantic to Newfoundland, instead of making directly to St Michaels for fruit, as had been expected. This second journey the ship was in ballast, and though the winds were favourable enough and they only got a couple of days' bad dusting in the Bay, yet the absence of a stiff cargo caused very much pitching and tossing, and Christopher, try as he did, could not conquer his weak stomach. He found little sympathy among the hands for'ard, and cousin Dick the skipper had more serious matters to occupy his mind than to consider the feelings of this raw youngster.

Christopher began to despair. He would stick the life a while longer for his father's sake, and his own pride's sake, but if things became no better there would have to be a change. A final stretch of hard weather was the finish of him. He had scarcely snatched a moment of sleep for nearly a week, and the whole time it had been orders to go aloft and repair some damage, or take in sail, or set sail, or bend new canvas in place of that which had blown away, until his mind was half crazy with the conflicting orders, and his body was dropping with exhaustion and pain.

Then two days before they reached London the vessel sprung a leak in her fore hold, nothing very serious, but enough to give work for hands at the pumps, until the ship was anchored safely in the river. This terrible back-breaking process on top of the fight against the gale in the Bay filled the young seaman's soul with hatred and rebellion.

He could not endure it further; he would cast himself overboard and end his misery rather than set off to sea again. So decided Christopher as the *Janet Coombe* signalled for her pilot and a tug, and they made their way slowly up the long grey fog-bound river to the docks of London.

So this was the city of fame and fortune, this was where

poor boys became Lord Mayors, and ragged urchins million-aires. Well, it was hard to see much of it in this light, with the grey mists creeping from the river and wrapping everything in its clammy hands.

There seemed to be many towers and buildings, somewhat dark and sinister in the gathering fog and twilight, and tall chimneys belching forth smoke; the sound of ships passing up and down, the sight of crowded wharves, the hooting of several big steamers who made the *Janet Coombe* look a smallish little pleasure-boat.

Inside the docks were the high masts and bewildering yards of the large clipper ships, side by side with the smaller fry, schooners and barquentines like his own vessel. The true city lay beyond all this, he supposed, away yonder where the dull lights flickered and the queer unmistakable throb of life sounded.

Christopher sighed, he knew not why, and turned to the work on deck. The ship luckily secured a berth alongside one of the wharves the following morning, and proceeded to unload.

All the cargo of fruit would be out of the hold in three days' time, and then up anchor and back to Plyn in ballast, for ten days spell ashore perhaps if lucky, and once more load with clay for foreign waters. So much did Christopher gather from the talk in the fo'c'sle, and a word dropped now and again by his cousin the skipper.

It was impossible to continue as seaman on the *Janet Coombe*. He loved and respected his father, but his way was not his son's, there was the truth of the matter. Now he must strike out on his own. There were other things in life besides the sea and a ship; there was nothing to prevent him making a name for himself in another sphere altogether. Uncle Philip had told him of London, and the path to fame for anyone who was ambitious. Well, Christopher Coombe was ambitious, and he would show his family and the whole of Plyn that he was not to be beaten. One day they would realize how right he had been to give up the sea; they would look with pride and respect to the man who returned to

226

his home town with an established position and a high reputation.

And thus it was that the afternoon before the *Janet Coombe*
weighed anchor, Christopher escaped from the ship, with never
as much as a backward glance at his father's vessel, nor a
thought to the white figurehead.

Christopher found himself alone in London, with about
five pounds in his pocket between him and starvation.

The first thing to do was to find lodgings for the night.
He was determined to avoid this quarter by the docks, that
smacked of sailorism and the sea, and taking an omnibus at
haphazard he found himself in the centre of the West End,
amongst the shops and the cabs. He was so interested in these
new scenes that it was dark and past six before he realized
how the time had flown.

There was nothing for it but to ask this policeman the
address of some cheap, respectable lodging-house, though he
felt fool enough to appear such an ignoramus. However, the
copper seemed a pleasant sort of chap, and he even bothered
to pull out his note-book and write down some names on a
slip of paper.

'All right, no trouble,' replied the man, and the boy was
impressed by his cheerful Cockney accent, and mentally determined to copy this in future, for it sounded something smarter
and quicker than his own West Country drawl. The first address
on his list was: 'Mrs Johnson, 53 Albany Street, Marylebone
Road'. He was advised to take an omnibus from Great Portland
Street, which would carry him straight to his destination. It
was a dark night with a hint of fog, and the omnibus took
some time to reach Albany Street, the horses being obliged
to walk carefully.

Christopher knocked at the door of No. 53, and presently
a woman came to the door, and turned up the gas in the
dingy hall.

'What do you want?' she asked sharply. She was a nervous,
rat-like woman.

'I was told I could find lodgin's here,' stammered

227

Christopher, slightly taken aback at her manner. 'Maybe there's some mistake.'

'No – it's all right. Come in, can't you, and let's take a look at you.'

Christopher stepped inside, while Mrs Johnson glanced at his mud-bespattered clothes.

'Hum, been tramping by the look of you. I only takes in lodgers who are clean.'

'The fault of a cab,' he said timidly, 'passed right close to me before I knew where I was. I'll brush it off, if I may, direckly.'

'You don't speak like a Londoner,' said Mrs Johnson suspiciously. 'What part of the world d'you come from?'

'I'm Cornish, m'am, by birth, but I'm come to London to look for work.'

'Oh! dear, you've no employment. Oh! I'm sorry, then, but I never takes people who haven't regular work.'

'I mean to find the first thing I can i' the mornin'. You'll find me very quiet an' steady, I assure you.'

'People can't be too careful who they take nowadays,' she said nervously, glancing at Christopher's torn finger nails. 'So much crime about. A decent person can't sleep in their bed. Where've you been to mess up your 'ands like that?'

'My ship docked four days ago,' sighed Christopher wearily, 'an' now I've left her, an' want to live ashore permanent. Does that satisfy you?'

So Christopher became a lodger at 53 Albany Street, rather damped and dismayed by his reception, but consoling himself with the thought that soon he would find work and be able to move to more comfortable quarters.

The following day he stepped out into Albany Street, a smile on his face and his spirits high. Who would seek work when there was so much to be seen, so far to wander, and no responsibilities?

Spellbound by all he saw young Christopher gave himself up to a fortnight of enjoyment. But in the third week of January, after he had paid his weekly bill at the lodgings, he found to his horror and surprise he had but one-and-ninepence in his pocket. For a few minutes he was aghast, and then he pulled himself together and vowed he would take the first vacant job he came across.

Thus it happened that when he passed the fishmonger's 'Druce', in Albany Street, and saw chalked upon the board 'Boy wanted', he made his way to the desk inside the shop, and demanded in humble tones to be given a trial.

So Christopher Coombe, of Plyn in Cornwall, became a fish-monger's assistant in a small shop in Albany Street, London, thankful to be rid of the demon of starvation, but scarcely proud of his new position.

He then wrote the following letter home, dated the twenty-fifth of January, eighteen hundred and eighty-nine.

Dear Father,

I am happy to say I have found a very good situation, and I intend to stick at this until I have a good cheque put by in the savings bank.

The line I am at present following is the fish business. I dare say you thought I was very foolish to run away from the ship, but I must tell you before I proceed that just at present I have no intention of returning home again yet awhile. It is very unpleasant to feel you may not think as much of me as you used to do, but I do trust that you have not altered in your affections. I am very distressed not to have heard from you or my brothers, and fear you may find it hard to forgive me.

London is a fine place, and I have seen many wonderful sights, but it is a sad feeling to think I may not see your dear face again for some time. I do hope you are enjoying the best of health as I am myself at present, and I sincerely trust you will soften your heart towards me. I will now draw to a close with my fond love to all, and shall still remain your affectionate son,
Christopher Coombe

PS – Kindly send me a letter in return if you please, dear father, c/o Mrs Johnson, 53 Albany Street, Marylebone Road, London.

This letter was placed in a box with the seal unbroken, and found, amongst many others, nearly thirty-five years later by Jennifer Coombe, in 1925.

230

## 2

The months passed, and Christopher was still an assistant at Druce's shop, glad to pocket his weekly wages, half of which went for board and lodging, but sadly disillusioned in the glamour of the city, which had been described so much better by Uncle Philip.

Besides this London life did not greatly improve his physical health. He was not exhausted and dog-weary as he had been on the ship, but accustomed as he was from boyhood to the pure air of Plyn, the warmth of the sun even in winters, and the fine sea breezes, he found the cold and the fogs of London infinitely disagreeable, the plodding round on wet pavements a miserable undertaking.

If only he could get a position as clerk somewhere, it would be a step in the upward direction. He could write a clear hand, and spell correctly, he had been bright enough at school in spite of his jibbing at discipline. Surely it would not be so very difficult to find a situation.

It was then that the idea of going to night-school and polishing up his learning occurred to him.

When the local evening classes resumed, Christopher took his place on the benches besides lads some years younger than himself and men old enough to be his father. Fortunately the schoolmaster, Mr Curtis, at once took a liking to Christopher, saw that the young man was a cut above the usual class who attended his school, and singled him out for some attention.

This fishmonger business was clearly so much waste of time, brains, and energy. They talked the matter over together, and the schoolmaster found Christopher had very vague ideas as to the kind of work he wanted.

231

Finally, after Christopher had attended night-school for six weeks, the schoolmaster suddenly thought of the Post Office.

Mr Curtis at once began to make inquiries, and a few weeks later, after the necessary applications had been made, Christopher found himself sworn in as a servant of the Government. He took up his new duties on 1 May in the big branch office in Warren Street. The schoolmaster advised him to stay here for three months on trial, and then, if he liked the work, and was keen to rise, Mr Curtis would prepare him for the necessary examination which he must pass before he could obtain a position of any authority.

It was now September 1889, and exactly a year since Christopher had left home. He had not heard from his father or any of his family, and though he continued to write it was in a half-hearted fashion. He resented the way he had been treated, as though he had committed some heinous crime, and was more determined than ever not to return.

In his capacity in the Warren Street Post Office, Christopher made the acquaintance of a young man of his own age, who seemed friendly, and the pair spent their free time together. During one of their conversations Christopher mentioned that he was lonely in his lodgings in Albany Street, and wished he could make the effort to move.

'Why did you never say anything of this before?' exclaimed his friend. 'You are a funny fellow. I gathered that you liked your own company and would not have moved for the world. Of course you must come to the place where I'm living. It's a highly respectable boarding-house, kept by a Mrs Parkins, a fine woman. There are three daughters in the family, she being a widow, and I must say I find no time to be lonely at No. 7. We're a very happy crowd indeed. It's about two minutes' walk from your present lodgings. Look here, what about coming along to tea tomorrow, Sunday, and I'll introduce you. Of course, Mrs Parkins is highly particular who she takes, but you being a friend of mine, don't you know? Didn't you tell me your father owned a ship or something?'

'Yes, and he was a master in the Merchant Service.'

'Oh! it's sure to be all right. Only you know what people are: must have everything genteel and just the thing.'

'Oh! quite, I perfectly understand.'

The following afternoon Christopher rang the bell at No. 7 Maple Street, and was admitted by a stiff maidservant. His friend, Harry Frisk, was waiting for him in the hall.

'These Sunday afternoon teas are just a wee bit formal,' he whispered nervously. 'Thought I'd better warn you, in case you entered a trifle too free and easy. Never fear though, I'll back you up. I'm a favourite with Mrs P.'

Christopher, slightly alarmed, was shown into the drawing-room and was aware of a group of people seated about the room, and a tinkle of spoons and cups.

'Mr Christopher Coombe,' said the maid in a loud voice. A tall, majestic woman with a lace cap on her head, and dressed in brown velvet, rose from the chair where she had been sitting.

'Mr Frisk has told us about you, Mr Coombe. I am pleased you were able to come this afternoon. Won't you take this chair here beside me. Edith, my love, pour some tea for Mr Coombe. Mr Coombe, my second daughter, Edith.'

Christopher bowed, red in the face, and balanced a slice of bread and butter beside his scalding cup. 'Thank you very much.'

'Mr Frisk tells us that you are doing so well in the Post Office, Mr Coombe.'

'I am doing my best,' he said modestly, and she bowed her head.

'Try a morsel of this marmalade cake. My boarders look forward to these Sunday teas because of it.'

A little murmur of polite laughter rose from the crowd.

'It's not only the cake, Mrs P., you know,' said Harry Frisk, with a jocular smile, anxious to show his familiarity with his hostess. He dug Christopher in the back.

'You just tell Mrs P. about your father in the Navy,' he suggested.

233

'How delightful. I am thrilled by anyone in the Service,' gushed Miss Edith. 'There's such a romantic flavour about the sea, I find.'

'Hush, my love,' frowned her mother, 'let Mr Coombe speak.'

To his alarm Christopher found that everyone in the room had ceased from talking, and had formed an audience.

'The Merchant Service, Frisk, not the Navy,' he began awkwardly. 'My father was master of a little schooner, but he's on the retired list now. I dare say you have heard of Plyn in Cornwall. That is my home.'

Nobody had apparently been aware of its existence until that moment, and he explained that the town was situated on an estuary in Cornwall, the other side of Plymouth.

'Ah! Plymouth,' cried Edith. 'Fancy, the Spanish Armada, mamma, you remember Lord Macaulay's poem.'

'Yes, indeed, Drake and the Hoe, he played bowls or something of the sort. Dear me, Mr Coombe, how very interesting. Being a Cornishman, you sing, I suppose?'

'Well, now, I hardly . . .'

'Oh! nonsense, no modesty now. All Cornishmen sing. What a pity that Bertha is not here, is it not, Edith? Bertha is my eldest girl,' she explained. 'She is away staying with relatives at Chichester. Dear Bertha has such a talent, and usually on Sunday evenings we have music. Delightful pastime, don't you agree with me?'

'Oh! assuredly, madam.'

'Never mind, when Bertha returns we can promise ourselves such merry little gatherings. I need hardly tell you,' she added in a lower tone, 'that Mr Frisk has explained something of your desire to join us in our home. Now that we have made your acquaintance, and you have been formally introduced, we shall expect you, of course.'

'I'm sure it's very good of you, Mrs Parkins.'

'Any friend who is recommended by dear Mr Frisk is welcome. Ladies and gentlemen, I wish to announce that Mr Coombe will shortly be one of us, and I'm sure we all hope he will never live to regret the day he took up his abode at No. 7.'

'Hear, hear – splendid, how very delightful,' rose the chorus.

'Mr Coombe, you must meet all our little group,' said Mrs Parkins, and she took him by the arm, while Harry Frisk followed officiously in their train. 'Dear Mr Frisk you already know. No further time need be wasted on him.' A polite smile from Christopher and a snigger from Frisk.

'You have met Edith, and this is May, our baby.' A fat, bashful creature of about nineteen sidled across the room, and held out a large damp hand.

'This is Mr and Mrs Arnold Stodge, who have been with us for many years.'

Christopher bowed to a thin, melancholy man, with a drooping moustache, and an even more melancholy lady, dressed in deep black with a shawl about her shoulders.

'Mr Stodge is a retired traveller,' continued the hostess.

'Indeed, how interesting. I suppose you've been all over the world, sir?'

'Commercial, you idiot, commercial,' whispered Frisk, scarlet in the face at his friend's blunder.

'Oh! dear – pardon – of course,' mumbled Christopher, colouring in turn.

'Here is Miss Davis, who is one of our most ardent musicians.' Miss Davis, a pale, earnest young woman with dark eyes, gazed at the young man searchingly, and inquired if he had heard *Faust*. 'No – I – I think not,' began Christopher nervously. What the devil did she mean? 'Miss Davis teaches music in the daytime, and entertains us in the evenings,' said Mrs Parkins. 'This gentleman on your right is the Major – Major Carter.' A large, pompous individual put up an eyeglass and stared haughtily for a minute, then turned his back.

'Awful stickler for etiquette,' muttered Frisk. 'It doesn't do to offend him.'

'On your left we have Mrs Crisp,' a small waspish little woman, with a pointed chin; 'Miss Tray, a keen politician,' a tall, frightening woman bore down upon him with pince-nez and prominent teeth; 'Mr Wooten, in the wholesale business,' a red-haired young man twisted his feet and giggled inanely;

'and Mr Black, in tallow.' The words suggested a mass of oil and grease, but Christopher shook hands with a stout, bloated old man, red-nosed and watery-eyed, who winked at him when his hostess's back was turned. 'And so you have met us all except dear Bertha, which will be a pleasure to come. And now, what about a little reading, everybody?'

In a few minutes the room was cleared and the chairs drawn in a circle. Christopher found himself between Miss Davis and the tallow merchant.

'We generally read from the poets,' explained Miss Davis kindly, 'so as to become accustomed to the beauties of the English language. It is Tennyson this afternoon.'

'Damned humbug!' breathed the tallow merchant, 'bores me stiff. Always go to sleep. Wake me up if anyone reads anything spicy. Get my meaning?' He put his finger to his nose and winked odiously.

'Mr Coombe, our custom is just to open a book and read haphazard,' said Mrs Parkins. 'Thus we get a fair amount of variation. Edith, my love, will you commence?'

Christopher, too nervous to laugh, bent over the book he was sharing with Miss Davis, and listened with embarrassment to the various members of the group as they read the verses aloud. When it came to his turn, and Mrs Parkins was gazing at him expectantly, he shut his eyes, fluttered the pages, and a little unfortunately opened the book towards the end of 'Guinevere'. Swallowing bravely, Christopher made a start in the middle of the page.

O imperial moulded form,
And beauty such as never woman wore
Until it came a kingdom's curse with thee –
I cannot touch thy lips, they are not mine,
But Lancelot's; nay, they never were the King's.
I cannot take thy hand, that too is flesh,
And in the flesh thou hast sinn'd; and mine own flesh
Here looking down on thine polluted, cries . . .

Christopher heard a snigger in his right ear. The tallow merchant had wakened up. The young man raised his eyes and noticed the flush on his hostess's face. She fanned herself nervously and frowned. The other members of the boarding-house moved uneasily in their seats. The two daughters sat with lowered eyes.

Flurried and embarrassed Christopher continued:

> I loathe thee, yet not less, O Guinevere,
> For I was ever virgin save for thee
> For love thro' flesh . . .

'Yes – well, perhaps that will do for today, Mr Coombe,' interrupted Mrs Parkins, rising to her feet. 'Miss Davis, dare I suggest a little music?'

Christopher, feeling he had committed some unforgivable crime, concealed himself in a corner of the room, where he was soon joined by Messrs Frisk and Black.

'I say old fellow,' began the first hurriedly, 'do choose your subject before you read another time. Just glance down the page, if you know what I mean. Frightfully sensitive woman, Mrs P., if you get my meaning. No offence, I hope?'

'Certainly not,' said Christopher, 'really, I'm sure I had no idea . . .'

'He! he!' chuckled the tallow merchant, 'you clever rascal. How on earth did you find that speech? Bless my soul, I've searched through the Idylls of the King, and never come across it. Well done, my boy. I can see things will look up now you're to join us.' He dug the young man in the ribs.

Christopher listened to Miss Davis's rendering of the Moonlight Sonata in bewilderment.

When the music was finished, and Christopher was about to leave, his hostess signalled to him to follow her for a few minutes' private conversation in her boudoir.

'Quite all right,' whispered Harry Frisk, 'this is the custom before a new boarder joins. She'll ask you what religion you practise and also tell you about something that happened here some years ago. A couple behaved very badly – no need to explain further if you get me. Damn bad form and all that sort of thing.'

Above in the boudoir Mrs Parkins motioned the young man to a seat.

'Mr Coombe, before you go I must ask you if you are a member of the Church of England?'

'Well, madam, my mother was a Wesleyan Methodist, but my father was brought up a Churchman. I've attended both services in my time.'

'Ah! well, I think that is quite satisfactory. You are, at least, neither an atheist nor a papist. We never could receive you here if such was the case.'

'No, madam, I'm sure.'

'Then, Mr Coombe, I trust, I hope that your morals are above reproach.'

'Please?' asked Christopher, a little puzzled.

'In other words, you are clean-living and clean-thinking?'

'Oh! exceedingly, Mrs Parkins.'

'That is well. You see, Mr Coombe, a woman in my delicate position as head of this establishment cannot afford to be too careful. Being a widow – in short, you understand me.'

'Quite.' He was lost, but no matter.

'In fact, because of what I have said to you I feel it my duty to acquaint you with an unfortunate occurrence that took place under my very roof three years ago. It so happened that it came to my knowledge quite by accident, indeed I might never have discovered it but for being obliged to descend down to the lower landing in the middle of the night. Mr Coombe, this is highly distressing to both of us, I'm sure, I found to my horror that two of my boarders, a young man and a – a woman, were' – she lowered her voice to a whisper – 'were cohabiting.'

She sank back in her chair and fanned herself.

'Dear me, how very shocking,' murmured Christopher.

'Oh! infamous. They were flung from the building early

the next morning, of course. But as the mother of three innocent young daughters, three pure gems, Mr Coombe, imagine my state of mind.'

'I can, Mrs Parkins.'

'Since this − this painful incident I have lived in perpetual
agony lest it should happen again; I have feared lest my own
girls should not escape the contamination. Mr Coombe, I can
place my confidence in you and never have it abused?'

'Certainly, madam, I assure you.'

'Then I need keep you no longer. Good-bye until next
Saturday, and welcome to No. 7. Liberty Hall, Mr Coombe,
to those who can be trusted.'

She bowed gravely, and Christopher took his leave.

The tallow merchant was hovering in the passage. 'He! He!'
he leered, 'been in the dragon's den? I'll walk with you to the
end of the road. Believe in an evening constitutional. So she's
been showing you the family skeleton, has she? Thought as
much. Don't listen to a word she says. Perfectly easy for a
young fellow like you to have some fun if he feels inclined.
Other pair of fools got found out. Their own fault. Used to
leave on the gas-light. Showed under the door. Prefer the dark
myself. Ha! Ha! bit of a dog in my day.'

Christopher, something of a prude, hastened his steps. What
an objectionable old fellow.

'Here! not so fast. Not as young as I was. Always ready for
fun though. We'll set things humming at No. 7, eh? Worst of
it is, such rotten poor material. Virgins every one of 'em, and
past their prime. No good to me. What about you, you rogue?
Bertha's the goods. She's the doings. Cold as ice, though. Made
of marble. See if you can thaw her, eh? He! He! Don't forget
to turn down the gas.'

'Good night,' said Christopher hurriedly, and crossed to the
other side of the street, leaving the tallow merchant on the
opposite pavement, waving his umbrella.

# 3

So Christopher became a boarder at No. 7 Maple Street, Liberty Hall to the favoured, though personally he found little enough freedom there. There seemed to be so many rules and regulations, and such show of etiquette, and this was not the thing, and that showed lack of breeding, and the other showed really deplorable taste. He began to feel he was a very difficult person to suit. He had detested the rough ignorant crowd on the *Janet Coombe*, his father's vessel, and longed for people of culture and understanding; now he had found them they were scarcely better, for they were narrow and pretentious, with small hearts and stilted views.

It was certainly a queer circle in which he had found himself, and though he worked hard at the Post Office it was a dry, tedious business, and he often sighed for the fresh air of Plyn, and the sound of the sea. Until, of course, Bertha Parkins returned to the boarding-house. Christopher never forgot the first moment he saw her.

He had returned from his work and entered the drawing-room where the boarders assembled before the evening meal. Mrs Parkins had hurried forward. 'My dearest Bertha is a stranger to you, Mr Coombe. May I present my eldest daughter?'

A tall, graceful girl turned from the piano where she had been looking over some music, and bowed distantly. 'I am delighted you have become one of us, Mr Coombe,' she said. Christopher gaped at her, blushing to the roots of his hair. Could she possibly be a Parkins? Why, she was beautiful and stately, like a princess. She was a picture, she was the drawing by Mr Marcus Stone in the dining-room, of a lady sitting in a garden dressed in white. How clumsy and awkward she must think him with his country manners and his Cornish accent. Her sisters could not hold a candle to her for looks. Such grace too, or deportment as Harry Frisk would say, and her simple, almost severe dress, her soft brown hair swept away from the high forehead.

Christopher was a curious young man. He was nearing twenty-three, and he had never as yet considered women except in the light of a relative. Now suddenly this cold, stately, utterly beautiful Miss Bertha had made her appearance, leaving him quite bewildered and a prey to a host of new painful and perplexing emotions. Firstly he was tongue-tied in her presence, he found himself unable to utter a word that seemed reasonably sensible or intelligent. At once he was self-conscious, and lost his ease, he was terrified lest he should make some idiotic social blunder, taboo at No. 7, that would cause her pain and displeasure.

He began to go to church regularly on Sundays, he read the same authors he found in the hands of his divinity, in order to exchange opinions concerning them, and then when she turned to him with an encouraging smile and asked him a question, he was covered in confusion and stammered something perfectly unintelligible.

Gradually, of course, his feelings became stronger. He found to his amazement that Miss Bertha was not above entering into conversation, accepting small bunches of flowers for her room, bunches which grew larger as his sentiments grew bolder; that she was willing to walk home with him from church on Sundays, exchange books and discuss Mr Gladstone without animosity.

Gradually Christopher realized he was in love. There was no use in denying it, he could not withstand this strange thing that had come upon him. He loved Bertha Parkins. He was miserable and unhappy when not in her company, his long days in the Post Office seemed interminable, until the evenings brought him back to her again.

Had the other inhabitants of No. 7 noticed his emotions, he wondered? They had. Mrs Crisp muttered her suspicions

241

to Mrs Stodge, Miss Davis sighed sentimentally as she dreamed some waltz on the piano. Miss Edith and Miss May whispered in corners, and Mr Black the tallow merchant listened at keyholes. He was the first to inform Christopher that the entire household was waiting for him to take steps.

'Here, Coombe,' he said in his familiar manner, 'this sort of thing can't go on. Doing yourself no good, nor the girl neither. Go and get her.'

'I don't know what you mean, Black,' said Christopher stiffly, 'nor to whom you are referring.'

'He! He! – you can't fool me, you dog. I've watched you. Can't contain yourself when a certain nameless one is present. She's not made of ice either. Soon melt, if you teach her the trick. By George, wish I were twenty years younger. Teach her myself.' Christopher turned his back. He would box the fellow's ears if he said another word. To drag Miss Parkins in the mud like that. It was at this moment that Harry Frisk came to his aid.

'I say, old chap, no offence, but – what are your intentions regarding a lady known to us both?'

Christopher swallowed and took a grip of himself.

'What do you mean?' he said faintly.

'Well, only it's devilish awkward for me. I mean, the girls have no father and no brother, and I sort of hold myself responsible. Mrs P. trusts me. What are you going to do?'

'I – I – what can I do?'

'Well, declare yourself, old boy.'

'I'm sorry, but I honestly haven't the courage. I've never thought of such a thing. She's far too good for me, why . . .'

'Oh! I don't know. You're smart enough. You've got a good position at the P.O. You could support a wife, I dare say.'

'A wife – good heavens, you suggest I should ask Miss Parkins to become my wife?'

'Why, yes. What do you think I meant?'

'I hardly know – forgive me, I must have been mad. You advise me to propose to Miss Parkins, to offer her marriage?'

'Certainly, old fellow. Damn bad form to do anything else.'

'Oh! of course – of course. She is the soul of honour, I – really – phew! old man, I am in a regular state.'

'Well, think it over. You can scarcely remain here without making a declaration. She must expect it.'

'Impossible. She cannot have the slightest suspicion.'

'I'm not so sure. Anyway, don't lose heart over it. Pull yourself together if you get my meaning. No offence?'

'Oh! None. Thanks, Harry.'

The weeks passed and Christopher Coombe had not yet summoned up enough courage to speak his mind.

Things might have gone on like this indefinitely had it not been for the return of Stanley from Africa on 26 April. Bertha had expressed a wish to join the crowd at Victoria Station and catch a glimpse of London's idol, and her mother had refused until Christopher timidly offered his escort. This, of course, was another matter; Mrs Parkins smiled approval, and her daughter flushed with pleasure. Instantly there was an electric feeling in the boarding-house that the great moment was approaching. Black, the tallow merchant, took an extra glass of wine at dinner, and tried to hold Miss Tray's hand under the table, much to that lady's indignation; effeminate Mr Wooten summoned up sufficient virility to play cat's cradle with May Parkins, and Mr Arnold Stodge read Ouida's new novel aloud to his wife.

Christopher and Bertha took up their usual positions by the piano to sing duets, while Miss Davis fluttered the music nervously.

'It is a wonderful thing how your voice, Mr Coombe, and Bertha's harmonize,' she murmured daringly.

Bertha lowered her eyes and Christopher's heart leapt in his breast.

Did it mean, could she possibly . . .?

Miss Davis struck the opening bars, and Christopher's light baritone joined Bertha's clear soprano.

O! that we two were maying,

What feeling the young man put into his voice, what passion into the words! If he had not the courage to propose, he could at least declare himself in song. Bertha was smiling at him over the top of Miss Davis's head.

He felt that until this moment nothing in his life had held any value at all. Plyn, the country, his father, the ship, none of these had existed, he had been born merely to look into Bertha's eyes and to read the answer to the question he dared not ask. He was swept with an affection for the boarding-house, for everyone in it, even old Black himself was a good fellow. And it was spring and he was twenty-three, and he was taking her tomorrow to see Stanley return; they would drive round Regent's Park afterwards in a hansom cab – they would, if he threw himself in the Canal afterwards.

> O! that we two were maying
> Down the stream of a soft spring breeze
> And like children with violets playing
> In the shade of the whispering trees.

'Charming, charming,' said Mrs Parkins, feeling for her handkerchief.

With hot trembling hands Christopher propped another sheet of music on the stand before Miss Davis.

'Play the last verse slow and very soft,' he muttered fiercely, and she nodded in sympathy, her heart beating.

With his eyes aflame, and tremor in his voice, he plunged once more into song—

> I will give you a fine silken gown,
> Madam, will you walk,
> Madam, will you talk.

Why must she shake her head in such determination. Could not she see that he was laying his very life at her feet?

Miss Davis pressed heavily upon the soft pedal, her fingers scarcely touched the keys.

With doubled ardour, his voice cracking with emotion, Christopher sang the last verse.

> I will give you the keys of my heart,
> And we will be married till death us do part,
> Madam, will you walk,
> Madam will you talk,
> Madam, will you walk and talk with me?

The following evening Christopher and Bertha were packed tight in the crowd gathered outside Victoria Station.

They caught one glimpse of the celebrated traveller, guarded from the cheering masses by a cordon of police, and then he was gone.

'What a splendid figure of a man,' exclaimed Bertha, her eyes shining. 'Don't you agree with me, Mr Coombe?'

'I scarcely saw him, Miss Parkins, but I take your word for it of course.'

They climbed into an omnibus that would take them in the direction of home. Christopher's brain was afire with plans. It was impossible to return at once, the opportunity of being alone with Bertha could not be wasted thus.

Presently they descended from the bus at the top of Baker Street, and Bertha was preparing to change into the next, when Christopher seized her arm.

'Miss Parkins,' he said hurriedly, 'surely there is no need to be so pressed. It is a fine evening; would you consider it very improper if I suggest we took a little turn in Regent's Park in a hansom?'

'Oh! Mr Coombe – I hardly think – perhaps – it certainly would be very delightful.'

'Then you don't object? Hurrah! Pardon my excitement, dear Miss Parkins, I scarcely know what I am about. If we walk along we shall soon pick one up, in passing.'

Ten minutes later, Christopher Coombe and Bertha Parkins were inside a hansom, driving briskly round the outer circle. Christopher glanced at his companion, muffled in her fur stole

245

although it was April, and her hands hidden in her muff. Her veil was fastened tight to her hat. Forgetting himself, entirely losing his head, he stretched out his hand and took one of hers from the shelter of the muff. To his wild delight she did not remove it. She sighed, and drew her fur closer to her chin. Feeling that the world would crash for all he cared, Christopher said not a word, and they proceeded round the outer circle in silence. This was pure heaven; never, never had he known such ecstasy of bliss.

He rose, and tapped on the ceiling. The cabbie lifted the trap and peered down. 'Once more round the Park, please,' cried Christopher firmly.

He sat down again, and nerved himself for the ordeal in front of him.

'Miss Parkins,' he began, 'Miss Bertha — I — can I call you Bertha?'

A soft pressure of her hand was his answer.

'You will hate me, despise me, for what I am about to say,' he continued, 'I have no right to weary you with my foolish notions. I'm not fit to touch the hem of your skirt let alone anything above.'

Good God — what was he saying? This was not what he meant at all.

'No — No — at least, not that — what I mean to say is — Oh! Bertha, would you rather — perhaps — shall we go home?' He pulled his handkerchief from his pocket, and mopped his brow.

'What are you trying to tell me?' she said gently. Modesty forbade her to go further than this.

'That's just it — I'm not sure — confound it. Bertha, dear Bertha, forgive my expression. I do not know what I want to say — what I am longing, burning to say in fact. For months I have struggled with myself but in vain. I am convinced that I am now going to earn your distrust of me for ever, that this is the moment when my future agony will begin, never to end.'

He paused, while she moved, ever so slightly, towards him.

'Bertha, could you ever, could you possibly look upon me without – could you ultimately learn to—' he choked, swallowed, blew his nose, and feverishly drew her hand to his lips.

'Mr Coombe – Christopher – what do you mean?' she murmured.

'Bertha – I – I am asking you to be my wife.' God! He had said it! For three minutes there was a pause, while Christopher cursed his brutish lack of tact. Then he drew her other hand from her muff and placed it upon his.

'Christopher,' she whispered, 'how did you guess?'

Guess? Guess what? He peered into her face.

'That I am yours,' she said, and hid her face in confusion. A wave of madness surged through Christopher. It could not be true. He had misunderstood. He . . . but no, she sat close to him and pressed his hand. His head swimming, he put his arm around her waist. Decorum fled to the winds, manners were forgotten, the 'genteel' ways he had learnt in the boarding-house existed no more.

'Put up your veil,' he whispered. She obeyed. Christopher struck his fist at the trap-door.

'Drive half a dozen times round the Park, and slow about it,' he roared.

Then he took Bertha in his arms . . .

And that is how Christopher Coombe declared his love for Bertha Parkins, in the year eighteen hundred and ninety.

247

# 4

—22nd, 1890                                32, York Road,
                                              Nr. Camden Town
My dear Father,
I have been thinking of home all day, and felt that I
must write and acquaint you with my great happiness,
since I have been married.

I received no letter from you in reply to mine,
telling you of my engagement, and fear it may have
gone astray.

I enclosed with my letter a photograph of my
betrothed, and was anxious to know that it had given
satisfaction.

I must confess that had I searched London throughout I could never find a better partner nor a more
respectable family than hers. I shall leave you to judge
my last sentence by the photo that will follow this,
which includes her two younger sisters who were
bridesmaids, and who were pleased to escort her from
the altar after the ceremony. I need hardly mention
they were taken in their bridal array.

My wife and I intend to have our photo taken
together shortly, which we will send to you. Our
wedding took place on the twenty-sixth of August at
Holy Trinity, Marylebone, and Bertha and I spent a
very enjoyable honeymoon at Harrogate; this I need
hardly say was her choice, for I would have dearly
loved to return to Plyn and show her to you all, but,
alas, it was not to be. I hope that this will be a pleasure to come, and when I have passed a further examination in the Government Postal Department, I shall

feel entitled to a holiday. Should I not succeed, however, I will quit postal work, and turn my brains to something else. It is a tiring tedious business. You will wonder why my wife and I were not married sooner no doubt. Well, her mother was most particular on a four months' engagement, and we carried this out to the very date, as you will observe.

We have now been married nearly three months, and talking it over last night we decided that it seemed but three weeks, so you can well imagine our happiness. I quite understand my wife's desire to live so close to her family, but I would greatly prefer to have her more to myself, which seems difficult, with the sisters and the friends from the boarding house running in and out. Still, I suppose this is natural enough. Bertha would not leave London for the world, so I could not dream of tearing her away. I so often long for the sight of Plyn, but it seems fated to be otherwise. I have given up the thought of hearing from you, and Albert and Charlie, you may tell Albie straight from me that he is no man and no brother for I have written to him many times asking after you, and I have never received an answer. Neither from him, nor from the others. I have done what I believed to be my duty and asked your forgiveness, but you seem to have hardened yourself against me. Please God in time I will prove to you that I am no weakling as you seem to consider, but an honest hardworking man, with a dear wife, and the hope of raising a family who will not be ashamed to bear the name of Coombe. Of course these are early times to predict as yet, and you will naturally think I have reasons for saying so, which is quite correct, I have but I must leave it until I write again when I will give you particulars. My suspicions may be unfounded, but I think not.

I often think out of so many Coombes I am the only one who has wandered to London, and settled down, but let me advise them that the cost of living is high, and it is not such a grand place as folk would make out, very dirty and noisy.

Well, dear Father, I have told you all the news I can think of.

I must draw to a close, wishing you good health, and fond love to all from Bertha and myself.

I remain,

Your loving son,

Christopher Coombe

After the honeymoon and the settling down in the new house, with her mother constantly at her elbow to advise her, Bertha retained, successfully she considered, her gentle state of passivity and her notion of privacy, causing through her ignorance an insurmountable barrier, with Christopher a barred and lonely spirit on the other side.

The influence of mother and sisters kept Bertha from responding to Christopher's need of her.

Left to herself, and Christopher as her only companion, she would probably have outgrown the customs and habits of the boarding-house, but the tenacity of the Parkins was too strong, and her upbringing and environment vanquished over her own scarcely perceptible emotions.

One of the first proofs, observed by the hitherto unenlightened Christopher, as to his wife's limited range of vision, was obtained in a very cursory manner, in a discussion on the Parnell-O'Shea divorce case. He had laid aside the evening paper and remarked how wretched it must be for a man of public character to have his private life drawn into the light, and used as a weapon against his career.

'Oh! Christopher, how can you say such a thing,' exclaimed Bertha. 'I am surprised at you for defending a man like Mr Parnell, who appears to be entirely lacking in moral sense.'

'That's as may be, dear heart,' he replied. 'I know little of him, except what people say, and that he seems an able politician and a leader of his party. But that his destiny, and maybe his country's, should crash because he has lived with this lady out of wedlock, seems to me highly unjust.'

'But Christopher, none of his party could possibly wish to follow him, or to place their trust in him, after he had done so terrible a thing. Their faith would die instantly.'

'Why, Bertha – just because the man has loved a woman?'

'Not because he loved her, though that is wrong in itself, seeing she was not at liberty, but that he gave in to this improper feeling and sinned in the doing of it.'

'Dearest, he must have had a very strong affection for this Mrs O'Shea, possibly he could not exist without her, she may have been necessary to him in every way.'

'Oh! nonsense, love, a man of strong will should control passion.'

'But I dare say the passion, as you call it, was only part of his feeling for her, bound up in a hundred other emotions, all equally deep.'

'Why, Christopher, they lived in sin – that is immoral and wicked. I wonder the papers dare print anything of it.'

'Yes, dear, I know the law of the thing is wrong, and must not be condoned. But after all, they only did without the benefit of Clergy or State, what you and I do – and if we love each other why . . .'

'Christopher – how can you?' She rose to her feet, scarlet with confusion, her eyes ready to fill with tears.

'Why – Bertha – my Bertha, what have I said to hurt you?' he asked, holding out his arms to her.

'Oh! I've never felt so – so humiliated in my life,' she sobbed, and rushed from the room.

Like every lover faced with his first quarrel, if it could be so called, Christopher was ready to blow his brains out, if by doing this he could make amends.

He was prepared for her to descend with her hat and wrap, declaring she would return to her mother, when half an hour later she entered the room, her tears dried and her manner calm, and asked him meekly if he had washed, as supper was

251

waiting. Christopher told himself that he did not understand women.

Before the birth of his son Harold in the early autumn of 1891, he had many instances of his wife's difference from himself. Bertha's condition was shrouded in the utmost mystery by herself and her family, and to her husband, accustomed to the healthy, open atmosphere of the homes of Plyn, this was quite inexplicable. In Plyn, such matters were discussed continually before company.

Christopher never forgot one evening returning home, very excited and pleased with life and the thought of the future, and carrying in his pocket a small woollen cap he had seen in some fancy shop.

He entered the parlour to find his wife, her condition obvious to the denset of persons, seated beside the tea table, surrounded by her mother, her two sisters and two ladies from the boarding-house, discussing the latest fashions.

He listened for a while, joining in now and again, and then when there came a pause he suddenly remembered his purchase.

He dived his hand into his pocket, and produced the miniature woollen cap. 'Look,' he said, smiling, holding up the cap for all to see, 'won't the little chap look a picture in this?'

There was a moment's horrified silence. Bertha flushed all over her face, the friends gazed steadily at their plates, while Mrs Parkins, rising to the occasion, stretched out her hand to the teapot.

'I am sure you would like another cup, wouldn't you, Christopher?' she asked brightly. Hastily he replaced the cap in his pocket. 'Thank you,' he said in an awkward voice, and tried to hide himself behind a slice of bread and butter.

What a stiff, unnatural atmosphere, and how difficult it was to know how to behave, according to the Parkins's ideas of decorum and good taste. Still, he must consider himself a lucky man to have married anyone with such high standards, and with such superior breeding.

252

The child was born in due course, and received the usual amount of praise and attention, and generally causing much fuss and commotion. The little Harold was closeted for hours with his mother and grandmother, while the father, an outsider of course, was treated with lofty scorn as one who had had no hand in the creation whatsoever.

In the summer Christopher sat for his further examination in the Government Postal Department, and failed to satisfy the requirements of the board. At first he was greatly concerned and upset, blaming himself severely for not having studied sufficiently, previous to the examination, but on thinking the matter over he decided it was just as well, and that this provided an excuse to leave Postal work altogether.

The Coombes managed to exist comfortably enough on Christopher's savings, through the summer and autumn, but the year closed dismally for him, for like many other people of his class he had amused himself that autumn by taking in financial papers, and had hoped to add to his savings by a clever piece of investment. He had, accordingly, placed some of his capital in the Liberator Building Society, and was preening himself on the thought of the approaching dividends, when suddenly there came the news of its failure and of the institutions known as the 'Balfour Group'.

He then wrote the following letter home.

My dear Father,
As it is such a long time since I wrote to you no doubt the right and proper thing to do is to ask you to forgive me for being so neglectful.

I do trust that you are quite well and comfortable at home, and that your health will be spared for many years and that the remainder of your days will be free from worry and trouble. I am extremely sorry for keeping you so long without a letter and I hope you do not worry yourself concerning us up here, and I am convinced that if you could only look in here sometimes and see my dear wife and boy you would

253

have a good opinion of both her and the child. I kept putting off writing, since I have done so many times without receiving a reply, hence my carelessness.

I hope my brothers and sister and my stepmother are well, and getting on in their different vocations.

I am sorry to say just at present I am out of work. I failed in my Postal examination, but cannot say this worried me considerably, as my health for the past six months has not been too good, though I stuck to my work as long as I could for my wife's and the boy's sake. I would like to get something in the open if possible, even if the money is a little less, but you must know from experience it takes a good bit to provide for a family, let one be as careful as one can be, and it doesn't pay to be idle long. I am pleased to say since I have been at home I feel a good deal better and hope soon to be quite myself again. I think I told you our boy was taken ill early in the year, but I am glad to announce he is a strong healthy lad now, and a great joy to his mother.

No doubt the country papers have been full about the great failure of the 'Balfour Group' concern, it has caused a lot of misery for the working classes, myself being affected also. I've never seen such a wicked thing, for in these times one cannot help speculating a trifle and I had the bad fortune to lose a certain amount of my savings. Now dear Father, this has made me very worried, and I cannot help thinking that it would be wiser if I left London, and came home again to Plyn, to settle down there for good and all. I have said nothing to my wife, but will await your reply to this, before telling her my decision.

I have been just over four years away from home, and not one reply have I had from you, and I must say I feel it very much. I do ask you most humbly to answer this letter, as to whether you approve my suggestion of returning to Plyn.

254

I know it is useless to keep worrying and grumbling over my family affairs, but just a few lines from you will make all the difference in the world, and may alter the whole course of my future life, and of those depending on me.

If you ignore this wretched demand as you have my others, then it grieves me to say that this will be my last letter home to you and I will have to say good-bye.

From your loving son,

Chris

Christopher Coombe waited four weeks for an answer, and when it did not come he went to his wife and told her that he had failed her as a husband, for they had very little money left, and his family could not see their way to help him.

She immediately sent for her mother, and Christopher stood with meekness and humiliation while the full torrent of Parkins's wrath was poured upon his head. The upshot of it was, that the house was abandoned, enough money having been scraped together to pay off the rent due, and the couple with the little boy were lodged at the boarding-house until the bread-winner had found work.

From this time onwards he obtained various temporary situations, but it seemed impossible for him to remain anywhere for any length of time. Another son was born in the summer of 1893, and much controversy had been caused over his name. Christopher had wished for Joseph after his unforgiving father, Bertha had declared for George, owing to the marriage that month of the Duke of York to Princess May; but finally the grandmother got her way and the boy was named Willie after the late lamented Mr Parkins.

So while Joseph Coombe languished in Sudmin Asylum, his son Christopher toiled and struggled in the City of London, his life made something of a burden to him by his in-laws, but remaining singularly attached to his cold wife and to his two little boys.

Thus Christopher Coombe, at the age when his father Joseph had obtained his Master's Certificate and became the proud skipper of his own vessel, was an assistant in a large drapery store, and the friendless inhabitant of a stiff boarding-house.

256

# 5

My dear Sister,

It is now eight years since I wrote home, and I said then it would be my last letter to Father and Plyn, but of late I have been sorely troubled with the longing to know that all is well with you and those whom I have never ceased to love.

I feel that I should have made greater allowances for Father, for his approaching age, and indeed the very affliction of his blindness should have caused me to think less harshly of his treatment of me. These years have been long and difficult, and at times I was well nigh stricken to the ground with despair that I should fail to provide for my dear wife and two boys. Then I remembered my father's own indomitable will, and his tenacity of purpose, these things had not failed him when he fought for the safety of his vessel at sea, nor had he shown cowardice when the doctor at Plymouth gave to him the realization of many years of blankness and dim horror. That my father had triumphed over the bitterness of frustration and the curtailing of his life of glory, I have never for one moment doubted; in my mind's eye I can see him standing upon the Cliffs of Plyn, a bold upright figure of great strength and beauty, facing with true courage and unfailing endurance, whatever Fate might hold in store for him.

The thoughts of him, Katherine, have been something of a banner to your wretched brother, during those evil times now happily ended; he was like a star set in the heavens that the old mariners would follow

257

in the vanished days, bringing them through danger and desolation to a quiet haven and safe anchorage. I resolved I would not break faith with his past proud trust in me, however little he might think of me in the present. So with this to guide me, and the continual presence of my young sons, real Coombe lads, every inch of them, and the reproachful, wistful shadow in my wife's eyes, I did not withdraw from the struggle, but managed after some little time to attain to a certain position, which enabled me once more to offer them a home. Before then we had existed mainly on the charity of my mother-in-law, which was a bitter blow to my pride, as you may easily imagine.

When all this trouble with the Boers started, I at once thought of dear brother Charlie, and trusted that though he did his duty to Queen and Country, he would be permitted to pass unscathed, returning finally to you all quite safe and sound.

The idea of breaking my silence did not occur to me until a few days since, when having occasion to enter the docks of London to transact some matter of business for my firm, I chanced to glance at the many vessels being at anchor, or passing down the river. Then to my astonishment I perceived a schooner in ballast, that a tug-boat had in tow, making her way down the centre of the stream; it was none other than the *Janet Coombe*. I was profoundly moved, and would have given ten years of my life to have spoken to those on board, but it was not to be. I shall never forget the shock of mingled joy and pain that came to me, when I saw in the distance the brave little figure-head, so much beloved by my father, and whom I forsook so heedlessly those twelve years ago. I resolved there and then that I would write to Plyn again at the first opportunity, but I was prevented from doing so by being sadly disheartened, as most of us were here in London, and no doubt you in the country as well, by the fresh losses to our armies overseas.

Then two nights ago Bertha and I were amongst those present at some musical gathering, a concert given in Queen's Hall. Once more my old longing rose unsuppressed in my heart, as I listened with tears in my eyes to some plaintive Irish song, whose sad verses recalled my dear absent home. It seemed to me that I was indeed looking upon the peaceful harbour waters, and hearing the hungry clamour of gulls; the sea was at my feet and the hills behind me, and through the air I could hear the chimes of Lanoc Church. For all I knew you believed me dead and forgotten, or travelled far away into some distant land. I left the building in a dream, my wife holding to my arm; and there in the streets we beheld a striking emotional scene, the whole population of London gone crazy apparently, with flags waving and men shouting like children for joy, while the newsboys ran amongst them crying that Mafeking had been relieved.

The tumult and rejoicing had swept us too, and this seems the first moment since, that I am free to be able to write to you. Fancy, you were a girl of sixteen or seventeen years when I last saw you, and now I take it you are a young woman of nine and twenty, married perhaps, with children of your own.

I write to you because I expect Albie to be at sea, and Charlie at the war. Father I dare not approach after my last unanswered efforts, but I enclose letters from the children to him, hoping that this may move him. They are strong, healthy boys, and a great joy to me and my dear wife. Now, Katherine, should this not reach you, of which I cannot but entertain doubts, I shall think most seriously of taking the train to Plyn and risking the consequences. If, on the other hand, you do receive this safely, then I shall be eternally grateful for an early reply. If you could but fathom

half the deep and earnest longing I have in my heart
to look upon all your dear faces again, you would find
it not difficult I believe to grant me this desire. Well,
no more at present, and I will now close with my
fond love to you, Father and all members of the
family, remaining as ever your affectionate brother.
Christopher

In this letter were enclosed the following notes from the
two boys:

Dear Grandfather,
I dare say you will be pleased to get a letter from us
and to hear how we are getting on. I am very glad to
tell you we are all very well at present and hope this
letter will find you the same.

I am sorry to think of Uncle Charlie fighting the
Boers and you must miss him sadly, we would not like
our Dad to be away from us long, but I think Uncle
Charlie must have an exciting time being a soldier all
the same. I shall be a soldier when I grow up too, but
if there is not a Boer left to fight I will come to Plyn
and help in the yard.

Dad has told us about Plyn.

Last week Willie and I took our lunch to Regent's
Park by the lake and pretended it was the harbour, I
am sure you would smile if you saw the big bag of
food we took for we are strong and hearty, Mother
says, with good appetites.

Well, this is all I think and I will send my love to
Auntie Kate, and Uncle Albie if he is at home, from
your loving grandson.
Harold Coombe

(eight years last September)

Dear Grandfather,
i am rather small to write letters but i will do my best
to write as well as Harold does i am rather good at
lesons Mother says so you will be proud of me i expect
wont you. Dad gave me a nice present of a fine ship in
a bottle i must try and keep it safe to show to you
when i see you. i would like to see you and Uncle
Albie and other aunties and uncles and some day i will.
Wud you like a photo of me i will try and find one for
you i am to be a sailor when I grow up how is the
*Janet Coombe*, now dear grandfather i must close hoping
you are well and fond love from your loving
grandson
Willie Coombe

(six years last July)

A few days later to Christopher's wonder and delight an
envelope came for him with the Plyn postmark. Not trusting
his emotion at the breakfast table he withdrew to his room
and read his sister's long letter. Katherine had not spared herself,
she had written clearly and fully a truthful account of everything that had taken place since her brother's departure thirteen years ago.

For some time Christopher Coombe sat dumbfounded by
the shock of this letter, and the news that it contained. That
he, seemingly, had been the means of driving his father to acts
of unprecedented cruelty and then to ultimate insanity was a
thought of such horror and desolation that he knew he would
never recover, never be able to pay back onefold of the peace
which he had deliberately robbed, but must live the remainder of his days with the burden of another soul upon his, and
go to his grave guilty of murder and the causing of misery
to many lives. There was no punishment heavy enough to
meet his case; those years of hard work, toil, and the threat
of poverty, were as nothing compared to the vast suffering of
his father.

261

On Friday evening Christopher sat in the corner of a third class carriage of the jolting train that was bearing him swiftly to Plyn.

The weather had been fair enough when he left Paddington but as the night advanced and the train sped towards the west an angry shower struck the carriage window, the wind howled, and he gathered from these signs that a sou'westerly gale would greet him on arrival at Plyn.

He snatched a few moments of sleep during the night, and then woke, pallid, unrefreshed, with a tremulous heart and shaking hands, as the train drew into the junction for Plyn. It was about seven-thirty in the morning, and the porter shouldered his box and placed it in the Plyn train. He was a young man, a stranger to Christopher, but the sound of his pleasant, west-country accent was like music to the ears of one who had not heard it for twelve years. Christopher Coombe, the wanderer who returned to his home.

The train shunted and groaned, the station-master whistled, and they were off.

The wide river stretching and turning away, the first sight of Truan woods fresh with their young green, the banks of yellow primroses clustered in the low valleys, and a glimpse of a blue carpet spread beneath the shivering trees, a carpet of bluebells and soft violets. The flaming gorse waved in the high hills, a lark hovered in the air, and the figure of a farmer with his team of horses paused for an instant on the skyline to watch the passing train.

Then the broad river widened, they were past the saw-mills now, past the farmhouse at the head of the creek, they were turning the bend and the white jetties swung into view, the tall dangling cranes, the masts of ships – sailing-vessels, steamers, dusty with clay. The rough harbour water, the weather-beaten horse-ferry making its way across to the farther hamlet, the sight of grey houses, grey smoke, wet shining roofs glistening in the morning sun – Plyn – home – home again once more.

The tears running down his face Christopher threw down

262

the carriage window. The wild wind tossed at his bare head, he breathed in the pure, salt-laden air, he caught a whiff of the open sea beyond the point.

Forgotten was London, forgotten were the long dreary years of toil and strife, of love, bitterness, desire, and frustration, these were things that had never counted, that had served as some evil dream to tear him from this place that was part of him.

He was home again, home to Plyn where he belonged, where he had always belonged before birth, before creation; Plyn with her lapping harbour water; her forest of masts, her hungry wheeling gulls, her whisper of peace and comfort to a lonely heart; Plyn with her own grey silent beauty.

Home; he tore open the carriage door and stepped upon the familiar platform. Nobody recognized him. He had been a careless boy of twenty-two when he sailed away, and now he was a man nearing thirty-five, who had suffered much and worked hard, a man whose fair hair was growing thin on the top, whose forehead was lined, and whose shoulders stooped. No, there was nobody here who knew him, no one he knew himself. There was a woman standing on the platform, with eyes red from weeping, and her mouth working strangely. She held her coat up to her chin. He did not know her though, and would have passed her by if she had not looked up at him oddly, with a half-glance of recognition.

She put out her hand timidly and touched his arm. 'Is it – is it you, Christopher?' she asked.

It was his sister Katherine.

'Why, Kate!' he started, 'I didn't recognize you, I wasn't thinking . . .'

At once she burst into a torrent of weeping.

'You're too late, brother, he's gone – he's gone.'

An icy hand clutched at Christopher's heart. 'What do you mean – Father – he's dead?'

'Lost – Christopher – lost last night and must be drowned. His cap and coat has been washed up on Pennytinny sands and the crabbers found the boat from the yard, cast adrift with

263

her boards broken. His body hasn't been recovered, it must be washed away, far out to sea.'

They clung to each other, brother and sister who had parted twelve years ago as boy and girl, and were now reunited, man and woman, after suffering and anguish.

'You're too late, Christopher, too late, he's gone . . .'

## 6

Christopher was kept too busy during these first days to allow himself to be weighed down by the shock of his father's death, there were many matters to which he must attend, bills to settle, and relatives to visit. The accounts seemed to have been kept very slackly at Ivy House, and Katherine told her brother, to his intense surprise, that since her father's illness Uncle Philip Coombe had possessed the handling of their affairs. Their wants had been very few, but at the same time the interest he had paid in to her quarterly from the shares in the *Janet Coombe* was certainly very little, and they had existed barely on Joseph's pension.

'But Father owned nearly all the shares of the schooner,' exclaimed Christopher, 'besides having interests in many other vessels. I know that for a fact, for he often told me so. He surely never sold any of his rights, did he?'

'Not to my knowledge,' replied Katherine, 'but then when he came over peculiar there is no knowing what he did not do.'

The next morning Christopher went down into the town to the office on the quay.

The name of Hogg and Williams still stood above the doorway, in spite of the fact that Williams too was dead, and that Philip Coombe alone held the power in his hands.

After sending in his name Christopher was kept waiting nearly twenty minutes, and finally when his patience was exhausted and he was about to leave, the clerk said that Mr Coombe was disengaged.

He found his uncle little changed, though he must be past sixty now. His face was as grey and colourless as ever, his sandy hair little streaked with grey. He looked up from his desk and motioned Christopher to a chair, as though it were only yesterday that they had parted.

'Well, nephew,' he said, 'I heard you were back again and wondered whether you would drop in and see me for old time's sake. You've altered tremendously. I should not have known you. And how is London? Did you make a fortune? I often searched the papers for mention of your name, "young Cornishman rises to sudden fame" sort of thing, but I never found you there.'

'I have not come to talk of my own affairs, Uncle,' answered Christopher, 'but of my dead father's, which I am told have been in your hands.'

'Quite so. Yes, I felt it my duty to relieve your sister, she seemed a timid, inexperienced sort of girl, with no knowledge of such matters. And my wretched brother – no doubt you know the whole story?'

'He was kept at Sudmin Asylum three years longer than was necessary, and at your express orders,' replied Christopher.

'Come, nephew, I am not going to quarrel with you. Your father was a raving madman in 1890, when you were enjoying yourself in London.'

'But my sister tells me he was never violent in any way – he never occasioned them bodily harm, until that night.'

Philip shrugged his shoulders.

'It merely proves that it is impossible to trust insanity,' he said. 'Of course your father would have broken out some time or other.'

'Not unless he was driven to it,' suggested Christopher. 'Who is to know what scene took place between you that Christmas Eve, eh – can you answer me that?'

Philip Coombe narrowed his eyes, his fingers tapped slowly on the desk before him. 'Have a care, nephew,' he said softly, 'you are playing a dangerous game. I am a powerful man in Plyn these days. Do you want to be arrested for libel?'

Christopher sat back into the chair from which he had half risen. It was impossible to get the better of his uncle.

266

'All right, Uncle Philip, you have won again. The past must be past, and it is I who will bear the blame. But let us attend to business. I wish to know the exact amount of my father's estate.'

'I must tell you that my brother was grossly careless in his affairs, I had a great deal of trouble to put them to rights. For instance, he owed this firm a considerable amount. I had to arrange this naturally, in my capacity as senior partner, and putting aside his relation to me. When all these various accounts were paid – well – there was very little left. I have all the papers quite in order should you wish to see them.'

'What about the shares in various vessels, and most particularly the *Janet Coombe*?' asked Christopher.

'The sums from these amounted to very little,' answered his uncle. 'And in fact I was obliged to sell his shares in the *Janet Coombe* in order to pay for his keep at the asylum.'

'You mean you made them over to yourself?'

'That is, perhaps, a more brutal way of putting it. You could scarcely expect me to pay for his internment out of my own pocket.'

Christopher seized his hat with trembling hands.

'God,' he said. 'I'll have the law on you for this.'

Philip laughed. 'You will find that extremely difficult and embarrassing to yourself. I have done nothing that is not perfectly within legal rights. Go read up the law, nephew, and return when you have done so.'

The nephew was beaten, and he had the sense to realize it.

'If there is a God above, you will be punished for this one day, Uncle Philip,' he said slowly.

'I am glad to hear your exalted opinion, nephew. You were always cut out for a failure, as I often told your father. So it is to be enemies, eh?'

'I could never be your friend.'

'Few men care to have me as their enemy, I give you my warning here and now.'

'I am not afraid of you.'

'Found your courage, have you? You lost it when you went to sea twelve years ago if I remember, and your father lost his reason at the same time.'

Christopher went out into the street without a word.

## 7

Christopher Coombe was a proud man when he brought his wife and sons home for the first time. They drove through the long street of Plyn, and the horse climbed steadily up the back-breaking hill to the house that stood, ivy-covered, in its plot of garden.

Christopher led his wife to the large bedroom over the porch. 'This is ours. Tell me that you are pleased with it all and that you will not miss London too much?'

She smiled at him, and shook her head.

'Here, Dad,' cried Willie, leaning out of the window, 'the ivy's thick here like a tree. Thick enough for climbing.'

'Come out of it at once,' called his mother anxiously, 'you'll be breaking your neck.'

Willie jumped unwillingly from the window, and turned his back upon the branches where Joseph Coombe, his grandfather, had climbed to greet Janet — long, long ago.

'Run and wash your hands, boys,' said their father, 'for supper will be ready.'

Bertha laid her coat and hat on the bed, the big double bed where Thomas and Janet Coombe had lain side by side, sixty, seventy years back.

'It's a nice room,' she said to her husband, 'it has such a happy atmosphere.'

Christopher sighed and laid his head against her cheek.

'I'm so glad we've come home,' he whispered.

Then they went downstairs to supper, leaving the room to the first stars and the shadows.

Once they were settled down and no longer strange to Plyn, Christopher took up his work at the Yard as business manager. He was touched by the way he had been welcomed home again, and was determined to assist his cousins and Uncle Herbert in keeping 'Coombe's Yard' on the same high level it had always been.

Never again, he feared, would it know quite the same prosperity it had experienced during his grandfather Thomas and his Uncle Samuel's time. Year by year now the steamships were growing in importance, big clumsy vessels of iron or steel, built for power and not for beauty.

It was strange how easily Christopher fell into his old ways of living after twelve years' absence, and stranger still, he considered, how now that his youth was past his one-time restlessness and discontent had also departed.

He saw now that it was he who had been narrow in the old days, not those around him, and that by forgetting himself and watching the lives of the people he had discovered an inner source of happiness which had, hitherto, been unpossessed.

When the *Janet Coombe* returned to Plyn, Christopher descended the hill at once to greet Dick, and to ask pardon for that day of desertion twelve years ago.

He was greatly moved to find himself once more on the deck of the old schooner. It was true he had known three months' hardship and misery in her, but she was a plucky, wonderful little vessel for all that. She was nearly forty years old, she had braved every kind of sea and weather, and had never belied her reputation for speed or shamed her builders, nor drowned a man who sailed in her. She had been the pride and joy of his father's heart, and a symbol of beauty to his own childhood.

He explained the grace of her lines to Harold and Willie as they pulled round her in a dinghy, and showed them the stately little figurehead beneath the bowsprit, who had not changed in all the years, save for the dimming of her white paint and the blue feather in her hat.

'That's your great-grandmother, boys,' said Christopher. 'She was a very splendid woman by all accounts and greatly loved in Plyn.'

'Did you ever know her, Dad?' asked Harold.

'No, sonnie, she died before I was born.'

'D'you think she's frightened up there when the sea's rough?' said little Willie awestruck.

'I've heard my father say she didn't know the meaning of the word fear when she was alive,' replied Christopher, shading his eyes with his hand to see more clearly.

'Grandfather was proud of the ship and her, I guess,' said Harold after a minute's silence. 'She looks alive enough now, don't she, Dad?'

'Yes, boy, I reckon she does.'

The three of them gazed up at Janet, high above their heads, her eyes gazing seaward, her chin in the air.

'Look, she's smiling,' laughed Willie.

Then they pulled away towards Plyn, leaving the ship to the ebb tide and the gulls.

# 8

I t seemed to Christopher these times that no day dawned alike in Plyn. He would rise in the mornings keen and refreshed, eager to get to his work and be out in the open, and content at the prospect of a full day in front of him.

He soon became very fond of his steady, kindly hearted cousins. Tom was another Samuel, James another Herbert, and Christopher respected and loved them as his father Joseph had loved his brothers. This work too, once fancied as monotonous, was varied and absorbing, it was like a miracle to watch the gradual growth and shaping into a stately vessel from what had been loose timbers and rough planks.

Christopher had long since got over his old distrust of the sea, and during the summer and even the fine days in winter when a boat could get outside the harbour, he would accompany the boys on some fishing or sailing expedition. He was now as steady in a boat as on the land. He was careful and safe, never reckless like Joseph had been, but with a keen eye to the winds and currents, and seldom going wrong in his estimate of the weather. Deep in his heart he felt he owed it to his father to give some measure of his life to the sea, and it was with this thought in his mind that he volunteered as a member of the Plyn lifeboat crew. His name and his steadiness won him a position, and it was a proud moment for Christopher when the offer of his services was accepted. He knew then that he had retrieved something of the honour that had left him when he deserted the *Janet Coombe*, and that Joseph himself would have looked into his eyes with love and forgiveness.

The sea and the earth were dear to Christopher because

he had discovered them so late, and because he had once known the lesser things, tawdry and valueless.

And side by side with his love for them grew his love for humanity, a great tenderness for simple people whose lives were unswept by restlessness and fever, who lived for their women and their children, for their little joys and sorrows, who worked daily through the long years at the tasks their forefathers had done, who climbed on Sundays the path across the fields to worship their God in Lanoc Church.

Christopher talked with them, and moved amongst them, he saw the beauty of the old people and the tenderness of children, he listened to their calm minds, he sorrowed at their partings and rejoiced at their laughter, he perceived the strength and kindliness of men, the instinct and loveliness of women. He knew that until now he had lived without wisdom, without truth, but from henceforth he would dwell for ever in the high places amongst the very humble, the very lowly, that he had been born only to come to this understanding, to give help to those who called unto him, to love with them, suffer with them, to go his way asking for no reward, no ultimate thanksgiving, only to gladden his heart with the light that shone upon the faces of these people.

# 9

In April 1906, Jennifer Coombe was born. Her coming was a great joy to Christopher. When the two boys were babies he had been passing through a critical period of his life, but now he had no worries, and there was nothing to prevent him from giving his whole time to this daughter of his.

She went to her father readily at quite an early age. Her serious little face would lighten at his approach as she grew older, and she would wave her hands when he returned from work in the evenings, making as he always did straight for her cot or her pram. Bertha she seemed to accept as a necessary person to wash her, feed her, and clothe her; she submitted to these attentions gravely and with a placid air of resignation. Bertha it was who taught her that she could do this, but she mustn't do that, she was a good girl if she swallowed up her food, and did not cry at bed-time, but she was a naughty girl if she bit her toenails or wetted her drawers.

But it was Daddy who lifted her on his shoulders and ran with her round the garden, it was Daddy who let her ride horses on his foot, and it was to Daddy she whispered she was sorry in the evening, if there had been some scene during the day.

It was pleasant to have a young child about the house, for Harold and Willie were grown to be young men now who shaved regularly and smoked, though the elder was not yet twenty-one.

Richard Coombe, who was now fifty, felt that it was too late for him to start afresh, and as long as he was fit and able, he would continue to skipper the gallant little schooner in her fight for freights.

Albert Coombe had left his barque and was gone into steam; he now commanded a five-thousand-ton vessel belonging to a company at Adelaide, and he spent most of his time in Australian waters.

Charlie Coombe had returned to England after the conclusion of the Boer war, and had put in a few weeks at Plyn, but he was soon away again with his regiment, and was now stationed in India.

Kate Coombe was married and had left Plyn to live in Yorkshire.

So Christopher had none of his own family with him in Plyn, he was the only one to remain faithful to his home. He seemed closer to cousins Dick and Fred, and Tom and James at the Yard, than he had ever been to his two brothers. Christopher seemed to have found his way into the hearts of folk. There was always a welcome for him and a smile in the poorer cottages. People felt that here was someone who had suffered and was made sweeter by his suffering, here was one who accepted life patiently and without pride, who offered his sympathy and understanding to any who made call upon it.

Christopher felt that he had indeed reached safe anchorage after his weary wandering. The future years stretched peacefully in front of him and the ever-growing wonder and beauty of little Jennifer filled his days with a blessed sensation of promise and fulfilment.

# 10

By the autumn of 1911, orders came few and far between down to the Yard. It seemed that no more schooners or barquentines were being built; owners were commanding iron and steel vessels from the up-to-date yards in the big ports, and the ever-sounding hammer and saw was infrequently heard in Plyn these days. The trade grew yearly for the clay, many more ships lay alongside the jetties than had done so in Christopher's boyhood.

The town thrived and flourished, land was thrown open for building, new houses were springing up where once had been fields, and wide highroads stretched across the country instead of the narrow winding lanes. Farmers went to market now on motor bicycles and Ford cars, the old gingles were scrapped and the ponies turned out to grass.

Herbert, now seventy-five, did little but shake his head and declare that Plyn had fallen upon evil times, and he withdrew from activities and contented himself in grumbling.

Tom and James, men of over fifty, who had been boys during the great shipbuilding boom, could but submit to fate and progress and put as bold a face on the matter as possible.

So it seemed as though there would be no young blood to follow on and continue the Coombe tradition, which saddened Christopher greatly at times, and he was often thankful that his father Joseph was not alive to see the decay and pity of it. His two boys, of course, now earned their own living, and could look after themselves. But it was a sad outlook all the same, for unless steady work could be continued it seemed as though the Yard would fall into total disuse.

In the autumn of 1911, with the prospect of a long winter ahead and a minimum of work, the Coombe cousins met at the Yard to discuss business. Christopher's heart bled to see the expressions on the faces of the two men, once so confident and determined, and now set in deep lines of worry and doubt. He would have given his own home to be able to be at that moment rich and prosperous, and order with sublime folly a fleet of schooners. They discussed plans for the coming winter from every conceivable angle of hope, but could hit upon nothing that offered certainty of employment. It was not until the meeting was about to break up, having arrived at no solution to their problem, when Christopher remembered Uncle Philip. After all, he was their own kith and kin their own flesh and blood, he had risen by his brains to a position of authority in Plyn, he was prosperous, surely he could, at seventy-two, with no ties or family of his own, hold out a helping hand to his people.

'I'd as soon draw blood from a stone as draw money from him,' said James Coombe grimly. 'The old skinflint, he's never given a penny to his relatives nor to charity, far as I can see. What's the use of makin' beggars of ourselves, to ask his charity, knowin' as 'twill be refused. My father reared fifteen of us, an' I know 'twas hard for him at times, but never a suggestion from Uncle Philip to put any of us boys in business. My brothers are scattered now, three at sea, two dead, one over to Falmouth, and one to Carne, none of 'em prosperous.'

'He might ha' offered poor Aunt Mary somethin', after my father and mother were taken, but he didn't even go to her funeral or see that she was buried decent,' said Tom.

'I know folks always said 'twas he who sent your own father crazy, Chris,' remarked James. 'Uncle Joe would ha' soon recovered if 't'addent been for Uncle Philip puttin' in his spoke. There's none know the trewth o' that Christmas Eve yet, nor never will, I reckon. Then keepin' him there at Sudmin those five years, 'twas shameful, an' desarvin' hard words, but he'll never get 'em, he's too wily for we by long chalks.'

'I know only too well the force of what you are saying,' said Christopher. 'No one can say I have any affection for

Uncle Philip. He drove my poor father mad. But he is a man of authority in Plyn and it would do no harm to turn to him now for help. After all, he can only refuse us.'

'I don't know,' said Tom slowly, 'he's that peculiar with his grudge agen his own folk, ther's no knowin' what he might conceive to harm 'em.'

'Come, but that's nonsense, Tom. A man of seventy-two is past makin' trouble for us or anybody else. Besides, for why?'

'Sounds foolish, maybe, but I wouldn't trust 'un now, no more than ever. I won't trust Philip Coombe till he's lyin' in his coffin, an' then I'll cross my fingers an' whisper a charm.'

'Tom's right,' muttered James, 'the fellow bain't human, he's an evil pisky what never did belong to Coombe blood – I'll lay my oath to it.'

'Yes – but listen here, something has got to be done and quickly – you know it both of you, sitting here and shaking our heads isn't going to bring employment and save the Yard. I'm not afraid of Uncle Philip, he's done me all the harm he can, in the past, and that's over, thank God. I'm going down to the office this very day to speak my mind.'

'You're a good fellow, Chris, but no good'll come of it – mark my words.'

Christopher would not listen to them, and that afternoon he made his way down the hill of Plyn to the office on the quay. He was admitted at once, and found his uncle standing on the hearth, warming his hands before a poor fire.

He showed no surprise at the appearance of his nephew. He rubbed his hands and smiled strangely.

'Well, you've come at last to see what I can do for you. That's it, is it not? I very rarely make a mistake, you know – very rarely.'

'I take the responsibility of this visit upon myself,' said Christopher steadily, 'my cousins were against it, being proud, independent characters. I have no such qualities, as you probably know.'

'So my brother Joseph's son admits his defeat. This humble attitude is very pleasing. Different to the old days. It's a sublime piece of irony that you should come to me in your trouble, after all that is past.'

'Ironic to you, maybe, Uncle, painful and bitter to me, and I do it for my cousins' sake alone.'

'Well, what do you expect me to do? Order a hundred-ton yacht for the races at Cowes next year? I suppose you think I'm made of money. Or perhaps you are hoping to build a schooner on the same lines as the old *Janet Coombe* which I shall probably scrap in a year or two. Want me to throw my money about just to give employment to a crowd of incompetents. Is that it?'

Christopher turned to the door.

'I see it is useless remaining any longer,' he said quietly. 'I'm sorry to have disturbed you, Uncle.'

'Hold on – hold on,' cried the man. 'Not so fast, I never said I wasn't going to help, did I? Not if the lot of you were starving would I give a penny to lift you out of it, unless it suited my purpose. Well, as it happens I have got work for you, and you may consider yourselves lucky. The whole business could probably be done much better and more thoroughly at Falmouth, but I am willing to risk it. You know the barque *Hesta*?'

'Yes, Uncle.'

'I've bought her, and want her re-classed. She's to be refitted altogether, and re-rigged as a three-masted auxiliary schooner. With a powerful motor she ought to be useful in coastal trade, though in all probability I shall lose on her. Now are you prepared down at the Yard to take this on?'

'Good heavens, Uncle, what do you suppose? This will be a godsend to us all.'

'You can take the winter over it, but I shall expect her to be completed by March.'

'Why, yes – of course, Uncle. How can I thank you? I was over-hasty just now I admit, and here's my apology for it.'

'Don't talk nonsense, fool,' snapped Philip. 'I'm giving you the work because I want it done, and that's all there is to it. Now you can clear out of here, and carry your precious news to your thick-headed cousins. I want the work well done, mind, no niggling and poor material.'

'No, Uncle. Good day, and good health.'

Christopher left his uncle's office with something of the boyish spirits that had been his over twenty years before, when he had set forth to sail in the *Janet Coombe* with the false hope of London to fill his dreaming mind. He had not changed so greatly after all.

Once again the hammers sounded in Coombe's Yard, the slip was busy with workmen, and on the beach beside the old wall stood a big vessel, stripped bare of all her gear, looking, with her plain hull and dismasted deck, for all the world like a ship newly launched.

Tom Coombe and his Cousin James worked with straightened shoulders and an air of authority, they could lift their heads once more in Plyn and feel they were doing real business at last, after so many idle months, and wasting their skill on little pulling boats and prams.

Christopher, as business manager, left the actual manual part of the labour to his cousins and their workmen, while he busied himself with the ordering of materials and all necessary articles, interviewing firms, writing letters to places up-country, and taking a great deal of trouble and interest in the whole concern. Uncle Philip had said he wanted the work well done, and so it should be, the Coombes would not spare themselves in their undertaking.

It was a custom in Plyn, and generally in the west country, to have terms of long credit. Folk trusted one another, and did not bother to send their account at quarterly dates, but waited until they had a need for their money, knowing that the necessary sum would be immediately forthcoming. The Coombes for generations had followed this old-standing custom, and had never found it at fault. They had always known with whom they were dealing, and orders went by word of mouth and never by written contract.

The winter months passed, and the days began to brighten. Soon the work at the Yard would be finished, and the ship ready for sea. She looked a fine, smart vessel now, and the

Coombes were proud of her. The first week in March, Christopher had a nasty attack of influenza, and was laid up in bed. Just before he was taken ill he sent the *Hesta*'s account up to the office, as the firms in Plymouth and elsewhere had begun to write for their money. Then when the influenza came upon him he left word with Tom to attend to the business.

A week after this when he was able to move downstairs, and was sitting before the fire in the parlour, Bertha came in with a worried face and said that both cousins Tom and James were outside and wished to see him on a matter of grave importance.

'Let them come in, by all means,' said Christopher in some surprise. 'I hope nothing upsetting has occurred.'

The two men entered the room, and Christopher saw at once by their faces that something of great urgency had brought them there.

'I wouldn't have disturbed you seein' as you'm poorly,' began Tom, 'but for a terrible thing that has happened. See here, this letter came for us this mornin'.'

Christopher took it from him and read the following:

To Thos Coombe and Sons

Dear Sirs,
With regard to your account for the re-conditioning of the barque *Hesta* we find you have grossly over-charged and far exceeded the limits intended by this firm. As you produced no estimate at the outset, and appear to have acted entirely on your own responsibil-ity without once consulting us, we do refuse here and now to pay such a sum, and you must make the necessary reductions or forfeit the entire proceeding.
Yours faithfully,
Hogg and Williams

Christopher turned the letter over in his hands and gazed blankly at his cousins.

'What does it mean?' he said stupidly. 'I don't follow at all.'

'It means one thing, Chris,' replied Tom slowly. 'It means that we're ruined.' He rose and paced up and down the room while James said not a word.

'But look here, cousins,' cried Christopher wildly, 'there must be some mistake. He can't refuse to pay, it's impossible, it's inhuman. Have you been down to the office?'

'I went direckly the letter was read by us,' answered Tom, 'straight down and demanded an interview. He didn't keep me long. He said as we'd been tryin' to rob his firm, that we'd deliberately gone about the work in an unbusinesslike fashion without estimates nor nothin', that he'd given no orders for such and such to be done, an' it was our own fault to ha' landed ourself in such a mess. He was'n goin' to pay, an' he'd have the law on his side if we wanted to fight. That's about the sum of it all, Chris.'

'So we came right along up to you to see as what you suggest,' broke in James.

Christopher looked from one to the other in bewilderment and horror.

'But we've only acted as Coombes has always done,' he said, 'we trusted people and people trusted us. This sort of thing hasn't ever occurred before. Ask anyone in Plyn, they'd say the same. Hogg and Williams can't do us like this – I say they can't, why . . .'

'Hold on, Chris,' cried James, ''tain't no mortal use in appealin' to folk. It's Philip Coombe an' the law we've got to fight now. It's a fight, or ruin as Tom says.'

'Aye, an' look at this, an' this,' said Tom fiercely, and he drew from his pocket bills from Plyn, Plymouth, London, and elsewhere. 'These are all floodin' in by every post, an' more to come. Goods and materials ordered in our name, for which we expected payment from Hogg and Williams to be able to meet 'em. He won't pay, an' we can't. It's ruin, I tell ye – ruin an' the finish to Coombes.'

He buried his head in his hands.

'It's not true,' murmured Christopher, 'it's not true, there must be a way out, I swear there must.'

The room was silent, and no man spoke. Tom took his handkerchief from his pocket and blew his nose. James whistled slowly between his teeth and gazed stubbornly into the fire. From the kitchen came the sound of Bertha laying the plates for lunch. Jennifer ran past the window calling to her mother. The three men in the parlour made no move. Then Christopher moved unsteadily from his chair and held out his hands to his cousins.

'We're all in this equally,' he said, 'and we'll fight or fall together. Uncle Philip may have the law, but we've got the truth. I'm not afraid.'

Then James shrugged his shoulders and laughed harshly.

'Who's ever got the better o' Philip Coombe yet?' he asked. 'Truth b'ain't no weapon for me, it's cunning an' sly dealin's that brings a man to prosperity these days. He knows what he's about, I tell ye – an' he's got us beat right from the start.'

The three cousins gazed at one another like dumb things, lost and helpless.

# 12

The next weeks were fraught with anxiety and distress. Christopher lay awake at nights, tossing by his wife's side, praying for some ray of light to show itself in the maze which had grown up about him and his cousins, and which threatened to entangle them for ever.

By day he worked with the lawyer, laying before the man every atom of evidence he could obtain to show that the Coombes had acted justly and within reason, and that the fault lay with the firm of Hogg and Williams.

The solicitor, familiar with all the machinery and quackery of the law, did his best to assemble a strong case from this scattered heap of muddled facts and material, but he warned his clients that his hope of success was small, that however sincerely and honestly they had gone about their business, legally they had acted wrongly.

On the fifth of April the case came up before the court at Sudmin. The cousins set off by car, hired from the Plyn Garage, along the same winding road that Joseph had taken, over twenty years before, in the little trap, beside the keeper from the asylum. The day was wild and stormy, and rain fell in torrents, the wind reaching gale force at times. The memory of the father was much in the mind of the son this day. The same man who had sent Joseph to desolation was sending Christopher to ruin.

At the end of the day Christopher learned that the action had failed. Hogg and Williams had triumphed, and Coombes must go into liquidation to absolve their debts.

Coombes ruined, Coombes in liquidation. The old sign would be torn down, and the yard sold. The slip, where so many brave and lovely ships had been built and launched, would fall into decay. One of the greatest traditions of Plyn would be no more.

It was a sad homecoming for Christopher that night. Half stunned by his misfortune and the ruin that had come to his cousins, he let himself into the house, scarce noticing the howling gale that tore at his clothes, nor heeding the angry sea that spent its fury on the rocks below.

Bertha came to meet him, and one glance at her husband's face told her the worst had befallen them.

He wandered hopelessly into the parlour, his streaming coat still on his back, and stood before the fireplace gazing before him.

Supper time came, and he had not moved. Harold was returned from his work and a late class, he had heard in the town the result of the case, and he went at once to his father and laid a hand on his shoulder.

'Don't worry, Dad,' he said gently, 'we'll pull through all right. Everyone is on your side. It won't be as hard as you think.'

Christopher raised his head and looked at his son. He tried to smile but the effort was pitiful. He could not respond to their sympathy, and his heart felt frozen. It seemed to him that he would never be able to feel again, that the shock had in some sort paralysed his nerves and left him without the sensation of emotion. He was beaten, finished. He could fight no more, feel no more.

The meal passed in silence. Little Jennifer was aware of the atmosphere; when she began a sentence in a loud voice about something she had seen during the day her mother bade her sharply to be quiet, and her brother frowned. She started and turned crimson, unused to a scolding for no reason, and lowered her head over her plate. She felt her lip tremble and her heart swell, the corners of her mouth turned down for all her efforts to prevent them. The tears welled up into her eyes. She tried to force her milk pudding down her tightened throat, but it would not go. She did not understand why they were cross with her. She choked suddenly and the spoon dropped on her plate. When Christopher saw her tears something seemed to move inside his heart; he rose from the table and left the room. He drew on his oilskins and his boots and let himself out into the blinding storm. Jennifer had cried. Everything else had failed to rouse him, the broken expressions on the faces of his cousins, his wife's sympathy, his son's helpful words, they all had failed to stir him from his lethargy of despair. But the tears in Jennifer's eyes – these had brought him to his senses once again: more than this, they had brought him to a cold, unwavering decision that was leading him from the house, down the hill, through the streets, up the road to his uncle's house.

Philip Coombe must die, and Christopher would kill him with his own hands. No turning back now, no softening of his heart. Through the streets of Plyn went Christopher, while the wild winds shook the buildings, and the lashing broke against the quays. There stood the bleak house at the end of the terrace, there was the light in the upper window.

Christopher cared not that he would swing for his deed. Tomorrow he would give himself up willingly to the hands of the law.

Uncle Philip must die. Christopher climbed the steps of the silent house, he clutched at the iron railing, and beat with his fist against the door. The wind shouted in his ear and the rain blinded him. Murder was in his heart, murder gleamed in his stricken eyes, love and compassion were dead intangible things, no longer possessed, no longer part of him. By killing Uncle Philip he would destroy himself. He knew this, he believed this, but he did not care.

'There's no salvation,' he thought, 'we're doomed both of us, Philip Coombe and I, but I'll suffer in eternity to have him suffer now. There's nothing can save him.'

For a moment he paused, preparing for one tremendous blow that should summon his uncle from the room above. As he waited a sudden startling crash sounded in his ears, followed by another and then another. Three reports flung into this

287

night of hell and chaos. Three rockets rose into the air, borne by the sobbing wind—

It was the Lifeboat Call.

In less than five minutes the crew was assembled on the quay, some half-clad, buttoning their oilskins, some fumbling with the strings of their sou'westers. Last of all came Christopher Coombe, staggering, breathless from his mad run down the hill. He took his place in line with the others, he jumped with them into the waiting boat, and pulled towards the lifeboat moored some fifty yards away. It was not long before the coverings were ripped aside, the moorings cast, and the men at their places on the thwarts.

Beyond the point a ship was speeding to destruction, there were live men on board who must be saved. This was the one thought in the mind of each member of the lifeboat's crew, the only thought. Christopher bent to his oar, the sweat pouring into his eyes, his arms nearly wrenched from their sockets. Gone was the lust for murder. He was filled with exultation. He had been born for this moment that was lifting him from desolation to the heights of splendour. Over the sweeping seas at the harbour mouth, beyond the bar, beyond the rocks, away to the helpless ship that should not call in vain.

He had no fear of the breaking sea. The knowledge of this was a triumph to him, something overwhelming and strange, he knew that in all his life he had never experienced the feeling of courage and strength that he now possessed. The forty-six years he had lived counted as nothing compared to this moment. The lifeboat call had come to him as a summons, a demand into the depths of his being, bidding him rise and enter the light, enter into promise and fulfilment. It seemed to him that the courage of his father Joseph had become part of him, that in some great and incomprehensible way they were together now, and fighting hand in hand. Someone had called to him out of the blackness of the night, someone had cried that his time was come.

288

All was forgotten save this finding of himself and his father Joseph. The dim shape of the stricken ship loomed out of the darkness, he heard the shouts and the cries of men, he heard the grim shaking of the torn rigging above the thunder of the breakers.

Then out of the mist she swept, desolate, forlorn, like a great and mournful gull with its wings broken, heading for the rocks. Christopher raised his eyes and saw the shuddering, trembling vessel, he looked at the bows and beheld the white figurehead, her hands at her breast, her proud face turned towards the surf upon the shore. Straight into his eyes she looked. As the ship plunged in the trough of the sea he read the white letters on the starboard bow – *Janet Coombe*.

The lifeboat drew alongside, borne on the swell of a big sea. The skipper stood upon the deck; he placed his hands to his mouth and shouted; 'We can save the ship yet,' he roared above the fury of wind and sea. 'We can save her if the tugs come quick an' get her in tow.'

'No – no,' cried the men from the lifeboat, 'jump now, all of you, jump for your lives. The ship must go.'

The schooner's crew tumbled like scared sheep into the waiting boat, but the skipper shook his head. Then Christopher rose from his place and clung to the rope's end that his cousin had flung. 'There's time yet!' he yelled. 'Look there!'

He pointed to the harbour entrance, where slowly round the point, plunging and rearing into the gigantic seas, came the lights of the two tugs.

'They'll do it, I tell you, they'll do it,' shouted Christopher, 'get on board, some of you, to lend a hand in making fast the hawser when they come.' The poor, frightened crew cowered in the boat, too exhausted and wet to move, while the men in the lifeboat hesitated, glancing from the tugs to the foaming rocks. They would never be in time.

'Stay in your place, Coombe,' ordered the coxswain of the boat. 'It's your life you'll be riskin' if you climb aboard that vessel. There's none can save her now.'

Another big sea lifted the ship towards the waiting rocks.

Christopher smiled, and catching hold of the rope's end he swung himself aboard the schooner, and stood by the side of his cousin Dick, the skipper.

The lifeboat hung away from the helpless ship, and the men lay on their oars, ready to stand by when she struck. The *Janet Coombe* was deserted save for the two cousins, who waited, silent and motionless, as the tugs drew nearer and the ship swept on to destruction. Christopher knew that they were not alone, he knew that Joseph was beside him giving him his courage, he knew that Janet was with him bidding him be calm. He had never known danger and now it was before him. The great cliffs stared up towards him, the smouldering surf rang in his ears like a wild sweet song. That moving thing in the mist was the tug, that flying, tearing rope was the flung hawser. Blindly, instinctively, Christopher and Dick worked in the darkness, yelling at one another, stumbling on the sea-swept deck.

There was a shudder and a crash as the ship struck the first ledge of rock – but the hawser held. A gigantic sea swept the face of the vessel – but the hawser held. Inch by inch over the tumbled breaking sea plunged the little tugs, with the *Janet Coombe* in tow, a jagged hole in her bottom, the hold fast filling with the churning water. Another sea swept Christopher from his feet and hurled him, face downward, upon a broken spar. Dick clung to the wheel, spent and exhausted. 'Give us a hand here, Chris,' he called. 'Just a hand, lad, for the worst is over now.'

But his cousin never moved.

When Christopher opened his eyes he saw the black skies above his head, and he felt the soft rain fall upon his face.

He was lying on the old cobble stones of the quay, and it seemed to him that the eyes of many folk were upon him, and that they were talking amongst themselves. He tried to move, and as he did so the blood rose in his throat and choked him. Then he remembered that he had been fighting, he

290

remembered one wild stupendous moment on the *Janet Coombe*, when the hawser held.

Someone wiped away the blood from his mouth.

'Did we save her?' he asked.

A voice spoke in his ear. 'Aye, you saved her, but she'll never sail again. There's a hole in her bottom, an' the keel clean ripped away. It's the mud now for the *Janet Coombe*, though you kept her from the rocks.'

'I'm glad for that,' he said, 'I'm glad she's safe.'

Now their voices sounded faint in his ears, and he could no longer see their faces. The sky was speckled with queer dancing lights. He felt very weary, very tired. People lifted his head and held him in their arms. They were all slipping away from him though, he thrust out his hands towards them and they were gone.

'Tell Father I wasn't afraid,' said Christopher. 'Tell Father I'll never fear the sea no more, for I've conquered it at last.'

# Book Four
## Jennifer Coombe (1912–1930)

Sweet Love of youth, forgive, if I forget thee,
While the world's tide is bearing me along;
Other desires and other hopes beset me,
Hopes which obscure, but cannot do thee wrong.

E. BRONTË

. . . And there are bosoms bound to mine
With links both tried and strong;
And there are eyes whose lightening shine
Has warmed and blest me long:
Those eyes shall make my only day,
Shall set my spirit free,
And chase the foolish thoughts away
That mourn your memory.

E. BRONTË

# 1

Jennifer Coombe was six when her father Christopher died. The horror and fear that this cast upon her was to become part of her childhood, and even when she grew up, with him already many years in his grave, the memory of the death haunted and tormented her, causing by its presence a strange, unaccountable dread of the future. She would always remember, somewhere in the dark desolate places of her mind, the night that he had gone from her, never to return.

It was like the coming of a great darkness upon the glory of her little day. Hitherto life had been a succession of months, a following of winter upon summer; moments when she could play in the garden for hours on end, and moments when she must stay in the house with her toys because of the wet skies and blustering winds. Living was a matter of routine to her. She awoke in the mornings with a song on her lips and a happy expectation in her heart, reaching for her teddy bear, and glancing across to the big bed where her father and mother lay. Only a tuft of Daddy's fair hair was visible, he slept on his front with his face buried in his hands.

When Mother had washed and finished dressing, she went downstairs, and then Jennifer's moment had come. She scrambled out of her cot, and climbed on to the big double bed. She tripped over Daddy's foot beneath the blanket, and he stirred restlessly in his sleep. Then she struggled with the sheet and curled in beside him, contented with the strange warmth of his body and the comfort it gave to her.

He opened one eye and seeing her there he smiled, and held her close.

'Hullo, Jenny!' he said.

At breakfast she sat beside him, and it was he who poured

the extra helping of cream on to her porridge, making the whole an island surrounded by a white lake. Then he was off, and away to his work at the yard, with Jennifer running to the end of the garden path with him, her short legs striving to keep in time with his long stride. She swung backwards and forwards on the creaking gate, watching his back as he disappeared down the hill, waiting for his turn as he reached the corner and waved his last farewell.

In summer-time he took her on to the cliffs by the Castle, and peering over his shoulder she saw the sea stretching away for ever like part of the sky, the sea whose murmur woke her in the mornings and whose whisper was the last thing she remembered before sleeping.

During the day the sound of it rang in her ears, summer and winter, always the sigh of the waves as they broke against the Castle rocks. When the rain came, and the mists, and the hollow echoing wind and sea shouted fierce and insistent, laughing at the wet gulls, Jennifer was never afraid. She could not imagine a world without the sea, it was something of her own that belonged to her, that could never be changed, that came into her dreams at nights and disturbed her not, bringing only security and peace. The sea was part of her life that could never be taken away from her, any more than her father could be taken from her.

When she lay in the narrow truckle bed at nights, her last biscuit eaten, and the last candle blown, she listened one moment to the hum and murmur of her father's voice in the room beneath. Soon, aware of the thin ceiling boards, he raised his voice and called up to her, 'Are you asleep, Jenny?' This was her last signal that all was well. She turned on her side, sighing for no reason, and fell asleep knowing that he would never forsake her, knowing that in the morning she would wake to see his fair tousled head buried in the pillow of the big bed beside her mother.

At last the day came when Daddy went to Sudmin. He started early in a motor-car with the uncles, and the novelty of this was exciting to her, but he forgot to wave his hand.

It was dark before he returned, and as she ran into the hall to kiss him he put her away from him gently, and went into the parlour. No one spoke at supper. When Jennifer could bear it no longer, and her mother scolded her, she burst into tears, and above her mug of milk she saw her Daddy's face, white and fearful.

He rose and went out of the room. She struggled to free herself from the table, calling to him to come back to her, but he never heard.

Then her mother carried her upstairs and undressed her without a word, tumbling her clothes off her and forgetting to fold them up, tucking her so tightly in her bed that she felt imprisoned.

The house seemed still and ghostly without the customary voice below; no star shone through the chink tonight, and the wind shuddered in the ivy branches. She cried softly to herself, her thumb in her mouth, the salt tears running down her cheeks.

Suddenly came a sound that she was never to forget, the sound of three rockets fired into the night.

As the last echo died away Jennifer held out her arms and screamed: 'Daddy – don't go from me, don't go from me.'

She ran out on to the passage in her white nightgown, distressed, tormented – frightened, she who had never known fear before. The house was ringing with voices and questions. Now her mother was running upstairs and seizing her in her arms. She was being dressed, she was fumbling with her gaiters, her thick coat was buttoned to her throat and a heavy shawl wound about her mouth.

Harold was swinging a lantern in his hands, he picked her up and handed the lantern to his mother. They ran down to the quay, they moved amongst a throng of people, calling, questioning, their voices carried away by the wind. And Jennifer pulled at her mother's skirt, 'Where's Daddy – where's Daddy?' but nobody answered her; once more they were running up the hill, to the high cliffs where dark figures moved amongst one another in the mist. The wind blew at her, the rain stung her eyes.

Now they were sweeping down the hill, now time disappeared in a hopeless confusion of horror, and now all that remained in the depths of a child's memory was the parlour in the early morning, the floor wet and muddied from the footsteps of many people; Mother, her face weird and twisted to one side stretching out her hand to Harold, and Jennifer herself peering round the corner of the door, looking beyond them to something that was covered by a blanket on the stiff horsehair sofa. . . .

The *Janet Coombe* lay at the entrance to Polmear Creek. The tide had deserted her, and she leaned pitifully on one side, half buried in this bed of mud and slime. Her bottom timbers had been torn from her by the jagged rocks at the harbour mouth, and the water gushed from her side, rust-coloured, like the blood from a living thing.

No longer was she part of the wind and the sea, no longer would she answer the call and pass away upon the surface of the water, free and triumphant. Adventure would claim her no more, nor beauty, nor the white skies; the singing gales would be a memory now. Gone was the stinging foam and the kissing spray, gone was the rattle of shrouds, the thud of canvas, the songs and the laughter of men.

Here her spars drooped listless and forlorn, her sails hung like rags upon the bent yards, and she herself was no more the pride and glory of Plyn but a shunned wreck, stricken and forsaken. A gull cried mournfully above her decks, and spreading his wings he took himself away to the high hills and the sun.

In the bows of the ship the figurehead of Janet gazed towards Plyn. She saw Jennifer, part of herself and belonging to her; she saw Jennifer, lonely for the first time.

# 2

'Coombes' had gone into liquidation, and today the sale had taken place at the yard. The shipwright's hammer would be heard no longer, it was the auctioneer who took command and a representative of the firm of Hogg and Williams. The place was filled with inquisitive folk who had come to watch the sale, and also the faces of strangers, men from Plymouth and elsewhere, shopkeepers and managers knowing nothing of the Coombe family but all bent on the same mission, to secure payment of the debts due to them.

Bertha Coombe sat before the fire in her parlour, her two sons standing on either side.

They scarcely noticed Jennifer in the corner of the room, white-faced and silent; anyway she was too small, she would not understand.

'It's a bare pittance, Mum,' Harold was saying, 'just enough to keep you and Jenny until she is big enough to earn her own living. I always imagined Dad had scraped together more than that, but it appears he drew from this pile to help the business down at the yard. All gone west now, of course.'

'There's no need to worry, though,' said Willie, 'I can spare some of my pay, and Harold too for that matter.'

Bertha fumbled for her handkerchief. 'I always was against him belonging to that horrible lifeboat,' she said, wiping her eyes. 'That terrible funeral, and that awful windy little church-yard . . .' She blew her nose and glanced at Jennifer, who was watching her with scared eyes.

'Run and find your pinny, Jenny, or you'll spoil your new black dress.'

The child obeyed without a word, and as she ran upstairs she made a little picture in her mind of the damp cold church-yard. Clutching at the banisters she saw her daddy's old mack-intosh hanging on a peg in the hall; it moved slowly, caught by a draught from the open door of the parlour, and she was afraid – she knew not why.

Once more she crouched in the corner of the room and listened to the conversation, catching the sense of it now and again, and then going off into dreams of her own.

And the voices went on talking.

'. . . every day I spend in Plyn makes me more and more miserable. You had better see to things here, Harold, for I really don't feel strong enough. Of course Jenny and I can go and live with mamma in London . . .'

Where were they going? What was going to happen? She sat tight in her corner, fearful lest they should see her and send her from the room.

'That seems the best way out of the whole business.'

Words, words – grown-up people's mouths moving rapidly, tall figures standing by the mantelpiece rattling money in their pockets, Mother in her armchair deciding what was to be done.

When she woke up in the mornings she would look towards the bed to see if he had returned during the night. But her mother lay alone, her face upturned to the ceiling and her eyes closed. There was no one lying there beside her with his hair rumpled and his head buried in the pillow.

The threat of London drew nearer, now it was the day after tomorrow, now it was tomorrow. The house had a strange unreal appearance. The carpets were up, and some of the furni-ture gone. Where the pictures had hung on the walls there was a large brown stain, and a row of little black nails.

The trunks stood in the bedroom filled already with their clothes, and wisps of tissue paper lay strewn about the floor. The wardrobe and the chest of drawers gaped open, empty;

in the corner of the room there was a small heap of things that mother had thrown away, a broken photo frame, an old glove, some pins, and a faded red rosette off one of Jennifer's shoes. These things looked dusty and forlorn. Jennifer turned away from them with a shudder and tiptoed from the room that had grown too large suddenly and too bare.

They had a queer supper that last evening, they had eggs and bacon, and potted meat with their bread because the jam was finished. Jennifer felt sick, and she had a cold ache inside her she could not explain. Only the thought of wearing her new boots in the morning prevented her from crying.

The Day had come. Mother got up early, about six o'clock, and started cramming the last things in the trunk.

Harold and Willie kept running up and down the stairs. 'What about the keys?' someone shouted from the hall.

Jennifer crept from room to room seeking some measure of consolation. It seemed to her that the doors and windows gazed at her reproachfully, the tumbled bed she would never sleep in again had been stripped bare, and was now a strange thing made of little grey wires with knobs.

There was an old pin in a crack on the floor, and underneath the washstand lay her dirty sand shoes which mother had told her she could leave behind. In the soap dish was a half-finished tube of tooth paste.

'. . . Move out of the way, Jenny. We shall never get off at this rate. No, you can't take that collection of rubbish with you . . . Harold – Harold – will you come up and strap the hold-all . . .?'

Jennifer pattered after them in her new boots, but somehow they felt different from what they had done in the shop. They were a little tight, pinching her. Suddenly she turned white, and the tears welled into her eyes.

'Mother,' she whimpered, 'Mother, I don't feel very well.'

The basin was fetched and she was sick.

'I don't want to go,' she screamed – 'I don't want to go.'

Mother kissed her, but the kisses were wet through the veil, and the gloved hand could not comfort her.

Harold and Willie stood helplessly by the door. 'I say — time's getting on. The bus'll be here in five minutes.'

Mother was dragging on Jennifer's frieze coat, she was cramming the tight velour hat on to her head, snapping the elastic under her chin. 'Oh! I don't want to go, oh! please, I don't want to go.'

But she was dragged downstairs, her teddy bear in her arms, and it seemed that the hall was full of people shaking hands with mother and there were jabbering voices talking too loudly.

They were in the bus now, and Jennifer tightly packed between Willie and mother.

The driver started his engine. 'Good-bye . . . good-bye . . .' She watched Ivy House left behind, empty and alone. From the open bedroom window the curtain was waving foolishly in the wind.

# 3

The earliest recollection of London to Jennifer Coombe was the call of bugles blowing from the barracks at the end of the street. They were the first things that woke her in the mornings, and the last things she heard before she fell asleep at night. In her mind they struck a note of incessant reminder that Plyn was far away, and that the sound of the sea would come to her no more. The bugles rang into her dreams, and she would wake with a start, and open her eyes upon the unfamiliar room with its massive wardrobe and its heavy curtains, and the chink of light that came to her from the window showed rows of slate roofs and thick chimney-pots stretching far into the distance.

Then there would be a sound on the landing outside, and the clang of a water-can in the passage. A knock on the door. Ethel the servant entered the room. She stumped across the floor with heavy footsteps, and drew aside the curtains with a crash. It seemed odd to Jennifer to be waited on, and she would have made friends with Ethel but for the fact of the brown mole on her chin. She slipped out of bed quietly and began to dress herself.

The gong would sound for prayers. Mother and Jennifer had to go downstairs and into the dining-room, and kneel at different chairs while the members of the boarding-house stole into the room. From her stool in the corner Jennifer could watch them coming downstairs, through a chink in the open door. She noticed that as soon as they reached the dining-room they put on different faces, something happened to their lips and their nostrils seemed pinched. Then there would be a rustle in the hall, and Jennifer cringed a little to herself, knowing that Grandmamma was just outside the door. Slowly she came into the room swaying from side to side, her great breasts heaving beneath her black dress, her white hair piled high on her head like a huge nest. As she moved she grunted to herself, and it took her nearly three minutes before she was seated in her chair, her bad foot on a cushion, and the Bible open before her.

Jennifer listened for the snap of her glasses, worn on a jumping piece of chain, and then the terrible voice boomed out – 'Our Father, which art in Heaven,' and a little chorus of voices followed her lead, anxious to do well.

The boarders gathered round the table for breakfast. She watched them over the rim of her cup, but if any of them met her eyes and spoke to her, she turned away and hung her head pretending she had not heard.

'Seeing so many new faces has made the child shy,' apologized her mother, 'she is generally such a talkative little creature.' And Jennifer clung to this weapon of shyness as a defence; she found that if she closed her mouth tight and gazed at the floor nobody took any notice of her and she was free to think by herself.

Only Grandmamma guessed that this was a trick. She knew that Grandmamma was watching her all the time. Once she had seen Jennifer take a piece of meat from her mouth and hide it under her spoon, and from that moment her eyes were upon her all the time, prying into her thoughts. 'Bertha, love,' said the terrible voice, 'I fear that the child is faddy about her food.'

'Why, no, Mamma, we have never had any trouble with her eating. You like the nice meat, don't you, Jenny?'

'Yes,' she mumbled, and sat quite still with her cheeks bulging, chewing the fat over and over, knowing in her heart that Grandmamma was not deceived.

'May I get down, please?' and then she slipped from the table and ran out of the room, pulling the last greasy bit of fat out of her mouth and hiding it in the pot of ferns that nobody ever remembered to dust, which stood by the entrance to the lobby. This lobby was the place where the gentlemen boarders washed their hands, and hung their coats, and left their wet umbrellas turned upside down if it was raining. The lobby was

at the end of the little passage by the head of the stairs leading to the basement. Jennifer liked the lobby. It had a familiar
feeling of security, the tweed coat on the hook smelt of Daddy,
and the mackintoshes were old and used as his had been. The
men left their cigarettes here sometimes, squashed on the floor.

Jennifer would wait for them to come out of the dining-
room, and once they were in the lobby they smiled and laughed
as though they were pleased to be free. They never patted her,
or said silly things, they treated her as one of themselves. They
were away from the house all day, and only came back in the
evenings. It made some sort of interest to lean from the
window and watch them mount the steps, and fumble in their
pockets for keys.

She went into the hall, biting her finger, looking away when
they said 'Hullo, you,' but pleased all the same. She followed
them into the lobby, and listened to their brisk voices talking
to one another. She liked the eager careful way they washed
their hands, turning them over and over and squelching them
with soap, and then they unbuttoned their trousers and passed
into the lavatory, taking no more notice of her than if she
had been a cat.

Ladies were never like this, jolly and happy together, they
whispered in her ear and took her quietly to a bedroom, closing the door very softly in case somebody should have noticed.

For a week the lobby was the chief interest to Jennifer, for
she scarcely went out of doors at all as Mother was supposed
to be 'settling down'. And then one evening Grandmamma
noticed that she disappeared from the drawing-room as soon
as voices sounded in the hall. She herself was going up to
speak to a servant, and as she passed along the hall, leaning
heavily on her stick, she caught sight of a small figure hanging on to the door knob of the lobby, with one of the boarders brushing past her into the lavatory.

'Jennifer.' She started in fright, and saw the huge massive
presence of Grandmamma peering at her from the staircase.

'Jennifer, whatever are you doing in the gentlemen's lobby?'

She flushed crimson at once, guilty as a criminal, and stole away before anything more could be said to her.

After tea Jennifer crouched with a picture book on her knee, but she never turned a page; she kept it there as a blind, listening the while to the scraps of conversation, expecting any moment that there would be a long silence and Grandmamma would say, 'You must tell us now, Jennifer, what you were doing in the lobby.'

Bed time came and nothing had been said, nor was it mentioned the next day, or the day after – but she never went along with the men again, and if someone said casually, 'Oh! I must have left it in the lobby,' her heart jumped and her face and hands turned hot.

The weeks passed by, and still they remained in the boarding-house with Grandmamma, and Daddy had not come.

No one ever told her anything, she had to listen to what people said to each other, or make it up for herself. Once mother read a letter from Harold . . . 'It seems queer to see the old home shut up. Willie sailed yesterday in great spirits, and I miss him tremendously. The yard is a most depressing sight, and both Cousin Tom and James are very cut up. It's rotten how things have turned out for them. The old ship is still on the mud, and likely to lay there till she's broken up. Poor Dad, I am thankful he will never know . . .' Here mother folded the letter and put it away.

What wouldn't he know? Why should Daddy never know? Jennifer looked at her mother sharply, but she had turned to Grandmamma and was talking about something else. Why did they never mention his name in front of her? There was some secret that they refused to tell, but they were too clever to be caught. They treated her like a baby. She was afraid to know this secret, and yet she must.

Jennifer hugged her knees and bit her nails. She was thinking out some plan whereby she could trick Grandmamma and Mother into a confession. Mother was sewing by the open window, glancing down at the hot, airless street and the buses. Grandmamma perched her spectacles on her nose and opened the evening paper.

Jennifer wandered towards her mother and pretended to play with the tassels on the curtain. She banged them backwards and forwards against the glass, knowing that this would cause irritation.

'Jenny, stop doing that.'

She obeyed sulkily, and then pulled at her mother's hand. 'When are we going home?'

No answer. 'When, Mum – when are we going home?' The voice was a whine now, pleading, grumbling.

'Don't be such a nuisance, Jenny. Go and find something to do.'

'But I want to know when we're going home?'

'We are not going home, child, we're living in London now, you know that perfectly well. Stop that fidgeting. Do you want to go somewhere?'

Jennifer moved away to the middle of the room. She saw her Grandmamma fixing her with stern disapproving eyes.

There was no way of escape. Plyn was lost to her.

Soon she would know the full truth, and terrified as she was yet she had to continue in her search for it.

She moved near the door, so as to be able to run the instant she knew. Grandmamma had laid down her paper and was yawning. Now was the time to catch her.

'Where's my daddy?' asked Jennifer.

No one spoke, and she felt little pricks of fear steal into her body.

Mother had on her awkward face, it was puckered and queer.

A flat patch of colour came on to Grandmamma's cheeks.

Jennifer twisted the handle of the door. She waited a moment, and then frightened at her own daring she spoke boldly, rudely.

'I believe Daddy's dead,' she said.

And when they made no attempt to scold her or reprove her, but gazed at her with strained, embarrassed eyes, she knew by the silence that this was the truth at last.

## 4

T he shipbuilding yard of Thomas Coombe and Sons
was empty of timber and gear. There was no longer
the clanging of the hammer, nor the high-pitched
song of the saw. Ships must go elsewhere to be refitted and
re-classed, yachtsmen must wander farther up the harbour in
search of a designer for their craft. The shed in the corner
of the yard was taken over by the engineer in need of premises; he set up his garage on the spot where the *Janet Coombe*
was built. Greasy young mechanics in stained overalls lounged
about the place with spanners in their hands, a Ford lorry
shunted in and out of the yard gates, filling the air with petrol
fumes and oil, air that once had been laden with the bitter
tang of pitch, barked ropes, and tar. The loft building had not
been sold, the big wide loft where Thomas Coombe and his
sons had chipped and chiselled at their models. His namesake and grandson Thomas, together with his Cousin James,
still clung to this place as a last remnant of their departed
trade, but they used it no longer as a workshop and as a
dwelling of inspiration, but as a boat store, humble and
insignificant. Motor boats were housed here during the
winter, and occasional small sailing craft used for pleasure in
the summer. Pulling boats and dinghies could be left here for
a small charge.

His father dead, his mother and sister gone to London, the
yard sold, and his brother away at sea, Harold Coombe had
no wish to remain a school-teacher in Plyn.

The house was sold successfully, lock, stock, and barrel, and
it was hurtful to pass his old home every day on the way to
the school and see other people at the doors, other children
at the windows. After some months of hard thinking and

consideration he resigned his position at the school, having first made certain of a post in London.

His last night in Plyn, Harold told his plans to his father's best friend and favourite cousin, the farmer Fred Stevens. Fred was forty-two now, and had stood staunchly by Christopher during the case of Coombes *versus* Hogg and Williams.

'I don't want to give up teaching, Cousin Fred,' said Harold. 'It may not lead to great things, but it's a fine job for all that and I'm proud of it.'

'D'you think you can stick the drudgery of it, working yourself to the bone with scarce a prospect of advancement, and in London too – crowded out with youngsters like yourself?'

'I'm going to have a shot at it anyway. It'll be a wrench leaving Plyn, but after all I was born in London, and lived there till I was nine. I shan't feel really strange. Then there's Mum and Jenny. Poor little kid, it's been rather tough luck on her. Not much fun for her in that boarding-house, along with my old grandmother.'

Fred Stevens whistled in disgust. 'I wish your mother hadn't run off in such a hurry. She and Jenny could have come here, and welcome. Norah was only saying so to me the other evening. It would have done John good to have a small companion. Only children stand in danger of being spoilt, what?'

'Not John,' laughed Harold. 'The lad has got his head screwed on the right way. I've had him under me in school and I know. He doesn't say much, but he thinks all the same. Good boy that.'

'Think so?' The father smiled.

'Yes – I think John will turn out all right.'

Soon after Harold rose to go.

'I'd better be clearing off now, Cousin Fred, though I hate to say good-bye. Think of me this time tomorrow night in London. I'll be wishing myself back again in Plyn before long. I'll try and persuade my mother to come down for holidays if I can, though it'll be a struggle. D'you think in a year or two she'll be fed up with town, and long for the country again?'

'You never know with women,' smiled Fred. 'Anyway, she can always send Jenny down here if the child is looking poorly and needs a change. Norah will take great care of her. And John can put on his best company manners, can't you, John?'

'Where is the boy? John?'

A head looked in at the window.

'Come and say good-bye to Harold. He's off to London tomorrow.'

The boy climbed in over the sill. John Stevens was eleven, and tall for his age, with long legs that didn't know what to do with themselves. His eyes were blue like his father's, and his fair hair toppled over his face.

'Sorry you're going,' he said abruptly.

'I'm sorry too, John, but things have turned out so and it's no use grumbling.' The boy nodded.

'Think you'll ever come back?'

'I mean to. I should feel rotten if I thought I was never going to see any of you again, all the family, and Plyn – and everything.'

'Of course he'll come back, he and Willie. In a couple of years' time you'll have made your fortune and be settling down here in retirement,' laughed Fred cheerfully. 'Willie'll be running some gigantic liner in here for his own amusement. How's he getting on with this wireless business, Harold?'

'Very well, Cousin Fred, and he seems dead keen. I don't follow it myself at all.'

'No more do I, but they say it's going to be darned useful. Well, good-bye, my boy, and good luck to you. We won't forget you in Plyn. Come back to us before long, and don't let London spoil you. Give my love to your mother.'

'Good-bye, Cousin Fred, and – thanks terribly for all you've done for us. Neither Willie nor I will ever forget – good-bye John, see you again some time, eh?'

'Sure.'

Then Harold walked through the Yard and was gone by

the farm gates. Young John looked after him and frowned.

'What are you thinking, son?' asked Fred.

'He won't come back,' said the boy slowly.

'How d'you mean, he won't come back? Of course he will. He may stick London for a couple of years, but he'll be home in Plyn soon after.'

'No,' said John. 'I reckon it sounds soft what I said, but when I get feelings like that they're generally right. Remember what I told you about Uncle Christopher? You laughed at the time, but I just kind of knew in myself.'

'Now listen, my son, you're becoming a regular little prophet of despair. Cut all that stuff out of your head, it's silly, see? It's unhealthy and morbid, and your mother and I don't like it. See?'

'Sure.' The boy ran away whistling and vaulted a stile. He fumbled in his pocket for his catapult, and took careful aim at a pheasant that was flying low over the cut stubbles of wheat. He missed it, of course. Then he strolled through the fields to a point of high ground that overlooked the harbour and Polmear Creek. Through the trees he could see the spars of the wrecked *Janet Coombe*, while below him to his right the evening mists gathered round the tower of Lanoc Church.

John Stevens stuck his hands in his pockets, and watched the scene through half-closed eyes.

'I can't help these feelings that come to me,' he thought. 'I know I'll never see Harold nor Willie again, like I know that the ship in the creek won't be broken till they take the figurehead away. Father and mother don't believe me, but one day somebody will understand.'

Then he heard a shout from some boys in the fields beyond, and he waved to them, laughing, and ran away down the hill forgetting his thoughts.

Harold was throwing his things into his trunk. He straightened his back and sighed, and looked out upon the harbour water through his lodging window.

'I'll come back,' he whispered. 'Mother'll get fed up with London, and in a year or two we'll all be living here again,

311

Willie, and Jenny, and I. Dad belonged here, and his father, and his grandfather. We belong too, we can't keep away, no more than Willie can stay from the sea. We'll come back to you, Plyn – in a year or two.'

Already he planned in his mind the happy years ahead, years of fulfilment and content; but he reckoned without knowledge and with only the bare substance of a dream.

In a year or two, he said, and it was then the autumn of 1912 . . .

# 5

Gradually Jennifer became used to living in London at the boarding-house. She began to feel as though she had always looked out upon those stretches of slate roofs and chimney-pots. The buses rumbled past her bedroom window, and from the distance came the whistle of the Metropolitan trains and the throb of the traffic moving citywards.

Bertha Coombe had easily slipped back into the ways she had known as a girl.

Unconsciously she remembered the early days of her married life, when she and her husband had lived upon the bounty of Mrs Parkins, such as it was, and how quiet and humble he had been, aware of his weakness and of his failure to support her and the boys. This was the man her mother had known, ignorant of the change that hard work and Plyn had made in him, and slowly she too began to regard him in this past light, taking her mother's attitude that she had been something of a saint to have stayed by him all those years. She still cried over his photograph and clung to her widow's weeds, but she talked of him now as 'poor Christopher', and shook her head sadly when his name was mentioned.

Harold, boylike and a little selfish, had stood a month at the boarding-house on his arrival in London, but no more. He had moved into lodgings nearby, resentful of the rules and regulations which his grandmother impelled at No. 7.

Willie made brief appearances every now and again, making shift with the boarding-house as his temporary home, but he grumbled in private to his brother, saying that he couldn't for the life of him see why they had come away from Plyn after all.

313

It was about this time that it was decided that Jennifer should go to day-school. At Plyn, of course, she would have attended the ordinary local board school like every other child, but such an idea as this shocked Mrs Parkins beyond measure, and rather than suffer the indignity of her grandchild receiving her education side by side with the poorest children of the district, she made inquiries about Miss Hancock's Private School in St John's Wood and offered to pay the necessary fee.

'She will soon get over her silly shyness when she mixes with young companions of her own age,' said Bertha. 'Sometimes I think she puts it on when she doesn't want to do something she is told. It's sheer naughtiness really.'

Grandmamma made a sucking sound with her teeth, and removed a piece of meat with her knitting needle.

'The child has been spoilt,' she announced, 'badly spoilt by her father, I should imagine. But then, what else would you expect?' She shrugged her gigantic shoulders and sniffed.

'Jenny dear,' said Bertha, 'run along.'

So Jennifer 'ran along', and went upstairs to her bedroom, and leaned out of the window watching the rain fall on the chimney-pots and the grey sloping roofs.

She shut her eyes tight and tried to make a picture in her mind of Plyn, but her old powers of visualization seemed to have deserted her, and when she conjured up the sea all that came to her was the wide beach and the pier at Clacton where Mother had taken her for three weeks in the summer. Even her old bedroom over the porch at Ivy House was confused now, and dim; she had forgotten the position of the bed and the pattern of the wallpaper. All she remembered was a fair tangled head on a pillow, someone who slept with his head in his hands and beside whom it was warm and comforting to lie – but his face was gone from her.

Somewhere a little girl ran barefoot on the sweeping hills with the sun in her eyes and the wind behind her, ships sailed away from the grey harbour waters to the open sea, and the gulls cried. Then she opened her eyes and the steady rain fell over London, the traffic rumbled in the street below, and the high, shrill call of the bugle summoned the soldiers in the barracks opposite.

Her first term at school was a success. She soon found that it mattered little how she did her lessons as long as her writing was neat.

In the middle of her second term a terrible thing happened which left a lasting impression on her mind. The principal complained of her and wrote to her mother, and for many weeks she crept about the boarding-house like a little criminal, aware of cold looks and shudders from her mother and grandmamma.

It happened that Jennifer had noticed a group of children in her form who sat apart over their milk and biscuits, and whispered in each other's ears. She crossed over to them and a thin giggling girl with curls called Lillias seized her by the waist and asked her if she would join.

'Join what?' said Jennifer.

'Our secret society for finding out things. It's a sort of spying game, and we tell each other secrets.' This sounded rather exciting.

'Could I be captain?' asked Jennifer.

'Yes, if you like.'

Lillias put her arm through one of her friend's and whispered something. 'Ooh!' said the other with round eyes. 'Do you really? How did you find out?' They clustered together in a group, nodding excitedly.

'H'sh – don't tell anyone.'

Jennifer fidgeted.

'What's your old secret, anyway?'

'Lillias knows,' came the whisper.

'Knows what?'

'How babies are born.'

A quiver of excitement ran through the group, with Lillias in the centre, proud and admired.

'Oh?' said Jennifer casually, 'that's nothing. Everybody knows.'

'Do you know?'

She hesitated a minute, uncertain of her answer. She had never considered the question before. At all costs she must keep to her status as captain.

'Yes, you silly,' she lied.

'Jennifer knows too!' was the exclamation. 'Tell us, quick.'

'You can tell them if you like,' said Jennifer graciously, and Lillias leaned forward, the words tumbling from her mouth.

'They don't come with angels at all, they grow inside people.'

'Oh! – how do you know?'

'I asked my sister, she's fourteen. And there's a funny word that tells you, I looked it up in the dictionary.'

Jennifer gazed at her in surprise. Was this true? What an extraordinary thing. For a moment she was taken off her guard.

'Pooh!' she said, 'I don't believe it. How could they?'

'There,' screamed Lillias triumphantly, 'then you didn't know after all.'

'Yes, I did – yes, I did,' shouted Jennifer. 'I was only pretending I didn't to see what you would say.'

The lame excuse was received in silence.

'Anyway,' she went on, 'I know more than any of you 'cos I've had a baby!'

'Oh! you fibber, you haven't. Why, you're not grown up.'

'Yes, I have,' said Jennifer, inventing rapidly, dazzled by her audience, 'I had one last summer but I gave it away to – to a friend.'

'No, you couldn't. Only married ladies have babies.'

'Well, I did. People said it was a miracle. I b'lieve someone put it in a paper, but I forget.'

'Jennifer! It's a story, you're making it up. What did it feel like? Did it grow inside you?'

'Oh! yes, easy as anything. I'm magic. Mother says I'm going to have another one in the holidays.' With this last bombshell the children melted away, awestruck, biting their fingers.

Later in the week when she was doing her preparation in her bedroom, her mother called her to come down into the

316

drawing-room. She found Grandmamma and Mother sitting in front of the fire with flushed pained faces, and Mother had a letter opened in her hands.

'Jenny,' she said gravely, 'here is a letter from Miss Hancock telling us about your naughtiness. Grandmamma and I are so unhappy we don't know what is going to be done.'

Jennifer's knees trembled. Whatever had happened? What had she done? 'What does Miss Hancock say?' she asked timidly.

'One of the parents wrote to her complaining that her child had gone home with horrid ideas and thoughts that you had put into her head. Miss Hancock spoke to this child, Lillias, I believe you have had her to tea here, and she cried and said it was all some secret game of which you were the head, and the idea of it was to find out about – about babies and things. Jenny – how could you.'

'It was only pretence,' stammered Jennifer, 'I didn't know really, I'd never thought. But Lillias was so boasting. I didn't do anything naughty, she said she knew how babies were born and I said I had had one, and that . . .'

'Jennifer!' Mother gazed at her in disgust.

Grandmamma sniffed, and then laughed grimly.

'What did I tell you, Bertha? I always knew the child had a nasty mind. Do you remember how she used to wait about the lobby for the gentlemen?'

At the mention of the lobby Jennifer blushed crimson.

'There,' said Grandmamma, pointing at her. 'Look at her guilty face. She owns up to it. She knew she was doing something wrong. A child of her age, with such ideas. Bertha, this is revolting.'

Jennifer twisted her hands in front of her, wretchedly distressed. What had the lobby got to do with babies?

'Jenny,' said Mother sadly, 'I don't know how I'm going to look upon you in the same way again. All this has shocked me so deeply that I can never forget it. To think my own little girl should have nasty, vulgar curiosity . . .'

She shuddered as she folded the letter.

'You must write to Miss Hancock and say how sorry you are, otherwise she will never take you back. Will you promise Grandmamma and me that you will never think these horrid thoughts any more?'

'Yes,' she whispered.

'You see, Jenny, it's made me so sad I feel I can't trust you.' She looked helplessly across at Grandmamma.

'Of course we know what branch of the family is to be blamed for this,' said Grandmamma slowly. 'Possibly it is too late to alter anything now. I wonder what other ideas the child has?'

She fixed her heavy, brooding eye on her granddaughter. Jennifer's eyes fell beneath the piercing glance. Nasty, vulgar curiosity, Mother had said. She must mean things like drawing pictures of naked ladies . . . She had done this – perhaps Grandmamma had found some of her old drawings. If only she could fly somewhere far away, and never, never come back . . .

Then Grandmamma played her trump card.

'I wonder what your daddy would have said to this.'

The room swung round before Jennifer's eyes, her heart thumped, and spreading out her hands helplessly she ran from the room, anywhere, away – away – seeking some possibility of escape.


In July, Grandmamma, Mother, Harold, and Jennifer went away for a fortnight to rooms in Swanage. It made a change from the dreariness of Maple Street, and she enjoyed the sands and the bathing, and the nearness of the glittering sea.

These sands were spoilt by all the people, though, by deck chairs, crying children, and barking dogs.

'Plyn wasn't like this, was it, Harold?' she asked anxiously, and he pulled her hair and laughed – 'Rather not.'

She sighed with a queer feeling of relief, and hoped he would not wonder if she had forgotten.

He forgot to build sand castles with her this summer, he

was always reading the newspapers aloud to Mother and Grandmamma, nothing interesting, but long, boring pieces about other countries.

As she rounded a sand house with her hands, and carefully placed a white shell for the door, she would hear him say – 'England'll have to decide one way or the other, you know, if it comes to a dust-up.'

Then she would seize hold of her bucket and run across to the edge of the sea to fill it, spilling little drops of water behind her as she returned.

Harold would tilt his straw hat over his face. 'I don't know, Mum, but it seems there's bound to be war. Of course it will all be over by Christmas.'

And Jennifer made a moat for her house, and sprinkled the water inside it to look real.

One day it rained, and they had to stay indoors at the lodgings. Mother and Grandmamma were sewing by the window, and Jennifer had her painting-book on her knee. She was painting a sailor in a bright blue coat, and she had smudged the colour on to the white page.

Suddenly Harold burst into the room, a paper in his hand, and the back of his coat wet from the rain.

Afterwards Jennifer remembered this picture of him, his head thrown back, his chin in the air, and a queer fluttering smile on his lips.

'Germany's started fighting Russia,' he said.

Jennifer went on with her painting.

# 6

A t first the war made very little difference to Jennifer's life. They came back to London after the holiday at Swanage, and by the end of September term had started and she was at school again. Grown-up people were making a great fuss, as they always did, and talking very big. During the autumn evenings Jennifer used to bring down her homework to a corner of the drawing-room – there was never a fire in her bedroom of course – and as she bit the end of her penholder and rested her head on her hands, trying to concentrate on the preparation before her, she would listen to the conversation round the fire in the centre of the room. Grandmamma had pinned a map of Europe on the wall, and this she dotted over with little flags to mark the advance of the enemy.

Grandmamma and Mother bought great balls of red wool and started to knit socks. Jennifer began a scarf, but she left it after a week.

It seemed to Jennifer that the war had made a new interest for grown-up people; they had started a fresh pretence of being important and were inwardly enjoying it, for all their serious words. It was amusing to watch them send away parcels to the trenches every week.

Grandmamma's question, 'Well, dear, have you forgotten anything?' and Mother's reply, 'No, Mamma, it's all here. Potted meat, biscuits, tinned sardines, and tobacco.'

She spoke briskly, and tying her parcel she snapped the string with a new pair of sharp bright scissors. It was only a game after all, thought Jennifer, watching her from behind an arithmetic book.

Gradually the men boarders began to disappear from Maple

Street, and they would come in one day in khaki, looking very tall and different. The women could not do enough for them then.

Everyone left off sugar in their tea, and Mother, not to be outdone, refused to touch any butter. Jennifer shrugged her shoulders. This war would not affect her, she touched neither.

She was only a little girl who took no part in conversations and must learn lessons every day.

On her way to school in St John's Wood she watched soldiers drilling in Regent's Park. Sometimes they marched in long columns in the streets, their arms swinging in time to their feet.

She liked the songs they sang.

> Who were you with last night
> Out in the pale moonlight,
> It wasn't your sister,
> It wasn't your Ma . . .

Often they called out to the children in perambulators wheeled by superior nannies in blue veils – 'Hullo, baby, how's nurse?'

They were jolly and full of fun these soldiers, they didn't care about Grandmamma knitting ugly socks, or Mother posting deadly parcels.

> Who – who – who's your lady friend,
> Who's the little girlie by your side?

They shouted this out with a roar, and Jennifer halted on the pavement, swinging her satchel behind her, and waved her hand to the men who waved back to her. These men understood how stupid it was to be serious.

Jennifer skipped along on her way to school, and that morning she realized that this war was something besides a string of words in the newspapers, it was something that could touch people. They were having a drawing-lesson in her form, and the mistress was Mrs James, a patient, ineffectual woman without authority.

In the middle of the lesson when Jennifer was behaving badly, standing on one leg and waving a ruler in the air, the wretched mistress calling to her to be good, someone came to the door, and said – 'Please, Mrs James, Miss Hancock wishes to see you.'

The room clear, the children indulged in an orgy of freedom, Jennifer leading the crowd over desks in a wild stampede. Ten minutes, twenty minutes, half an hour passed, and still the mistress did not return.

Jennifer seized the chalk and drew a feeble picture of a donkey on the blackboard, with 'Mrs James' written underneath. The children screamed with laughter. Flushed with success she rubbed it out, and was about to start another when the door opened and one of the elder girls appeared.

'Will you please be quiet, all of you,' she said gravely, 'and sit down at your desks. You can start your homework. Mrs James won't come back this morning. She has had a telegram to say her husband has been killed. She's gone away in a taxi.'

The room was suddenly silent.

The children sat down at their desks and opened their books without a word. The chalk fell from Jennifer's hand. She looked at the pencil on the mistress's desk that Mrs James had laid aside hastily when she was summoned. She pictured her hurrying along the corridor to the study, wiping her chalky hands on a handkerchief, and opening the door, and seeing Miss Hancock with a telegram in her hands.

A nervous, plain little girl called Lucy began to cry noisily from her desk at the back of the room.

'Oh! it's beastly,' whispered Jennifer, 'beastly . . . beastly.'

And she remembered Harold in his uniform, waving to her from the window of a packed train at Waterloo Station, and she was afraid.

Children often stayed away from school now for a week, and when they returned they wore black bands round their arms.

This meant they had lost somebody at the front. The food was horrid at the boarding-house. The bread was a dark brown colour, there was no jam, and margarine instead of butter. They had rice now, no potatoes, and stuff called swedes instead of cabbage.

If pudding was sour it was sweetened by little white tablets named saccharine. Jennifer began to forget what the old food had been like. She forgot also what sort of suits men wore in the days before the war. Everyone had khaki now. It was difficult to imagine anything else.

She wondered whether Daddy would have gone to the war if he had not died. She tried to remember his face and his figure, but all she could ever see was the tangled hair on the pillow. Even his photograph failed to remind her. He belonged to another time, long, long ago. There was something pathetic in the fact that he would never know about the war. His infinite wisdom dwindled in her eyes, and she saw him smaller than he had been before, smaller and shrinking in value, a pale shadow compared to the living stalwart presence of Harold and Willie. Already she herself was older, superior to him.

He was a tombstone in a churchyard now, and the churchyard itself a far, forgotten place.

Jennifer pushed the photograph carelessly behind the ornament on the mantelpiece, and ran down the stairs, her satchel on her shoulder, humming 'Tipperary', a song he had never sung.

Harold was killed in March.

She returned home from school in time for tea, and directly the front door was opened she knew what had happened. The servant's expression was scared, and she fumbled with the handle of the door, avoiding Jennifer's eyes. There was a man's hat lying in the hall. She looked into the dining-room and saw that tea had not been laid. One of the boarders came out of the drawing-room, and as soon as she saw Jennifer, her mouth worked queerly, and she stepped back again, closing the door softly. The rims of her eyes had been red.

A pain came into Jennifer's heart. She must not let the servant know that she had guessed.

'Where's Mother?' she asked.

'Upstairs with your granny — she's — she's not very well, I think,' said the woman, and slipped away silently to the basement. For a moment Jennifer hesitated, wondering whether she could creep from the house and run somewhere far, run so that she would never have to find out whether this thing was true. Terrified lest she should meet someone who would tell her she went along to the downstairs lavatory, and locked the door. No one would find her here. She knelt on the floor and prayed. 'Please, God, don't let it be Harold or Willie, please God, let it be just my imagination.' Then she rose and waited, her ear to the door, listening for footsteps.

In about twenty minutes she heard a slow, heavy footfall descending the stairs. It moved across the hall and went into the drawing-room. Then the door closed. All was silent. Jennifer knew that it was Grandmamma. Stealthily she opened the lavatory door and stepped into the hall. It was no use, she could not wait any longer. She must know the truth. She stole up the staircase to her mother's bedroom, and with her heart thumping and her hands clammy with sweat, she crept inside.

The room was quite dark, and the curtains were drawn.

Faintly Jennifer could make out the figure of her mother on the bed. She stood by the door, holding her breath, terrified that she would be seen. The blind flapped against the window pane. There was a little sound from the bed, and the figure moved.

Mother spoke, in a thick swollen voice that she had never used before.

'Is that Jenny?'

'Yes, Mother.'

There was a silence, and she waited, her heart thumping . . . thumping; her throat dry.

Her legs suddenly began to tremble.

'Harold's been killed, darling . . .' the voice trailed off, smothered and lost.

324

'Yes' – whispered Jennifer. 'Yes – I know.'

For one moment she longed to go to the figure on the bed and creep next to her, holding her very close, making by this humble effort of consolation the beginning of friendship, love, and understanding. She did not know that the whole of their future might depend upon this moment.

Jennifer was too shy.

She stole from the silent room and crouched in the passage outside, the scalding tears blinding her eyes, running down into her mouth . . .

Jennifer woke with a start. It seemed as though the gun had sounded next to her, close to her ear. Once again the report rang out, shaking the very walls of the house with its vibration. She sat up in bed and reached for her dressing-gown. This signal to which she was so accustomed never failed to waken within her a smouldering whisper of dread, a cold senseless touch of babyish fear. Then the maroons began. Screaming, whistling, they lifted their voices, filling the air with a hideous cry of panic, stirring the slow and sleepy part of her to action, causing her to jump from her bed and run crazily to the door, stuffing her fingers in her ears. Already the three servants were tumbling down the staircase from their cheerless rooms beneath the roof. Their figures were clumsy and grotesque. Impossible to connect the cook, the martinet of the boarding-house kitchen, with this lumpy, moon-faced woman, clutching her flannel dressing-gown to her with trembling hands. There was something painfully intimate about seeing her thus, something almost shocking. Jennifer smiled politely, but avoided her eyes. Mother appeared on the landing, helping Grandmamma, a monstrous, horrible figure in a red dressing-gown.

The boarders came out of their rooms. The women in various stages of undress, hair screwed anyhow, grease at the corners of their noses, and the only two men of the boarding-house who were left, old Mr Hobson, kicking his stomach before him as he walked, and Mr Weymes who had only one lung and could not fight, his long red nose sniffing the air, his pale eyes seeming to apologize for the fact, 'Really, you know, it isn't my fault that I'm here.'

They went down into the cellar, where campstools and rugs were already prepared, and huddled together they seemed a preposterous little group, the women nervous, the men over-smiling, their faces yellow and strange in the dim candlelight.

Jennifer sat next to her mother, her teeth chattering. Funny – she wasn't afraid but – but she could not keep her body from shaking like this, nor her teeth from rattling. They went on, in spite of her efforts to control them. It was the silence that was unbearable, the straining her ears to listen, and wondering what was happening up in the sky above.

'Hark! did you hear that?'

One of the boarders spoke sharply.

The air was filled with sound now. First the terrible split-ting echo of the Hampstead gun, followed by the low thun-der and steady rumbling of the others. Jennifer closed her eyes and pressed her hands against her tummy.

It was something that would never stop, that would go on for ever, that she would know to the end of her days.

While the guns paused for a moment it seemed there came a high thin humming, steady and unmistakable, the hum of distant bees, crowded together in a flock, moving slowly. Somebody whispered in the darkness, 'There are the Gothas – they're right above our heads.'

Once more the guns broke out, deafening the world with the explosion.

It seemed to Jennifer that she had sat in the cellar from the beginning of things, that never, since she could remember, had there been anything in her life but this. One day, so she was told, it would be ended. One day there would be no war.

Now she was twelve, she was old, she understood.

The war had killed Harold and Willie. Once they were alive, laughing with her, playing with her, she had touched them, knowing them to be true, then all that was left of them were two telegrams, two letters from strange officers. However

326

much she called to them in lonely moments, they would not come. Soon their photographs would seem unreal, like the photograph of Daddy. They would be dead people. She herself, as a grown-up woman, would glance towards them casually, seeing their faces younger than hers, faded, curiously old-fashioned – 'Yes, those were my brothers.'

They would not even have the reality of an old toy, found in a forgotten cupboard, dusty and reproachful.

The guns were quieter now, from time to time there came a low rumble and a fierce short clamour, then they ceased again, muttering distantly a grumble and a threat.

Jennifer saw herself growing up and leaving Daddy and the boys behind, passing beyond them, to strange fancies and new thoughts, remembering them in quiet moments as belonging to a list of discarded things, children's books at the back of a shelf, the illustrations torn, boxes of cracked paints, an armless teddy bear – jerseys she had outgrown.

And Plyn, a queer blurred vision of the sea, high hills, and a path across the fields.

The horror of growing up, the horror of no longer laughing at really funny things, nor caring to run wildly, forgetting to pretend you are a boy, walking dully instead of slashing at trees with your sword. Never seeing again the fun of kicking autumn leaves in the gutter, stamping in puddles, banging a stick along railings, turning chairs and dust-sheets into camps, making food out of twigs and grass and pulling the petals off daisies for potatoes. No more to stroll hands in pockets, humming a tune, sniffing adventure round the corner.

Jumbled and confused the thoughts scattered themselves in Jennifer's mind as she crouched on her campstool, her eyes closed, her teeth chattering. Soon she would be old with the noise of the guns in her ears, London her home, Daddy, the boys, and Plyn the dead dreams of a forgotten year, and running by her side the shadow of a little girl who wanted to stay young.

Everything was silent now, the rumbling and the muttering had ceased. Suddenly, with the suggestion of a whisper,

like a faint far echo, came the sweet muffled call of a bugle.
Two little notes, twice repeated, losing themselves in the
distant streets.

'All clear' . . . 'All clear' . . .

# 7

Jennifer stayed at school until she was seventeen. She was twelve at the end of the war, and during the next five years she developed rapidly in mind and body, throwing aside her old childish shyness and timidity and becoming aware of her own latent will-power. At school she worked when she chose to give her mind to it, but remained throughout curiously detached as though she considered education merely a way of spending her time. Her teachers could make little of her.

Jennifer left school at the end of the summer term of 1923, and after the annual dreary holiday at the seaside, Felixstowe this year, she found herself back at No. 7 Maple Street with the prospect of empty days before her. Grandmamma, who merely sat in a chair in the drawing-room now and directed operations from there, advised her to help her mother with the business of running the boarding-house, and to be thankful that owing to her own generosity there was no need for her to tramp the streets looking for work.

'At the same time, Jennifer, I trust you realize what a lucky girl you have been all these years, receiving that splendid education, treating this home as your own, and now at the age of seventeen enjoying such liberty as your mother never had at your age, I can assure you.'

Jennifer glanced up from her book. She had grown so used to these speeches that they had little effect on her.

'I don't know about the liberty,' she said. 'The only difference is that I go about in the tubes and buses alone and Mother didn't. Otherwise I should think I lead very much the same sort of life.'

Grandmamma sniffed.

329

'Nonsense, nonsense,' she muttered, 'I don't approve of all this running about at all.'

Bertha snapped a piece of cotton in two. She was embroidering a camisole.

'I think it would be good for Jennifer if she made some really nice friends,' she announced. 'I wish you'd kept on with that Marshall girl, dear, she might have asked you to stay. I believe they had quite a place in Herefordshire.'

'What's that?' asked Grandmamma, peevishly, 'what's that? I can't hear what you say, you mumble so.'

'I said it's a pity Jennifer hasn't some nice friends who would ask her to stay,' shouted Bertha.

'What nonsense! Isn't the child happy here? Why should she wish to go tearing off somewhere? She's only just home from Felixstowe. There's too much going away these days altogether.'

'Still, Mamma, she has no young companions she seems to care about. Of course I had Edith and May in the old days, and anyway we always found plenty to do. No, it's a great pity you haven't more friends, Jenny.'

'Don't worry, I'm all right,' said Jennifer scowling, hating to be discussed. 'I don't want any friends. I hate girls, I always have.'

'What does she say, Bertha? Why doesn't she speak up so that I can hear?' Grandmamma stamped the floor with her stick.

'Jenny says she doesn't care for girls, Mamma, that was all.'

'Doesn't care for girls? What a stupid thing to say. What does she mean, I should like to know.'

'Yes, tell us, Jenny. You are always so reticent in your opinions.'

'Oh! nothing, Mother. I don't know why exactly. They're rather fools I think, at least they all were at school. Always giggling and whispering. I like people who either do a thing openly or keep quiet about it.'

'Do a thing openly, what do you mean, child?' Grandmamma pricked up her ears suspiciously. 'You shouldn't be so

330

mysterious in your conversation. Explain yourself.'

'Only an expression, Grandmamma. It doesn't mean anything. It would take me months to give you all my reasons for disliking girls.'

'Well, Jenny,' said Bertha cheerfully, 'at least you don't know many boys to compare them with, but I dare say you will as you grow older. I should like you to meet some really nice young men – after all, you are sure to marry one day.'

'I don't want to marry.'

'Oh! every girl says that at your age, I'm sure I did myself. You wait and see. It's just a pretence, being shy of men.'

'Shy?' Jennifer smiled. 'I'm not shy of men, I like them. Don't know many, but I see them walking about the street. They're more human than women, same as dogs.'

'What's that? What's that? What did she say?'

'Jennifer doesn't mind men, Mamma. She says they're like dogs, she sees them in the street.'

'She sees what? How perfectly disgusting – didn't she call a policeman?'

'No, Grandmamma, you didn't hear properly. I said men were human.'

'Well, everybody knows that, child, but it's no excuse for filthy behaviour. So that's why you like to go about London alone. Bertha, I don't approve of this at all.'

'It's all right, Mamma. Jennifer was joking.'

'H'mph! Joking, don't see any joke. The child knows too much, that's the trouble.'

Bertha changed the conversation.

'What are your plans for the week, Jenny?'

'Haven't got any. I thought of walking along the Embankment tomorrow, and seeing if there were any ships.'

'What a funny thing to want to do.'

'I like it.'

'Don't get spoken to by any roughs.'

'Nobody ever speaks to me, I wish they would.'

'What's that? The child wants to be assaulted by roughs? Bertha, I forbid Jennifer to go off on this expedition.'

331

'Very well, Mamma. Jennifer, you heard what Grandmamma says.'

'Yes. I heard.'

'Still, it's a pity to spoil your day. I was thinking of doing some shopping tomorrow afternoon. You can come with me and we'll have tea afterwards at Whiteleys.'

To their surprise Jennifer burst out laughing and walked from the room.

'Oh, dear! I hope Jenny isn't going to be difficult,' said Bertha thoughtfully.

Grandmamma sniffed, and settled herself in her chair.

'She needs watching, in my opinion; I don't like the look in her eye. The child's a dark horse.'

So they dismissed her from their minds.

Jennifer, who believed in fair play, stood exactly two months of idleness at the boarding-house, and then decided she could bear no more. It was absurd to say her mother needed her help in running the place, on the contrary, she would have been fussed at interference.

Bertha realized that the girl had nothing to do and was bored, but she seemed to think it was the fault of her character and could not be changed. Poor Christopher had been the same as a young man. Always restless and dissatisfied. It was most unfortunate that Jennifer should have inherited this fault. Bertha did not see what could be done about it. She herself had been so very different as a girl. Still, there it was; such a pity Jennifer had no hobbies to make some sort of amusement. Painting or music now. However she was very young, perhaps she would meet some really nice man with plenty of money . . .

She talked the matter over with Grandmamma, and they both agreed that this was the only thing for Jennifer. 'That's why I'm so anxious for her to make friends,' argued Bertha. 'She is so obstinate, and will not go out of her way to make herself agreeable. That Marshall girl at school had a lovely place in the country, and would have introduced her to no end of people. She might even have hunted.'

'Hunted? Nonsense, nonsense. No girl secures a husband by hunting for one. Jennifer is only too ready to make herself cheap as it is.'

'No, Mamma dear, you misunderstand. I mean hunting on horseback, after foxes you know.'

'Oh! well, why don't you say what you mean? Hunting indeed, what nonsense.'

'I am afraid Jenny has rather an unfortunate manner with strangers,' continued Bertha. 'She will give people the impression she is laughing at them. Even with people she knows it's the same. All the boarders here, for instance. I'm sure everyone is very nice to her, but she has such a quick tongue. I believe she would frighten off any man who wished to make an impression.'

'Humph! that's all a pose. Still waters run deep. She seemed on very familiar terms with Mr Tupton the other evening. I was watching her.'

'Oh! Mamma, they were only discussing horse-breeding. Quite harmless.'

'Harmless? Glad you think so. I call it a decidedly intimate subject to be discussed between two people of the opposite sex. There's no knowing what might be said. Men are always ready to twist words about and cause confusion.'

'I hardly think Horace Tupton would do that, Mamma. He is very serious-minded, and must be well over fifty.'

'How ignorant you are, Bertha. That's just the age men become foolish with young girls. I shall never forget a most unpleasant occurrence that happened to me years ago in a railway carriage, and I was married too. However, that is not the point. The point is, I wouldn't trust Jennifer at all. She may have introduced this horse-breeding subject and led Mr Tupton to believe heaven knows what.'

'Oh! dear, so you really think so? I shall certainly tell her to be more careful in the future.'

'If we want to see Jennifer married, Bertha, I must confess she is not setting about it in the right way. No nice-mannered man would dream of proposing to a girl who showed such a familiarity with the facts of life. He would be repulsed at once. He might suspect almost anything. Horse-breeding, indeed, what nonsense.'

At that moment Jennifer walked into the room. She was smiling, and carrying her hat in her hand.

'Hullo!' she said, 'I've got a job.'

Bertha started from her chair in astonishment.

'Jenny – what on earth do you mean?'

'She's got what, she's got what? I can't hear a word you say.' Grandmamma leaned forward angrily, her chin wobbling with emotion.

'I've got a job,' repeated Jennifer. 'I start tomorrow morning at nine o'clock.' She balanced herself on the arm of a chair and watched their faces.

'I don't think it's at all nice of you,' said Bertha immediately. 'And I simply don't understand your attitude. To go off calmly on your own and arrange your plans as though you were twenty-one and independent, while Grandmamma and I sit here worrying over you and wondering what's to be done, and . . .'

'Yes, but Mother, listen a minute. You and Grandmamma sit here and worry but you don't do anything. After all, why should you? So I just went out and did it for you.'

'But there's no need for it,' persisted her mother. 'Grandmamma sees you have everything you want, I'm sure. Why, that pretty hat you have, that was new three weeks ago. The whole thing reflects on me, it looks as though I didn't want you here in the daytime. Jennifer, you have hurt me very much.'

'Mother, please don't make a scene. There's nothing scandalous in getting a job surely. Why, everybody does something nowadays. Quite rich girls who live on big allowances – they're all doing it. I know it wasn't considered the thing years ago, but you said the other day the war had changed everything.'

'What does she say, Bertha?'

'Oh! dear, oh! dear. Jennifer says although it was consid-

334

ered shocking years ago quite rich girls think nothing of doing it now. She says everybody does it.'

'Doing it? Doing what? I never heard of such a thing! What a wicked, immoral statement. Can't they wait until they are married, good gracious, why I . . .'

'No, no, Mamma. Jennifer says all girls have jobs since the war. I don't know what to think about it. If only poor Christopher was alive — I wonder what he would have to say.'

'Daddy would be pleased,' said Jennifer hastily. 'I know he would, so it's no use shaking your head like that, Mother. And anyway, I've got the job, and I'm going tomorrow morning at nine o'clock, so why must we go on talking it over. Nothing you say will make me change my mind.'

'You are a hard, obstinate girl, Jenny. I had no idea you would grow up so callous to my wishes. I wish I knew where you get that horrid, wilful streak from — your daddy was never like it, nor the two boys. I shall begin to think you take after your cruel, disagreeable grandfather.'

'Who's talking about her grandfather?'

'Not Papa, dear, I was referring to poor Christopher's old father who treated us all so shamefully.'

Jennifer slid off the arm of her chair. 'I don't seem very popular so I'll go upstairs.'

'Wait, Jenny, you haven't told us what it is yet, this precious job.'

'Yes, Jennifer. Come now and confess, unless it's something you are too ashamed to admit.'

'Oh! it's nothing to be ashamed of. I'm going to be an assistant to a vet — a sort of kennel maid.'

There was a moment's horrified silence. Jennifer slipped quietly from the room.

'A kennel maid,' Bertha gazed helplessly at her mother. 'Can you imagine anything more appalling? She might pick up fleas or anything. Messing about all day with unhealthy animals. I have never been so worried in my life. Really, sometimes I wonder if I ought to take Jennifer to see a doctor, she may be the smallest bit peculiar. Oh! Mamma, what are we going to do about this business?'

'Peculiar? What nonsense, of course she isn't peculiar. I'm wondering what sort of aged man he is, this vet of hers . . .'

The following day Jennifer, in a white overall, was helping a sad-faced middle-aged man, also dressed in a white coat, while he made an injection in the side of a pitiful screaming cat that had been run over two minutes before. The man asked her if she could stand it.

'Yes,' said Jennifer, clenching her teeth.

She put out her arms for the whimpering, bleeding cat, and held it close to her, with calm, accustomed hands.

For eight months Jennifer was an assistant to Mr Macleugh, the veterinary surgeon in Baker Street, but at the end of that time he was obliged to give up the work because of his health.

Her mother and grandmother realized by now that it was hopeless to argue with her, she went her own way. It took them many weeks before they became used to her job as kennel maid.

When Jennifer's career as a kennel maid came to an end she looked about her for something else. She returned home one day with the news that she was selling stockings behind the counter at the Army and Navy Stores. Bertha looked at her painfully. 'Sometimes I think you behave like this only to hurt my feelings. After your splendid education, to go and sell stockings in a shop—'

'I never learnt a thing at school,' said Jennifer, 'except that it didn't pay to tell tales. I can't remember the names of the rivers in China or the exports of India, or how to parse a sentence, or what was the Reform Bill. Since I've left, I've learnt what to do if an animal is in pain, which is surely more use than all the rest put together.'

'But where is all this leading to? That is what Grandmamma and I want to know. I dare say it is very nice to be useful

336

with animals, but really – for a girl with your upbringing, to be selling stockings behind a counter.'

'Daddy used to be a shopwalker in the old days when you lived in London, you told me so once.'

'That's rather different.'

'How?'

'Your poor Daddy started life in rather humble circumstances, you know that perfectly well. You cannot remember your relatives at Plyn, but they were all rather – well – rough country people. I felt it a great deal at first. Your Daddy was superior to them in every way, that was why he ran away from sea. But as a young man he had very little money, and he was obliged to better himself as best he could. Unfortunately he was never very strong. Besides, there were not the opportunities open for young people in his day. It's quite another matter for you. You've been brought up as a lady, and you do nothing but throw your chances away. Look at the people you must mix with in this shop.'

'Oh! I don't know, Mother – the girls are very jolly, most of them. And I don't feel a bit ladylike – what a ghastly expression anyway, like commence.'

'Commence? I don't understand, what do you mean?'

'It doesn't matter.'

After two months at the Army and Navy Stores, Jennifer became sick of stockings, and amused by the advertisements of 'Nippy Chocolates', she spent three weeks as a waitress in Lyons, only to be dismissed for her number of breakages. This distressed her not at all, and her next job was that of saleswoman or advertiser to a firm who were about to launch a new type of carpet-sweeper upon the market. Jennifer was obliged to go from house to house with a small dispatch case filled with leaflets, a note-book, and a fountain pen, and after ringing the front-door bell engage the bored householder in a sparkling conversation as to the merits of the 'No-Dust' carpet-sweeper, without which no home is complete.

Unhappily the 'No-Dust' sweeper failed to make an impression in the homes of England, and Jennifer was once more without a job. She had saved money enough now to indulge herself in some way. Her mother suggested a good, serviceable fur coat, and Grandmamma a leather-bound edition of the works of Sir Walter Scott, but Jennifer had no particular wish for either. In a moment's madness she nearly bought the model of a full-rigged ship, displayed in the window of a curiosity shop, and then closing her eyes and hurriedly walking away she found herself opposite an office with a brass plate on the door – 'Typing and Shorthand Taught. Private Lessons.'

Jennifer went inside, and arranged to take the full course which included book-keeping and accounts. This would give her something to do until Easter.

In spite of this she was not happy. Always there was something lacking. It seemed to Jennifer that there must be more in life than the things she had known, there must be more than this occasional laughter, these little sorrows, this common irritation, that evidence of good-will – the dull or funny incidents of day to day. There was no depth of satisfaction in them, no real comfort.

Depression hung heavily upon her and the sensation that she belonged nowhere. She had no corner in the atmosphere of the boarding-house, she could not adapt herself to that way of thinking and living.

London was still the bleak city she had hated as a child, the boarding-house was still the cheerless shell of a home that held no welcome.

It seemed to her that there was no way of escape.

After Christmas a newcomer arrived at No. 7 Maple Street. He was a man of about sixty, whose profession was vaguely understood to be 'something in the City'. His manners were almost too faultless, his choice of expressions correct to the last degree of verbosity, and he became the brightest and most glorious feature of the boarding-house. His name was Francis Horton. Jennifer loathed him at first, but soon decided he was too ridiculous to be of any consequence, and watched with amusement the approval he met at headquarters.

'Such a distinguished person,' said Grandmamma, 'quite

*comme il faut*, my dear Bertha. Really one of the old school.'

He was soon admitted into the intimate sanctity of the boudoir. The evenings were not complete without Mr Horton sitting between the two women, while Jennifer crouched in a rocking-chair by the bookshelf. His manner towards them was at once deferential and familiar, eager to assure them of his infinite respect, yet mingled with the spice of male superiority.

'Well, ladies,' he would begin in his smooth, silken voice, too carefully modulated to be natural, 'and how have you spent your day? Mrs Parkins, allow me to arrange that cushion for you – h'm? No trouble at all, I assure you, a positive pleasure. Well now, here we are, all assembled. Tell me what you have been doing.

'Oh! it's been very quiet as usual, Mr Horton,' said Bertha. 'I do my best, you know, that everything shall run like clockwork.'

'I am sure you do, Mrs Coombe. You think of everybody before yourself. What pretty work this is – can a mere male be permitted a glimpse?' He bowed gallantly towards her, and fingered the piece of embroidery in her hands.

Bertha laughed, and pulled it away, a new note of affection in her voice.

'Really, the curiosity of you men . . .'

Jennifer glanced from her book, noticed her mother's silly gesture and the bold, rather swimming expression in Mr Horton's pale blue eye.

She lowered her head, hot and uncomfortable, wishing she had not seen.

'What's that? What's that? What did Mr Horton say?' Grandmamma leaned forward in her chair.

'I perceive that Mrs Coombe is an excellent needlewoman, dear lady. So rare an accomplishment these days. "A stitch in time,' h'm? You know the old saying. And what is Miss Jennifer about? What is our silent one doing in her secluded nook? I fear your daughter is a great book-worm, Mrs Coombe.' He shook his head in mock reproof.

339

'It's no use trying to make Jenny sociable, we have long given up that hope,' sighed her mother. 'There are no manners in the younger generation. Put down that book for once, dear, and make yourself agreeable.'

'Yes, come along Miss Jennifer, and join our cosy little circle. "All work and no play," h'm? You know the rest?' He over-laughed, and flushed slightly at the temples.

He disliked Jennifer. He was afraid she considered him a middle-aged fool.

'I am always alarmed, Mrs Parkins, that your granddaughter will take down my remarks with this shorthand of hers.'

'Take down your . . . with her hands? What's that, Mr Horton? What's that?'

'You misunderstand Mr Horton, Mamma. He was afraid Jennifer will write our conversations in shorthand.'

'Oh! I see, of course. Yes, what nonsense it is, this typing and the rest of it.'

Her misunderstanding had caused a little flutter in the circle. Jennifer stared straight before her, biting her cheeks to contain her laughter. Mr Horton was once more bending towards her mother, twisting his absurd moustache.

'Isn't it marvellous how time flies – but really, really marvellous? Do you know, I have already been amongst you five weeks today?'

'What's that? What's he been doing with you for five weeks?'

'I have been your resident, Mrs Parkins, dear lady, nothing more nor less than your proud resident. I was just saying so to Mrs Coombe. Delightful, quite delightful. À propos – excuse my poor French – à propos I am in favour of making some small celebration. I propose a little party, just us four, you know, and a visit to the theatre.'

'Theatre? Nonsense, nonsense, I'm not up to going to a theatre, Mr Horton. Actors don't speak clearly these days. Take Bertha, Mr Horton, take Bertha.'

'Mrs Coombe, would you honour me?'

'Oh! delicious. Jennifer, you will come too, of course.'

'Thanks, terribly, but I'd rather not. I – er – I think I'm

getting a cold. Such a nuisance.' Jennifer lowered her eyes.

'Then it will be you and I alone, Mrs Coombe? You have no objection, I hope.'

Jennifer saw that her mother was blushing. She felt a little sick. She pushed back her chair, and moved once more towards the bookcase.

'Ah! Miss Jennifer, you don't approve, I see.' The silken voice followed her across the room.

'I promise you I will take great care of your dear mother; she will be a very precious trust, and she will be all the better for a little amusement.'

'As long as she's amused,' said Jennifer brightly, 'it's not my affair.'

As she left the room she heard his voice continuing: 'What kind of piece would you care to see? I enjoy a humorous performance myself. I always appreciate clean, healthy humour.'

As time went by the celebration became a weekly event. Jennifer was never asked again. Day by day she watched the intimacy gradually increase between her mother and Mr Horton. She watched his effort at gallantry, and her self-conscious acceptance of it. She noticed his methods of singling her out for especial attention, and her change of manner whenever he entered a room. She saw the beginning of his air of proprietorship, the authority that crept into his voice, and her way of asking his opinion on any subject, of relying upon his advice.

She was an unwilling witness of their glances and of their conversations. She could scarcely bear to sit in the same room when they were together for the embarrassment and the boredom that they caused her. Her mother must be a fool to feel any affection for this man. She made herself out a martyr too. Jennifer overheard her.

'My life has been full of ups and downs,' she had said. 'My poor husband never understood the sacrifices I made for him. I gave him the best years of my life. He gambled away our early savings, and I knew years of great wretchedness. Then he was a little more fortunate, and offered myself and the boys some sort of a home. We spent twelve years, as you know, buried in the depths of Cornwall. I never grumbled, because I believe in making the best of everything always. The people were kind in their fashion, but of course they were an entirely different class, you understand.'

'You poor, dear thing,' he said, taking her hand.

'My happiness was wrapped up in Christopher and the children, to see that they were content prevented me from thinking of myself.'

Jennifer hurried away. It was beastly, nauseating. She could not bear it.

How could Mother speak about Daddy in that careless, off hand way, when he had slaved and toiled for her. Given him the best years of her life! What about Daddy? He had given her nothing apparently. He had stood by making no attempt to understand her.

Poor darling – poor darling, and all she could remember was a fair head on a pillow, and a figure raising his arm to wave to her from the bottom of a hill. . . .

Daddy . . . Harold . . . Willie. All gone, all forgotten as though they had never been, and Mother mouthing at this stranger with his silly sheep's eyes.

Perhaps she was hoping to marry again. After all, why not? Nobody forced her to remain a widow.

Obviously that was what was going to happen. She would become Mrs Horton, the wife of this fool. Her mother who was fifty-five. Revolting, horrible picture . . . How could women, after they had loved one man, ever think, look, at anybody else? Even if their husbands had been dead for years they must remember. It was sordid, unattractive. She tried to imagine what the future state of things would be like. Perhaps they would move to another part of London. Mr and Mrs Francis Horton, and she, Jennifer, his stepdaughter. Odious sense of familiarity. 'Your mother and I have decided, my dear . . .' The three of them sitting round the breakfast table.

'Another cup of tea, Francis?'

'Thank you, Bertha love, I have had sufficient.' His beastly smile of possession, aware of himself, and she fluttering, tremulous, eager to please.

And Jennifer condemned to watch them, conscious of the falsity of the whole position. She could not imagine how she would act under the circumstances.

The days passed, and nothing had been said. Jennifer began to look about her for another job.

She had just passed her nineteenth birthday. Apparently London was overcrowded with girls wanting to be typists; she almost despaired of ever finding a post. She would read the lists of 'Wanted' in the *Daily Telegraph*, but none of them seemed particularly suitable or worthy of notice. Life was rather a grind, and not so terribly amusing; she wondered why she was bothering at all. That idiot Horton had a tiresome way of seizing the *Daily Telegraph* before anyone else in the house, and reading it from page to page. She determined to prevent him by rising earlier in the morning, and running through the advertisements while they were waiting for breakfast.

The third morning that Jennifer did this she stopped halfway upon the stairs, a few steps from the drawing-room. The door was open, and she saw Horton with his arms round her mother. He had obviously just kissed her, and not for the first time. Her mother was patting her hair, and making a silly little face in the glass.

'Francis, I think we ought to tell them,' she was saying, 'people will begin to talk.'

'If you wish it, my Bertha, I propose that we make the announcement official at breakfast this morning. Wedding bells in the offing, h'm? What a sensation it will cause.'

'I think Mama is expecting it, but I don't know about Jenny.'

'Oh!' he laughed, 'leave Jennifer to me. She won't be any trouble, I assure you. A little firm handling is needed, that is all. We will soon be firm friends, you know. A father's will, eh?'

'Francis – how wonderful you are.'

Jennifer heard no more. She went upstairs and into her mother's bedroom. She took the faded, rather dusty photograph of Christopher Coombe from behind its vase on the mantelpiece. Then she glanced out of the window at the rows of chimney-pots stretching over London. The bugle summons rang out from the barracks across the street. 'Listen, Daddy,' she said, 'what do you suggest I do?'

' . . . And so, my very dear friends one and all, I have the extreme pleasure of informing you that your dearly-loved and respected hostess, Bertha Coombe, has done me the honour of consenting to become Mrs Horton.'

Cries of surprise, gratification, and polite approval came from the little crowd of boarders assembled in the dining-room. 'Isn't that just too romantic for words . . . we had no idea . . . heartiest congratulations . . . you're a lucky man . . .'

'I suppose you are all anxious to hear when the happy event will take place,' he continued. 'Well, I don't mind admitting it will be soon, very soon. Naturally, I am impatient, and I trust my dear wife-to-be shares my sentiments.'

Bertha nodded, and smiled up at Christopher's successor.

'I do not propose to rob you of her for long. Just a three weeks' honeymoon in some quiet corner, and we will continue to live here as before.'

'What's that, what's he going to do in a quiet corner?' whispered Mrs Parkins. 'Tell him to speak up, Bertha.'

'Hush, Mamma dear – he was referring to Ventnor.'

Horton was losing himself in a sea of eloquence.

' . . . Not only has she made me the happiest man on earth, but she has saved me from a drab and lonely bachelorhood, she has prevented me from straying and wandering in the paths of life with no fixed purpose, a rolling – er – stone gathers no – and so on, or in other words better to wear out than to rust out . . .' He broke off in some confusion.

'Go on dear,' murmured Bertha, 'it's beautiful.'

'What I mean is, dear friends, that I trust I will bring as

344

much content to her as I know she will bring to me.' He sat down amidst a chorus of applause.

'But where is Jenny?' asked someone.

'Hasn't she congratulated the happy pair?'

'Yes – where is Jennifer?'

Her seat at the table was empty. No one had noticed this before.

'Jennifer is late for breakfast,' said her grandmother. 'What is she up to? Some nonsense or other.'

At that moment Jennifer came into the room. She wore a tweed coat over her jumper and skirt, and a brown squash hat tilted to one side. In her hands she carried a couple of small suitcases, and a disreputable old mackintosh hung over her shoulder, covered with ink stains.

'Jennifer,' exclaimed Grandmamma, 'what is the meaning of this?'

'Jenny – what is it?' cried her mother. The boarders gaped up at her, interested but confused.

Lastly Mr Horton, in his new dignity, rose from the table.

'Dear Jennifer,' he began, 'I think you owe your mother an explanation. Why this – er – costume? And those portmanteaux?'

They waited for her answer.

'I'm going away,' said Jennifer.

'You intend leaving us, making your departure in this absurd high-handed way?'

He watched her face incredulously.

Grandmamma shook with anger, and Bertha fumbled for her handkerchief.

'Listen to me, Mr Horton,' said Jennifer, 'what I do and where I go is my affair. I hear you are going to marry my mother: that's your affair. I hope from the bottom of my heart you'll both be happy. Let's leave it at that, shall we?'

'But Jenny – one moment, I don't understand.'

'Don't you, Mother? Well, it doesn't matter very much, does it? You want to lead your life in a new way, and I'm going to do the same with mine. I've had just over thirteen years

345

of the present one, and believe me it's enough. I'll send you a picture postcard from time to time. Good-bye – everybody.'

'Stop her – stop her,' said Grandmamma, purple in the face. 'There's some man at the bottom of this; she's no better than she should be. Find out where she is going?'

Jennifer waved her suitcase in farewell.

'I'm going to the place where I belong,' she shouted. 'I'm going home to my own people – home to Plyn.'

# 8

Jennifer had exactly five pounds, six shillings, and fourpence halfpenny when she left No. 7 Maple Street. She lugged her two suitcases along with her into various buses, and arrived at Paddington with three-quarters of an hour to wait before the twelve o'clock train should bear her away from London for ever. Thirty-two shillings and sixpence of her capital went on her third-class ticket, and three shillings more on a cup of coffee, two rashers of bacon, and a banana, for she had eaten no breakfast. During this wait she had time to think over her crazy flight from the boarding-house. It had been her home since she was six years old, and she had left her mother without one pang of regret. 'I must be terribly unnatural,' thought Jennifer sadly. 'But it can't be helped. I was probably born without a heart; I believe some people are.'

She sat, rather aghast at herself, watching the movement of people about the platform, the roll of trolleys, the bustle of porters, the sudden shrieks and shuntings of departing trains.

Thirteen years before she had arrived here, at this very station, clinging to her mother's hand, subdued, tearful, utterly bewildered by the lights and the clamour, and it seemed to her now that those years had counted as nothing in her life, that she was still unchanged and unaltered from the child of six years old, who had felt herself alone. Jennifer sat in the corner of the carriage, and the train bore her swiftly from the city she detested, the roofs of houses stretching to the horizon, the crowded, threaded streets, the roar and clatter, the luxury, poverty, and squalor, the narrow faces of men and women; the train carried her past flat meadows and small hedges, glimpses of a narrow river, scattered towns, and a dull make-believe of country.

Later her spirits rose within her, strangely disturbed and content, for the flatness was left behind and they came upon rolling hills and a high white skyline, paths leading across the downs, sheep wandering in a thin unbroken line, and groups of labourers who raised their hands and waved.

And then suddenly, with no warning, the breathless grey sweep of the sea itself, breaking beneath the passing train, the high red cliffs of Devon, children who ran barefoot upon the shingle, and little boats like toys rocking against the tide.

They were in Cornwall now, her own country, and a weird, bewildering mixture of rugged hills and low, sweeping valleys, grey scattered cottages, tall forests, and swollen streams. In her excitement she got down at the wrong station, the junction for St Brides, and she had the anguish of seeing the train steam away in the distance, and her left with her luggage upon the narrow platform, some fifteen miles from her destination.

Ruthless and extravagant, careless of her money, Jennifer walked out of the station and found her way to a garage, and in less than twenty minutes she was being driven through the lanes towards Plyn in a hired and battered Ford.

Heedless of the white dust she took off her hat and let the wind run riot in her hair, she ignored the noisy engine and the fumes of petrol, and leaning forward she caught the scent of trees and hedges, primroses upon the banks, campion and flaming gorse, earth and the sun and the rain, and a distant shimmering tang of the sea.

They came upon the summit of a rolling hill. Down below, like a still lake in the valley of mountains, gleamed the wide grey waters of a harbour. A town was built up upon the farther hill, rising away in terraces to the cliffs. Old jumbled houses clustered together, the smoke curling from their slate chimneys. There were cobbled stone quays at the water's edge, and steps leading to the doors of the cottages.

A ship was leaving the harbour, she was steaming past the entrance, and making her way slowly and majestically to the open sea. Three times she blew her siren, and the sound travelled up into the air and was echoed by the surrounding hills. Hovering over the masts of the ships at anchor the gulls cried.

The driver of the Ford turned in his seat to Jennifer and pointed. 'Look there,' he called, 'that's Plyn.'

He jammed on his brakes and the car descended the steep, stony hill. Here there were whitewashed cottages on either side, and ducks and hens wandering in the ditches. Then a long stone wall and a cobbled slip and beyond this the wide expanse of harbour stretched to the sea, with the grey houses gazing down upon the shining water.

Jennifer left the car and leaned against the rough stone wall, and with one sweeping glance it seemed to her that she could gather to herself the whole of Plyn, she could break down the barrier of years that had meant separation and a dumb solitude; with a sigh and a strange awakening of her heart she looked upon that which was lost to her so long; and the peace so often sought came to her shyly, softly, like a message of hope.

Jennifer paid her car and crossed the ferry. She wandered through the long narrow street of Plyn, her suitcases in either hand, uncertain as to her direction or for whom she must inquire.

She remembered in some queer intuitive way that Ivy House was beyond the town, that it lay some little distance up the farther hill towards the cliffs and the open sea. And as she reckoned this there came the realization that Ivy House was hers no longer, that it had belonged now for many years to others of whom she knew nothing, that they could scarcely give her welcome without warning, and twilight was falling, and she was virtually a stranger in her own home.

Now she stopped, tired, hungry, a little dispirited, craving some welcome. Scarce knowing what she was about she laid her hand on the arm of a passer-by and questioned him.

'Tell me,' she asked him, 'is there anyone in Plyn with the name of Coombe?'

The man gazed at her curiously.

'Which Coombe is it you'll be wantin', my dear?' he

inquired. 'There's several Coombes in Plyn, scattered here an' there you know.'

Jennifer tried to summon up her courage. Forlorn and weary, she could remember no relative who had known her as a child, there had been uncles, cousins, many of them she was certain, but their Christian names and their faces were unknown to her.

'I'm not sure,' she said unhappily. 'It's – it's some years since I was here. I feel a little bewildered, and scarcely know where to turn.'

'There's the two Miss Coombes who keep the shop yonder opposite the Bank – might they be of help to you? They're the daughters o' Samuel Coombe, but he's been dead many a year. They're elderly ladies, very good sort o' persons. Would you care to try there?'

'Oh, yes!' said Jennifer quickly. 'They might be able to advise me in some way. I feel rather abrupt to disturb them, are you sure they won't mind? Perhaps it would be better if I went to a hotel.'

'Are they relatives of yours, my dear, by any chance?'

'Yes – at least I hope so. My name is also Coombe.'

'Well, then, Miss Mary and Miss Martha will make you welcome for sure. There's the place just opposite, with the queer-shaped knocker on the door. Good night to you.'

'Good night – and thank you.'

She walked across the street and tapped upon the door. She felt nervous now and shy, uncertain of what she should say. Mary and Martha – she was sure these names formed some link in her memory. Aunt Mary – Aunt Martha – was it Harold who had mentioned them once, long ago? Even so, how could she be sure that they would know her?

The door opened, and a tall white-haired old woman with soft blue eyes and pink cheeks waited on the threshold.

'Is that Annie Hocking with my paper,' she began. 'Oh! I beg your pardon, miss, I didn't see proper in this fallin' light. Shop's closed now; were you wantin' anything particular?'

Jennifer, the hard, cool, resolute Jennifer, who had left No.

350

7 Maple Street with such assurance, was trembling now, a little girl again ready to cry.

'Excuse me,' she said. 'I am sorry to worry you, but I wasn't quite sure what to do or where to go. Could you tell me – was Christopher Coombe any relation of yours?'

The woman stared at her blankly for a moment, taken by surprise. Then her face cleared, and she smiled.

'Yes, indeed,' she answered. 'He was my first cousin, an' I looked after him an' his brothers as lads, me an' my sister between us. Aunties, he called us always.'

'Oh!' said Jennifer, the tears rising in her eyes. 'Oh! I'm so glad, so glad. You won't remember me, of course, but I'm his daughter – I'm Jennifer Coombe.'

'Why' – the woman's face puckered up strangely, she took a step forward – 'you'm never Jenny – poor Christopher's little Jenny?'

'Yes.'

The woman called over her shoulder: 'Martha – come here quick; why, did you ever? Who'd ha' believed it possible!'

Another old woman, the living image of her sister, but shorter and stouter appeared from the back room.

'What's all this to-do?'

'Why, here's Christopher's little girl – grown up an' big. You remember Jenny, Martha?'

'That's never Christopher's girl? Merciful Lord – whatever next. There now – I can scarce believe me eyes. Where you'm sprung from, my dear – so sudden after all these years? Come inside, my dear, an' let's have a peep at you proper.'

They led her into the little black kitchen overlooking the harbour. The curtains were not yet drawn, and through the window Jennifer could see the shadows of evening fall upon the water and the lights of the ships at anchor. The room was small and cosy. There was a cheerful fire burning in the low grate, and the table was laid for a simple supper – bread, cheese, and hot pasties. The room was lit by four candles, they flickered and danced in the cool air that blew gently through the open window. A cat lay stretched upon the hearth, licking its

351

paws. There was an old-fashioned dresser in the corner of the room, crowded with china, and a clock ticked above it, solemn and slow. On the hob above the oven a kettle hummed softly.

Suddenly from without came the churning sound of water stirred by a ship's propeller, the grating, hollow rattle of the chain, a whistle and the hoarse cries of men.

Jennifer heard the sounds, she listened as though to the echoes of forgotten dreams, she saw herself a child leaning from the bedroom window carried in her father's arms, stretching out her hands towards the distant lights. She looked around the little room, she saw the homely comfort of the fire, the quiet flickering candles, the shadows playing upon the ceiling, the simple cottage furniture, the waiting meal, the faces of the two old women smiling, tender, holding out their hands to her in welcome.

Jennifer turned from them, blinded by tears, ashamed of her foolishness, but helpless, immeasurably content.

'You don't know what this means,' she said, 'but this is home to me, home at last.'

# 9

The following day there was much to be said and discussed. The aunts would have the whole story of Jennifer's running away, and her reasons; they inquired of this London they had never seen and how irksome it must have been for the poor child to have borne it so long; and how these thirteen years had changed the little girl they had known, and then the war and such unrest, and they had heard of Harold's death but not of Willie's; what sadness and misery it was for sure, and many were gone from Plyn never to return, the place itself greatly changing according to some but scarcely spoilt for all that.

Then Jennifer in her turn inquired what relatives were living, but though she heard many names, and uncle this and cousin that, she admitted they meant nothing to her.

Later she walked in Plyn and to her dismay found she remembered little, save the angle of the place here and there, the slope of the hill leading to the cliffs, the Castle ruin, the path across the fields to the church. The town itself seemed unfamiliar and quaint, but no less dear for all her short memory.

It was the harbour that delighted her most, the ships, the sailing boats, the glimpse of the jetties near the station, the wide grey sweep of water and the chink of open sea beyond the entrance.

Then she stole away up the road and through the fields, to the tower of a church she could see rising above the slope of the hill.

Jennifer came to Lanoc.

She wandered among the graves searching for the one she loved. For some time she looked about her in vain, and lastly she arrived next a thorn hedge and an elm tree, and here were many stones bearing the Coombe name, some plain and recent, others ivy-covered, worn with age.

Here was Herbert Coombe and his wife, here was Mary Coombe, Samuel and his wife Posy; there was someone named Elizabeth Stevens and her husband Nicholas, there were sons and grandchildren of these people. Close to the hedge was a stone that seemed older than the others, it was sunk a little, and the ivy so clustered about the writing that Jennifer had to break some of it away to see the blurred and faded name.

'Janet Coombe of Plyn, born April 1811, died September 1863, and also Thomas Coombe, husband of the above, born December 1805, died September 1882. Sweet Rest At Last.'

There was no stone older than this, and she wondered if these were the first Coombes, the founders of the family. A little away to the left were two single graves, near to one another. Here lay Susan Collins Coombe, dearly beloved wife of Joseph Coombe, and the other grave, smaller, unkept, was also his wife's, 'Annie, wife of Joseph Coombe, died 1890, aged twenty-four years.' Joseph himself was not here. Was it he who had been her grandfather, and whom her mother had spoken of as selfish and cruel? Poor Annie, aged twenty-four—

Then at last she found that for which she had been seeking, apart, on a rising slope of ground, with the letters cut clear and strong against the white stone. 'Christopher Coombe, son of Joseph and Susan Collins Coombe, who gave up his life fearlessly on the night of 5 April 1912, aged forty-six years.'

Jennifer knelt down and smoothed away some of the tangled grass, she found an empty pot amidst some rubbish by the side of the hedge, and this she filled with water from a tap next the church, and placed inside it the daffodils she had brought for him.

Then she stood up, and looked upon the little group of graves, these last resting-places of her people, so quiet and peaceful in the still churchyard, unmolested save for the blossom that fell from the trees in the farther orchard.

And Jennifer turned, knowing them free from trouble and distress, and went home through the fields to Plyn.

Half-way down the hill she asked a passing boy the exact whereabouts of Ivy House, but he shook his head and said there was no such house in Plyn. She insisted, however, saying she had lived there before the war, and he called to a woman across the road, 'D'you know anything of Ivy House, Mrs Tamlin? The young lady says she lived there, but I've never heard of it.'

'Oh! that's Seaview she'll be meaning,' answered the woman. 'It was called Ivy House once some years ago, I believe.'

'No ivy on it now, miss,' grinned the boy. 'It's a fine new-looking place. Mr and Mrs Watson are the present owners. Look, that's it, away yonder, standing in its own garden.'

Jennifer walked uncertainly towards the square, middle sized house, surrounded by a trim box hedge.

There was a green gate, and a trim path leading to the front door. This door was also painted a bright green. The roof was obviously new, the old grey slates were gone, and shining black ones in their place. No ivy now on the face of the house, but to relieve the bare appearance the owners had stuck a couple of pillars of eastern origin beneath the lower windows. Where the wash-house had been they had built a small conservatory, and facing the garden, leading from the original parlour, the path had been constructed into an attempt at a verandah.

A woman was lying in an orange hammock, with a Pekingese dog in her lap, and an elderly man was stooping over a flower bed, snipping at something with a pair of scissors.

He rose and wiped his forehead with his handkerchief.

'I think it would be wise if we spread a little lime here, my dear,' he called to the woman, and seeing Jennifer staring at him over the hedge he frowned and turned his back. The dog began to yap excitedly.

'Quiet, Boo-Boo,' cried the man, and then said in a tone, unnecessarily loud, 'He's a good little watch dog all the same. He knows when strangers are about.'

355

Jennifer turned and ran down the hill, her eyes burning and her heart throbbing while she was aware of something sticking in her throat which she could not control.

Seaview. But that was only a phase of time to those new people, they could not alter the truth. They imagined that the place belonged to them, to change it as they willed, but somewhere there was no hammock, no yapping dog, only a little girl waving to her daddy, swinging backwards and forwards on the garden gate.

That day Jennifer helped her aunts with the shop, but she was scarcely needed, for the business was simple and easy, and they were both well accustomed to the work for all their sixty-nine years of age.

In the evening Jennifer begged them to tell her something of the old days in Plyn, of her father as a boy, of her grandfather, and of the worries and cares that had been part of their life.

One by one Jennifer conjured up the scenes of the past, she saw the men and women whose name she bore live out their little lives, knowing sorrow, joy, suffering, and despair, loving and hating one another, and so pass away out of the scheme of things, realities no more, nothing but the grey tombstones in Lanoc Churchyard.

Janet – Joseph – Christopher – Jennifer, all bound together in some strange and thwarted love for one another, handing down this strain of restlessness and suffering, this intolerable longing for beauty and freedom; all searching for the nameless things, the untrodden ways, but finding peace only in Plyn and in each other; each one torn apart from his beloved by the physical separation of death, yet remaining part of them for ever, bound by countless links that none could break, uniting in one another the living presence of a wise and loving spirit.


'It seems to me, then, that Uncle Philip set himself against my grandfather from the first, and because he hated him he carried the bitterness on into the next generation – Daddy, too, had to suffer.' Jennifer was filled with anger and loathing for this old man who had brought such ruin and misery to her family.

'I'd like to make him suffer now,' she said. 'I'd like to bring fear to him as he has done to others. We don't know anything about death; why should he be allowed to go free now, just because he's so old, and nobody has the pluck to stand up to him? I believe that's the truth of the whole matter. No one has the pluck.'

'Oh! your Cousin Fred stood up to him, an' bravely too,' interrupted Aunt Martha. 'When he was a young man it was he took your grandfer' from Sudmin, and it was he spoke him to his face in the office hard by after your dad died, full seventeen years later. Fred was a good friend to Christopher an' Uncle Joseph.'

'I wish I could thank him, but wasn't it he who was killed in the war?'

'Yes – poor man. Which year was it, Mary? – 1917, I'm thinkin'. He left a widow an' boy, but Norah didn't long survive him. The boy though – well – there's a regular Coombe if you like. He's our celebrity in Plyn these days.'

'Yes, indeed,' smiled Martha, 'we'm proud o' John. John's the talk of all folk now.'

'Why, what does he do?' asked Jennifer. 'I seem to remember playing once with a boy called John, but he was older than me.'

'That 'ud be John all right, when he was up to the farm with his family. I mind your dad would take you there visitin' at times. Well, John's a great lad, a splendid lad. He tried to get to France in a little boat during the war, only a young chap he was, bare seventeen, but not a fear in his heart, bless him. Off he started at dead o' night, in an old tub scarce seaworthy it appeared, but luckily he was found off Plymouth somewheres, an' sent back home with a caution.'

'Oh! what a shame!' said Jennifer. 'Then he never got to the war?'

'No, my dear, he didn't, he was under age you see. Well,

then his poor mother died – such a to-do, there was John left with the farm on his hands, an' a tidy sum of money in the bargain.

'So what d'you think he does, Jenny?' cried Martha excitedly, her cheeks flushing with pride.

Jennifer shook her head, smiling at the two old women.

'I'm sure I can't guess.'

'He sets brother Tom an' Cousin Jim up in the yard again which hadn't been used since the trouble o' the licadation, an' he himself goes off over the country to learn his trade, findin' out this, an' improvin' on that, and back he comes four years ago with every trick at his fingers' ends, an' since then he's done nothin' but build yachts, build yachts – from winter till summer, with orders comin' through to him from all over the place, an' Plyn in quite a ferment over the whole business. Why – look through the window, my dear, to the right of the harbour, see that huge ship there, stretchin' to Polmear Point, see them buildin's an' sheds, those cranes, an' the tops of masts – well, that's John's yard, Jenny – built beyond the original Coombes' Yard, but ten times as big. There now, did you ever see anythin' like it?'

'Has he really done all that in four years? He must have worked like a navvy. What's that mast tipping up behind the crane?'

'Why, that's the new 100-ton sailing cruiser he's havin' built. There's two of John's boats racin' at Cowes this year he tells me, two smaller ones built in his second year. They belongs to some gentlemen over to Falmouth. They'll be comin' here for the Regatta in August for sure.'

'So I suppose they've gained back all their losses, and are making more money now than they ever did in the old days.'

'That's right, my dear, that's right. An' brother Tom lives in a fine big cottage now, with a fair sized garden, and Jim next door with his married daughter. They're elderly men now, of course, like ourselves, but they still work – why, I've never seen such workers as they, did you, Mary?'

'No – I declare, but then it's all John's doing. He's the one.

Ah! Jenny, if only your dad could ha' lived to see this, my dear.'

'He would be proud and happy, wouldn't he?' asked Jennifer. 'Just to know that everything had come all right. He wouldn't mind the changes do you think?'

'O' course not, he'd be surprised no doubt, but 'tis a change for the better as everyone can see.'

'What does Uncle Philip say to all this?'

'Turns up his nose, you may be sure, an' ignores the whole proceedin's. If he'd been younger no doubt he'd ha' worked against it, puttin' in his evil spoke.'

'I think I shall go and see my fine Uncle Philip,' said Jennifer frowning. 'I'm not afraid of him.'

'Why, deary me, you'd never do that, would you? Mercy on us, he'd eat you alive.'

'I'd be willing to risk that!'

'There now, well, really. I wouldn't advise it, would you, Martha?'

'No, indeed, I wouldn't.'

'He's a fierce, irritable old gentleman, my dear, he only sees his head clerk I believe, an' those who has interviews on business. Why, Maggie Bate was workin' there till she left last week to be married. Typin' an' that, you know. She was proper scared of him, an' he'd never as much as spoken to her. It's difficult to get people to work for him. Has anyone taken Maggie's place, Martha?'

'No – not as I know.'

'Typing?' said Jennifer. 'Do you suppose they're looking for anybody else?'

'I couldn't say, but I should think it were possible. Few girls are willin', I dare say, with the scanty pay they get.'

'Well, I've got to get some sort of a job in Plyn, haven't I? Why shouldn't I try for this one?'

'Can you use a typewriter machine, Jenny?'

'Rather. I've just finished a secretarial course in London.'

'There now! – did you ever! Mercy on us, how the girl has grown up. I shouldn't go to your Uncle Philip all the same, my dear. I doubt if you'd care for sittin' all day in that nasty office, an' him maybe disagreeable.'

'No, Jenny, don't you go.'

'Oh! but I want to – I want to have a shot at it. I can always try something else if it's hateful. Perhaps I could speak to the head clerk, there'd be no need to come in contact with the old man at all. Not until later . . . Listen – it will be rather exciting. What's the name of the place?'

'Hogg an' Williams, on the quay. But you'd better not do it, Jenny?'

'Oh! yes, I shall. You see.'

The following morning Jennifer set out, and turned to the square red-brick building on the little cobbled quay. Above the door were the faded letters, untouched by paint, 'Hogg and Williams.'

She pushed open the door and went inside. An office boy stepped through a swing door on the right, and inquired her business.

'I want to see the head clerk, please,' she said.

'Mr Thornton? What is it you require?'

'I wanted to know if there is a vacancy for a typist, in place of – of a Miss Bate I think.'

'Oh! well, wait a minute, will you?'

The boy came back in a minute with the head clerk, Mr Thornton.

'I hear you are inquiring about the vacancy,' he began. 'As a matter of fact, we have a lot of work on hand and are rather anxious to fill the post. But if you don't mind my saying so you seem very young, and we can only use a person of experience.'

'That's me,' said Jennifer. 'Typing, shorthand, and the rest of it. I'd be very obliged if you'd give me a trial at least.'

'I'd like to be fair, of course,' he answered smiling. 'Your name, by the way?'

'Coombe – Jennifer Coombe.'

'Oh!' He looked rather taken aback. 'Are you any relation to Mr Coombe?'

'I may be some distant connexion,' said Jennifer carelessly. 'It's a common enough name in Cornwall, isn't it?'

'Quite so – quite so. The old gentleman has many relatives of course, but I think he sees none of them. He is very retiring, you understand.'

Two days later Jennifer came face to face at last with her Uncle Philip.

It happened that she had overstayed her time in order to finish a heap of letters. Her companions, the other clerks, left the office at five o'clock as usual and Jennifer imagined she was alone in the building save for the caretaker, who lived on the premises. She finished her letters at a quarter to six, and was about to leave when she noticed the door of her uncle's room, the private room, was half open.

Curiosity proved too much for the great-granddaughter of Janet Coombe, she walked along the passage and pushed open the door, and then stood, a little surprised at the figure that met her eyes.

Seated at his desk was an old man, his pale face heavily lined and wrinkled, his body bent and crouched with age but pitifully thin like the skeleton of a human being, his hands clasped together seemed the trembling claws of a bird, and the extreme pallor of his face and the white sparse hair stood out strongly against the drab black of his clothes.

Was this Uncle Philip? Was this weary, crumbling old man her father's enemy?

'Philip Coombe,' she said softly. He looked up, and saw standing in the doorway of his office the figure of a girl, her hands clasped to her breast, her chin tilted in the air, her dark hair brushed away from her face and her brown eyes fixed upon him.

He made no answer, he caught at the sides of his chair with his trembling hands, and stared back at this vision which had come to him out of the buried past. There were no more years, no time, no grim and satisfying death; this was Janet herself who stood before him, Janet who flamed in the bows of her vessel, Janet as he had seen her in his dreams

361

as a boy, Janet who had preferred Joseph to himself.

And Philip looked upon the figure shrouded by the shadows in the doorway.

'Why have you come?' he said. 'Is this Joseph's revenge, long waited for and planned?'

'Why do you speak of Joseph,' asked Jennifer, 'have you forgotten Christopher his son?'

'I had no quarrel with the son,' cried Philip, 'he deserved all that came to him. Am I to be held responsible for the poorer members of my wretched family, for the failures?'

Jennifer saw the sneer on her uncle's face, and was angry.

'You call Christopher Coombe a failure, do you? A failure because he lived simply, spending his time with the people in the cottages, the labourers in the farms, the fishermen. He was a failure because he was loved by people, loved, respected, and mourned. And you – you call yourself a success? What have you ever done for anybody in the world? You're hated by everyone in Plyn, you're only left alone because you're an old man, useless and feeble, too helpless to be of value.'

Philip leaned forward in his chair, breathing heavily, his eyes narrowed.

'Who are you, in God's name?'

Jennifer smiled. To think that people had been afraid of this trembling old man. He didn't even seem to know who she was.

'Who do you think I am?' she asked contemptuously. 'A ghost, someone out of your past? Look at you, shaking with fear in case I touch you.'

He rose unsteadily, leaning on his stick, and walked slowly towards her, peering into her face.

'Who are you?' he whispered. 'Who are you?'

She threw back her head and laughed as Janet had done, as Joseph had done, as Christopher had laughed before her.

'I'm Jennifer Coombe,' she said. 'I'm the daughter of Christopher your failure.'

He looked at her strangely, still uncertain, still wandering in his mind.

'Jennifer – I knew no Jennifer. Did Christopher have a daughter?'

She nodded, puzzled, struck by his behaviour.

'Yes,' she told him, 'I am Jennifer. I've been working in your office for two days. I had some curiosity to see the man who ruined my father and my grandfather.'

Once more Philip was master of himself.

'I must congratulate you on your fine performance then, no doubt,' he said. 'You should have been an actress. May I ask who gave you the permission to come into this room?'

'If you think you can frighten me you're making the biggest mistake of your life,' answered Jennifer. 'I don't care if you're the head of this firm or not, you happen to be my great-uncle and I'm not at all proud of the fact. Now, naturally, you'll dismiss me, but I expected it. I only took the job to have things out with you. Now I've met you I realize you're not worth it, that's all, just not worth the trouble. Good-bye, Uncle Philip.'

She turned and walked out of the room.

'Stay,' he cried, moving after her. 'Stay, come back.'

'Well – what do you want?'

He stroked his chin and looked at her.

'I have enjoyed this interview,' he said slowly, 'enjoyed it very much. I was in need of a little mental amusement. So you are my great-niece, are you? Not at all proud of the fact. What a pity. Well now, supposing you do me the extreme honour of dining with me tonight.'

'Dine with you?' Jennifer considered the matter. 'What! in that awful old house in that dreary terrace?'

'Yes – I'm sorry it does not meet with your approval.'

'Well – I might. I don't see why not.'

'That is decided then? I shall expect you at eight o'clock punctually.'

'All right. I'll be there. See you later.'

Jennifer left the building extremely surprised at the state of affairs. She had expected fury, or at least dismissal, instead of which he had calmly invited her to dinner. 'He's probably potty,' she thought to herself.

She put her head in the back sitting-room of the shop.

'Uncle Philip has asked me to dine at his house,' she told them. 'I thought it only genial to accept, though it rather bores me.'

The two old women stared at her aghast.

'Philip Coombe has asked you to his house? You'm jokin' of course, Jenny.'

'No – honest I'm not. I was surprised myself. I told him a few home truths and he asked me to dinner. Personally I think he's mad. I'm not in the least afraid of him.'

'But there's no one ever goes to his house, Jenny – he's never asked no one. He's got somethin' up his sleeve, depend upon it. I wouldn't go, my dear.'

'Of course I shall go. Good evening, I won't be late.'

Jennifer walked up the hill in high spirits. This was something of an adventure. She rang the bell of a grey and gloomy house, and was shown into a fair sized, barely furnished room. A small fire was burning in the grate. From the way it was smoking Jennifer guessed it was many years since it had been last lit.

Her uncle was standing in front of the fire. To Jennifer's amusement he had changed into a dinner jacket, of very old-fashioned cut, probably taken from some fusty cupboard, and unworn since the last century.

'Good Lord – I didn't know you were going to cope,' she said. 'I haven't brought any evening dresses down here.'

'What you are wearing is delightful,' he told her, and she supposed he was making her some sort of compliment.

The dinner was better than she had expected. They started with fish, and went on to a vague hash, flavoured with onion, followed by what he termed 'steam pudding'.

Afterwards they had coffee, and he handed her cigarettes, obviously bought for the occasion. 'I never smoke myself.' he told her. They talked a little while of various matters of Plyn and of the clay industry, and then after a slight pause he cleared his throat, and rubbing his hands softly together and avoiding her eyes, he began to speak once more.

'I must admit to you I have an object in asking you here this evening. The idea came to me very suddenly. I am an elderly man as you see. I may have few years, or only a few months in which to live. It is lonely here at times for an old man like myself. Now this is what I propose. That you live here with me for good – in fact – I propose to adopt you, become your guardian – what you will.'

'You must be crazy,' said Jennifer. 'Why, you don't even know anything about me. Besides, after the way you treated my father and my grandfather to calmly turn round and adopt me – whatever for?'

'My reasons are my own. Possibly they may be connected with what you have just said. My treatment of your father and your grandfather.'

Jennifer grasped something of his meaning, and was filled with contempt. In some mysterious way she had frightened him down at the office, she had shaken his faith in himself, and now he wished, not for any fondness of herself but for his own sake, to make some amends to her, daughter of Christopher, granddaughter of Joseph, in case there was any truth after all in the legend of existence after death. In case there was immortality. By adopting her he would acquit himself of what had been. She would be his means of salvation. From no love, no real atonement, but from a hidden terror. That was his reason. He wished to use her as a screen to his fear.

Jennifer thought rapidly.

'Would I be free to do as I wished?' she asked. 'Could I change this drab, gloomy house and try and make something out of it?'

He considered the matter for a moment. Jennifer knew he was thinking of the expense.

'Yes,' he said. 'Yes, you can be completely free. As to the house, you may alter it as you wish.'

'In that case,' said Jennifer slowly, 'in that case, Uncle Philip, I'll say yes. But I want you to understand that I come to look after your house. I refuse to treat you as my guardian, or for you to call me your adopted daughter. There must be no question of it.'

'So that is a bargain, eh?'

'Yes – Uncle Philip – we'll call it a bargain.'

She shook hands with him for the first time.

# 10

News travels fast in a town such as Plyn. The following day it was all over the place that Christopher Coombe's daughter, a girl fresh arrived from London, had met with her great-uncle Philip, the terrible, dreaded Mr Coombe of Hogg and Williams, and she was to live in Marine Terrace with him as his companion.

The theory was that this Jennifer Coombe was nothing more nor less than a common fortune-hunter making up to the old man who had ruined her dead father; she expected to be made his heiress.

Over in his shipbuilding yard word came to John Stevens of the amazing happenings in Plyn, but he was too busy with his yachts and his plans for the future to be greatly interested. When old Thomas Coombe told him the news with much excitement and shaking of his head, John, who was busy over some blueprint in his office, took his pipe out of his mouth and smiled.

'After his money, is she? She'll be a clever girl if she gets it. I don't see Philip Coombe parting with a halfpenny.'

'Why, John, it's the truth I'm tellin' you. There's that there house up to Marine Terrace all painted already, new curtains in t'window, an' the gal orderin' him about from pillar to post.'

'She must be an unholy terror, unless the old chap's in his dotage at last. Is that the child who used to live at Ivy House? Harold and Willie's young sister?'

'That's her, John. Bin educated in London – quite a young lady my sister was tellin' me. They took to her seemingly, but I don't know – sounds a queer sort o' concern to me.'

'Well, Cousin Tom, we haven't time for young women of fashion making up to disagreeable old gentlemen, though I dare say it's all very intriguing. D'you mind coming and casting an eye over this print?'

So he dismissed the matter from his mind.

At twenty-four, John Stevens was a very strong-minded and resolute young man. The dreamy boy had grown into one of the most efficient and enterprising of people; he had set out to build up a business and to make it well known through the whole of the west country, and he was succeeding. In a year or two his name would be among the best yacht-builders of the day, challenging the big firms on the north and the south coast. John had few thoughts for anything but his work, and he had long got over his old habits of dreaming and star-gazing, of seeing into the future, of feeling disaster and death.

John the boy had lain on the hills watching the sea, John the man wrote in his office or stood in his yard directing his workmen. John the boy had climbed aboard the wreck *Janet Coombe* and dreamt of the past, his eyes fixed on the little white figurehead in the bows, John the man waved aside sentimentality and possessing now the entire rights of the vessel, Philip Coombe being weary of the whole concern and selling his share for a small profit, he was considering breaking up the ship when he could spare men to the task. So it happened one Sunday afternoon in the middle of the summer, towards the end of June, this downright determined John Stevens was distinctly annoyed to find a recurrence of his old boyish symptoms, in other words the urge came upon him to leave his plans, to go from his office, and to walk across the hills to Polmear creek. From time to time the ship made claims upon him such as this, and John resented these claims. He resented any suggestions of weakness. That a figurehead should possess any powers over him at all was preposterous.

Janet Coombe was a decided nuisance. She was always bent on telling him what to do. Of course it had been she who had suggested starting the ship-building yard, but now that this was accomplished he was hanged if he would listen to her any more. It was all his imagination anyway, she was only a bit of painted wood.

He turned frowning to his work, a pencil in his mouth, his hair ruffled. He reached for a textbook at his side. He read a couple of pages but the words jumped up and down before his eyes. He looked out of the window and saw the blue sky and the glittering harbour. He heard the gulls crying on the Castle rocks.

'Oh! – hell,' said John, and threw his book across the room.

Two minutes later he was walking up the path that led to the fields, and Polmear creek.

Jennifer pulled her boat close to the ladder and made fast the painter. The tide was on the ebb, but they were only neaps and she would not find it aground when she was ready to return. She put her hands on the shaking rope ladder, and swung herself over the bulwarks on to the sloping deck. She looked around her curiously. This was the first visit she had ever paid to the schooner, and she had already been in Plyn over two months.

The glass on the skylight roof was smashed, and scattered about the deck. The winch was broken, pieces of broken spars and odds and ends of tattered gear lay unheeded in the scuppers. Part of the shrouds were gone, and the top of the mizzen mast had been carried away.

Some things remained strangely intact, the hoops around the masts, the wooden belaying pins in their sockets, the pumps.

Jennifer peered down into the dingy fo'c'sle, the notice clear cut on the bulkhead 'Certified to accommodate 6 seamen'. There were three cots still hanging, an old saucepan lay on the floor, and tucked away in one of the cots were the coverless pages of a magazine. Men had lived here, slept here, the little space had rung with their laughter and their song. Now all were gone, forgotten, dead perhaps. A drip of moisture from the deck above fell upon her hand. The atmosphere was chill and queer. As she turned to climb the ladder, she saw the photograph of a woman pinned upon the wall. A cutting from a newspaper of the year 1907. Someone had scratched a heart beneath it with his knife, and pierced it with an arrow.

On the deck she looked into the tiny galley; the oven was still there, and two empty bottles. One cracked plate remained in the rack.

The wheel stood as it had done thirteen years before when Dick Coombe had helped bring her into harbour, and Jennifer was standing on the very place where Christopher had fallen, his back crushed by the falling spar.

She made her way down the companion-way into the cabin.

First she came to the mate's hole, a space no bigger than a small cupboard, and from thence into the main cabin, or cuddy, a room about six or seven foot square, a swinging table in the centre, a built-in bench, and lockers on either side.

A sliding door led to the master's sleeping cabin, a cupboard scarce two feet larger than the mate's, but with the addition of a wash basin. Here Christopher had sobbed himself to sleep as a lad, on his first sea voyage from Bristol, while Joseph his father tramped the deck above, bewildered and embittered by his son's distress. Jennifer sat down at the table, her chin in her hands. A clock was still nailed to the bulkhead, the hands had stopped at twenty-four minutes past nine. The lamp still swung in its gimbals, the brass dim and discoloured. There was a calendar of 1912 hanging beneath it. The cabin smelt damp, rotten; through the floor boards the water crept at high spring tides.

The drawer in the table was filled with charts, yellow now with age, and dirty and well thumbed. Joseph had sat here once, and spread the charts upon the table. He had marked them with his seal – 'Joseph Coombe, Master.'

Jennifer rose, haunted and wretched. She opened the lockers and found them filled with indiscriminate objects. There were some old books, paper, sodden with the damp, and a man's cap.

She passed into the captain's cabin and rummaged around in his lockers. Here she found a bent tooth-brush, a collar stud, and one sock, in the corner of a drawer a small worn prayer-book. On the fly-leaf was written 'To Dick, from his loving father Samuel Coombe, May 1878.'

The highest locker Jennifer found she could not open. She pushed and pulled, but it stuck firmly, and then finally after one determined wrench, it opened. She soon saw the reason for it. Inside was a large wooden box of some depth. She lifted this out, and carried it into the cuddy, placing it upon the table. On raising the lid and looking inside she found it to be full of papers, documents, and bundles of old letters.

One by one she laid them on the seat beside her. There were bills of sale here, bills of lading, documents relating to the ship's cargo, to the freights at various ports, accounts of passages, a few rough pages from the ship's log.

Here was Joseph Coombe's Master's Certificate, the piece of parchment that had given him and Janet the happiest and proudest moment of their lives. Here was a faded photograph taken in 1879 of Joseph and Susan with their four children, Christopher, Albert, Charles, and Katherine.

There were letters of Joseph's and of Dick's, about the ship's record passages, there were bits and pieces of detail making in one stupendous whole the sketchy outline of the *Janet Coombe*'s history.

As Jennifer wandered amongst these forgotten things she saw again, in the reading of them, the proud sway of a ship upon a lifting sea, she heard the singing canvas and the straining masts, she heard the shouts and tramping of men upon the deck, she saw the figure of Joseph, his dark hair and beard wet with the spray, his voice crying some order – and carried away by the wind.

She heard the scream of a gale and the thunder of the sea. She saw Joseph throw back his head and laugh.

Then she looked around her in the cabin, she heard the drip of the moisture from the deck, she saw the broken glass and rusted nails upon the sodden floor – mournful – mournful.

Beneath all the letters, at the bottom of the box, was a small bundle tied with a piece of worn tape. Something in the handwriting clutched at Jenny's heart. She had seen that writing before. It was in books of her mother's. The writing was Christopher's. The envelopes were addressed to Joseph Coombe. She turned them over and found the seal unbroken. They had never been read.

She felt she had the right to read these letters that had come like this out of the past.

Now for the first time in her life Jennifer learned the truth of Christopher's early days in London. The last letter was dated 22 November 1890, never read, never answered. Condemned to lie in this box for over thirty-five years until his daughter found it.

The tears were running down Jennifer's face now, she rocked herself backwards and forwards in distress.

'Oh! my darling,' she said, 'my darling.'

She had not heard the footstep on the deck, nor the soft creaking of the ladder, and as she raised her eyes from the pile of letters on her lap she saw that someone was standing in the cabin doorway, looking at her. For a moment neither of them spoke. Jennifer, too startled to move at first, saw Christopher with his long legs and fair ruffled hair – like a vision this flashed before her and was gone, and instead was a young man she had never seen before.

John had ploughed over the dry mud to the schooner, he had noticed a small boat on the starboard quarter fastened to the ladder, floating in a foot of water.

'Trespassers,' he thought, and climbing aboard had made his way down to the cabin. There he stopped, his eyes narrowing, his heart thumping, for surely there was Janet Coombe herself kneeling against the table, her hands clasped, her dark hair brushed away from her face.

Then the vision was gone, and he saw this stranger was only a young girl with the tears running down her face.

'Hullo,' said John.

'Hullo,' said Jennifer, wiping her eyes with the back of her hand.

'You've been crying about something?'

'Yes.' He stepped forward and noticed the box on the table.

'How did you manage to get that drawer open?'

'I wrenched it until it came of its own accord.'

'I thought I'd jammed it too tight ever to be moved.'

'Did you put the box in there, then?'

'Yes – about half a dozen years ago. Before then it used to lie on this bench you're sitting on. I was afraid it might get damaged, or that some curious fool would come across it. I see now it wasn't safe even in the drawer.'

'Do you mean I'm a curious fool?'

'I don't know anything about you. Have you put the letters back?'

'Most of them. I'm going to keep these.'

'Which ones are they? Do you mean to say you've been and broken the seal? Isn't that rather a filthy thing to go and do? I put them at the bottom on purpose. They belong to someone who is dead – who died over twenty-five years ago.'

'I know that.'

'You do, do you? You make a habit of reading dead people's letters?'

Jennifer turned away, the tears in her eyes.

'I never want to do it again – there's so much unhappiness, so much that is pitiful, that I'd rather not know the truth.'

'Was it these letters that you were crying over when I came in just now?'

'Yes.'

He came and sat on the bench beside her.

'Why should they make you cry?'

'I don't know who you are – or why I should answer you. You called me a curious fool just now, let's leave it at that.'

'I'm sorry – that was rude of me. But you see, this ship belongs to me: I was furious that anyone who was a stranger, who didn't understand, should come aboard at all.'

'I do understand.'

'These papers have given you some idea, I suppose. The ship is bound up with the lives of dead people, men and women who loved one another – and now there's nothing left. It was very wrong of you to open the sealed letters.'

373

'How can it be wrong when they are mine?'

'What are you talking about?'

'Those letters were written by my father to my grandfather.'

'Then you are Jennifer?'

'Yes – I'm Jennifer. Are you John?'

'I'm John.'

'Do you want a handkerchief, Jennifer? I've got one here you can use. It's fairly clean.'

'Thanks.' She took his handkerchief and blew her nose, then wiped the tears from the corners of her eyes.

'Now you look better. I've been rather beastly to you. I'm terribly sorry.'

'It's all right. How were you to know who I was.'

'I don't know – I might have guessed. So you're living with Philip Coombe? How do you get on with him? You seem to be the only person who has ever managed him.'

'I think people have been frightened of him so long that it's become a sort of legend. He isn't frightening at all. He's just a wretched old man who is afraid to die.'

John made no answer to this. He fumbled about in his pocket.

'Do you mind a pipe?'

'No.'

For a minute he busied himself in filling and lighting it. Then he spoke again.

'Listen, Jennifer. Don't think any more about those letters. It was all long ago, wasn't it? You're upset because you feel your father was never forgiven. I can remember him here in Plyn. I was only a small boy at the time, but he gave me the impression of being the happiest, gentlest creature in the world, utterly content and at peace. Really at peace. He didn't worry about his father Joseph. He knew that everything was all right. I liked him tremendously, he was my own father's greatest friend.'

Jennifer touched his arm.

'You can read these letters if you like. Read them with me now.' He glanced at her sideways.

'Can I? That's rather sweet of you, Jennifer.'

374

She spread them out in front of her and they sat with their shoulders touching, their chins cupped in their hands.

When they had finished Jennifer put them away without a word.

'How did the box come here?' she asked afterwards.

'It belonged to your grandfather. It was always kept here. Then when Dick Coombe became skipper he used it too. Those letters of your father must have been slipped in when Joseph Coombe went to Sudmin.'

'Daddy must have written other letters, I wonder what happened to them.'

'Destroyed, I suppose.'

'I suppose so.'

'Do you want to keep the box?'

'No – let's leave it here, where it's always been.'

He got up and taking the box he put it away in the drawer. Then he came back, and looked down at her curiously, his hands in his pockets.

'So you and I are cousins, Jennifer?'

'Vaguely – but several times removed.'

'No – not so damned removed.'

Jennifer laughed.

'Come on deck – I want to show you something,' he told her. They climbed up the ladder and walked forward to the fo'c'sle head.

'Give me your hand,' said John. He pulled her up beside him by the bowsprit. They both leaned over the bows of the ship. 'You haven't met Janet Coombe, have you?'

'No,' said Jennifer.

'There she is, below you.'

Jennifer looked upon the figurehead in the white dress, the old-fashioned hat, the dark hair pushed away from the pale face, the eyes gazing seaward, the chin in the air.

'Oh!' cried Jennifer, 'I wish I'd known her, I wish she wasn't dead.'

'She isn't dead.'

'Isn't she?'

'No – she knows we're here, both of us.'

'I believe she does.'

They smiled at one another.

'Jennifer, do you realize anything?'

'Realize what?'

'Do you realize you're exactly like her?'

'Like the figurehead?'

'Yes.'

She laughed. 'Am I really?'

'H'm. How odd,' he broke off suddenly, and leaned against the bulwark, his chin in his hands.

Jennifer went and stood next to him. 'What are you thinking about?'

'Wondering what made me come out to the ship today.'

'I'm glad you came,' she told him. 'After all, we ought to know each other, being cousins.'

'We aren't terribly removed, are we?'

'No – not terribly.'

They looked down into the shallow water, watching a crab settle on the bottom. John picked up a piece of glass and threw it down. They laughed as the crab scuttled away.

'Jennifer, I believe I remember you as a child.'

'Do you?'

'Yes – I'm sure you were brought to tea at the farm sometimes. Rather shy and timid.'

'Was I? I believe I remember you too. There was a boy called John played with me once in a field. He kept running ahead, and I couldn't keep up.'

'I bet that was me.'

He kicked the side of the bulwark.

'Jennifer – tell me why you've gone to live with Philip Coombe?'

'I don't know – as a sort of subtle revenge.'

'Don't see where the revenge comes in myself.'

'No – you wouldn't. Nobody would but me.'

'Is it terribly subtle?'

'Terribly.'

376

He could not help smiling at her grave face.

'You ran away from home, didn't you?'

'I ran away from London – Plyn is my home.'

'You love Plyn very much?'

'H'm.'

'So do I.'

They looked across the harbour and watched the gulls.

'How old are you, Jennifer?'

'Nineteen.'

'You look younger.'

'No, I don't.'

After a minute he spoke again.

'Would you like to come and look over the yard some time? That is, if you've nothing better to do. It might interest you.' He spoke as though he didn't care twopence whether she came or not.

'Yes – I'd like to very much.'

'Don't bring Uncle Philip with you.'

'Do you think I would?'

'Jennifer – listen. If he gets trying – if you suddenly loathe the sight of him – will you come and tell me?'

'Right, John, I will. You mean – I can vaguely count on you should I get depressed or . . .'

'No – not vaguely. Definitely. Always at any time.'

'It's awfully nice of you,' said Jennifer. She whistled and looked at her watch.

'I ought to be getting back.'

They walked to the ladder in silence.

'Can I take you anywhere in my boat?' she asked.

'No – I can get back across the fields.'

She climbed down the ladder into the waiting dinghy.

'Wait a minute,' said John. He looked so stern and cold that she was almost afraid of what he should say. 'Listen – supposing we make this a sort of weekly business? I mean – come out here every Sunday and talk.'

Jennifer hesitated. He sounded so bored with his idea she hardly cared to agree.

377

'Do you mean that?' she asked.

'Sure.' Then he smiled.

'That's a bet then?'

'That's a bet.'

'Good-bye – Jennifer.'

'Good-bye – John.'

Now that Jennifer acted as her uncle's companion there was no point in her continuing as typist in his office. She had no need of money. What he allowed her for housekeeping expenses was more than enough for her wants. Jennifer was not naturally extravagant but on seeing the pain it gave her uncle to part with as little as a shilling, she doubled the expenditure, knowing for his own sake he dared not refuse. He had fixed it in his mind that this great-niece of his should be the barrier between him and terror, that while she was present Janet and Joseph could not get to him. He clung to her from fear.

So, though he watched her spend his money he said nothing. Jennifer knew that every penny she threw aside hurt this old man, and she continued, recklessly, laughing, remembering how Christopher had suffered.

This was the subtle revenge of which she had spoken to John.

After the house in Marine Terrace had been done up, painted, redecorated, and refurnished from top to bottom, she turned her attention to Plyn itself. The mission, the hospital, the poor, all these claimed her attention under the official patronage of her uncle, and when a scheme was brought forward to raise a sum in order to acquire large spaces of the headland for the public, as a safeguarding against building, the name of Philip Coombe headed the list of subscribers.

And all the while Philip Coombe watched little by little the crumbling of the wealth he had secreted for himself, he watched this girl with Joseph's eyes and Joseph's ways do as she pleased, spend as she pleased, and he hated her.

Jennifer saw the expression in his narrow deep-set eyes, she saw his wrinkled hands clutch the side of his chair, she saw the thin mauve lips pressed tight together – she knew the horror he had of her and she smiled inwardly, caring not at all.

Jennifer had no worries, the time was passing pleasantly for her. She wrote to her mother telling her of the happenings of Plyn, of this living with Uncle Philip, of the freedom and amusement of life in general, of her friendship with her cousin John. Her mother's reply was typical, neither cool nor particularly warm, surprised that she should have so made up to her father's enemy, but glad that she was comfortable in his house, and after all, she had always heard he was a gentleman which Jennifer must naturally appreciate with her own education and upbringing. Plyn of course was delightful in summer, but no doubt she would find it very different with the approach of winter, though probably in her position as Philip Coombe's niece she would have invitations to parties and dinners, which she, Bertha, had never experienced, poor Daddy having no social position. Meanwhile Francis and herself had settled comfortably down once more at No. 7, after a delightful three weeks at Ventnor, and she was certain that her life in future would make up for all those lonely years of widowhood and even before. At last someone really understood her, and though she would always remember poor Daddy with affection, she knew now what true love meant, she and Francis being everything to each other.

And Jennifer must look upon Francis as a real friend and adviser; if she returned to London she would find a ready welcome from them both.

Bertha added in a postscript that poor Grandmamma was seedy, and though she had not forgiven Jennifer she had insisted on reading the letter. She had seemed very perturbed about this Cousin John, and wanted to know what he and Jennifer found to do on a lonely old wreck, miles from sight of anyone, and quite out of earshot, on a Sunday afternoon. She did not like the sound of it at all. There was no knowing what a hot-headed

379

young man might take it into his fancy to do.

Jennifer shouted with laughter over the postscript, but frowned as she saw the words at the bottom . . . 'anyway, Jenny dear, although Grandmamma exaggerates, I hardly think the idea of these meetings very nice myself. After all, you are so young and with nobody to look after you down there. I should not care for you to come to any understanding with this young man – boat-builder or whatever he is – especially as he is a cousin.'

'What idiots they are,' thought Jennifer, putting the letter in her pocket. 'Boat-builder sounds like a plumber, the way she writes it. John's the cleverest yacht-designer in the country. Besides, we're not very close cousins if it comes to that. And anyway I loathe the way people jump to conclusions – it's filthy.'

She walked very fiercely down the hill, furious with the world in general, and seemed surprised when she found herself at the yard entrance. John was standing in the middle of the yard, talking to his foreman. His clothes were white and dusty, as though he'd been messing about in shavings. His fair hair flopped over his right eye, one hand was waving in the air, and his long legs looked as though they didn't know what to do with themselves.

Jennifer knew this attitude. It was the one he used when he tried to explain anything. She waited patiently until he should finish. Presently he caught sight of her. His hand dropped, his legs untwisted, and he walked away with the foreman far too carelessly to deceive anyone but himself. 'Yes,' he said loudly, 'Yes – er – what I've been trying to point out is this, that . . .' but when he was out of earshot he looked at his watch in some surprise and said 'I'd no idea it was so late. Look, I'll see you about that business in the morning,' and left the foreman in the yard, scratching his head and wondering.

John strolled across to the gate – casually, yawning a little.

'Is that you, Jennifer. I thought p'raps I saw you, but I wasn't sure.'

'Are you very busy?'

380

'Lord no – finished for the day,' he lied.

'Good.'

He swung himself up on the gate beside her.

'What have you been doing with yourself?'

'Nothing much. I'm depressed. I've had such a beastly letter from Mother.'

'Oh! – what about?'

'I'll read it to you if you like. It's all about this awful husband of hers.'

'Well, hang it, Jennifer, I s'pose she's fond of him.'

'How could she be after Daddy?'

'But your father's been dead nearly fourteen years – I know it sounds queer to you, but there's no earthly reason why she shouldn't care for somebody else.'

'John – you just don't understand. After being married to the most perfect man in the world to go and end up with an awful pompous, fatuous fool like Horton . . . it's utterly beyond me.'

'Of course it's beyond you. How can you expect to follow her feelings. Possibly your mother was never terribly happy with your father. This chap, though he may be a fool, happens to suit her, understand her – I don't know. Anyway, she was probably lonely.'

'Lonely?'

'Yes – lonely, Jennifer.'

'How dreadful, I never thought of that.'

'You're always telling me she never made any attempt to understand you. Did you ever make any attempt to understand her?'

'No – I – I suppose not.'

'Well then—?'

'Oh! John – how terrible. Shall I go back to London now, this minute?'

'Don't be an idiot. It's too late now, besides she's happy with this husband of hers.'

'Do you really think p'raps she didn't get on with Daddy?'

'Maybe not. I mean, they may have been awfully sort of

381

devoted but never well – absolutely – I can't explain.'

'I know what you mean. Never really indispensable.'

'H'm.'

'It must be dreadful to be married to a person and not sort of feel that if they went away you'd be sick all day in a basin.'

'I don't think one would do that, would one? Personally – of course I don't know anything about it – personally if I loved someone and they went away I wouldn't be sick, I'd just feel everything in life would be utterly pointless, un-worth-while – there would no longer be any object in working, thinking. And yet one would go on – just the same.'

'Would you do that? Oh! I wouldn't. I'd be sick at first, and then I should get very angry, and dress up as a man and join the Foreign Legion.'

'You'd soon be discovered.'

'No – I wouldn't, I'm strong, I'm quite thin – I don't look like a girl.'

'Who says so?'

'I say so.'

'Then you're a bloody fool.'

'John!'

'Sorry – let's change the subject. Read me your mother's letter.'

She did so, leaving out the postscript.

'I shouldn't worry, Jennifer.'

'I don't. It's only I can't understand it. That awful man . . .'

'He's obviously very attractive to her.'

'If you could see him.'

'Some women fall for the most amazing men. Fellows with spots, and bad teeth, who smell.'

'John – don't be filthy.'

'It's true – I think all men are terrible anyhow.'

'You look pretty repulsive yourself at this moment, I must say. Where's that dust come from?'

'Wood shavings.'

She brushed it off with her hands.

'John – are we going to the wreck on Sunday?'

'Sure.'

'It's fun rather, isn't it?'

'H'm.'

'John – d'you suppose Janet Coombe was happy with Thomas?'

'I wonder. I think she was probably too wrapped up in Joseph to care for anyone else.'

'And Joseph probably never cared for either of his wives really – he was thinking about her, or worrying over his son.'

'And your father Christopher thought so much about you that he rather forgot his wife.'

'Isn't it awful, John? All these people loving one another and being prevented somehow, from absolutely understanding, from it being perfect. They went away – or they died – or they quarrelled – or they lost each other. Somewhere – something went wrong for them. They had a kind of loneliness the whole time. I feel the same – I shall always miss Daddy.'

'Do you honestly think so?'

'Yes – I don't know.'

'You're happy at Plyn, aren't you?'

'Oh! terribly – I never want to leave Plyn again.'

'What is it then?'

'I can't explain. A doubt of the future, an uncertainty, a vague fear . . .'

'What sort of fear?'

'A fear of being afraid – that sounds crazy, doesn't it? Sometimes I wake up in the night and feel there's nothing before me – but nothing – nothing – emptiness and mist. And I walk about laughing all day pretending I don't care and really just longing to be safe.'

'Jennifer – promise me something.'

'What?'

'Promise you'll always tell me things like this. When you're frightened, lonely – or when you're happy – come and tell me.'

'I believe I could tell you anything, John.'

'There's no reason for you to be afraid, Jennifer. It's only because you were left alone when you were a child. You were too little to understand. And now you feel you'll never grow out of it, but you will. Jennifer – don't ever be frightened or lonely again.'

She rubbed her face against his sleeve.

'It's nice knowing you, John. You're safe.'

'Always think that, won't you?'

'H'm.'

'Coming to the wreck, Sunday?'

'H'm.'

'All day – bringing pasties and cider.'

'H'm.'

'Not unhappy, are you?'

'No.'

'Well, what are you hiding your face about?'

'I don't know.'

She slipped off the fence, and ran away from him without looking back.


Jennifer did not find winter at Plyn either gloomy or cheerless. She knew that this was where she belonged. Jennifer belonged to Plyn, she was Christopher Coombe's daughter, she had been born here, her home was here, she moved and dwelt amongst friendly simple folk because her nature demanded their kindliness and their company.

These were her true surroundings. She had been deprived of them too long, lonely and frustrated.

Jennifer knew that had she stayed in London she would have drifted heedlessly wherever her casual fancy called her, little caring what should become of her. And now she was in Plyn, and so far removed from that other life that it seemed another world and she another being.

Plyn was necessary to her; she loved the sea, the shelter of the hills and the valleys, the comfort of the harbour, the wide grey sheet of water, the sight of the clustered houses, the church tower, the coming and going of ships; the crying of gulls, the peace of continual beauty, the love and kindness of the people who understood. It seemed to her that she possessed the companionship of those who were part of her, the very air rang with their voices, and their footsteps echoed on the hills.

She could see Christopher's figure outlined against the sky, his fair hair blown by the light wind, his eyes tender as he watched the life in the cottages below. She heard him whistle to his dog, and then disappear over the brow of the hill in the wake of the setting sun.

Harold and Willie ran with her across the fields, they taught her to dive from the projecting rock in Castle Cove, they shouted with laughter as she shivered on the brink.

It was Harold who guided her to the gull's nest in the cliff; it was Willie who showed her how to spin for mackerel. They walked three abreast, over the stretching hills, arguing, discussing . . .

Other voices were with her too, the voice of Joseph when she sailed a boat, making her careless of time and weather, setting her blood on fire with the zest of the stinging spray and the wet wind. Joseph who taught her the triumphant power of a sou'westerly gale, the thrill of a lifting sea and a straining mast, the weird exultation of danger.

But there was one who understood her best, one from whom she withheld no secret, one who soothed all irritation, all idle questionings, all vague perplexities, all hidden doubts.

On the sloping fo'c'sle head of the wrecked *Janet Coombe* Jennifer would lie, her cheek against the bulwark, her hand upon the bow-sprit; and beneath her a white figurehead gazed seaward, not a painted wooden carving with patched colouring chipped and old, but someone who was part of Jennifer herself, someone who cried and whispered in the depths of her being, someone who was loving and infinitely wise. Someone who knew that restlessness came from a rebellious mind, that fancied loneliness was the outcome of an awakening heart, that sleeplessness was due to the hunger of instinct, that dreams were the prelude to fulfilment, that fear was the tremor of a spirit craving completion – and that the cause of these things and the sweet anguish and torment within Jennifer was the sight of John climbing down to her from the hills above.

## 11

Philip Coombe rarely went to the office now. His business was left almost entirely in the hands of his head clerk, as nearly forty-five years before the senior partner Hogg had done in entrusting it to him.

Philip was eighty-seven.

He sat all day in the front room overlooking the harbour, in his house in Marine Terrace. This was the room where Annie had visited him twice a week in the last months of her life, this was the room where Joseph had struck him to the ground. It was to this room that Christopher should have come, with murder in his heart, when the storm raged and the rain and wind shattered themselves against the window.

Now nearly fifteen years had passed since then, and opposite him in this room of memories sat a girl in the likeness of Janet, with Joseph's eyes and Joseph's hair, a girl who held no fear of him, who laughed and sang, a girl who waited for him to die that she might seize upon his money, who already scattered it far and wide, careless, triumphant, holding him in her power.

This was the Jennifer he saw before him. Someone who embodied in her person the souls of Janet, and Joseph, and Christopher, someone who watched him day and night that he might not escape from their keeping, someone whose presence was a continual reproach and a reminder, tormenting his memory, a haunting spirit. Yet he dared not turn her from his door, he dared not bid her be gone and be lost to him, for then he would be enveloped by the presence of unseen things, of whispering voices, of soundless footsteps; he would turn in his chair and feel the gathering shadows about him, the clustering of dark, malevolent thoughts, the existence of shrouded figures, motionless, behind him, their breath fanning his fore-head, and then creeping nearer, nearer, seizing upon him with cold, abhorrent hands . . . Better a living hated form, better a real physical detestation than an unknown horror.

Thus Philip clung to life and to the nearness of Jennifer whom he loathed, rather than lose himself in the fear that waited for him, that loomed close, so close.

And Jennifer watched this old and trembling man, crouch-ing before his fire for all the midsummer days without, his wrinkled hands like the claws of a bird, rubbing slowly one against the other.

He spoke seldom, addressing her when he did so with unfailing courtesy, inquiring after her health, and expressing a hope that she was finding everything to her satisfaction.

Then he moistened his thin, racked lips with his tongue, and turned his narrow, deep-set eyes away from her hated face, back to the glow of the little fire, the coals sinking in upon one another, fanned by one single blue flame.

'She is wondering when I shall die,' he thought, 'she is wondering if I have made my will, and where it is hidden.'

And Philip schemed how he could prevent her from robbing him of his wealth. He had made no will, therefore if he died leaving none behind him the value of his estate would go to his next-of-kin. Jennifer — his next-of-kin. Jennifer, or the other Coombes scattered about Plyn. All day he puzzled the matter.

While Jennifer, ignorant of his fancies, leaned out of the window, seeing nothing but a fair untidy head and a pair of long legs walking towards her, heard nothing but a whistle and a distant shout, and a voice which called 'Jenny, come down,' cared for nothing but to walk with her hand in his, singing snatches of songs, to stand on the hill with her cheek against his shoulder. 'Do you want to bathe, sweet, or shall we just muck about in a boat and fish?' and to answer 'I don't mind, John,' knowing he felt the same. To be half-asleep on the thwart beneath the blistering sun, the line dangling in her careless hand, and to open one eye and see him laughing at her, waving a glistening wriggling fish, 'Wake up, you lazy little beggar, and do some work'; to pull home away from the path of the setting sun, wrapped in his jacket so much too big for her that the sleeves hung down below her hands, weary, happy, saying no word, and smiling at him for no reason . . .

'Tomorrow's Saturday – I'll get away from the yard at two-thirty, and we'll have the whole afternoon out here. Is that all right for you?'

'Lovely. You'll bring the bait?'

'Sure.'

'I'll bring the cigarettes.'

'Not cold, Jenny?'

'No.'

'Been dull at all?'

'Frightfully.'

'Same here. God! I'm sick of the sight of your face.'

'Are you, John?'

'H'm. I look up, and see you in front of me and think hell – this woman again.'

'What else?'

'Want to know? It bores me terribly never thinking of anything but you, day and night . . .'

And that was how John Stevens told Jennifer Coombe he loved her, in the year nineteen hundred and twenty-six.


Throughout the year Philip Coombe was planning to exclude Jennifer and the Coombes from inheriting his wealth.

In spite of his age and his dawning insanity, his brain was still astute enough to reckon the state of his present financial affairs, and whilst his niece followed her lover on the hills above Plyn, the uncle examined papers, files, and documents, checked figures and compared accounts.

Although Jennifer had barely lived eighteen months under his roof, she had compelled him to part with at least a quarter of his private income, on voluntary donations and subscriptions.

'The Carne Infirmary is badly in need of funds, Uncle Philip,' she would say. 'I met the hon treasurer yesterday, and I said I was certain you would be only too pleased to help them out of the present difficulty.'

'The Carne Infirmary?' he would ask guardedly. 'I did not know there was such a place. The treasurer was possibly exaggerating. I should think no more about it.'

'The appeal was quite genuine,' she answered. 'If you care to write out a cheque I will see that it is posted tonight.'

He would hesitate a moment, tortured by the thought of that money slipping through his fingers, gone from his power for ever, and then glancing at her face he would see the shadows watching him over her shoulder, the pale motionless shadows waiting until she should turn away and leave him to their hands.

'Certainly – yes – I will sign the cheque this evening.'

A quarter of his private income was gone in this way, frittered, wasted. Somehow she must be defeated. He knew now that his end was near and that there was no time to be lost. By November his plans were complete. Once more Plyn saw the bent, well-known figure, wrapped in his black coat and muffler, walk slowly through the street to the office on the quay.

Every day for a week Philip Coombe sat in his private room at the office, and not even his head clerk knew what he was about.

Even when a man named Austin, a stranger to Plyn, arrived by appointment and stayed with the head of Hogg and Williams for half a day, it caused no comment, Mr Coombe giving his employees to understand that the stranger was a shipowner.

In reality, he was a wealthy ship-broker from Liverpool, with whom Philip Coombe had long been in correspondence, and the reason for his five-hour interview was to discuss the final figure of the sum which would terminate the existence of Hogg and Williams, and see the birth of the firm James Austin, Ltd.

Philip Coombe stipulated the amount, and he won, as he

390

had always won, and seizing the pen he signed the agreement making over the firm he had owned for over forty years to the stranger from Liverpool. The contract was secret, and would be held so for the space of a month, after which official declaration would be made.

There now remained his private investments and his separate banking account, his bonds and securities, which must be with-held from the possible enjoyment of his next-of-kin. To sell whatever stock he possessed and to withdraw his securities from the bank was a matter of comparative simplicity. Before three weeks Philip Coombe had the entire remainder of his fortune, in bonds, shares, and actual Bank of England notes, in his own possession under his personal supervision in the house in Marine Terrace.

To see, before his own eyes, the written testimony of his wealth, to touch with his own hands the very presence of his power brought Philip Coombe to the highest summit of exultation, and he stood in his room of memories, a weird triumphant figure, gazing upon the documents and paper at his feet, laughing softly to himself, clasping and unclasping his small and wrinkled hands. Death would come to him, but these things should perish with him. He would pass away, unloved and unremembered, but his treasures would pass also, never to fall into the hands of others, never to gladden the hearts of the people he despised.

For a moment he had forgotten the warning shadows, but as the light faded from the room and the shades of evening crept across the floor he was aware of voices murmuring from the doorway, their stealthy footsteps in the passage outside. He strained his ears to catch the echo of their sighs.

'You cannot escape us,' they whispered, 'we are waiting for you. Nothing can keep you from us, there will be no hiding-place for you, no rest, no peace.'

Philip shrunk against the walls of his room, he put his hands over his ears that he might not hear their voices, louder now and pressing, a riot and confusion of tongues. They were close to him now, they hovered above him with outstretched hands.

He seized his stick and beat against the air, and it seemed to him that they twisted and writhed with the pain he caused them, filling the room with lamentation.

Then he laughed aloud and trembled for joy, and into his mind came his last supreme decision.

The moon rose over the harbour, streaking the water with a path of silver. The lights of Plyn danced and twinkled in the darkness. The chimes rang out the hour from Lanoc Church.

'Jenny, sweet, don't go back tonight, come home with me.'

'But John, darling, don't be absurd, why should I suddenly, for no reason.'

'Because I want you to so terribly, because something tells me that if you don't you'll be taken away from me, and we shall lose each other for ever.'

She put her arms about him, and laid her cheek against his face.

'You know there's nothing can take me from you, John, why do you ramble round with your silly little fears, looking for a danger that can't exist?'

'Oh! I admit it, I'm a fool tonight, dithering, hopeless, anything you like, but come with me, Jenny, just this once.'

'No, John.'

'Darling, this isn't any beastly selfishness on my part, I'm not trying to put over a brilliant attempt at seduction – if you want to be by yourself you can have my room and I'll lock myself up in the lavatory, but every instinct I possess tells me to keep you beside me tonight, to be near you – in case anything should happen.'

'John, if I came to you there would be no locked doors – you'd find yourself shut up with a very immodest and abandoned woman – but it isn't that, it's giving way to a foolish fixed idea you have in your mind for which there can be no earthly reason.'

'Jenny – I've told you about my damned premonitions, haven't I? I've told you that when I sense danger it's infallible

– I'm always right. Sweet, there's danger for you tonight, danger in that gloomy blasted house, danger with that loathsome uncle of yours . . .'

'You're crazy, John. Uncle Philip is a weak, doddering old man, he hasn't the strength to harm a fly, he always goes to bed by half past nine. What could he possibly do to me?'

'I don't know – I don't care – Jenny, my Jenny, come home with me tonight. I want to hold you so you can't get away, I want to tell you everything I've ever dreamt about you, so much, so much . . .'

'John, don't make me weak and helpless. I won't give way to your creepy, haunting fears.'

'Jenny – let me love you.'

'No, John.'

'Come back, Jennifer, don't go – Jennifer – Jennifer.'

She ran away up the steps of the house, laughing over her shoulder. 'Go home and be good. I'll see you tomorrow.' Then she slammed the door and was gone.

When Jennifer was inside the house, with the door between her and John, she closed her eyes and rested her head against the wall, her nails digging into the palms of her hands.

She had refused to go back with him when she wanted to more than anything in the world. Just for the sake of a senseless flickering spirit of independence, a cold sprite within her mind who laughed at love and denied emotion, who saw ridicule in all things, and who suggested surrender as weakness and loss of freedom. Knowing it to be false yet she had persisted in listening to this cold voice, and now she was all alone, and John half-way home in all probability. Sighing and yawning she dragged herself upstairs, seeing by the clock in the hall it was already half past ten.

She undressed slowly, sitting on the edge of her bed, and gazing in front of her. John would be prowling about the yard now, seeing that all was quiet for the night, he would light his last pipe before climbing to his funny rooms over the office. Jennifer pulled on her pyjamas savagely and turned into bed, her face buried in the pillow.

393

She must have slept some five hours when she awoke to a blinding flash of light in her eyes. She sat up, dazed and stupid, and saw her uncle standing beside the bed with a flash-light in his hands. He was fully dressed, and when she was about to exclaim he put his fingers over his lips, and glanced half fearfully towards the door.

'Hush,' he whispered, 'we must not make a sound or they will hear us. Be quick, put on your dressing-gown and follow me.'

What did he mean? Were there burglars in the house? Jennifer fumbled for her dressing-gown and her slippers.

'Are they downstairs?' she asked. 'Is it impossible to get to the telephone? Perhaps if we make a noise it will scare them.'

He shook his head and laid his hand on her arm. 'Come with me.'

He led the way into the front room, and to her surprise she saw that the lights were switched on and a large fire was burning in the grate. On the table there was much litter of papers and official documents, and what seemed to her to be pile after pile of bank-notes.

'Whatever have you been doing with all these, Uncle Philip? Surely – why, I don't believe you've been to bed at all. What's the matter? Are there no burglars, then? I don't understand.'

'Don't be alarmed, Jennifer,' he answered. 'I am going to explain everything to you. Will you please sit down?' She did so, gazing up at him in astonishment, while he stood with his back to the fire rubbing his hands together.

'You see those papers scattered on the table?'

'Yes, of course. What about them?'

'There's money there, Jennifer, stacks of it, bundles of it. All my money, shares, bonds, securities – crisp Bank of England notes. It belongs to me, do you understand, to me and to no one else.'

'What are you going to do with it?'

'That is the question I was waiting for. You want to know who will inherit all this, you want to know who will have the right to spend it when I die. See, your fingers are itching to stretch towards that table – I know you – I know you. You think all that is going to be yours, eh? Don't you, don't you? But you're wrong, see, you won't touch a penny of it, not a farthing.' He trembled with excitement and pointed his finger at her.

'You've been considering yourself an heiress all these months, haven't you? No use in denial, I've seen you, I've watched you. But you were mistaken, hopelessly, miserably mistaken. Look at me – I say – look at me.'

He laughed, high pitched and shrill, he leaned towards the table and seized some of the papers, tearing them across, fluttering them before her eyes. 'There – there – there goes your precious inheritance.'

Jennifer made no answer. She knew now that her uncle was mad, she knew now that she must move warily, carefully, lest he should do himself and her some irreparable harm.

'Uncle Philip,' she said softly. 'Supposing we talk all this over in the morning. You're tired now, come along to bed.'

He turned his narrow eyes upon her and smiled slowly. 'No. I understand you too well. You think I am an old man to be fooled by you. I know you. As soon as my back is turned you creep down here and steal what doesn't belong to you. No, I have been too clever for you. Much too clever!' He made his way across the room and opened the door. Jennifer was aware of a queer, pungent smell that came from the passage, a smell of burning. She rose to her feet instantly, and crossed to the door.

'What is it, what have you done?'

The air was thick with smoke, it travelled up to her from the staircase, and from the hall below. She saw the glint of flames as they caught at the woodwork of the staircase, and licked the strips of paper from the walls.

At once she remembered the two servants sleeping in their rooms at the top of the house. Then her uncle pushed her back into the study, locking the door.

'No – you must not go,' he cried, 'you must come with me. I will not be alone, or they will break through to me and

395

strangle me. We must keep them out, help me to keep them out, Jennifer.'

He seized the tongs and tore a flaming log from the fire. He set alight the curtains, the carpets, the papers on the table, while she watched him, grown stiff with horror, unable to cry out. The flames made their way from the curtains to the wall-papers, burning fiercely now and bright, destroying all that stood in their way.

Philip snatched the books from the shelves, he hurled them one by one into the centre of the room. The air was thick with smoke, the black smuts danced before Jennifer's eyes, she watched the fire spread across the room, licking the ceiling, while moving amidst it was the figure of her uncle, laughing, sobbing, his hair singed, his hands outstretched flinging the books and the papers about him in confusion, feeding the hungry leaping flames.

Jennifer flung herself against the door, which resisted all her efforts, shouting at the pitch of her lungs. Then the smoke entered her throat, she sank to her knees, coughing, choking, the tears running down her cheeks. She groped about on the floor for the key of the door which her uncle had thrown aside, and at length she found it, and fitted it to the lock. But when she opened the door it was to be driven back by the swirling, driving smoke from the passage outside, and the heat of the burning staircase.

She heard something crash in the room behind her, a tall cabinet leaned from the wall, splintered and charred, and fell into the waiting flames.

'Uncle Philip!' she cried. 'Uncle Philip, come away, come away!'

He heard her voice, and stumbled towards her, swaying, suffocated.

'Get back, Joseph, get back from me, I say.' He brandished a chair above his head, he flung it towards her, knocking her sideways, bleeding and stunned into the passage outside. She stumbled to her feet and fought her way to the staircase leading to the rooms above. She heard a scream of terror, and looking back for the last time she could see through the open door of the study the bent figure of her Uncle Philip, his clothes alight, his hands outstretched, running round and round in circles, with the flames at his feet . . .

She clung to the banisters, sick and giddy, dragging herself away from the fire below, knowing dimly that there was no escape, no means of safety. Part of the landing beneath her crashed, and she saw the floor sink into itself and crumble away.

There were no walls left to the study now; it had vanished, gaping, blackened, and charred – and her uncle was gone.

A cloud seemed to come upon Jennifer, seizing her throat, blinding her eyes, and she was falling, falling, part of the roaring flames and the crumbling stones.

When John heard the door of the house slam, and knew that her good night was final, he turned away and walked down the terrace, impatient with Jennifer, angry that she had not listened to his words.

He felt restless and unhappy, he knew that if he went to his rooms now sleep would not come to him. When he arrived at the yard he wandered towards the slipway, and after gazing at the still harbour water and the clear starlit sky above, he cast off the painter of his dinghy, and jumping into the boat he seized the paddles and began to pull away rapidly up harbour. He had no difficulty with the tide, for it was just about slack water, and the little boat shot away into mid-stream under his powerful stroke.

John hoped that with this exercising of his body something of the fear and care in his mind would pass from him, leaving him in the end both weary and untroubled. He tried to persuade himself that this feeling that held sway over him was nothing but the physical want of Jennifer, that his efforts to make her return with him were due to that alone, and to none other. His suffering now was the result of frustration.

He argued thus, knowing there was much truth in his self-accusation, but knowing also, in the depths of his reason, that he had another and more powerful motive. There was fear within him for her safety. Some danger threatened her, of which he had no knowledge, some horror was preparing to tear apart their happiness, bearing her away to the lost and lonely places. His hidden powers of foresight had risen swiftly, silently, against his will they had taken firm hold upon him, and now he was a prey to fear, with no means of protecting she who belonged to him, and who had laughed aside his strange warnings.

Unconsciously John was pulling towards Polmear Creek; the dark form of the wrecked schooner cast her shadow on the water. He made fast the painter, and climbed aboard. He went below to the black cabin and sat on the bench against the table, his head in his hands. Here he had seen Jennifer for the first time, here she had turned her first startled gaze upon him, her dark head thrown back, angry at his intrusion, the tears upon her cheeks. Here they had read her father's letters, their shoulders touching, her hair brushing his cheek.

He remembered, with a strange thrill of pleasure and pain, that here he had also kissed her for the first time, she standing upon the companionway – between the cabin and the deck above, looking over her shoulder at him standing below, and he, blinded by something he did not understand, had caught her in his arms and carried her to the cabin, and there they had clung to one another, bewildered and lost, while he had whispered against her mouth. 'Oh! Jenny – Jenny.'

Afterwards they had sat upon the bench, looking at each other with new eyes, Jennifer wondering and silent, and he, triumphant, miserable, unable to keep his hands and his lips away from her. Later, when they were accustomed to one another, they had laughed at those early moments of feverish confusion, and they had agreed that they must be the first pair of lovers to make the cabin of a ship their trysting-place.

John rested his face upon his hands, and the thoughts jumbled in his brain, and here he slept awhile, awaking some few hours later, cold and ill, knowing he must be gone.

Once more he climbed down into his waiting boat, and as

he gazed at the white figurehead above him, it seemed to him that she whispered a message with her lips, that she counselled him go quickly if he would save Jennifer, for the danger was come upon her and she had need of him.

He turned his eyes upon the town of Plyn, shrouded in the quiet of the night, and when his gaze travelled in the direction of the terraces he knew.

For there, out of the darkness, leapt the vivid streak of a flame.

When John reached the house he had to fight his way through the crowd of people, shouting and crying in the road outside.

The engine, small and inadequate, was of little use against the terrific force of this fire, and though the men worked furiously, tirelessly, playing their hoses upon the burning buildings, the sheet of water hissing into the air, beating against the walls, it seemed they could not quench those fierce and hungry flames that turned and twisted into the sky.

John laid his hands upon one of the firemen, shouting in his ear above the roar and crackle of the flames, 'Are they safe? The people of the house – are they safe?'

The man shook his head, his eyes scared, his face ashen. He pointed to the escape, placed against one of the higher windows.

'There's two women brought down, the servants of the place, but the walls are falling – the other floors must be rotted through by now – look there – Mr Stevens – look there!'

A cry rose from the mass of people assembled in the terrace, and one of the firemen lifted his hand and shouted: 'Keep back there – keep back, I say!'

Part of the front facing of the house collapsed, crumbling in a molten mass of smouldering bricks and charred burning wood. The men began to drag the escape away from the doomed building.

'No, no!' shouted John. 'There are living people inside, I tell you. You must get to them – you must, you must.'

Once more the escape was flung against the high windows.

399

'Come back, Mr Stevens,' yelled someone, 'come back, there can't be no one there alive – it's too late – the flames have got them.'

Deaf to their cries and warnings John climbed up the escape to the rooms of the burning house. He flung himself inside one of the windows, and a cloud of smoke swept upon him, filling his lungs, dazing his brain.

'Jennifer . . .' he cried. 'Jennifer . . . Jennifer!'

He felt his way forward, until he stumbled against a rotting, crumbling staircase, where the angry flames leapt at him from the passage beneath.

'Jennifer,' he called helplessly. 'Jennifer – Jennifer!'

Then he saw her lying where part of the stairway was giving way. It seemed to him that she was slipping with it, slipping away from him into the chaos of horror and fear, down into the hungry flames.

He reached forward and took her in his arms, and as he fell on to the landing above he saw the stairway where she had been lying disappear before his eyes, swept away by the fire that mounted steadily towards them.

Someone seized hold of his arm, someone shouted in his ear, and he knew that they were being dragged forward – forward – out of the blinding, suffocating smoke to the cold pure air of the open window, to the moving heavens and the falling stars, to the cries of the people who waited below, their faces upturned . . .

When Jennifer opened her eyes she saw John kneeling beside her, and she smiled, holding out her hands to him. And as he held her, she hiding her face against his shoulder with no knowledge of what had passed, he raised his eyes above her head and saw that the house where they had been was no more now than a crumbled shell, outlined against the dark sky.

## 12

Jennifer stands on the hill above Plyn, looking down upon the harbour.

Although the sun is already high in the heavens, the little town is still wrapped in an early morning mist. It clings to Plyn like a thin blanket lending to the place a faint whisper of unreality as if the whole has been blessed by the touch of ghostly fingers. The tide is ebbing, the quiet waters escape silently from the harbour and become one with the sea, unruffled and undisturbed. No straggling cloud, no hollow wind breaks the calm beauty of the still white sky. For an instant a gull hovers in the air, stretching his wide wings to the sun, then he cries suddenly, and dives, losing himself in the mist below.

Three and a half years have passed since the night of the fire, the night when it seemed to John and to Jennifer that they would be separated for ever. The years have passed swiftly, bewildering and sweet, and now the horror and anguish of that time is no more than a dim memory to both of them, bringing no threat to their present happiness, no suggestion of fear and trouble to their peace and content.

Few changes have found their way to Plyn. The blackened, gaping building on Marine Terrace is demolished, and the last bricks cleared away, and a new house has been built there in its place, and has been taken over as a private hotel for visitors in the summer months.

The faded board with the letters 'Hogg and Williams', that once swung above the red brick office on the cobbled quay, is gone now, and painted in gold lettering on the door is the sign of 'James Austin, Ltd.'

The town of Plyn is as prosperous as ever; every day

throughout the year ships enter the harbour and make their way up to the jetties by the entrance to the river, the sound of their sirens echoing in the air, thrown back by the surrounding hills. One of the most striking parts of this modern Plyn is the large ship-building yard, which extends beyond the original premises to the opening of Polmear Creek. There is no ugliness in its growth, no offensive iron girders, no unsightly structure; John Stevens's Yard is a forest of small masts, the ground a mass of great timber, and inside the hanging sheds can be seen the smooth but unfinished shapes of boats.

These racing yachts are famous throughout the West Country, and their designer one of the best loved and respected men in Plyn.

Jennifer turns, and sees John coming up the hill towards her. She smiles, and goes to him.

'What are you doing up here?' she asks him. 'Don't you know you ought to be in the yard, slaving away for the sake of your wretched wife and son?'

He laughs and pulls her towards him. 'I don't care if there are fifty million people watching, I had to follow you, and tell you how sick I am of you. Do you know we've been married three years ago today, Jenny? It seems like centuries.'

She runs her fingers through his hair, pulling it over his eyes.

'D'you remember the bells pealing from Lanoc, and how angry we were when we didn't want anyone to know? And we thought we'd be romantic and go by boat up Polmear Creek to the church, and then half-way the engine stopped!'

'Yes – and I thought "Thank God I needn't marry the woman after all."'

'John – I've been moody, and trying at times – have you ever regretted it all, seriously I mean?'

'Jenny, sweet . . .'

'Funny to think we'll be together always, John – never caring for or wanting anyone else. Funny to think our fathers and mothers loved, and our grandfathers and our great-grandfathers

'– perhaps they all said the things we've told each other, up here, on the top of Plyn hill in the morning sun.'

'Why think about them, sweetheart? I feel selfish today – I only want to remember us – not all the little sad tomb-stones in Lanoc Churchyard.'

She clings to him suddenly, looking the while over his shoulder.

'A hundred years ago there were two others standing here, John, the same as us now. People of our blood, who belong to us. Perhaps they were happy like we are happy, long, long ago.'

'Think so, Jenny?'

'Oh! John, people can say whatever they damn well please about work, ambition, art, and beauty – all the funny little things that go to make up life – but nothing, nothing matters in the whole wide world but you and I loving one another, and Bill kicking his legs in the sun in the garden below.'

They wander down the hillside without a word.

Their house is five minutes' walk from the yard. It stands on the slip-way, part of the original loft, added on to and extended, where Thomas Coombe first made the models of his boats. At high tide the water creeps above the slip, wash-ing its way to the doorway of the house.

Bill is two. He is lying on his tummy, tugging at the grass with his hands. Jennifer picks him up under her arms, and smacks his fat behind.

John tickles his nose with a piece of straw, and Bill sneezes, shouting with laughter.

Across the harbour comes the sound of hammers, of wood cracking beneath the blow of axes. It is the sound of work-men breaking up a wreck in Polmear Creek. She is no more than a hulk now, a few battered timbers.

Jennifer raises her eyes to the great beam that stands outside the room facing the harbour.

This is Bill's nursery.

Placed against the beam is the figurehead of a ship. She leans beyond them all, a little white figure with her hands at her breast, her chin in the air, her eyes gazing towards the sea.

High above the clustered houses and the grey harbour waters of Plyn, the loving spirit smiles and is free.

Bodinnick-by-Fowey
October 1929–January 1930